Whispers on the Ice

Whispers on the Ice

Elizabeth Moynihan

Writers Club Press
San Jose New York Lincoln Shanghai

Whispers on the Ice

All Rights Reserved © 2000 by Constance E. Moynihan

No part of this book may be reproduced or transmitted in any form or by any means, graphic, electronic, or mechanical, including photocopying, recording, taping, or by any information storage retrieval system, without the permission in writing from the publisher.

Writers Club Press
an imprint of iUniverse.com, Inc.

For information address:
iUniverse.com, Inc.
5220 S 16th, Ste. 200
Lincoln, NE 68512
www.iuniverse.com

This book is a work of fiction. Names, characters, places and incidents are products of the author's imagination or are used fictitiously. Any resemblance to actual events or locales or persons living or dead is entirely coincidental.

ISBN: 0-595-16397-1

Printed in the United States of America

I dedicate this book to those who have dreams and find the courage to make them a reality.

And, to Mom, who always believed in me. I love you.

About the Author

Elizabeth Moynihan

Having fulfilled a lifetime dream, and completed her first novel, Elizabeth is busy completing the sequel to WHISPERS ON THE ICE. A transplanted Californian, she calls the mid-west home, and is married, and the mother of two.

Chapter 1

"Twenty-four year old, Olympic Gold Medalist, and World Champion figure skating star, Aleksei Rocmanov, is resting comfortably after breaking his leg while mountain climbing with friends in Yosemite National Park. Aleksei's coach, Frank Whittaker's oft-heard comments that 'Aleksei's devil-may-care attitude regarding his off-ice activities would eventually catch up with him, and land him on his butt in the hospital' apparently have come to pass. Doctors expect the skater to be released from the hospital tomorrow, with a recovery period of approximately eight to twelve weeks, barring any unforeseen complications. However, knowing this skater's tendency toward pushing the envelope, and his lack of patience, don't be surprised to see him back on the ice in half that time. This is Mark Foster, Channel 5 news. We'll see you back here at ten o'clock."

Everyone broke into cheers and applause as the packed hospital room erupted into noise at the end of the sports broadcast.

"Coach, is that anyway to talk about your favorite athlete? You make me sound like an accident waiting to happen," Aleksei growled good naturedly, his dark eyes flashing mischievously as he threw a handful of smuggled popcorn toward his coach of eleven years.

Aleksei's six-foot two-inch frame barely fit the hospital bed, his long legs reaching beyond the end of the mattress, the sheet forming a tent over his feet. His broad shoulders nearly spanned the width of the twin-sized bed, his elbows reaching into air as he folded his hands and rested his head on his hands. The full, firm muscles of his chest and shoulders flexed visibly through the fabric of his hospital gown as he sought a comfortable position against the pillows. His face was the stuff that women envisioned in their fantasies; a strong chin, a full upper lip that begged to be nibbled on—and often was—and frequently displayed a rakish smile, a straight nose, high cheekbones and his trade-mark ebony-black eyes. Eyes that gave away his every emotion, whether flashing dangerously in anger, smoldering in passion or sparkling in mischievous wickedness, as they were now.

"If you'd listened to me in the first place, you wouldn't be here now. We're looking at a twelve week training delay because of your latest stunt," Whittaker stated gruffly, more than a little serious.

His coach, Frank Whittaker, was a good six inches shorter than Aleksei and outweighed him by at least seventy-five pounds. His hair had thinned and grayed, his speed had slowed and he didn't look as good in tight pants as he once had, yet he was still considered to be one of the best coaches in the world. Aleksei continued to prove that fact each time he stepped on to the ice and brought home another championship. In his hey-day he'd won his own fair share of figure skating competitions, but had decided his real love was in teaching and so he'd taken Aleksei on as a student more years ago than either of them could remember.

"You heard the sports guy, I'll be back in half the time they're expecting," Aleksei responded smugly, running his hands haphazardly through his dark, wavy hair.

"You hope you will. You're not some young buck any longer that bounces back like a rubber ball. Your bones don't heal like they did ten years ago!" Coach Whittaker referred to the time when Aleksei had tried ice hockey without the pads and broke his shoulder when he'd been checked into the wall by some kid.

"That was just being stupid and cocky," Aleksei stated.

"And this wasn't?" his coach argued, waving his arm toward Aleksei's left leg, fully encased in a heavy cast, now covered with questionable comments and pictures from his friends still crowding his hospital room.

"My leg was fine until Viktor fell on it," Aleksei argued, pointing at his friend, now filling his mouth with garbage pizza. Viktor only smiled, shrugged and continued eating.

"Aleksei, you're missing the point," Whittaker stopped, took a deep breath and trudged on. "Your off-ice escapades are catching up with you. I can't keep wondering if every time I see you leave at the end of the season I'll get a call from some hospital administrator letting me know where to come pick up whatever is left of you. You're going to have to make a decision to either skate or be a wild-man. I'm not going to wait for those calls any longer."

Abruptly the room became silent; thirteen pairs of eyes all focused solely on Coach Whittaker.

"What exactly are you saying?" Aleksei asked quietly, his voice dangerously low.

"You have a choice to make, Aleksei. You come skate with me on my terms, under my rules, or you find yourself another coach. It's time to decide what's important."

"Clear the room!" Aleksei demanded, his tone leaving no room for questions. Within seconds the room was empty save for Aleksei and the only coach he'd ever known. Fixing Whittaker with an unflinching gaze, he stated clearly, "That was un-called for."

"I disagree. You need a wake-up call and shocking you seems to be the only way to get through that sludge you call brains. You take everything as a joke, Aleksei, and there is not a damn thing funny about any of this," Whittaker cursed angrily.

"I've never looked at my skating as a 'joke.' It's my life, Whittaker, and I have you to thank for it. But I can't live by ultimatums. I have a right to an off-ice life. No one can eat, drink and breathe skating all the time. There has to be more to life than that. I have a right to more than that!"

"I agree, you have a right to a life other than skating but not things that can take away everything you've worked your entire life to attain. Your body is a God given gift and you can't keep taunting him to take it away. Where will you be when you fall off the next cliff and they don't find you or if they do manage to find you you're so mangled you never walk again? Where will you be then? Is putting a little zing in your life worth losing everything?" Whittaker ran his hands through his hair in frustration. "Christ, Aleksei, get a dog, or a hobby, write a book or God forbid, find a girl—but stay the hell off of mountains, motorcycles and bungi cords. Life can be exciting without being life threatening!" he roared.

"Whittaker, I'm on a damn bus for nine months a year touring. Hardly the makings of a stable relationship with either a wife or a dog."

Whittaker shook his head in frustration. "I didn't say a wife—I said a girl. Someone to hang out with, be friends with, maybe even soften your hard edges a bit," he suggested.

"Generally speaking, soft edges are not what the girls I meet seem to have any interest in," Aleksei replied smugly.

"I have no desire to know about your sex life, what I hear is enough to send me running screaming in the opposite direction as it is! Find a …" he scrambled for the right words, "a companion; someone you can talk to, laugh with, share books and go to movies with. Share popcorn—not necessarily a bed," he suggested.

"Sounds rather boring," Aleksei grumbled.

"Right now, I want you boring. Boring and in one piece."

"Suppose I take your advice? Where would you suggest I find such a paragon of womanly virtue?" Aleksei demanded, scowling at Whittaker's smug grin.

"Leave everything to me. I've got a few ideas."

"That's what I'm afraid of," Aleksei grumbled. "The last time I 'left everything to you', you forgot my skates in the locker room in Canada and I had to run through that maze of tunnels back to the dressing room to get them."

"That's hardly a momentous occasion, and it warmed you up quite nicely, as I recall," Whittaker offered.

"Yeah, it warmed me right up, especially after I tripped over the 'Ice Queen' and her blade sliced my leg open," Aleksei complained.

Aleksei's comment drew Whittaker's undivided attention. The less than complimentary title had been attached to only one person he knew of. "It was Jordan Jamison you body-checked?" Whittaker choked in disbelief.

Aleksei cast a bewildered look at his coach. "This is old news, coach. I told you she tripped me."

"No, you said some 'snotty bitch' tripped you," Whittaker corrected.

"Same thing," Aleksei answered, shrugging his wide shoulders. "They shouldn't let babies compete anyway."

"She's hardly a baby," Whittaker mumbled, making notes in his ever-present notebook. "Why she must be about sixteen or so."

"Which would have made her twelve at the time. Like I said—a baby."

Whittaker sent Aleksei a disgusted look and silently scribbled more notes. Aleksei watched his coach; curious at the frantic writing and felt the small hairs on the back of his neck start to tingle, surely a bad sign if past occurrences were an indicator. "Whittaker, what are you up to?" Aleksei questioned suspiciously, his voice low.

Whittaker looked up from his notebook, scratched his head with the end of the pencil and with great enthusiasm stated, "If it can be done—you're about to become half of a pair."

"Bull shit!"

"No bull shit here, son. Your body won't hold up to the rigors of singles right now, but dollars to donuts, you can make it as half of a pair."

"I've—we've—never even done pair skating in an exhibition. Come on, Whittaker, I'm the biggest of all the male skaters. Who's going to risk letting me partner them? For that matter—who's missing a partner? No one worth a damn's available." Aleksei prayed his last statement was true.

"Let me worry about that. I'm the coach—the one in charge—remember?"

" Yeah, I remember, and let me tell you, it's starting to scare the hell out of me!" Aleksei stated firmly, shaking his head at his predicament.

"Good, you should be scared. It'll give you an edge!" Whittaker declared reasonably and left the room to head for the pay telephone.

*   *   *   *   *

Jordan Jamison skimmed effortlessly over the frozen surface of the ice rink. Her petite form, now covered in a sedate black and white warm-up suit, hid the curves of her journey toward womanhood that she was still becoming used to. There were still days when she was certain it had been easier not having breasts; they somehow always seemed to be in the way and it took having to re-learn certain jumps and spins to reacquaint herself with her center of gravity. Thankfully, her hips still retained their slim, boyishness, but when she looked at her training films it seemed her bottom had grown more curvaceous, and heaven knew if her legs got much longer, she was going to scream. Still, all in all, she was basically happy with her figure. Her skin was peaches and cream, her eyes varying from emerald to forest green; depending on her mood, her lips full and soft; a warm shade of peach. But her crowning glory, she felt, was her shoulder-length head of softly waving shades-of-copper hair. Now worn up in a snug French-braid to keep it out of her face, she absently pushed an errant strand behind her ear and slowly circled the ice, warming her muscles in preparation for the rigorous practice session to come with her partner, Bob Hanks. For the last four years the two had been skating partners, winning several titles and now contemplating competing for a slot on the up-coming Olympic team. Jordan, too serious at the age of sixteen continued her warm-up slowly, cautious to a fault that her muscles be completely warm and ready to skate and thus avoid possibility of an injury due to being cold and stiff. Unlike Bob, who thought he knew everything at the age of nineteen, who would come in, put on his skates and proceed to toss her around like a rag doll until he warmed up and could better judge his throwing and lifting power. With Jordan barely hitting five foot two on skates and weighing all of ninety-five pounds, her partner at almost six feet tall and eighty pounds more than she had all too often thrown her into the boards more times than she cared to count. She'd long ago quit looking for bruises and simply opted for thicker stockings to hide the telltale marks of her numerous assisted falls. She often wondered why she didn't just get another partner but the difficulty of re-training with another partner terrified her in such a way that she simply stuck it out with Bob. Now, Bob was an hour late and Jordan continued to slowly circle the ice and run through their program in her mind.

"Jordan…" A voice over the loud speaker called.

Jordan gracefully slid to a stop, a little rooster tail of ice flying up in front of her, and looked across the ice and through the window dividing the front office from the rink.

"Bob's not going to make it," The voice cautiously stated.

Jordan spread her arms and shrugged her shoulders, mouthing the word *why?*

Jordan watched as Mindy, the Office Manager at the rink continued her conversation on the phone with Bob. When she suddenly dropped the phone and cast a quick disbelieving glance at Jordan then quickly picked the phone back up to finish the call, Jordan cautiously made her way across the ice toward the office. The small hairs at the back of Jordan's neck signaled a catastrophe in the making. Jordan skated to the open door, slipped her blade guards into place and quickly crossed the rubber-covered floor to the office. Mindy's loudly voiced "you son of a bitch!" greeted her as she opened the door, followed quickly by the resounding bang as she slammed the phone back into its cradle.

"Mindy…" Jordan asked softly, numerous questions in her green eyes.

Mindy heaved a huge sigh, ran her hands through her hair for lack of another way to stall the inevitable and bluntly stated. "That bastard left you for Chanelle Watts."

*   *   *   *   *

Coach Whittaker had stayed at the hospital with Aleksei and continued to outline the various points that Aleksei would have to follow to maintain their coach/athlete relationship (which was closer to a father/son relationship than either one cared to admit). During the hours since the early sports report they had alternately yelled, cursed, threatened, argued and laughed to get their opinions across, causing nurses to check the room more than once to insure no blood had been shed. Eventually, the noise had lessened and then finally disappeared completely into a comfortable silence as Whittaker watched the final news of the evening and Aleksei thumbed through an old **People** magazine and listened with one ear.

"Next up—sports—with more information about Olympic Skater Aleksei Rocmanov and up-and-coming skater Jordan Jamison. This is Mike Foster, we'll be right back."

"Now those are two names you haven't heard in the same sentence before," Whittaker joked out-loud.

"Fire and ice," Aleksei mumbled in return, casting a quick eye toward the TV.

Again, the sports reporter appeared on TV, all perfect hair, makeup, and dental-enhanced smile. The same report that ran earlier was repeated with some additional comments from friends stating his mood was good, and he was resting comfortably.

"It's good to know we'll see Aleksei up and skating again soon but unfortunately it looks as if Jordan Jamison's Olympic plans have just been lost. According to sources close to Ms. Jamison, her partner of four years, Bob Hanks, has terminated their partnership and become the skating partner of Chanelle Watts. That, of course, leaves Ms. Jamison very little time to find a new partner, let alone prepare for any bid in the upcoming Olympics, even if they are over three years away. We'll keep you advised of any further developments on both these stories. Next up, Roger with the weekend's weather forecast."

"Poor little thing," Whittaker commiserated with a shake of his head.

"Little is right. I'm surprised they have skates that fit her," Aleksei grumbled, continuing to thumb through his magazine.

"She just looks small on the ice next to that putz Hanks," Whittaker growled.

"Christ, Whittaker, she looks small off the ice too, even without the putz!" Aleksei argued. Remembering their little encounter in Canada that left him with six stitches still rankled and he absently rubbed the small scar on his un-cast leg. Amazingly enough, her furious expression still came to his mind's eye clearly; her dark green eyes flashing fire, her cheeks blushing darkly, despite her stage make-up, her gorgeous mouth casting aspersions on his heritage and his ineptness that had obviously caused the upheaval. Whittaker's voice suddenly brought him back from his memories.

"Still, she's a beautiful skater; reminds me of Ekaterina Gordeeva when she was younger."

"Only smaller, if that's possible," Aleksei qualified.

"I bet she could win Gold with the right partner," Whittaker stated, steepling his fingers beneath his chin, deep in thought.

"The Olympics are over three years away. They'd have to make it through U.S., Nationals and World Championships for a berth. Hell has a better chance of freezing over than that happening," Aleksei stated matter-of-factly.

"Not with the right partner," Whittaker re-emphasized.

"You're repeating yourself, Whittaker."

"Just thinking out-loud."

"Mr. Whittaker, visiting hours ended over an hour ago. I'm going to have to insist you leave now. Mr. Rocmanov needs a full night's sleep if he plans to leave tomorrow," a very serious, very large nurse stated from the doorway.

"I was just leaving," Whittaker stated, nodding good-bye to Aleksei and walking toward the door.

"His release papers will be signed by ten o'clock. Don't be late," The nurse stated firmly.

"Ten o'clock it is. I won't be late," Whittaker agreed and walked away whistling an indistinguishable tune.

Shaking her head in disapproval, the nurse directed her gaze to Aleksei and smiled in pleasure. "Is there anything I can do for you Mr. Rocmanov?"

"If it isn't too much trouble, I sure could use some ice water," Aleksei asked softly, his lips curving into a sexy smile.

As usual, the response was immediate. "Of course, Mr. Rocmanov. Is that all?"

Aleksei's smile widened to display perfectly straight, gloriously white teeth. "The ice water is more than enough, thank you."

With a quick smile of her own, the nurse rushed away to fill his request, her crepe soles squeaking on the gleaming tile floor.

Aleksei raised his muscled arms over his head and stretched, feeling the tension leave his upper torso for the first time since he'd entered the hospital. Folding his arms and resting his head against them, he closed his eyes and sent a quick, silent prayer heavenward. This time he'd gotten out with his life, but could he count on there being a next time? All of Whittaker's words crashed and echoed through his mind, replaying over and over. His coach was right—it was time to grow up. Now all he had to worry about was what Whittaker had in store for him over the next twelve weeks and why that pondering expression appeared in Whittaker's eyes when he'd watched the report on Jordan Jamison?

With a sudden foreboding, he had the feeling life, as he knew it was about to change. And more drastically that he could ever imagine.

*   *   *   *   *

"Chanelle Watts?" Jordan whispered in disbelief, horror clearly written on her expressive face.

"That's what he said. He feels his chances for Olympic Gold are, how did he put it? 'Supremely better if his partner is closer in stature and maturity to himself than with a child.' Or some shit like that," Mindy growled, stalking about the small office like a caged animal.

Chanelle Watts had been Jordan's good friend, up until three years ago when Jordan had introduced her to Bob at a party celebrating Chanelle's sixteenth birthday. Bob had agreed, under protest, to take Jordan to the party, preparing to simply drop her off and pick her up two hours later. However, upon meeting the amazingly physically mature and lovely Chanelle Watts, he decided to stay. That Chanelle was five foot eight and more curvaceous than a sixteen year old had a right to be didn't seem to bother Bob. In fact, it seemed to Jordan, that he spent the better part of the evening ogling Chanelle's breasts than actually talking to her. To make matters worse, Jordan teased him for two weeks after the party that he couldn't tell her what color Chanelle's eyes were when she finally managed to drag him away from the party. That she was right didn't matter to Bob, because he couldn't tell her what color eyes Chanelle had, but he had turned nasty and said he didn't have time for such childish games or partners and to grow up or he'd find another partner. When she stated that she was only thirteen after all, he had threatened once again to quit partnering her if she couldn't act older and at that moment she had learned a hard lesson in life. To blend in, you often had to lose part of yourself, but in the end, it would all be worth it, or so she believed. So at the age of thirteen, she turned into an old lady, meticulous in her manners, her speech, the way she always maintained her composure and that was when sports commentators began to notice her sudden maturity and dubbed her the 'Ice Queen'.

Jordan's presence and skating matured to a degree where anyone who didn't know her age assumed she was simply a very small woman; granted, missing the expected curves, but not everyone was full figured like Chanelle. All the music Jordan picked was serious, often melancholy, never requiring her to smile during a performance and thus allowing her to concentrate on her skating and landing the throws that Bob fiercely threw her into. Enduring his endless criticism of her abilities and how Chanelle could do this or that, never satisfying him in any way, but she never stopped trying.

Now, her last four years work was dissolving before her eyes. All because her partner had found her lacking yet again somehow. He moved on to what he believed to be a perfect partner, abandoning Jordan, but not before digging the proverbial knife in one last time.

"Where's Dee?" Mindy asked, referring to Jordan's coach and guardian, as she watched Jordan's eyes cloud with conflicting emotions.

Jordan appeared baffled by the question, shaking her head in confusion then suddenly remembering. "She had to run over final details for our costumes. She should be home by now," Jordan suggested, glancing quickly at her watch; Ten forty-nine p.m..

Mindy quickly dialed Jordan's number, frowned at the busy signal and hung up. "Get your things—we're out of here. Dee will know what to do," Mindy hoped out-loud. Dee had been there when Jordan's mother had died and her father hadn't been able to face seeing his wife every time he looked at his daughter. It wasn't that her father didn't love her. He diligently sent little gifts and cards to her frequently. Still, he hadn't been the same since her mother had died, seeming to want to slip silently away to join his wife, never thinking about what his behavior might do to an eight year old girl. He couldn't deal with the burden of an eight-year old questioning why God took Mommy and why daddy seemed to be slipping away too. That was when Dee had volunteered to take guardianship of Jordan, already having known and coached her since she was five, and ready to answer any questions she might have about anything at anytime. It had been a blessing to both Jordan and Dee.

"Yes, Dee," Jordan agreed softly, still numb with confusion.

*   *   *   *   *

As Dee Carlen listened intently to the voice on the other end of the phone, astonishment and disbelief shifted across her features. One moment she would agree, the next offer suggestions as to an alternative. Jordan and Mindy watched in stunned silence, as Dee grew more animated and excited. Neither Jordan nor Mindy had ever seen Dee act this way. After what seemed an eternity, Dee ended the conversation, hung up the phone and with the biggest smile Jordan had ever seen, announced confidently, "Jordan Jamison, we've found you a new partner and a Gold Medal one at that!"

"We who?" Jordan inquired cautiously.

"A friend of mine who thinks—no actually has decided—that it's in the best interest of his athlete to become 'half of a pair' and get this, and I quote, 'get respectable and responsible!'" Dee explained, excitement taking over completely. "He saw the news report tonight and decided on the spot the two of you could very well be the next 'G & G' skating duo."

"As far as I'm aware, there are no male skaters looking for new partners. Who, on earth, is that good and available?" Mindy asked curiously, knowing of no one other than Chanelle's ex-partner and not even Dee would partner Jordan with that flunkie.

"You won't believe me when I tell you!" Dee could barely contain her excitement, clapping her hands together then finally calming enough to gently hold Jordan's pale face between her hands while she regained her composure.

Jordan's emotions shifted from hope to terror waiting for her coach and friend to tell her whom she was about to be paired with. "Aleksei Rocmanov," Dee proudly announced.

Jordan's eyes grew wide and her mouth dropped open in astonishment. Mindy whooped in excitement and danced circles around Jordan exclaiming her approval.

"He's a monster!" Jordan whispered, her face completely colorless, her dark eyes wide in disbelief.

"He's gorgeous!" Mindy squealed in delight.

"He'll kill me," Jordan worried out loud, her voice a soft whisper.

Dee immediately sensed Jordan's concerns about their differences in size and reassured her all would be well and that they would have the opportunity to meet each other in two days.

"He won't do it," Jordan predicted, shaking her head, remembering their unfriendly run-in in Canada.

"Yes he will." Dee confirmed, nodding her head to emphasize her statement. "Whittaker's promised he'll be there."

"He's a single," Jordan protested, looking for any way out of this seemingly crazy suggestion.

"Not any longer," Marina replied.

"According to whom?" Jordan questioned hotly.

"His coach—and I'd say that's a pretty accurate source."

"Doesn't Aleksei have the right to decide if he's a single or not?"

"Not according to Frank Whittaker."

"I was under the impression you still had a right to choose what you wanted to be in the U.S., something about amendments, and freedom of choice," Jordan grumbled sarcastically, trying to control the growing urge to run as fast and as far away as possible. "Obviously, while I wasn't looking, democracy went out the window."

"Don't be such a snot, Jordan. You have the freedom to say 'no'. I'll be the first to say I think it's a mistake if you don't skate well together. I've never made you do anything that could hurt you—I won't start now. All

Whittaker and I did was set up a meeting so the two of you could meet and we could see how you fit each other."

"Rather like trying on new boots," Jordan mumbled. "Besides, we already met—in Canada. Remember?"

"Let's try it without bloodshed this time, okay?" Dee suggested, smiling as Jordan blushed in remembered embarrassment over the incident in Canada.

"I'll do it—but only because of all you've done for me," Jordan conceded.

"Damn—for the chance to get my hands on Aleksei Rocmanov, I'd even take my dusty old skates out of retirement and take a few turns around the ice." Mindy exclaimed, pretending to skate as wobbly as she could across the thick carpet, all the while batting her eyelashes at an imaginary partner, then slipping ungracefully to the ground.

"Heaven help, Mr. Rocmanov," Dee laughed, helping Mindy from her sprawled position on the floor, laughing all the while.

"Heaven help me," Jordan whispered quietly and cast a quick glance toward heaven.

*   *   *   *   *

"I've got your walking papers." Frank Whittaker waved the hospital release papers at Aleksei, a Cheshire cat smile creasing his face.

"How about coach release papers?" Aleksei questions, a scowl creasing his brow as he reached for the crutches beside the hospital bed.

"Amazing how fast TODAY gets their information, isn't it?" Whittaker asked with a sheepish smile.

"Yeah—amazing. Especially when it's a direct quote from a reliable source."

"Well, you know, son, they don't have truly reliable sources that often. So when they do get one, they run with the story like the wind!"

"You'd better hope like hell you can run like the wind when I get this damn cast off my leg," Aleksei threatened meaningfully.

Unfazed, Whittaker just shrugged and smiled that annoying smile he couldn't wipe off his face, frustrating Aleksei even further. "I'll worry about that when the time comes."

"According to TODAY, I'm meeting with my new partner tomorrow."

"By God, those news people can get it right on occasion.

"Is this a private meeting?"

"As private as it can be with cameras and news people around."

"Whittaker, I could…" Aleksei began, running his hand through his hair and rubbing the suddenly tense muscles in his neck. "Why are you doing it this way?"

"This way both Dee and I can be sure the two of you will be on your best behavior. Generally speaking, you can manage to hold your own at a news conference and I'm hoping your expertise and maturity will help ease the way for Jordan. Who, by the way, is certain you are entertaining thoughts of maiming her in one way or another."

Aleksei's look was one of pure disbelief. "Maim her? She's the one that put the lovely gash in my leg—not the other way around."

"Be that as it may, she's under the impression that you hold grudges and it's just a matter of time until you exact your revenge on her," Whittaker explained patiently.

"Tell her I don't pick on little girls," Aleksei stated in a dangerously low voice.

"Tell her yourself—tomorrow. But I wouldn't use those particular words. You've only got one good leg left," He chuckled, holding the door open and pointing with the papers. Now, are you ready to blow this joint?"

"Do I have a choice?"

"You always have a choice."

"Yeah, right. That's why I get to go play nice-nice with the 'Ice Queen'. God only knows what parts of my body she'll try to slice off this time," Aleksei complained loudly.

"Come on now, Aleksei, how much damage can one little girl do?"

Aleksei cast a deadly look at his coach and stated, "You'd better be damn sure you have plenty of bandages on hand and I want to see papers indicating she's up to date on her rabies shots."

Whittaker's loud laughter echoed through the hospital halls as they headed for the parking lot.

Chapter 2

Bright lights, reflectors and electrical cords crisscrossed the living room of Dee Carlen, where the soon-to-be first-time interview between new skating partners Aleksei Rocmanov and Jordan Jamison would take place. Dee's tastes ran toward the simple and comfortable, shades of off-white with splashes of color via pillows, flowers and pictures made the room comfortable yet fashionable. Yet with all the electronic paraphernalia scattered about, it was a wonder any of the home's decor showed at all.

The front door remained open, as more equipment was moved into place and storage cases were hauled outside to the porch. Aleksei and Coach Whittaker arrived early (at Whittaker's insistence), and skirted the wires and tripods. Aleksei finally gave up the attempt to maneuver through all the cords and wires and simply leaned against one wall out of the way as he nonchalantly watched the cameramen set up their equipment.

"He's here," Jordan whispered to Dee from where she peeked around the closed door that led into the kitchen. Through the wooden shades of the door, she could watch Aleksei unobserved by any and all.

"I know," Dee answered, filling a tray with coffee, cups, cream and sugar.

"They're not supposed to be here for another hour," Jordan mumbled nervously.

"They're early," Dee explained simply, grabbing a handful of spoons and placing them on the tray.

"Aleksei's never early," Jordan argued, casting another quick glance at the handsome man leaning against their living room wall.

"Well he is today. Jordan, if you're so anxious to meet him, quit peeking through the door like some voyeur and go say hello."

"This is anxiety, not anxiousness, you're witnessing," Jordan hissed, pressing a delicate hand to her pounding heart.

"Doesn't look like that to me, but what do I know," Dee countered, hoisting the tray and making her way toward the door Jordan was blocking. "Excuse me, miss, but move aside."

Jordan automatically pushed the door open. Unfortunately, she didn't notice the pile of cables on the floor and stumbled forward, clutching at air and catching hold of a reflector tripod that immediately collapsed and caused a domino-effect to the other four reflectors stationed in a neat semi-circle around the sofa set up for the interview. When the dust settled and all was quiet, Jordan looked over her scene of destruction and then glanced at Aleksei who continued to lean casually against the wall, a sardonic brow lifted in amusement, his dark eyes gleaming brightly as he struggled to keep the smile from his lips.

With all the chivalry of days past, standing on his good leg, he swept a grand bow and stated: "Ladies and gentlemen, I present to you, my new partner, the 'Ice Queen'!"

Jordan's eyes widened in horror, but never left Aleksei's. With a brilliant smile, she flipped her middle finger at him, silently mouthed a clear *fuck you* and picked herself up out of the nest of tangled cables beneath her, and regally left the room.

The entire camera crew stood stock still, mouths hanging open in astonishment.

"Anyone for coffee?" Dee casually offered, looking for any takers.

"Is it loaded?" someone asked on a laugh, the moment of tension dissipating like mist touched by the sun.

Dee sighed and shook her head. "No, but give me two minutes. I've a full bottle of whiskey and I think we may all need a little fortification to get through this interview."

The coffee tray was set on the table and Dee disappeared into the kitchen and returned, as promised with a new bottle of whiskey and several shot glasses. "I decided why ruin perfectly good whiskey with coffee," She stated and poured out several shots of the fine liquor and passed out the drinks to eleven crewmen, Frank Whittaker and finally to Aleksei, who still leaned casually against the wall. "You might need this to dull the pain of what's to come," Dee encouraged, holding the glass to Aleksei. Quickly she tossed back her own drink, breathing slowly as the warmth of the liquor filled her chest and settled comfortably into her stomach.

Aleksei followed suit, tossing the drink back, his eyes never leaving Dee's and handed her back the glass. Dee smiled at his show of macho. "You've made an enemy," She stated simply.

"You?" Aleksei asked, his voice deep and warm from the after effects of the whiskey.

"No. You'll come to wish it were me—but no. It will take a lot to get Jordan to forgive you for your…" Dee searched for the right word, "arrogance."

Whittaker choked on the chuckle he tried to hide, smiling at the disgruntled look Aleksei tossed at him.

"You owe her an apology," Dee stated.

"Bull!" Aleksei countered.

"You humiliated her in front of everyone."

"She told me to 'fuck off'."

"Aleksei…" Whittaker warned softly.

"So now we have two stubborn children, each refusing to admit they were wrong. Where does that leave us? I was under the impression that you were the mature one in this pair. Perhaps I was wrong," Dee ended, poking Aleksei in the chest with one finger to emphasize her point.

"Well, I hope we can come to some sort of truce, because if I'm not mistaken, the head honchos have just pulled up and our little interview is about to get underway," Whittaker stated, pushing the sheer drapes aside and looking out the windows.

"Well?" Dee asked bluntly, tilting her head back to look up into Aleksei's face as he pushed away from the wall and stood his full height of six foot two inches tall.

Casting a quick glance at his coach, he returned his gaze to the expectant eyes level with his chest. "Where do I sit?"

Dee and Whittaker both released their breaths and Dee pointed to the love seat in front of the newly set-up reflectors and lights.

Aleksei limped cautiously over the cables and sank into the comfortable love seat, gratefully accepting a hassock a considerate cameraman offered to rest his cast leg upon.

"Will she show?" Whittaker asked Dee quietly as they watched a pretty girl apply powder and make-up to Aleksei's already handsome face.

Dee smiled knowingly, inwardly cringing at what might transpire now that the first volley had been fired. "Without a doubt. I'm more concerned with the amount of blood Aleksei will lose this time. He won't get away with just a scratch like he did in Canada," Dee stated matter-of-factly.

"You knew about that?" Whittaker asked in amazement.

Dee laughed at Whittaker's expression. "Everyone knew about it!"

Whittaker's expression told her otherwise.

"Take heart, Frank, I'll keep you advised of every single, mundane, detail that concerns this pair."

"If they don't kill each other today in front of the entire viewing world."

"You don't need to worry about that today. There's a curiosity they have about each other that needs answering before any real damage occurs. Something's pulling them toward each other and I personally think they're both protesting just a little too much for any real dislike to be there. It's all part of the testing process—pushing each other just to see how far they can before the other pushes back."

"I hope you're right," Whittaker agreed.

Dee smiled and moved forward to greet the numerous reporters entering her small home, graciously offering *unloaded* coffee to them and making everyone comfortable as they made final preparations for the interview.

Aleksei sat comfortably on the love seat, the last touches of powder having been applied and waited for his 'new partner' to reappear.

Introductions were made and everything was ready to begin—with the exception of Aleksei's still missing partner. The same make-up girl that had flirted all the while she powdered Aleksei's nose, called down from the top of the stairs announcing Jordan was on her way.

Everyone looked up expectantly and suddenly Jordan was greeted with an audible gasp of surprise. The young woman standing at the top of the stairs looked nothing like the *little girl* who had earlier caused such an uproar. Her legs were encased in sheer black stockings ending in impossibly high heels seemed to make her legs go on forever. The short black mini-skirt barely covered her shapely little bottom and the black chiffon blouse emphasized more than distracted from the lacy camisole which displayed more cleavage than Aleksei could have guessed at. Her shades-of-copper hair was piled loosely on the top of her head with a gold and black barrette, wispy tendrils escaped to lay softly against her slightly flushed cheeks. Light make-up enhanced her green eyes, now shining dangerously bright, flashing in challenge even as her full lips curved into a sultry smile of welcome for Aleksei, much as a spider probably welcomed a fly. With a casualness she didn't feel, she slowly made her way down the staircase, her eyes never leaving Aleksei's face and smiled to herself when she saw him sweep his tongue over suddenly dry lips.

Reaching the bottom of the stairs, she accepted a crewman's helping hand to escort her to the love seat. Glancing uncertainly at the small amount of room Aleksei had left for her, she carefully seated herself on the low arm. Aleksei watched in amusement, having given great thought as to how much room to leave her. He had to give her credit for having courage. He'd figured she would have just squished into the remaining corner and disappeared. But surprisingly, she'd just seated herself like a queen on her throne on the arm of the love seat; her long legs crossed elegantly; innocently seductive. Jordan Jamison had certainly earned the title of 'Ice Queen'.

The interview began easily enough.

"Aleksei, what made you decide to leave singles competition?" a reporter inquired.

"The decision was made based on a number of things; primarily though, on my ability to physically maintain the high level rigors of singles competition. At this point, the doctors are uncertain if there will be any limitations I may experience in regard to my jumps, they just aren't certain how my leg will hold up. In pairs, I'll be the strength behind Jordan. It will be my job to present Jordan to the world. If I do my job right, the audience will barely notice me."

Murmurs about the impossibility of Aleksei ever being invisible were whispered, notes were scribbled down rapidly.

"Jordan, are you concerned with the difference in your sizes. Didn't you have difficulty with that point with Bob Hanks? And, unless looks are deceiving, Aleksei's larger than Hanks was."

Jordan looked at Aleksei and smiled warily. "As you all know, my ex-partner had a tendency to misjudge his power and I spent more time than I would have chosen checking out the boards on an up-close and personal basis. I can only hope that experience won't be repeated."

"How do you know it won't?"

"Until we actually skate together and become accustomed to the feel of each other, I won't know. However, I have every confidence in Aleksei and look forward to going back to sheer tights for competitions."

Aleksei's eyes clouded briefly at the cryptic statement, reminding himself to ask her about the comment later, but his attention was pulled back to the interview on the next question.

And so it went on for the next hour, question after question, cautious answers from Jordan, generic answers from Aleksei. Finally the interview was over, until one of the reporters asked for a picture of them together. Their first official photograph as a *pair*.

Aleksei watched as Jordan nervously tried to escape the request. Despite her womanly appearance, she was still just a sixteen year old all dressed up, even if she did look twenty-two. Knowing how reporters could be, he cautiously lowered his cast leg to the ground and stood, reached for her hand and effortlessly pulled her to her feet and against his chest. Even with her hair fluffed and piled high, and the ridiculously high heels, the top of her head didn't reach his shoulder.

Camera's clicked, and whirred, flashes of light from the reflectors causing streaks of white to blur Jordan's vision and make her dizzy. Feeling herself start to tilt, she reached for Aleksei to steady herself and found herself suddenly swept into his arms and cradled gently. Jordan shook her head slightly, trying to clear the bright spots that still flashed before her eyes and turned her head toward Aleksei's softly voiced "close your eyes and count to ten slowly."

Obediently she complied and when she re-opened them, the spots were gone and Aleksei was watching her expectantly.

"Better?"

Silently she nodded yes.

"Good," He answered, smiling easily, then returned his attention to the reporters before them.

"How's she feel?" The question came somewhere from the left of the group of reporters.

Aleksei bounced her slightly, testing her weight and smiled at the group before them. "Hopefully, her skates will add enough weight to her that I can tell when I'm holding her," he teased, releasing her legs and gently placing her back on her feet.

"How about you Jordan, any comments about your new partner?"

Jordan tried to calm her racing heart, tried to ignore the heat that threatened to melt her legs beneath her as she leaned casually against Aleksei. "I can only hope we don't have to skate in any arenas with low ceilings. I have the feeling I'm going to be seeing some spectacular views of the audience during our lifts and throws."

"Better than the boards, though, right?" a reporter asked.

Jordan looked up at Aleksei, their eyes catching and holding, hers pleading softly for safety and his acknowledging her unspoken question.

"Jordan's days of crashing into the boards are over. You all are going to have to find another pair for those pictures," Aleksei promised, his voice deep and sure.

Jordan smiled in appreciation and prayed he could keep his promise.

"If there are no further questions, we have a cake to celebrate the new pairing of Jamison and Rocmanov and we'd be thrilled to have you join us in wishing them well," Dee offered, moving cautiously around the camera equipment spread around her living room, into the kitchen.

Everyone expressed their agreement and began gathering up equipment and electrical cords to make moving around the small room safer and easier. In short order, most of the cords were neatly wrapped and piled near the front door.

"Whittaker, give me a hand would you?" Dee called from the kitchen.

"I've got it," Jordan offered, rising a bit unsteadily to her feet, still not completely comfortable in the heels.

Whittaker nodded his thanks and sat on the arm of the couch she just vacated. Whittaker and Aleksei watched as she walked around the couch and into the kitchen.

"Girl's got a great set of legs," Whittaker stated in appreciation.

"Her ass isn't bad either," Aleksei added.

"Remember, Aleksei, she's sixteen. We don't need that kind of trouble."

"I said she had a nice ass, I didn't say I was going to jump it," Aleksei scowled at his coach, his voice full of disgust.

"Just so long as we understand each other," Whittaker re-emphasized.

"Whittaker, what would I want with a sixteen year old? My leg may be in a cast but that doesn't mean I have to go begging scraps if I want a woman."

"Jordan isn't 'scraps' and at this moment, she doesn't look sixteen. I just want you to remember this is a business arrangement and it's in both your interests to keep in that way."

"I thought there was intimacy involved in pair skating?"

"There is, but it's more a blending of skating styles, personality compatibility, and the physical capability to skate together. Occasionally you get lucky, and reach a point where you're hearts, souls and minds meet and then you're unstoppable! It doesn't mean your goal should be necessarily getting into each other's knickers, not that it doesn't happen with a lot of skaters. But in this case, that particular thought better not even cross your mind. That's one scenario I don't even want to contemplate, if you get my drift? You've got a lot to learn, and a short time to learn it, son. I'd suggest you do your thinking with your brain!"

"And I suppose Jordan's going to do the teaching," Aleksei scoffed, remembering both sides of Jordan, the kid in the baggy sweats and the vixen in black. For some reason, he felt safer with the kid in sweats.

"Jordan's been a pair all her competitive life. She can teach you a lot if you let her."

"It doesn't seem right somehow that a kid can teach me about intimacy. I've been intimate with plenty of women."

"There's a difference between being intimate with a woman and having intimacy, Aleksei. And I think that kid is going to show you the difference," Whittaker decided, nodding his head in affirmation as he watched the subject of their discussion come through the kitchen door with a tray full of cake.

Aleksei watched his new partner push her way through the door, bottom first, stepping to the side and letting the door close behind her. Carefully she held a tray full of slices of celebratory cake. She looked at him tentatively, a small smile gracing her soft lips. His expression was dark, a scowl causing his eyes to narrow and the corners of his mouth to pull down slightly. Her smile slid away to be replaced by teeth that worried her full lower lip. Still, she remained motionless, until Dee pushed unknowingly through the door and shoved Jordan, and the tray of cake abruptly forward. With a shriek, the tray flew forward as Jordan tried to catch her balance on her overly high heels, failed miserably, and fell toward Aleksei.

People dodged flying cake slices, knocking over the few remaining light reflectors and assorted suitcases of equipment. Aleksei, at the mercy of his broken leg, could only wait for the dust to settle. As he watched, Jordan sailed toward him, tripping over one of the reporters who had had the misfortune of stumbling over his video camera, and now lay shielding it from destruction, Jordan hurtled past him and directly into Aleksei's lap.

Aleksei grunted as Jordan landed across his lap, one elbow dangerously close to his groin. Jordan's breath caught at the hard impact, and she dropped her forehead to the cushion as she regained her breath. The sudden realization that she was laying across Aleksei's lap had her face turning three shades of red and she slowly slid from his lap until her knees rested on the carpet, then finally cast a glance up at Aleksei.

"Is this your typical landing or are you just having a bad day?" he asked, his tone serious, but his eyes sparkled devilishly.

"I've had better," Jordan stated softly.

"Landings or days?"

"Both," Jordan answered, the hint of smile gracing her soft mouth.

"Glad to hear it," Aleksei answered, one eyebrow raising sardonically. "So, where's my piece of cake?"

Jordan shook the remaining cobwebs from her mind and glanced about her, her eyes widening as she viewed the scattered pieces of cake all about her. With a final look at Aleksei's arrogant smile, she plucked a piece of cake from where it landed on the ottoman beside Aleksei's cast leg, held it in her opened palm and sweetly stated. "Here's your cake!" and smeared the sticky cake over his face. Cameras clicked and flashed as pictures of Jordan Jamison on her knees before Aleksei Rocmanov smearing chocolate cake over his face joyfully was captured forever on film.

Aleksei's deep growl caused Jordan to push to her feet and take a quick step out of his reach. Bravely she stood three feet away from him, hands on her hips, chin raised defiantly, her eyes flashing fire and glared at Aleksei, silently daring him to say something.

"Fire and Ice," Frank whispered to Dee, shaking his head in worry as he thought about the road ahead of them. It didn't promise to be an easy one.

"Finding gold has never been an easy journey," Dee stated confidently. "When was the last time you saw a miner not covered in mud?"

"Trouble is, my dear, we won't be wallowing in mud. It's starting to look like blood is going to be our chosen cover."

"Just in the beginning," Dee stated with finality, smiling at the look of surprise Whittaker threw her. "They're establishing boundaries. They'll come to an understanding."

"Boundaries, huh?" Whittaker's look was one of pure skepticism.

"Give them a week," Dee offered.

"He's off the ice for at least six," Whittaker reminded her.

"He's off skates for six weeks! He'll be on the ice with Jordan, in a chair if necessary. But he will be on the ice. He needs to learn the way she moves. He can start to learn that by watching her. In six weeks there shouldn't be anything he doesn't know about her," Dee finished, moving forward to further separate the new 'partners' and thank the media for their patience and expertise.

Whittaker stood back and watched as Dee whispered something to Jordan and urged her toward the kitchen. Jordan cast a final haughty look at Aleksei, who now sat casually wiping the cake from his face and onto a plate someone had handed him. Under Dee's instructions, suddenly everyone had a job to do and couldn't do it fast enough.

It was only seconds later that a sopping wet dishtowel flew threw the air with unerring accuracy and hit Aleksei smack in the middle of his chest. Ice cold water from the towel splattered everywhere and Aleksei let out a battle cry of surprise that had everyone turning toward him in fright, then stepping back when he slowly got to his feet. With deadly intent, he limped the short distance to the kitchen door in which Jordan stood defiantly, drying her hands with another dishtowel.

Everyone in the room held their breath as they watched Aleksei come to stand directly before Jordan, towering over her by a good foot, his dark eyes flashing dangerously. Jordan unflinchingly held her ground, despite having to tilt her head back to see his face.

Silently they studied each other; deep green eyes meeting flashing black, their chests rising and falling as Aleksei fought the urge to wring her neck and Jordan fought the urge to run for her life. Jordan's tongue darted out to moisten her dry lips, the motion immediately drawing Aleksei's attention to her full, soft lips. Slowly he leaned toward her, his eyes returning to hers and holding them captive. Closer and closer he came, causing her breath to catch and hold. Towering over her, he took the forgotten dripping wet towel he held and wrapped it around her neck, the ends trailing over her chest and dripping wet trails into the 'v' between her breasts. The abruptness of his movement and the sudden coldness of the wet towel caught her by surprise and she gasped at the sensation, despite his heated words as they caressed her upturned face.

"Don't think you can win at this game, little girl. You're out of your league," he hissed, his voice deadly.

"You're wrong, Aleksei. You're in my league now. And you can't win without me. Like it or not, if we want to go to the Olympics, we're stuck with each other," Jordan countered. Pushing the wet towel off her shoulders, she ignored the thud it made as it fell to the floor behind her, sprinkling the backs of her legs with cold drops of water.

"I didn't ask to be your partner," Aleksei argued.

"Ditto," Jordan agreed.

"I don't even like you."

"Tell me something I don't already know."

"I won't bow to your 'Ice Queen' status. You're no better than I am and I won't be a baby sitter," Aleksei stated.

"And I won't let you bully me. I know more what we're doing that you'll ever know but I'm willing to share that information if you can quit being such an ogre. This is a business partnership and nothing more. If you can agree to that, you've got a partner. If you can't—get your ass out of my house!" Jordan stated firmly, her voice steely, despite it's softness.

Aleksei watched her, admiring her courage and tenacity and stepped back, giving her room to breathe easier. As everyone watched the pair, Aleksei offered his hand to her. "Looks like you've got yourself a partner."

Jordan accepted his hand, her fingers wrapping around his and shook hands in agreement. She was surprised at how soft and warm his large hand was, she would have thought it would be cold at least from the wet towel he'd held, but his palm felt hot. The current of warmth that passed between them as they touched was not lost to either of them and Jordan quickly took a step back.

"Remember, our partnership isn't cast in stone yet. You may still be out on your ass if you can't keep up," Jordan reminded Aleksei.

"I've got stamina to spare," Aleksei countered, smiling arrogantly at Jordan's flustered frown at his double entendre and then wondering if he'd wasted the effort and she hadn't understood his small attempt at a joke.

"I'm only interested in your stamina on the ice. What you do off the ice is your business, but you'd better have your legs under you when they're supposed to be," Jordan stated without humor.

Obviously Jordan had understood Aleksei's comment, and found little humor in it. Whittaker smiled at her statement and turned to Dee, whispering, "Girl's got balls, I'll give her that!"

Dee smiled at the statement and nodded in agreement. "Now, let's see if Aleksei's got balls to match!" and proceeded to clean up the disaster area that was her living room.

"Damn, this is gonna be fun!" Whittaker exclaimed, clapping his hands in anticipation and following Dee's example, began helping her clean up.

Chapter 3

The first week Aleksei sat center ice, on a hard, metal folding chair, watching Jordan literally skate circles around him. Jordan refused to make eye contact with him, let alone speak to him, still thoroughly embarrassed at the debacle their announcement had caused. After the infamous news conference, pictures the following morning showing the gentleness of Aleksei as he held her, Jordan smearing cake over his handsome face and then their heated face-off and eventual hand-shake, landed them on the front page of every newspaper across the country. Questions arose in abundance as to the possibility of such an obviously mismatched, volatile pair managing to make it through a breaking-in period let alone a simple competition. The concept of them as Olympic hopefuls was too much to imagine. Even Jordan's ex-partner had made comments insinuating that the breakdown of their partnership had been due to Jordan's volatile temperament. Aleksei had spent the better part of an hour howling in laughter over that remark. As far as he was concerned, anyone known as the 'Ice Queen' didn't have a 'volatile temperament' to be worried about. And if nothing else, she was true to her nickname. The air of indifference she directed at him came straight out of Canada.

Jordan had numbly skated through her practice sessions, hitting every jump and spin without fail, edging with technical perfection, but failing to bring any life to her skating. It was like watching a lifeless doll skate a program. Dee watched in patient silence, mentally taking notes of the behavior of the two skaters toward each other and pondering what format their first pairing should take.

Week two continued on in the same manner, with the exception that occasionally Aleksei would wickedly taunt Jordan, his remarks mean and cutting. Jordan, sensing his game, refused to respond in kind and that caused Aleksei's mood to grow even darker; his temper and patience reaching their limits.

By the end of week three, Jordan and Aleksei threw all common sense aside and were openly battling verbally; aspersions pertaining to their heritage, skating abilities and physical appearances topping their hit lists.

"You know, Aleksei, you don't look any where near as *big* as all the girls in the dressing room constantly bragged about," Jordan insinuated slyly, gracefully gliding past him in his hard, metal chair.

Aleksei smiling in warning, reaching muscular arms over head as he stretched, his chest swelling as he took a deep, calming breath, trying to lose some of the tension the days of sitting and listening to her barbs had caused. "Believe what you hear in that regard, little girl," He called confidently, his eyes glaring dangerously. "But I would like to know why you look so much smaller lately than when you had that little black get-up on for the interview. Lose part of your anatomy with the blouse?"

"Wouldn't you like to know?"

"Not particularly. I generally tend to lean toward women with real curves and more particularly, those of legal age."

"Only generally?" Jordan chided while executing a perfect sit-spin six feet away from him, her spin causing his dark hair to blow softly in the breeze she created.

Aleksei's only response was a dangerously, dark scowl.

Jordan continued to skate circles around him, each pass getting daringly closer, ignoring his words of caution that she 'back off' or he wouldn't be responsible for his actions making her taunt him even more.

Patiently he waited for her to make that pass that would put her within his reach, imagining what would best put her in her place. The mental picture of her laying helplessly over his lap, screaming in outrage, as he smacked her shapely rear-end made him smile dangerously in anticipation.

Sure enough, as he'd imagined, he was able to grab her arm as she started past him. In surprise, she tried to jerk away from him, actually surprising him when she pulled him out of the chair to his feet, making him slide several feet before he gained his balance. With virtually no effort, he pulled her screaming in outrage against his chest and lifted her into his arms.

"You bastard, put me down!" Jordan railed, twisting as she sought her freedom, the razor sharp blades on her skates flashing brightly through the air.

"Weren't you ever taught any manners?" Aleksei growled, easily controlling the ninety-five pounds of squirming body in his arms while balancing on his good foot and wondering briefly how to reach the chair several feet away. "It isn't nice to call people names, brat!"

Jordan screamed in frustration, the sound echoing off the high, metal ceiling. Still she thrashed wildly, one blade coming dangerously close to Aleksei's good leg when she managed to twist and actually free one leg. For a brief second, she felt her freedom was imminent, only to be spun about abruptly and tossed over his broad shoulder seemingly without effort like a sack of potatoes, both her legs now held completely shackled against his broad chest by one muscular arm. The sudden motion and hard landing as her stomach met his shoulder made her both dizzy and breathless. One moment she was upright, the next she was hanging upside down and looking at the ice. The stinging slap as his large hand landed on her unprotected bottom got her attention and she pushed against his back, trying to slide down the front of his body and out of his grip. Despite her frantic efforts, she was unable to escape his muscular grip. Frustration and anger guiding her, Jordan continued to scream her outrage to the world, adding words that Aleksei was surprised she knew, let alone considered using.

Without a word, Aleksei abruptly released her legs, catching her around the waist just before her feet hit the ice, his breath catching as her body slid down the front of his, astonished at the sharp stabs of awareness her small, firm figure caused.

Their breaths caught when Jordan's sudden stop caused her to fall against Aleksei as she sought her balance; her sharp nails digging into his muscular arms as she slipped slightly on the ice.

Aleksei looked down at Jordan, seeing only the top of her head, shaking his own in bewilderment as he wondered how they would ever skate together. The top of the little brat's head barely reached his shoulder, but her shining copper-colored hair bewitched him and even now he could smell the light fragrance that surrounded her. Still, how would they ever match their strides, despite her extraordinarily long legs? The only advantage he could readily see was it would be nothing to lifting her. Hell, he'd hoisted heavier beer kegs. And, despite her attitude, she was decent enough to look at when she cleaned up, unlike now, after their little disagreement.

Jordan couldn't draw her eyes away from his chest; immensely wide, rock hard and covered with dark, curling hair that peeked out the 'v' of his shirt; couldn't make her hands release the muscular arms so warm beneath her fingers. Her knees still felt like jelly; refusing to support her and the creep hadn't even struggled when he lifted her despite having one leg in a cast. And why did he have to smell so damn good? Jordan shook her head trying to clear the dizziness from her numb mind. She had to restore her thoughts to the rational and reasonable, and stop thinking about how Aleksei felt against her.

"This won't work." She stated suddenly, abruptly releasing Aleksei's arms and turning to skate away, only to catch her toe pick against Aleksei's cast and find herself falling backward to land flat on her butt.

Aleksei could only watch her legs fly from beneath her and keep clear of the flashing blades. Crossing his arms over his massive chest, he cast an amused look her way and stated tauntingly. "Not if you can't stay on your feet around me, it won't," Aleksei offered.

Jordan narrowed her eyes, clearly understanding his insinuation about the Canadian incident. "That wasn't my fault."

Aleksei shrugged nonchalantly. "Maybe it was—maybe it wasn't. Doesn't matter much, since you're still the one on your ass."

"You're a shit, Rocmanov!" Jordan stated firmly, swatting away Aleksei's offer of a hand-up and gracefully getting to her feet. "You're mean, and you're irritable and you're definitely obnoxious and you think entirely too much of yourself!" she ranted. *And you're gorgeous, and you smell wonderful and you feel so damn good!* she thought to herself.

Aleksei listened patiently, enjoying the way her eyes flashed in her fury, the way her hands never stopped moving, remembering their warmth as she had held him moments before and wishing she would touch him again. Hearing her voice, musical and sexy despite her anger. "Fine, I think too much of myself and you're a spoiled bitch," he countered, "That should make us a great match-up."

"According to whom?" Jordan stormed.

"All the great pairs had moments of dissension. It's a part of the process of bringing differences together to make one perfect blend."

"What a bunch of bull shit!" Jordan choked out, laughter escaping despite Aleksei's serious expression. "We aren't making a meal. We're two people so obviously wrong together that it will never work."

"The 'Ice Queen' has spoken," Aleksei taunted, and bowed deeply despite his broken leg.

"Don't even go there, Rocmanov," Jordan warned, her eyes darkening dangerously.

Unperturbed, he shrugged well-built shoulders. "I told Whittaker babies shouldn't be allowed to compete, but he convinced me otherwise. You've just proven I was right. You're not ready to handle a man for a partner. You'd better go find yourself another boy, someone you can push around."

"You didn't think I was a baby when you copped a feel during that press conference," Jordan stated dangerously.

"I was just trying to figure out what parts I'd have to worry about tripping over on the ice when they fell off," Aleksei answered tauntingly, turning around and carefully limping across the ice toward the doorway.

"Don't you turn your back on me, you coward. I'm not through with you yet," Jordan demanded, following after him.

"I've got better things to do with my time than baby-sit the likes of you!" he told Jordan, then shouted to the ceiling, "Whittaker, this fiasco is over!" and continued to limp slowly toward the boards.

Jordan screamed in frustration and picked up her pace to skate around him and come to a quick t-stop before Aleksei, causing him to look down at the ice particles she threw against his ankles. "I am not a baby!" she stated emphatically, poking his chest sharply to make her point. "I've skated since I was four; I hold several titles, I've been through more partners than I care to admit and after the last three weeks I refuse to start breaking in a new partner all over again."

"You're sixteen—a baby," Aleksei repeated, somehow managing to hold his arms at his sides despite his urge to wrap them around her small, shapely form. What was wrong with him? She was just a kid.

Jordan growled in frustration, ran her hands through her already tussled hair and angrily placed her hands on her hips. "If I wasn't sixteen, what would your answer be?"

Against Aleksei's better judgment, he surrendered to his raging testosterone. The little girl before him certainly didn't look sixteen, her curvaceous figure and knowing eyes didn't number her sixteen. Without a word, his hands slid into her hair, his palms carefully, yet firmly held her face as he pulled her mouth to his, his warm tongue pushing determinedly into her mouth and sweetly mating with her own. Surprised at his sudden movement, Jordan's hands grasped his forearms as their lips met, her nails digging in as Aleksei plundered her mouth. Sound thundered in her ears, blocking out all outside interference, the blood rushing through her body and her own labored breathing was all that reached her.

As abruptly as he'd pulled her against him, he released her. His hands swiftly moved from her head to her waist to steady her. The only outward sign of any shared passion was the sensual fire burning deep in his dark eyes. "Fine – we'll give it a try. But don't ever expect me to bow to the "Ice Queen!" He warned dangerously, releasing her and limping the final distance off the ice.

Jordan wrapped her arms around herself, hot and cold at the same time. Something had changed between them, she wasn't sure just what yet but she needed some time to analyze things and regain control. For the moment she was satisfied in simply having the last word and as haughtily as possible stated, "Agreed. Nobody leaves. But you're still an arrogant bastard, Rocmanov."

Aleksei turned, treated her to a brilliant smile and gracefully bowed. "Thank you, your highness. I'll take that as a compliment."

"It wasn't meant as one."

Smugly, and with a look that took her breath away, he answered in the most sensual tone she'd ever heard. "Yes it was!" Without another word, Aleksei limped toward the locker room.

* * * * *

Whittaker watched, unknown, from the bleachers, sensed a tentative truce and looked forward to the next battle of wills. They certainly weren't the calm serenity of Gordeeva and Grinkov but who knew, time could make all the difference in the world. And God knew Aleksei and Jordan looked damn good together.

It was a start!

Chapter 4

Aleksei cast occasional glances at Jordan as she worked on the stairmaster, grimacing as he turned the page of the People magazine he was reading while he shifted position on the hard folding chair.

"You'd think Whittaker could have scrounged up a more comfortable chair for me to sit on. I've been on this damn thing for eight weeks," He growled.

Jordan's look, a mixture of amusement and disgust, stated clearly that she would trade places with him in a minute. For the last eight weeks, she'd continued her daily regiment, both on and off the ice, alternately wishing she were the one on the cold, hard chair and knowing what lay ahead for Aleksei when the cast came off. The brief stint she'd experienced with a removable cast when she stress fractured her left ankle had side-lined her for three weeks (actually two weeks, three days, but she hedged on the time-frame) had nearly driven her crazy. At least she'd been able to remove the cast and sleep decently. Aleksei, on the other hand, hadn't the luxury of removal, despite the threatened self-removal with an electric knife, and the dark circles beneath his eyes stated clearly his sleep was anything but peaceful.

"You just keep in mind how much you hate that chair when they take that boat anchor off your leg. You may decide it's not so bad being side-lined and find yourself another mountain to jump off of," Jordan groaned in relief, silencing the buzzer that announced this portion of her workout over.

Aleksei raised one eyebrow sardonically, throwing the towel that she had draped over his cast leg to her and dropping the magazine to the floor. "I can't imagine being side-lined another day. The last thing I intend to do is 'find myself another mountain to jump off of!'" he growled, pushing himself easily up and limping over to where she leaned against the wall. Wiping her face dry and draping the towel around her neck, the ends rested loosely against the damp, pink skin of her chest, enticingly displayed by the scoop neck of her leotard.

Aleksei's gaze was drawn to a lone drop of sweat that left a trail of moistness as it coursed its way down her long neck and ever closer to the swelling cleavage displayed above her leotard. Unconsciously, he licked suddenly dry lips as his mind brought the image of his tongue following the same path as the slowly moving drop of moisture to his mind, making his breath slow and shallow. Jordan's repeated question finally drew his attention.

"What?" he mumbled, shaking his head to clear the picture from his mind.

"I said, when does that thing come off?" she inquired again, nodding toward the cast, then stretching around him to retrieve her water bottle from the table he leaned against. The softness of her leotard-clad breast as it brushed against his shoulder made him grind his teeth in building frustration.

"Not that I'm anxious, but one hour and thirteen minutes, give or take a few seconds," he answered, glancing quickly at the gold watch he always wore, a gift from Whittaker.

Jordan laughed softly, the sound sweet and carefree. "You won't miss it?" she teased, giving the cast a fond pat.

"About as much as I miss single beds."

I didn't know you knew there was such as a thing as a single bed," Jordan questioned haughtily; raising deep green eyes to meet Aleksei's calm, dark ones.

"I'm perfectly aware there are such things, I just happen to prefer a bed with more room."

"Yeah, I don't suppose your friends would appreciate having to share a small sleeping area."

"When I have friends sharing my 'sleeping area', they generally aren't sleeping!" Aleksei taunted, chucking her chin as if she were a two-year old.

"Hands off!" Jordan complained and swatted his hand away. "You may have another hour and thirteen minutes to screw off, but I've still got arms to do." and off she walked to the next torture machine.

"Why don't you hold off on *arms* and let me get a few lifts in. That way you can't complain that I didn't do anything today," Aleksei suggested, limping over to a large mat set before a wall of mirrors.

Carefully he lowered himself to the mat, removed his sweatshirt leaving only a cut-off T-shirt that showed off his muscle-toned stomach and laid on his back, stretching his arms over his head, displaying even more of his wash-board stomach. Jordan watched him quietly, frowning when he looked expectantly her way and stated, "Well?"

"Do you really think it's a good idea to get all sweaty when you're going to the doctor in an hour? The nurses really don't deserve that kind of treatment."

"Stop stalling. I promise I won't *sweat*," Aleksei growled, snapping his fingers impatiently.

Jordan slowly made her way to him, stepped carefully over his legs to straddle his narrow hips, then cautiously dropped to a kneeling position and leaned forward to place her hands on the floor above his shoulders.

"Ready?" Aleksei inquired, a devilish gleam in his dark eyes as he stretched his neck backward to allow his eyes to meet hers.

"You're running out of time," Jordan hissed, her mood growing surlier by the moment. "Do it or get the hell away from me."

"My, but aren't we suddenly cranky. Forget your coffee today?" Aleksei teased, grasping her hips securely and easily lifting her upward.

Jordan gasped in surprise at her sudden loss of balance and grasped the hands holding her hips. "I wasn't ready," she complained.

"You're the one who told me to hurry. It's not my fault you weren't prepared," he stated nonchalantly. "Arch your back, your balance is too far forward," he suggested, watching their form in the mirror on his left.

Jordan immediately did as instructed lifting her chin upward and arching slightly, her legs crossed tightly at the ankles, her arms beautifully spread.

"That's it," Aleksei said, approving of the beautiful lines her petite figure made. "Now if we can get it on the ice."

"We'll see soon enough," Jordan stated, glancing at their reflection in the mirror.

"Ready for motion?" Aleksei asked, his eyes meeting hers in the mirror.

Jordan nodded and maintained her position as he easily lowered her until their bodies nearly touched, her breasts perilously close to his face, then reversed his movement and pushed her into the air. Jordan watched their movements in the mirror, her mouth suddenly going dry and her breath catching.

Aleksei watched their movement also.

As clear and bright as the blue of a summer sky, his thoughts played as clearly in his mind as if he were watching a movie. His eyes darkened as he felt the warmth of her beneath his hands and became aware he had only to turn his head slightly and her breasts would brush his lips. The sudden rush of heat at the thought of such a thing baffled him and he pushed her upward faster than planned, his hands losing their firm hold on her. With a small shriek, Jordan lost her position, arms flailing wildly the short distance to fall solidly on Aleksei. His own breath whooshed out of him as their hips met squarely, her legs coming to rest between his spread legs, her soft breasts melting against the heat and strength of Aleksei's chest. Jordan's forehead fell forward into the curve of Aleksei's neck, the soft material of his T-shirt caressing her cheek. His intoxicating fragrance, slightly spicy and all male, made her close her eyes to fight the dizzying sensation that threatened to overwhelm her. Her breath came in short, shallow gasps.

Aleksei fared no better. Her softness melted against him. The sudden thought that she didn't look this soft crossed his mind and he smiled as he remembered comments from friends about her being nothing more than a piece of wood, hardwood at that! A lot they knew. It was all he could do not to grab her sweetly rounded butt and grind his hips against her own. That would certainly add another dimension to their barely restrained civility. Here he'd been hoping they could find a middle ground on which to build a working relationship and suddenly the thought of ripping her tight little leotard off her was uppermost in his mind. Definitely time to hit the showers.

"Are you okay?" he finally managed to gasp out, shaking his head to clear the disturbing path his thoughts lead him, his breathlessness betraying his deeply intoned question.

Jordan answered with a small nod, her eyes wide, afraid to speak let alone move. She didn't even want to address the feeling of rightness as she lay sprawled full length, or at least all she could reach of him, her blood raging through her veins even as she tried to steady her erratic breathing and thundering heartbeat.

"You're sure?" he asked again, closing his eyes as she moved her cheek against his shoulder, her hair brushing his face, the remnants of the soft fragrance she wore teasing his senses.

Again she nodded. But still she didn't move.

Aleksei couldn't stand much more of this. His steely determination to remain still was rapidly disintegrating. His need to touch her, everywhere, was becoming perilously close to overwhelming. He flexed his hands at his sides in an effort to release some of the tension surging through his body. "Jordan?" he questioned softly, deeply.

Finally she spoke. "Yes?" she whispered her voice husky and unsteady, a warm caress against his neck. Still she remained perfectly still.

"Can you move?"

"I think so…but I'm not sure."

Aleksei rolled his eyes in frustration; his hands desperate to touch her resumed their frantic flexing. "What do you mean you're not sure?" he asked, his frustration deepening his voice yet another notch.

"I mean I'm not sure!" she hissed softly, a gentle moan escaping her parted lips when his hands finally could resist no longer and came to rest on the outside of her rib cage, his thumbs settling perilously close to her breasts.

"Then let me help you," Aleksei offered, lifting her up and off him slightly, his breath catching as her legs tangled with his as he eased her to one side. Without thought he followed her until he found himself hovering over her, his spread legs entrapping hers, his elbows supporting his weight. Beneath him, she looked like a small child.

Jordan kept her eyes closed, afraid to look at him, unsure what she would see. She only knew she couldn't bear to see amusement or disinterest. It was safer to keep her eyes closed, to keep her dreams to herself. Now was the time to regain control of her breathing and her pounding heart.

"Jordan." The whispered word caressed her face, scattering all thoughts of regaining any sort of control. Slowly her eyes glided open to reveal the mysterious deep green of an enchanted forest.

Aleksei's mind went blank, the earlier image picking up where it had left off, drawing him ever closer to Jordan's flame.

"Dear God," Aleksei gasped huskily, his body melting deeper into hers, one hand lifting to slide into her tangled, auburn curls.

Slowly he lowered his head toward hers, his lips parting slightly as his tongue wetted dry lips. Her own lips parted in answer as she watched his mouth slowly descend, holding her breath as she awaited the moment she would finally feel his full lips on hers. Time stood still, blood pounded through their veins; everything around them faded into an out of focus collage. Jordan lifted her chin slightly as Aleksei's lips dropped the final distance to her awaiting mouth. Their breaths blended, their eyes held then drifted shut, their lips whispered together.

A door slammed loudly against the wall!

"Aleksei, it's time to get that damn boat anchor removed. Off your ass, and out the door!" Whittaker bellowed, then turned around and left, the door slamming closed behind him.

Jordan and Aleksei broke apart instantly, Aleksei rolling off her, sitting up and placing his back to her. Jordan sat up, the mirror reflecting Aleksei's stiff posture and her own wide-eyed countenance and ragged breathing. Jordan watched as Aleksei got easily to his feet, despite the full leg cast then turned to her and silently helped her to her feet. Without a word, Aleksei turned and limped from the room, silently acknowledging Jordan's 'good luck' with a nod. The only outward sign of his frustration was the resounding sound as both doors he exited through slammed against the walls.

"I second that motion," Jordan mumbled, then headed back toward the stair-master. Even a cold shower wouldn't take care of the torrent of sexual frustration rushing through her now. Hopefully, sheer exhaustion would do the trick. "Come to mama," she growled and punched in the settings on the machine. "Mt. Everest ought to do the trick!" she growled and proceeded to begin her climb.

✴ ✴ ✴ ✴ ✴

Aleksei reclined casually on the examining table; his head resting on his crossed arms, as the nurses carefully sawed the cast from his leg, laughing easily at some joke he'd told, their work seemingly undisturbed.

"How's the leg look?" Whittaker asked the doctor, nodding toward the x-ray the doctor was reviewing.

"Very good—but I wouldn't expect any quads out of him for at least another nine months, maybe a year," the doctor suggested, sliding the x-ray off the screen and into an envelope.

"That won't be a problem—his quad days are over," Whittaker stated factually. "In fact—his singles days are over. He became half of a pair six weeks ago."

"I'd read something to that effect in the newspaper. But I've discovered you can't always believe what you read," the doctor quipped.

"Well this time they got it right. He's now part of Jamison and Rocmanov," Whittaker explained.

"Sounds like part of a law practice."

Whittaker laughed, nodding in agreement. "I don't care what it sounds like, as long as it works."

"Will it?" the doctor inquired, scribbling notes in Aleksei's file.

"I think the potential is there. They're both proven skaters. A semi-truce has been called so hopefully they won't kill each other this week but they haven't actually 'skated' together yet."

"Due to his leg." the doctor finished the thought, still scribbling notes.

Whittaker glanced back at Aleksei, watching his reaction as the nurses made the final cuts and carefully removed the cast, then the padding and cloth covering his lower leg.

"Who'd you say his new partner is?" the doctor asked suddenly.

"Jordan Jamison," Whittaker answered, his eyes taking in the doctors surprised look and nodding in agreement.

"Will it work? He's got to out-weigh her by over one hundred pounds and have over a foot on her," the doctor guessed.

"So you know her."

"Treated her after her partner threw her into the boards. Luckily it was just a hairline fracture, and her partner then wasn't that much bigger than she was. On the ice together, they looked pretty equal. But I'll tell you, when I had her on the table, she wasn't a whole lot bigger than a peanut!" the doctor's stated, concern clear in his voice.

Whittaker chuckled softly at the doctor's comment. "Well, you don't have to worry about that *'peanut'*. The first time she met Aleksei she flipped him off. You could say she fired the first shot and it took them a good three weeks to get to where they could be on the ice together and not go for blood."

"I thought you said they haven't skated together yet?" the doctor asked.

"They haven't. Aleksei has been sitting on the most uncomfortable steel chair I could find for him, center ice, watching her literally skate circles around him. I figured it would be good for the boy to see how she moves, and who knows, maybe make him a little humble. Besides, just because he was fool enough to jump off a mountain doesn't mean she should fall back on her training. He's just going to have a whole lot of catching up to do," Whittaker stated.

"Can he do it without further injury?" the doctor asked seriously, watching Aleksei as the nurses carefully applied lotion to his dry, scaly leg.

"That's why he's now part of a pair, less strain on that leg. I won't lie to you; it's not going to be easy getting him back to a hundred percent. But if you could see how Jordan rides his ass and taunts him, he'll do it just to get the chance to exact revenge on the *'peanut'*."

"Why do I have the feeling there's more here than you're telling me?" the doctor inquired with a knowing smile.

"Suffice it to say, you don't have to worry about Jordan's well being," Whittaker offered.

"What about Aleksei's well being?" the doctor asked.

Whittaker shook his head sadly. "As far as I'm concerned, Aleksei's well being flew out the window when he took on that little bitty spitfire and expected to win the war. Far as I can tell, he hasn't even won a battle yet!"

"What's it called, 'artistic differences'?"

"I'm sure you've heard them referred to as 'fire and ice'?" Whittaker asked the doctor. At the doctor's affirmative nod, Whittaker continued. "And what happens when 'fire and ice' come together?" he questioned.

"Lots of steam?" the doctor suggested.

"Exactly!" Whittaker stated, poking his finger toward the doctor. "And if you'd seen them just before I brought Aleksei over here, you'd know we're just about to experience some serious skating."

The doctor smiled at Whittaker's enthusiasm and shook his hand. "Good luck. Let me know if you need a hand cleaning up the carnage," he offered, turning as Aleksei approached them on crutches and accepted his outstretched hand.

"Thanks, Doc," Aleksei stated, smiling in appreciation, his hand extended. Even the stiffness in his ankle and the itching skin from his knee down couldn't ruin his good mood.

"I recommend you take it real slow on that ankle. No jumps for at least eight to ten weeks and then only if the limp is completely gone. If you feel any grinding or extreme pain, I want you back here immediately," the doctor stated firmly, shaking his hand in return.

"I know the drill, Doc." Aleksei agreed, "your nurses gave me thirteen pages of instructions and threats of severe torture if I screw up."

"It pays to have a properly trained staff," The doctor confirmed, smiling at the nurses as they straightened the examination room.

"Good luck, Aleksei," the nurses chimed, smiling and waving as Aleksei made his way carefully out the door and down the corridor toward the lobby.

Whittaker again shook the doctor's hand. "I'll see that he follows all thirteen pages of those instructions," He promised, then nodded to the nurses and followed his athlete down the hall.

* * * * *

The music of Romeo and Juliet swelled sweetly, bringing tears to Jordan's eyes, as she listened to both the music and her coach, Dee, describe the program she and Aleksei would skate. The program that could possibly get their names back to the forefront of everyone's minds. Despite Jordan's concern over every pair known to mankind having used this piece of music at one time or another; Dee was convinced it was the perfect piece for Jordan and Aleksei. Dee and Whittaker had choreographed the program, working together, effortlessly it seemed, and now Dee walked Jordan through it mentally. Explaining where the lifts would be, where the throws would land, spirals, footwork, holds, all in minute detail until Jordan could actually see the program in her mind. Jordan could almost feel it in her body and wished she could realize it with Aleksei and that, more than anything, made her anxious. He was her partner—nothing more—one more partner in a long line of them. In all actuality, probably not the last one she'd have. And yet, something felt different this time. There was a connection between them. Dee called it chemistry. Whittaker called it a perfect pairing. Aleksei called it a glutton for punishment. Jordan called it…she wasn't sure what she called it anymore. At the beginning it had been a desire to see him grovel at her knees, begging for the opportunity to skate with her, touch her, lust after her. Now, somewhere along the line the rules had changed and she was the one needing to touch, lusting after him, wanting him. And it made her crazy! Never had she been so out of control of her emotions. Wasn't she the one they called the 'Ice Queen'? Wasn't she the one everyone deemed untouchable? Now she felt like an icicle looking for a place to melt and the power of Aleksei's inner flame drew her ever nearer, threatening the wall of ice that protected her heart and her soul from hurt and pain. Was she brave enough to risk the chance of exposing her true self to Aleksei or would he, like all her other partners, laugh at her and carelessly throw her dreams and desires back in her face? Quickly brushing away a tear that slowly trailed down her flushed cheek, she cast a glance at Dee, who silently watched her, lifted her chin determinedly and quietly, yet firmly announced. "We'll kick their butts if we can get Aleksei up off of his."

"Did I hear my name being bashed?" Aleksei asked softly, his deep tone sexy and deep. Without a word he took in the startled, almost frightened, look in Jordan's wide eyes, the shiny trail of tears on her flushed cheeks. "Did I miss something?" he asked cautiously, his eyes never leaving hers.

"How long have you been… When did you get back?" Jordan asked uneasily, turning her back to him abruptly and wiping the tears away hastily.

Aleksei started to move toward Jordan but caught Dee's barely perceptible shake of her head, her mouthed 'no' and that stopped him in his tracks. Nodding in acknowledgment, he easily answered "Only just."

"Good," Jordan mumbled in response.

"Good to know I was missed," Aleksei replied sardonically.

Jordan looked over her shoulder at him, amazed once again at his size, wondering how they could ever skate together, how she would survive his throws. Then deciding at that second they would find a way. A decidedly wicked light entered her tear-shined eyes, "Were you gone?" she asked haughtily, her gaze slowly traveling up and down his body, her eyes widening when he stood a little straighter, foregoing leaning on the crutches.

"How soon they forget," he replied huskily, his tongue quickly wetting his full lower lip, his eyes darkening at their shared memory of only an hour before.

Jordan was dumbstruck, her breath suddenly gaspy, her mouth dry, her blood boiling in her veins, legs threatening to collapse. "While you've been lounging about being ogled and pampered by nurses, I've been hard at work. Therefore, if you'll excuse me, I've got a whirlpool waiting for me," she stated, a small crease forming between her eyes as she scowled and tried to clear the vibrant image of them tangled together on the exercise mat an hour before.

"Great idea! The doctor said the water would be good for my leg. Give me ten minutes and I'll join you," Aleksei suggested, raising an eyebrow, daring her to run like a frightened rabbit.

"Yeah, whatever," Jordan returned as blandly as possible, one shoulder shrugging in what she hoped was nonchalance, wishing she could gracefully escape. The last place she wanted to be, feeling like she was about to explode, was in a whirlpool with the very person that made her feel so out of control. How do you control emotions you have no control over? How could she survive another encounter with the heat that was Aleksei, no wonder he was called 'fire'. His soul burned hot and fiery, consuming everyone and everything he directed it toward. And now, those dark, fiery eyes were looking at her and she felt about to be devoured.

"Give me ten minutes to get undressed," Aleksei stated deeply, his eyes holding hers captive, his comment off-handed to Whittaker and Dee but crystal clear to Jordan.

Jordan swallowed convulsively. " I didn't think you wore enough clothing that it took you ten minutes to strip? I don't know if I can stand the anticipation that long." The comment was meant to be casual but came out huskily, causing both coaches heads to turn and look at her questioningly.

"I'll help you, Aleksei," Whittaker stated, steering Aleksei toward the men's locker room, casting a last glance at Dee and Jordan.

"Jordan?" Dee questioned softly, laying a comforting hand on her shoulder.

"No problems. I'm okay," Jordan answered quietly, squeezing her hand reassuringly. With a quick smile cast over her shoulder at her coach, she stated, "Dee, I love the music," then made her way toward the women's locker room and the awaiting whirlpool.

* * * * *

Jordan silently walked into the steaming whirlpool, the water swirling noisily, bubbles rushing from the bottom of the pool as air was forced through the jets, their power gently easing away the pains of her workout. Slowly she eased her body into the steaming water, smiling in ecstasy at the high temperature of the water, warmer than normal, but forever grateful for Dee's thoughtfulness. There was just nothing better than a steaming hot whirlpool. Leaning her neck against the cool tiles, her eyes drifted dreamily closed, a soft smile graced her lips. Within seconds, she was daydreaming.

Aleksei silently limped toward the whirlpool, soundlessly watching the vision before him, feeling his body respond to her and wishing he had more than just the towel draped around his hips. But his ankle was throbbing, along with other things, and all he could think of was slipping into the heat of the swirling water and losing himself in it.

Cautiously he made his way into the water, holding the handrail. Two steps in, the high heat of the water suddenly hit him. "Damn, I didn't know the hot-tub had been turned into a soup pot and I was the soup of the day." *he swore, holding his position as he tried to acclimate to the water's heat.*

"Don't be a baby," Jordan mumbled, her head still reclined and her eyes closed. "It feels great."

"*I'm sure it will after all my nerve endings are fried. But right now, it's frigging hot!*" *he growled deeply. Gingerly he eased down another step; his breath hissing out as the water crept up another six inches, causing the bottom of his towel to float away from his legs until it sank into the water.*

Slowly she lifted her head, her eyes opening languorously then snapping wide when she viewed nothing but his wide shoulders, bare chest covered in curly black hair, flat, narrow stomach then a skimpy white towel barely covering his hips. An off-handed comment died on her lips, now parted slightly as she struggled for a full breath. Her arms that had been floating weightlessly on the bubbles, suddenly became heavy, sinking to lie helplessly at her sides. Her eyes stared, glazed and unblinking at the beauty of the man before her.

Aleksei returned the gaze, his eyes never leaving hers, as he slowly limped his way, through the waist deep swirling hot water to stand before her. The steam swirled around her, flushing her cheeks and causing small tendrils of hair to curl around her temples. Her eyes darkened to a deep forest green, glazed and uncertain, questioning and knowing at the same time. She gently chewed her lower lip, coloring them an even deeper shade of pink than normal, drawing attention to her already delicious looking mouth. Aleksei groaned softly at the display of total femininity before him. Whether she knew it or not, she was slowly torturing him. Making his blood boil hotly, testing every ounce of control he had or ever would have. Slowly he sank to his knees before her, his good leg taking all his weight when pain suddenly shot through his newly uncast leg. The insignificant burn he felt from the water briefly took his mind off of the pain of his leg, but not the pain Jordan was causing him. Slowly he inched forward on his knees, stopping when his belly pressed against Jordan's knees. The water made him weightless, all pain from injury gone, his blood boiling in his veins, the sound of the jets blanking out everything. Time stood still and yet their gazes remained locked. She looked so small, like a sprite resting in a steaming spring. Even on his knees, he was taller than she was. Slowly he leaned forward, placing his hands against the cool tile on either side of her head. Wordlessly he watched her, scarcely breathing yet feeling the need to gulp deep breaths of air. Sensuously he ran his tongue over agonizingly dry lips, his eyes darkening further while he watched Jordan's response to this small gesture.

She couldn't quit watching his mouth. She felt helpless against the silent sensual calling she felt from Aleksei. Her own tongue darted out, wetting lips in response, a silent yes to his request.

"Jordan," His voice whispered, huskily, sensuously.

She raised her eyes to meet his, her breath catching at the dangerously, wanting look in his eyes. She held his gaze, unflinchingly, achingly, then slowly closed her eyes in surrender.

Aleksei released the breath he'd held since he called her name, and leaned slowly toward her. A whispered, "Yes," escaped her lips, mingling with his breath just as their lips met. Their kiss was one of sweetness, one of welcoming, unhurried. Unlike the fiery near-kiss of earlier, this kiss promised more. There was no feeling of urgency this time, no this-is-all-there-will-ever-be. They melted together, becoming one. Magically, strength returned to Jordan's arms and before she knew how it happened, her hands were slowly sliding up Aleksei's muscular arms, coming to rest on his broad shoulders. Aleksei's large hands gently found her face, his palms resting carefully against her high cheekbones.

Slowly they pulled apart. Aleksei placed a small teasing kiss at the corner of her mouth before he fully left her. Jordan shyly opened her eyes. A soft smile slowly spread across her kiss swollen lips as she looked into Aleksei's dark eyes.

Without a word, she gently pulled him forward, wrapping her arms around his broad, muscular back. Aleksei easily followed her lead and wrapped his arms carefully around her petite form, once again amazed at how small she actually was. With a soft sigh, she laid her cheek against his shoulder, breathing in the scent that was uniquely his own and smiled peacefully as she felt his hand slide into her hair and gently hold her head.

Aleksei's breath escaped in a hiss as he cautiously stepped into the steaming water, holding the rail for support as he limped down the three steps. "I thought there were medical reasons for keeping the water below the boiling point." He stated grumpily as the hot water crept up his thighs.

Jordan's eyes snapped open worriedly at his first words, hoping against hope he was wearing more than the small towel she'd envisioned him in only moments before in her dream. The pair of Speedos he wore lessened her concern only minimally. "It was your decision to share my whirlpool, so don't complain about the temperature. Beggars can't be choosers," Jordan stated, closing her eyes to block out the vision of Aleksei's broad, muscular chest and the dark swirls of hair that covered all that strength. The washboard stomach, the long, muscular legs that led to a patch of material that was certainly too small to be considered a bathing suit and did nothing but enhance the maleness it sought to cover.

"I don't beg," Aleksei answered firmly, continuing to cautiously sink to the seat, grimacing as the steaming water inched up his broad chest.

"Instead you complain or demand until you get your own way," Jordan stated slowly, her voice soft and drowsy, the heat of the swirling water melting her tensions away.

"I've found it's the best way to get things accomplished."

"Try being nice. That works too," Jordan suggested sleepily.

"Not on you," Aleksei grumbled.

"You've never tried," Jordan countered softly.

Aleksei looked at Jordan, saw the pulse beating steadily against her throat, matching the beat of his own heart. Her head still rested against the rim of the whirlpool, her eyes remained closed, her soft pink lips parted slightly as she breathed slowly. The rest of her was hidden beneath the swirling water and surging bubbles. The urge to lift her from the swirling water and feel her against him was nearly overwhelming. Again he had to remind himself she was only sixteen, a child, but still it wasn't a child's body he had held and lifted and carried as they worked together.

"Jordan, kiss me," Aleksei whispered, his voice so deep it was more his tone than his request that snapped her mind from its mindless floating.

"What?" she gasped, her mind trying to catch up with the blood that now raced madly through her body. Did she really hear him correctly or had she merely wished the request in her dreams and somehow confused the two?

Aleksei cursed himself for even thinking let alone voicing aloud his desire. How had this slip of a girl, who infuriated him at every turn, suddenly have him on his knees and begging for a kiss? He'd never had to beg for sexual favors in the past. In fact, more often than not, he was turning women away. A fact he was not always proud of, but still, a part of his past and something that had kept his name in print. After all, even bad publicity was good, as long as your name was on everyone's tongue you wouldn't be forgotten. It was only when they forgot about you your career was over. And Aleksei had made sure his name was never forgotten. Now, with Jordan, he wanted to move on and start a new chapter of his life and career and amazingly enough, it was going to happen because of a slip of a sixteen year old girl. A sixteen year old girl who was wiser than time itself and infinitely more mature than he was himself.

"I said… show me, Jordan," He stuttered, holding his breath as he hoped she hadn't heard his original request.

Jordan shook her head slightly, confusion evident in her deep green eyes as they searched Aleksei's dark, shining ones. "Show you what?"

"Show me how to be a pair. Show me how to skate with you," He requested huskily.

Jordan raised one eyebrow, her expression expectant.

"Please," Aleksei growled sardonically.

Jordan's face lit up, a broad smile gracing her beautiful face and laughing eyes. "Now was that so hard?" she inquired sweetly.

That wasn't but I could show you something that is! Aleksei thought silently, shifting his position to try to relieve the building pressure against his Speedo trunks. "Don't push it, Jamison. I only grovel so many times a year and this year's quota is almost up," He stated darkly.

"I'm sorry. I'll try to curtail my enthusiasm at your groveling to a minimum. I've just never had anyone ask me to be their partner before. In the past, I was always the one asking and making the concessions. This is something new for me too."

"Great, we'll learn together then. If it's okay with you?" Aleksei asked, cautiously pushing to his feet and starting for the stairs. "Nobody leaves, right?"

"Right," Jordan agreed. "Done already?" she then asked, walking to Aleksei's side.

Standing beside him, the top of her head reached him mid-chest, again reminding him how much his strength could harm her. "I'll never hurt you, Jordan," He promised deeply, his words and tone making her raise her eyes to his.

"Do I look worried about that possibility, Rocmanov?" she asked knowingly, a serene, womanly smile gracing her full lips.

"I just wanted you to know that I do take your safety into consideration—despite the times I seriously consider murdering you. I just wanted you to know," Aleksei stated softly, his deep voice full of conviction.

"Okay, thanks," She answered quietly. "By the way, how's the leg?" she asked, nodding toward the leg he favored.

"Skinny, scaly and weak. But give me a few weeks and it'll be good as new," he quipped, a happy smile lighting his eyes as he rubbed his hand down his weak leg and felt his own skin instead of the cast he'd come to hate.

"If you say so."

"I do and the sooner you learn I keep my word the sooner we'll be standing on a podium collecting gold," He stated seriously.

"I'm beginning to realize that," She responded softly, lifting her chin at his sardonic expression and raised eyebrow, daring him to taunt her. "I'm man enough—woman enough—to admit when I may have misjudged someone."

"Is that what you're doing? Are you saying you misjudged me?"

"I wouldn't go that far. I'm just saying the jury is still out and I need more evidence before I make a final determination as to your worthiness," She concluded, making her voice as snobby as she could and still not dissolve into laughter at Aleksei's astonished expression.

"I've got to get out of here before I overcook—whether from your outrageously snobby opinions or the fire you obviously have going under this kettle," he called over his shoulder as he carefully limped his way up the stairs and out of the steaming water. "Later," He offered.

"Okay. Later," She returned, hoping it wouldn't be too much later as she watched his tall form make its way slowly to the locker room doors, until he was out of sight and then sank to her knees in the swirling water. "He's too damn gorgeous!" She growled softly, wrapping her arms around her middle in an attempt to slow the blood roaring through her veins and stop the excitement that threatened to explode from within. Abruptly she rose up, lurching toward the steps and climbing the three feet to the landing. Without a second thought, she loudly announced, "Dee, I'll be in the shower and there'd better be plenty of cold water!"

Her wet feet barely made a sound as she marched across the floor and into the women's locker room.

* * * * *

From across the room, unbeknownst to Aleksei and Jordan, Whittaker and Dee had watched the couple. Each of them lost in their own thoughts. Each pondering the wisdom of this unusual attempt to create a pair team out of two such volatile and differing personalities. Each questioning the reasons behind their beliefs that something wonderfully beautiful and magic could be made by Jordan and Aleksei. The silence suddenly broke when Whittaker clapped his hands together and stated without doubt, "Dee, that program's going to work just fine!"

Dee decided to reserve judgment on Whittaker's statement and remained silent, sending a simple wish toward heaven that Whittaker was right, and she hadn't sent Jordan into the lion's den.

Chapter 5

Over the next three weeks, Aleksei spent the better part of twelve hours a day pushing his body to its limit and demanding his healing leg regain its strength immediately. Over that same period of time, he decided if he had a dime for every time he found himself sprawled on the ice when his leg refused to support him, he could retire now, and forget all this foolishness. Then he'd hear the nearly soundless whisper of sharp blades on ice, feel the spray of tiny particles of ice as Jordan slid to a graceful stop beside him and held her hand out to him in assistance. Looking up into her smiling, concerned eyes, he'd feel her hidden strength as she helped pull him to his feet and was again reminded that he was doing this not only for himself but also for her. Patiently he'd stand still, his body aching with both pain and lust as she'd brush the ice from his legs and back and well shaped bottom, giving the last a final playful swat of encouragement before she skated silently away to continue her own practice session. On occasion, Aleksei was fast enough to catch her before she zipped away and kiss her hand gallantly, thanking her for her support and encouragement. It also gave him a very appealing view of her scantily clad bottom as she skated away from him.

Everyone agreed the pair would learn and perfect their lifts off the ice before they attempted the dangerous moves on it. Aleksei had refused the use of a practice harness, at Jordan's request, stating it was too easy to get tangled in the long ropes. Jordan's slight weight wasn't a problem for him, as he'd been lifting her even when his leg had been in the cast. Aleksei's quick glance made her realize he remembered their encounter the day his cast was removed, and she flushed a soft pink with embarrassment.

"It's a matter of balance, timing and gravity." Whittaker stated, as they watched training films of World and Olympic champions Gordeeva and Grinkov in a small room off the main office. "Watch where he places his hands, the position of his hips and legs as he lifts her. It doesn't get any better than that," he murmured, shaking his head in both wonder and sadness at the loss of such a great skater. "Makes you wonder what God's got in mind when he calls someone that young and talented home."

"Don't go soft on me now, Whittaker. We've got a job to do," Aleksei stated firmly, his eyes never leaving the tape as he watched Sergei Grinkov lift his young, beautiful partner through various lifts and throws, seemingly without effort.

Jordan watched Aleksei as he absorbed every nuance of the training tapes, mentally and literally taking quickly scribbled notes on a small pad before him, moving his hands as he imagined the positions of the different lifts. Occasionally she would state her opinion regarding a specific hold or difficulties she had experienced on a specific lift or throw. Aleksei would acknowledge her comments, nodding silently, his eyes never leaving the video screen.

The next day they agreed to try their first lift, a fairly simple platter lift. Aleksei stood facing Jordan, his hands on her waist, listening as Whittaker fired instructions at him.

"If you're both ready? On the count of two, Jordan, help him out with a small jump, keep your hands on his shoulders and let him get you up and over his head. You know the drill—but this is for his benefit."

Jordan smiled as Aleksei rolled his eyes at Whittaker's dig and then winked reassuringly at her.

"One...two..." Whittaker counted off, holding his breath as Aleksei easily lifted Jordan over his head, his elbows locking into position as she arched her back and lifted her legs straight behind her.

"*How's the leg, Aleksei?*" Whittaker asked, noting his sudden shift of weight to his good leg.

"Nothing I can't manage," Aleksei answered tensely, looking up into Jordan's concerned eyes.

Jordan's eyes reflected his pained expression. "Whittaker, get the harness ready."

"No!" Aleksei refused, determined not to be the one to hold their progress up. Cautiously, he unlocked his elbows and brought Jordan safely to the ground, walking slowly on his healing leg to stop the muscle spasms that shot shards of pain to his hip. "We already agreed the harness wasn't for us."

"*Then we'd better come up with another idea because I won't have you ruining your leg for the sake of a stinking medal. It's not worth it as far as I'm concerned,*" Jordan stated hotly, flinging her arm at Aleksei as he limped in small circles. "*Have we all lost our minds? He's risking his career for something he didn't even want and we're letting him. I can't believe I ever agreed to this madness.*"

"Nobody forces me to do anything I don't want to do!" Aleksei growled at Jordan, catching her hand as she tried to stalk past him and pulling her forcefully against his tall, muscular form and holding her arm behind her back to keep her against him when she tried to pull away. "I thought you knew me better than that?" He asked softly, the warmth of his breath stirring the wayward strands of hair at her temples.

Jordan sighed shakily, her forehead coming to rest against his chest, the blending aromas of his after-shave, the earthy seductiveness of well-warmed muscles through his shirt and the spiciness of his soap making her too aware of him as a man. How could she be so torn between wanting to ravish him and yet protect him as a lioness would her cub? When had she lost sight of the Gold medal she had spent her life reaching for? When had her priorities changed from wanting to be the world's best to wanting what was best for Aleksei, despite what it could mean to herself? "I'm beginning to think I don't know much about anything anymore," Jordan murmured softly, her voice falling away to a whisper.

Aleksei released her wrist and folded both arms around her small, shapely form, resting his chin on the top of her head. "You know more than I'll ever come close to knowing. I need you close just so I don't come off sounding like a complete idiot," he teased, hoping to break the tension that filled the workout room.

Jordan's smile was shaky, but it was a smile. "Not everyone can be smart and gorgeous," She quipped, pulling back to look into his dark eyes and then wriggling against Aleksei's hips when his fingers ran down her ribcage.

Aleksei's eyes flashed darkly at Jordan's wriggling intimacy, causing her breath to catch and her own eyes darken with passion. *If only we were alone,* Aleksei's eyes promised silently. Without his eyes leaving hers, he stepped back from her, his hands a sensuous promise as they slipped from her hips. "So what's our next option?" he asked his coach.

Whittaker looked from Aleksei to Jordan and then to Dee, who nodded her head in agreement at his unspoken suggestion. "I say we hit the pool." Without another word, he spun on his heels and headed for the door.

"We'll see you pool side in ten minutes," Dee stated firmly, then followed Whittaker's quickly moving figure.

Jordan and Aleksei exchanged confused glances, confused by their coach's behavior and the explosive physical attraction that had sprung so hotly and suddenly between them. They were partners on the ice and struggling to find a truce off the ice. Where had this fiery hormonal explosion suddenly come from?

Jordan backed up a step, her hands fidgeting as she tried to still their nervous fluttering. "We've got ten minutes," she murmured softly, her voice husky and whispery at the same time.

Aleksei nodded. "I heard." His own voice sensuously deep.

"Okay, then..." Jordan began, only to lose her train of thought when Aleksei took a step toward her, his eyes darkening; a wicked, beckoning light flickering dangerously in their ebony depths. His very gaze held her captive, made her heart pound heavily, her legs immobile. Unblinkingly, she watched him move slowly toward her, stalking her as a panther would its prey.

He stopped just before her, near enough to touch her but not. His hands captured her fluttering ones, his fingers weaving with hers, their pulses matching pace as their hands blended to become one. His passion-darkened eyes held hers, daring her to break contact. As if hypnotized, she returned his gaze. Inch by enticing inch his mouth lowered toward her slightly parted lips, his breath warm and sweet as it blended with her own shallow breaths. She felt intoxicated, dizzy with a need she was uncertain of, a want for something she couldn't name. Shakily she tried to close the remaining inches to his mouth, rising to the balls of her feet as she sought the promise his kiss offered. His hands controlled her own, shifting position and wrapping around her back to rest lightly at her waist. Easily he urged her balance forward; causing her to lean against his passion hardened frame, all doubts of his arousal gone as she could feel his heat strongly against her center. His lips closed the remaining distance, his mouth devouring hers upon contact, his tongue delving deeply into her mouth as his hips pressed heatedly against her own answering motion. Flashes of bright light flared behind her closed eyelids, her mind going empty to all but the raging emotions exploding within her. Her hands flexed convulsively, seeking to hold something stable, something that wasn't crumbling beneath this onslaught of physical power. His hands held hers steady; firmly yet gently, forcing her to feel without the benefit of touch. His kiss deepened, seeking more from her, demanding the walls she'd built around her heart crumble to dust and be replaced by the trust, loyalty and strength Aleksei promised. Jordan struggled to regain control. She couldn't possibly relinquish so much so soon to someone she barely knew. Despite her body's sensual response to his own, she had to stop this head long rush into recklessness that threatened to pull her into its center that was the total, encompassing, pure heat of Aleksei. With a strength that surprised her, she managed to pull her mouth from Aleksei's, whimpering at the loss of intimacy. Gulping in deep breaths of air, her breath caught again as Aleksei's deeply voiced Russian words heated her ear, words she didn't understand completely but were nevertheless crystal clear by their urgency and tone. Jordan's legs threatened to fold beneath her slight weight as Aleksei continued his assault on her senses. His heated mouth, wickedly suggestive words and dark eyes overwhelmed her tenuous hold on the control she believed would save her.

"Aleksei…" she gasped, her last thoughts of control drifting away like mist off a waterfall, her only worry touching that which Aleksei offered then teasingly held just beyond her reach. "Oh, God. Aleksei…" Lights shimmered around her, Aleksei's hands grazing over her body, his touch sending jolts of electricity to her very core. Higher, she flew, her body weightless, her soul free, reaching for Aleksei…

"Jordan? Jordan? Breath for me. Come on now, quit screwing around," Whittaker's voice reached her from what sounded like miles away.

"Is she okay?" Why did Aleksei sound so far away, too? They'd been so close to reaching each other. Their souls had almost blended. What the hell was going on?

"Dammm…" Jordan groaned softly, her chest rising as she took in a full breath of air, keeping her eyes closed as she focused on regaining her breath and trying to reach the shining star she'd been so close to touching. Consciously she knew she'd had the wind knocked out of her and the best thing she could do was relax and wait for her lungs to refill. However, her body still screamed for the impending physical release she'd been on the verge of experiencing and at the moment she'd have gladly given up breathing—hell living—to feel the shattering explosion of release that had been at her fingertips.

"Jordan, do you hurt anywhere?" Whittaker asked, concern clear in his deep voice; the voice that pulled her back to earth and replaced the freedom she had felt as she flew toward the stars with Aleksei and exchanged it for lungs that burned for oxygen. Damn!

"Should I?" she finally answered weakly, rolling to lay on her back, her knees pointing toward the ceiling as she covered her eyes with her arms. Relax, relax, relax she repeated to herself, feeling her lungs expand and contract with each slow breath.

Whittaker's voice held a smile. "Hopefully not, but considering you did your best to take off Aleksei's shoulder I thought I should ask."

Jordan raised her arms enough to peek out from beneath them and watch as Whittaker carefully checked her ribs. "What are you talking about?"

"My *fucking* leg didn't hold!" Aleksei growled from across the room, where he scowled back and forth between Whittaker kneeling beside Jordan to Dee where she stood keeping him from her, frustration and anger coming through loud and clear.

"It's not the first time I've been dropped, I'm sure it won't be the last," Jordan stated matter-of-factly.

"The hell it won't!" Aleksei blasted back.

Jordan allowed Whittaker to help her to a sitting position, breathing slow, deep breaths as her body got back into sync with itself. Allowing herself a slow perusal of Aleksei, she shook her head to clear the final remnants of her obvious hallucination. Aleksei continued to pace, his limp lessening as he moved restlessly. "Rocmanov, falling is part of skating. I would have thought you understood that. It's not as if you haven't taken a spill yourself," Jordan suggested, rising slowly to her knees and finally to her feet, foregoing Whittaker's offered assistance.

Absently she ran her hands through her tussled shades-of-copper hair, re-securing the barrette, which held it out of her face. Her body still hummed, balanced on the edge of she didn't know what, shifting from a need to explode to one of dissolving into nothingness. The need to touch and reassure Aleksei overwhelming and yet the fear of doing so almost tangible. The whole situation was unsettling, to say the least.

"No shit, Sherlock. I've fallen more times that I care to admit, but I've never been the direct cause of someone else being hurt."

"I'm not hurt," Jordan stated, straightening up then weaving slightly as bright flashes of light exploded in her head.

Aleksei rushed to her side, easily brushing Dee out of the way and caught Jordan from the back as her knees began to give way. Her back rested against his chest, the muscles of his forearms brushing against the undersides of her breasts. "Right—you're not hurt," his voice stated in a disbelieving tone over her head.

"Rocmanov, shut the hell up," Jordan complained weakly, her hands ineffectively pushing against his arms where they rested around her waist. "You're giving me a headache."

"That's it—you're going to the hospital!" Aleksei stated, sweeping her into his arms then staggering as his leg again refused to hold him and they both hit the padded floor in a tangle of arms and legs.

"God dammit, Rocmanov. What are you trying to do, kill me?" Jordan raged, untangling herself from his still clinging arms and sitting beside him.

Aleksei had the grace to look embarrassed and raised himself to his elbows, trying to ignore the pulsing pain surging through his weak leg. "So much for chivalry," he suggested, his eyes flashing impishly, then wincing when Jordan punched him in the shoulder in frustration.

"The next time you decide to be chivalrous, be sure you can keep from dropping the lady. I didn't ask for your help, in fact, I didn't even want your help!" Jordan fumed.

"You said you had a headache."

"I said 'you're *giving* me a headache'. There's a difference."

"You could have a head injury," Aleksei suggested.

Jordan looked at Aleksei in disbelief. "You're right!" she suddenly agreed. "I'd have to have a head injury to believe we could ever skate together successfully. Whittaker, take me to a fucking looney bin. I've obviously lost my mind!" she screamed, frustration turning her eyes a fire-filled emerald and her cheeks a deep rose. She rose to her feet, willing herself to stand tall and steady.

Aleksei followed her up, favoring his good leg but still towering over Jordan. "Jordan, I'm just worried about you," He allowed, refusing to believe it was any more than concern over their skating partnership, he didn't dare consider the aspects of a personal relationship.

"Well, don't be," Jordan stormed, pushing his arm away as he reached for her. "So help me, Rocmanov. You try to *help me* again and you won't have to worry about the next time you drop me—you won't have the arms to get me up in the air in the first place!" She vowed, lifting her chin challengingly and walking away.

Aleksei appreciated the view as she stormed away from him, despite her anger her shapely bottom still swayed enticingly and he smiled a wickedly appreciative smile.

Whittaker caught the look and shook his head knowingly. "That boy's a slow learner when it comes to that little girl," he commented to Dee. She still stood silently next to Whittaker trying to make heads or tails out of the little scene that had just played out before them.

"Did any of that make sense to you or have things changed to the degree that we're somewhere out in left field without the new rule book?" Dee asked in a bewildered tone.

"I was kind of hoping you had all the answers," Whittaker countered semi-seriously.

"We're in deep shit, Frank!" Dee stated, chewing on her lower lip as she pondered their predicament.

"I don't know about you, but I'm digging out my old waders," Whittaker stated, moving forward to meeting Aleksei as he limped toward his coach.

"Now what?" Aleksei demanded, absently rubbing his shoulder where Jordan had punched him. It hadn't been a hard hit but she'd known exactly where to do it and he could feel the knot beginning to form.

Whittaker looked at Dee. "The pool?" Dee agreed with a nod.

"We're going swimming?" Aleksei asked in disbelief.

"Something like that," Whittaker acknowledged and urged his skater slowly out of the workout room.

"Terrific, first she beats me up and now she's going to get the chance to drown me. I don't see how my day can get much better," Aleksei growled.

"Give it a chance. I'm sure there's a way," Whittaker suggested, lightly punching his already sore shoulder and walking forward to join Dee.

"I'm holding my breath," Aleksei mumbled darkly, rubbing his sore shoulder and doing his best to ignore the knot he could feel growing beneath his fingers. Maybe the pool wouldn't be such a bad idea. He could only hope.

Fifteen minutes later, after downing four Advil and changing into his Speedos, his belief that a training session in the pool wouldn't be such a bad idea was shot to hell when Jordan emerged from the locker room wearing a simple scoop-necked black leotard and black bicycling shorts. Despite the fact she was fully covered, as she climbed into the water, the material seemed to shrink, emphasizing every nuance of her shapely figure, leaving virtually nothing to his imagination. The skin-tight fit immediately ignited his imagination and his body and he was grateful he was already waist-deep in the semi-cool water.

He listened to Whittaker and Dee explain what they planned to do and how they wanted the training session to go, and when asked about questions, received none. Jordan already knew the drill. It would be simple. The lifts would be learned, without the fear of landing on anything harder than the water and the water would aide in supporting Aleksei's weak leg. Everyone had a job to do and got ready to do it.

Jordan stood before Aleksei, the water reaching just below her breasts, teasing her already taut nipples, trying to ignore the fact that Aleksei's gaze kept wandering to her breasts. "Keep your mind on your job, Rocmanov."

"I am," Aleksei growled, his voice deep, husky.

"Put your palms on her hip bones. You're going to have to get wet Aleksei." Whittaker called from pool side. "You have to lift her with your legs which means you're going to have to get under her."

"Christ," Aleksei groaned, doing as he was told and sinking into the water until it reached his neck, placing his palms against her hip bones, his fingers wrapping around the softness of her hips and holding her securely. Her skin felt hot despite the coolness of the water and the two layers of thin cloth separating his skin from hers. It was sheer torture and he was dying.

"Jordan, put your hands on his shoulders, for now. When he gets you up…"

"If he gets me up," Jordan interrupted, ignoring Aleksei's snort of disagreement.

"When he gets you up…" Whittaker repeated, "you can let go of him."

"Yeah, yeah, yeah," Jordan grumbled.

"Don't be a bitch," Aleksei warned.

"Don't drop me!" Jordan shot back, her eyes widening at the suddenly dangerous glint lighting Aleksei's ebony eyes.

"Shall we try it?" Whittaker suggested, casting a look at Dee for any further ideas.

"Looks good to me," Dee replied. "Let's do it."

"All right, children. On the count of two," Whittaker stated and counted off.

Jordan pushed lightly off the pool floor and Aleksei lifted her effortlessly, despite the water pouring off her sleek body. Locking his elbows, he held her steady over his head, nearly ten feet off the ground, his weak leg secure beneath him with the support of the cool, crystal clear water.

"Spread your arms, Jordan," Dee called out and she released her light hold on his broad, muscular shoulders, her hands suddenly cold after the heat of his skin. Automatically she spread her arms wide, arched her back, crossed her shapely legs at the ankles and held her position. Perfect, as expected.

"That's the position, Aleksei. How's she feel?" Whittaker asked, looking to Dee for agreement and receiving it.

Aleksei looked up, the water from her body dripping into his eyes and he shook his head to clear his vision. "Like a seal."

Whittaker smiled at his description and Jordan's snort of offense. "Well that's got to be the prettiest looking seal I've ever seen. Count yourself fortunate you're not having to lift a manatee over your head," Whittaker offered, quickly ducking away from Dee's censoring expression.

"Other than that, how does the position feel? Is your leg holding okay?" Dee questioned, taking over the questioning.

"Yeah, no problems, at all," Aleksei answered, bending his elbows slightly and shifting Jordan forward and backward to get the feel of her weight shifting over his head. He'd been right—she didn't weigh as much as a full keg of beer.

"Good, then you can bring her down," Dee stated, turning to say something to Whittaker.

The sudden shrill scream and loud splash echoed loudly off the high ceilings as the two coaches turned to see Aleksei stepping away from a thrashing Jordan. As she gained her footing on the pool's bottom and stood, she pushed her clinging hair from her face and screamed in rage at her antagonist. Aleksei stood a short distance from her, his arms crossed against his muscular, broad chest, his expression clearly stating he was more than ready to continue the battle of wills between them.

"You moron," Jordan sputtered, wincing when her fingers tangled in her hair and pulled.

"They said, 'bring you down'. They didn't say *how*," Aleksei offered smugly, his eyes flashing mischievously, his lips twitching as he fought to control his urge to laugh out-loud.

Whittaker wasn't so controlled and laughed uproariously, ignoring the scathing gaze of contempt she directed at him. "You find this Neanderthal behavior acceptable, even funny?" Jordan fumed, wading through the hip deep water until she reached the side of the pool. Her mind whirled madly as she tried to imagine ways to torture Aleksei, without stooping to his level of physical theatrics. She knew there was no possible way to out maneuver him physically. As much as she'd like to push him under the water and sit on his chest—for say two or three hours—the prospect of finding yet another partner and starting all over was enough to slow her urge to maim and destroy. No, there had to be a better way to put him in his place and make him see he'd picked the wrong person to play 'anything you can do, I can do better'. She had no intention of playing his 'male superiority games'. She may only be sixteen but it was time he learned she wasn't going to tolerate his 'macho attitude', he'd made the mistake of picking on the wrong member of the 'weaker sex'!

"Dee, would you take these please?" Jordan asked, wriggling out of the clinging bicycle pants and tossing them up to her coach, winking bravely at Dee's astonished expression. Her leotard may have had a simple scooped-neck, but that's where any attempt of it being conservative ended. The legs were high-cut, fashionably called a *French-cut* and left much of her skin visible. The shape of her legs and bottom were such that the back of the leotard could have been a thong, for as much of her bottom remained covered. When she glanced over her shoulder at Aleksei, she almost lost her nerve. Never had she seen such a look of hot, blatant desire on a man's face. But it was time to stand her ground and show him he couldn't push her around. If it meant stooping to such measures, then so be it. After all, as the saying went, 'all is fair in love and war' and this was most definitely turning into a war. "Are we going to continue this training session, Rocmanov, or are you not up to it?" Jordan taunted, walking toward him slowly through the swirling, crystal water.

If you only knew how up for it, sweetheart, his body screamed ferociously despite his silence. "Whenever you're ready," Aleksei managed in as bored a tone as he could manage, despite his tongue feeling like cotton and his body hardening painfully in response to her near nakedness. How had the tables shifted so suddenly? How could he be standing in thousands of gallons of water and still feel as if he were about to burst into flames and turn to dust? Why couldn't the water be another twenty degrees cooler? That would take care of any carnal thoughts. But then again, he knew he could be chest deep in snow, naked, and still feel the sensual fire that flamed in Jordan rage through him and set him ablaze. His only chance to survive the balance of this training session was to concentrate fully on the job of learning to lift Jordan and ignore the fact she was a semi-naked, child-siren, set on bringing him to heel. The fact that at the moment it looked more and more as if she'd won this skirmish, didn't sit well with his ego. Thankfully, it made him all the more resigned to ignore the thoughts that urged him toward forbidden territory and prove to Jordan that her body didn't tempt him at all. And if he managed to pull this off, he had beachfront property in Arizona he was interested in selling. Casting a quick glance skyward and silently asking for divine intervention, he walked deeper into the cool water, concentrating on everything but the small amount of fabric that made up Jordan's suit.

Whittaker watched the pair, shaking his head as he watched them come together, glance tentatively at each other, then look away when their eyes met. Definitely time to turn up the burner a bit, he decided and threw caution to the wind. "Okay, kids. Next lift on the agenda is what I like to call the layback…" Whittaker began, ignoring Jordan's gasp of dismay and holding up one hand to stop any additional comments. "Now, Jordan, take your position."

"Whittaker…" Jordan pleaded, casting a frantic look toward Dee, who simply shrugged, the gesture clearly stating *you're on your own*.

Whittaker wiggled his finger in a circular motion, and slowly she complied. Aleksei watched, a confused frown creasing his brow until he heard his coach's instructions. "Aleksei, both palms on her bottom, fingers wrapping toward her hips. Be sure you get under her again so the water supports that leg and pay attention, she's going to be slippery."

"Excuse me!?" Aleksei croaked in disbelief, twisting to face his coach and casting his own pleading expression.

Whittaker ignored his unspoken plea and again wiggled his finger, indicating he turn around. "You heard me. Positions, please."

Aleksei turned to face Jordan's shapely rear end, barely covered by the shimmering, black clinging fabric. His fingers flexed nervously, their tension climbing up his forearms and toward his shoulders. Seeking to stop the tension that threatened cramps, he rolled his massive shoulders, crossing his arms and stretching the muscles until he relaxed. Jordan remained still and silent before him, her own shoulders working out knots of tension. She could feel the heat of him as he stepped behind her, their bodies mere inches apart.

"Ready?" he asked softly, awaiting her answer.

She nodded once.

Aleksei flexed his hands once more and lowered himself into the water until it reached him mid-chest, his feet braced slightly apart. He placed his hands on her skin, cool against the heat of his palms, his fingers wrapping around her slim hips and holding steady. Jordan grasped his wrists and suddenly she was airborne, water pouring from her sleek body. She tottered back and forth, certain she was going back into the water over his shoulders but he held her firm, adjusting her weight and balance and holding her steady.

"Well?" Aleksei inquired loudly, shaking water from his face where it dripped from Jordan.

Whittaker looked from the pair to Dee and back again.

"Jordan, let go of his wrists," Dee stated, content with the position her arms took and the steadiness of their lift. "That's it," Dee approved, then suggested, "Jordan, try a lay-back."

"A what?" Aleksei asked, adjusting Jordan's weight forward as she straightened her legs forward and lay back as if on a bed.

"A lay-back," Jordan stated, groaning when her weight shifted farther back and Aleksei staggered a step backwards.

"Sorry," Aleksei mumbled, regaining control of her weight and holding the position. "We're going to do this on the ice?" he asked in disbelief.

"Hard to believe isn't it?" Jordan answered, returning to a sitting position and looking toward their coaches. "Well, what dismount are you looking for?"

"I know I'm not going to like the one he chooses," Aleksei mumbled to no one in particular.

"Aleksei, a little pop up, half twist and catch her against your chest, but not too soon or you're going to have her knees in your chest."

Aleksei groaned, remembering the position Gordeeva and Grinkov had used and grimacing as he thought about her warm, silken skin sliding against his own, mere scraps of material separating their bodies from one another, their own will power barely keeping the firestorm that threatened to overthrow them at bay. Aleksei did as instructed, tossing her easily another foot into the air. Jordan lifted her arms, aiding his powerful lift and twisted, sliding down the front of his muscled torso before his arms came around her waist to catch her and hold her tightly against him, her feet a foot off the floor of the pool. Both their breaths caught, whether from the abrupt stop or the sudden flaming of passions as their near-naked bodies met. Their eyes locked; ebony and forest green, searching, questioning, wanting, retreating.

Aleksei relaxed his hold and Jordan slid the remaining inches to the pool's floor, her breath held as she nervously nibbled her lower lip with straight, white teeth. Slowly Aleksei's arms released her waist and she stepped back, running her hands down her slim thighs and finally breaking the trance of Aleksei's gaze.

Tentatively she looked at Whittaker who looked from Jordan to Aleksei and back again.

"It needs work. Again," He boomed, turning to walk toward Dee, ignoring the groans of discontent drifting over the gently lapping water.

"You're wicked!" Dee stated, attempting to keep the smile at bay.

"Yeah, well ain't it a bitch?" Whittaker answered, a wicked smile lighting his eyes.

"How long do you intend to torment them?"

"As long as it takes."

Dee cast a glance at the pair in the pool; the intense vibrations of their ever-changing emotions toward one another filled the air with palpable electricity. "Shouldn't be too much longer," She decided.

Whittaker snorted in amusement. "Not long at all," he agreed. Casting his attention toward the athletes, his loud demand echoed off the high ceiling. "All right, children. Show me something beautiful!"

Aleksei resumed his position beside Jordan, sliding silently into the water and placing his hands as platonically as he could manage on her shapely rear-end, a hiss escaping his lips as his palms made contact with her silken, wet skin. With an easy lift, she was up and over his head, finding her balance quickly as she followed Whittaker's loudly bellowed instructions and slipped into the requested lay-back position. Aleksei cast a quick look upward, ignoring the drops of water that slipped from her shiny black swim suit on to his face and believed there was nothing more beautiful that the dripping wet nymph he held securely over his head.

* * * * *

Seven weeks after the cast was removed, Aleksei and Jordan officially began their practices together. As much as Aleksei had wanted his leg to hold, it refused to do so and the pair had spent nearly two weeks in the pool learning their lifts before they had felt confident enough to move back to the padded floor. Unlike their first attempt at a lift on solid ground, Jordan was safely lifted and returned to her feet harmlessly, she only hoped it would go as smoothly on the ice. The pair were both excited and apprehensive about moving on to the ice but knew their time was running out if they had any hope at all of making the upcoming competitions. Nervously, they agreed to move out of the safety of the padded room and on to the unforgiving surface of the ice, each saying a quick prayer for mercy.

Initially, they were walked through the program, much as Dee had walked Jordan through weeks earlier. Aleksei was several weeks behind Jordan as far as actually having had ice time with the music. Jordan already had the basic program down, she knew where the lifts and throws and holds would be; Jordan had simply been waiting for Aleksei to fill in the blanks. Aleksei had had the time to watch Jordan as she learned the program. Watching her skate over the last several weeks had given him more information than anyone could have ever told him. He knew how she moved, which side she was most comfortable on, the way her arms drifted downward on a given sequence. Without Jordan knowing it, Aleksei had had Whittaker videotape some of her practices and Aleksei then had practiced separately, late at night, trying to make up for lost time. The major competitions were drawing nearer and Aleksei didn't want to be the reason they couldn't compete. After several nights of midnight practices, he'd decided he was ready to try an actual run-through of the routine.

Jordan raised questioning eyes to her coach. "Are we ready?"

Dee looked toward Whittaker, shaking her head slightly in thought. "I think we should walk-through it a few more times," she suggested, frowning at Whittaker's casual shrug.

"I'm ready. We don't have the time to waste anymore," Aleksei stated, his deep voice sure.

"If he says he's ready, let them try it," Whittaker suggested, crossing his arms across his chest, and leaning against the wall surrounding the rink.

"That's easy enough for you to say. Jordan's the one that will be dropped on the ice and hurt if he's not ready!" Dee stated heatedly, casting a hot look at Aleksei.

"Wouldn't be the first time she's been dropped," Whittaker remarked without thinking.

"You asshole!" Dee managed to shriek before Aleksei's deadly calm, deep voice stopped her tirade.

"That won't happen!" He vowed solemnly.

Aleksei offered his hand to Jordan, waiting patiently while she looked from his hand to her coach to Whittaker then back into his eyes. "Want to skate?" Aleksei offered, his eyes promising her she'd not be disappointed or harmed.

Jordan placed her hand in Aleksei's, smiling softly as his fingers closed carefully around her palm. "Start the music, Dee," Jordan requested and together she and Aleksei skated to center ice.

"So help me, Whittaker. If she gets hurt there won't be a safe place for you to hide on this planet!" Dee threatened, shaking her head in concern and frustration as she turned on the CD player and slipped their program's music disc into the machine.

"Give me a little credit, would you? Do you think I'd risk either one of them if I didn't think they were ready?"

"Jordan's ready, but from what I've seen, Aleksei's still got a good two weeks to go," Dee stated, setting the volume and track buttons.

"You haven't seen what I've seen." Whittaker stated cryptically, again shrugging at her questioning look. "Just watch," he stated simply.

"You'd better be right!" Dee threatened.

"When have I ever been wrong?" Whittaker asked smugly.

Dee rolled her eyes in disbelief and turned her eyes to the ice.

Jordan and Aleksei had assumed their opening position center ice, she with her hands joined together over her heart, her right leg crossed slightly behind her left leg, resting next to his left supporting leg, her right toe-pick holding her securely in place on the ice. Aleksei stood behind her, his chest nearly against her back, his right arm crossed over her upper chest and holding her left shoulder gently. His left hand softly caressed her left hip. His right cheek rested lovingly against the top of her head. His right leg continued the line of her extended right leg where it brushed against his left.

Patiently they waited for the first notes of music to fill the air before they began, and as they waited, the hair on Dee's neck tingled and she cast a knowing look at Whittaker. "What don't I know?"

"Just watch," Whittaker stated and nodded toward the ice.

"Aleksei?" Jordan whispered, she too waiting for the music.

Aleksei gave her a soft squeeze and whispered back. "Believe in the story and let the music bring you to me. I won't let you fall."

Jordan nodded slightly in agreement and both breathed a deep sigh.

The notes of Romeo and Juliet slowly filled the arena and Jordan and Aleksei began to slowly move, circling each other tentatively, like new lovers, unsure, anxious, yearning to be close yet aware of the differences between them. Gradually they came closer, touching playfully, sensuously, maturing in their love as the music moved on, carrying them. Lifts were made seemingly without effort. Throws were landed perfectly. Somewhere during the routine, Jordan and Aleksei became one and it was impossible to tell where one skater ended and the other began, and like Gordeeva and Grinkov, their hearts began to beat as one, and there was magic.

Dee couldn't believe the performance going on before her eyes. The couple covered the ice at a frightening speed. Aleksei lifting Jordan over his head as if she were a feather, turning without fault or weakness only to gently return her to the ice. On and on the program continued, the lifts flawless, the throws defying time and distance as the pair sped across the ice. As the heartbreaking strains of the finale draw near in the cold air, Dee felt the tears slowly glide down her cheeks as she watched Aleksei slowly slide to a stop on his knees on the ice with a seemingly lifeless Jordan in his arms. Carefully he placed her on the ice, laying his cheek against her heart then lovingly running his hands over her face. Abruptly he raised his arms toward the heavens, pleading to join his love. His arms dropped hopelessly and he gently lifted Jordan from the ice, holding her limp form to his and burying his face into her neck. Without effort, he stood and skated as if dancing one last time with her, spinning and dipping, the music following suit. Suddenly he slid to a stop, her death brutally real to him. With a final soft kiss to her lips, he lifted her over his head in one last appeal to be with her. As the music whispered its final strains they both collapsed to the ice, their arms around each other, their lips gently touching, their eyes closed as if in death.

The arena was completely silent, Dee and Whittaker held their breaths, unable to believe the beauty of the program just skated.

Silently Aleksei and Jordan lay on the ice, unmoving, the final whispers of the music having dissipated. The only evidence of their strenuous performance, the rapid puffs of their foggy breaths hovering the ice as their breathing slowed and returned to normal. Jordan's mind slipped easily into her ever-strengthening dream of Aleksei as she felt her blood rushing through her veins and sought to regain her breath.

Aleksei effortlessly lifted Jordan to her feet, missing the softness of her body against his, then stood himself.

"You've been practicing!" Jordan accused, smiling broadly.

"Maybe a little," Aleksei teased back, ruffling her hair affectionately.

"Maybe you could use a little more practice," Jordan taunted, quickly skating out of his reach when he grabbed for her.

Aleksei raced after her, easily catching her, lifting her and spinning her around until she was breathless. "What part needs practice?" he asked deeply, his eyes darkening sensuously as his breath mixed with hers.

"This part." Jordan whispered, then pulled his mouth down to meet hers. Her lips parted at the first touch of his lips, her breath blending with his as his lips covered hers, gently caressing their softness.

"Jordan," Aleksei whispered softly, easily lifting her off her feet then setting her back down. Expectantly he looked into her upturned face, smiling gently at her amazed expression.

"I can't believe what just happened!" She gasped, her breath still a bit shaky. How did you do that?"

Aleksei shrugged nonchalantly. "It's no big deal. I just paid attention to your skating during practices and wanted to skate a clean program for you. I wanted to make our first program something special," he answered honestly, his voice deep with emotion.

"Well, you succeeded, Mr. Rocmanov. I'm truly stunned and amazed. You make me feel very special," Jordan whispered, tears of gratitude filling her eyes and slipping down her cheeks. No one had ever given her such a gift.

Aleksei leaned down and gently kissed the tears from her cheeks, unknown emotions of protectiveness surfacing as he wrapped his arms around her small form and held her close, his chin resting on the top of her head as they stood center ice in the silent arena. "It was my pleasure, little one," he offered quietly.

"Don't go soft on me now!" Whittaker bellowed, his booming command causing them to pull apart. Jordan and Aleksei smiled into each other's eyes, an unspoken change between them evident in their eyes.

"What's the problem, Whittaker?" Aleksei growled, knowing in his heart the program they had just skated had been something close to magical.

"No problem. I just want you to take a look at the tape. You'll see the hunger there between you through the whole program. I want to keep it there," Whittaker stated matter-of-factly.

"Why would we change anything? I can't imagine the program feeling any more 'right,'" Aleksei stated, holding Jordan's hand as they skated toward their coaches standing by the door to the ice.

"Denying them time together could end up being a dangerous thing," Dee stated.

"Dangerous is good too. We'll have to keep them apart if necessary," Whittaker decided.

Dee stared in astonishment. "You know what happens when you try to keep people in love with each other apart."

"In love? Dee, what are you talking about?" Whittaker grunted, casting a quick eye toward the couple nearly upon them.

"A pair couldn't skate a program like that unless there are deep feelings involved. That wasn't just a performance, that was a statement as to the beginning of a love that I don't think they're even aware of yet. Watch them together, Frank. Something is building between them and I think they deserve the chance to discover it," Dee quickly stated.

"That's not love—it's lust!" Whittaker classified.

"Don't be such an idiot, Frank. Aleksei's been nothing but a gentleman…" Frank raised disbelieving eyebrows at Dee's comment, remembering all too well their skirmish at Dee's house. "Granted, the news conference was a little rocky, but be that as it may, you can't stop an avalanche once it's begun," Dee stated.

"No, but if they're separated, other than when they're training, it reduces the risk of things happening." Whittaker suggested.

"As in, they can only be together during practice? You know that won't work. Think about it, if it was you, would you stand those conditions? They know right and wrong. We need to give them a chance to explore what they're feeling. They're smart, maybe they'll just turn out to be very good friends."

"I don't know, Dee. I say let's try it my way. Maybe we can get the point across once they see the tape. It says it all. If we can keep that intensity, we can't lose."

"I don't know. I still say it's not fair to Jordan and Aleksei."

"Show them the tape. We'll discuss it after they've seen it."

"I can't wait for that discussion," Dee could only mumble, knowing how Jordan and Aleksei would take the suggestion that they would only be allowed together during practice, to keep the intensity in the program.

* * * *

"Screw the intensity…" Aleksei suggested darkly, the look in his eyes dangerous as they looked directly at Whittaker then softening perceptibly when they slid to Jordan.

Jordan returned his look with a soft smile and looked to Dee. "What's your opinion?" Jordan asked calmly.

Dee glanced from Jordan to Aleksei to Whittaker, scowling slightly when Whittaker urged her to agree with him. "I think we have something very special here and Whittaker is afraid…"

"Dammit it, I'm not afraid…" Whittaker cut in.

"Whittaker *believes* it would be in your best interest to keep your exposure to one another limited to practice sessions only. He feels…" Dee tried to explain calmly, only to be cut off abruptly by Whittaker.

"For Christ's sake, Dee, they're not babies!" Whittaker turned his fiery look from Aleksei to Jordan then back to Aleksei. "I don't want you wasting your energy melting the sheets, I prefer you save that sexual tension for the ice! Once you see the tape of the program you just skated, you'll see for yourselves what I'm talking about. I worry that once all the mysteries you see in each other are discovered, the magic we saw today will melt as quickly as a snowball in hell!" Whittaker growled testily.

Aleksei and Jordan sat in dumbstruck silence, Jordan's eyes wide in astonishment; Aleksei's darkening in disbelief.

"You think this is about sex?" Aleksei questioned deeply, his voice dangerously soft.

Jordan cast a quick glance at Dee, her cheeks blushing softly, her teeth gently tugging her lower lip. Dee's answering glance made her lower her gaze downward to watch her fingers lace together in an effort to stop their nervous fluttering.

"Not as far as I'm concerned," Dee answered surely.

"I wish I could be as certain," Whittaker stated, watching Aleksei steeple his fingers, a motion he recognized as a firm indicator that Aleksei was reaching the limits of his toleration.

"Whether or not Jordan and I end up romantically linked has nothing to do with our skating. We are partners, first and foremost, and both of us are very aware of that obligation."

"I'm not worried about your individual skating abilities. I'm perfectly aware of your capabilities, and your limitations. What I want from the two of you is your promise that after you see the program you just skated, you will be able to repeat it, a hundred times if necessary and leave me feeling the same damn way!" Whittaker demanded.

"That's asking the impossible, Whittaker, and you know it. There's never been a pair in history that hasn't had down time," Dee stated.

"I'm not talking injuries, illness or vacation time. I'm talking I don't want a program suffering because you're fighting over some piddly-shit thing like he didn't send the right flowers or she didn't put out when he wanted it. Can the two of you promise me that won't happen? I don't want to have to deal with another Steuer and Woetzel scenario!" He growled; referring to the German pair team whose reputation for constantly being angry with one another was renown.

"We're not Germans, Whittaker," Aleksei responded.

"No—you're stubborn—it'll probably be worse!" Whittaker complained.

"Give us a chance to prove ourselves," Aleksei stated, reaching over to gently pull Jordan's hands apart and lace his fingers with hers. "Give us the chance to become a skating-pair, hopefully the best in the world. If anything else comes of it, it will simply be icing on the cake.

Whittaker looked from one to the other. "How much time are you talking about?"

Aleksei looked from Jordan to Whittaker to Dee. "What's the earliest competition we can qualify for?"

Dee and Whittaker exchanged glances. "The Nationals in nine weeks." Dee answered.

Aleksei's gaze returned to Jordan, the question clear in his dark eyes. Jordan's soft, answering smile was all Aleksei could hope for. "Nine weeks. If our intensity on the ice drops below your expectations, we do it your way. If it stays—we do it our way," Aleksei stated, offering his extended hand in agreement.

Whittaker looked from one to the other before finally accepting Aleksei's outstretched hand. "Against my better judgment, I'll agree. But one bad performance—we do it my way."

Aleksei and Whittaker shook hands, each firmly believing they would prove the other wrong. Aleksei released his coach's hand, gently shook Dee's hand and softly kissed Jordan's cheek.

"We can do this," he softly whispered into her ear, squeezing her hand to reinforce his belief and reassure her of their choice.

"I never had any doubt about it. Nobody leaves, remember?" Jordan stated quietly, yet firmly, then cast a quick glance and prayer heavenward.

Chapter 6

The nine weeks passed in a blur, practices lasting all day and well into each night. Whittaker pushed the limits of their endurance and patience to their very maximum. Jordan and Aleksei had little time for thinking about their blossoming feelings let alone encouraging them. They had to settle for quickly stolen hugs, longing glances and one gentle kiss that had been over far too soon as far as Jordan was concerned. And Jordan's heart melted every time Aleksei slid his hand into hers, their fingers weaving together and forming an unbreakable bond. Thankfully, Aleksei took every opportunity to hold her hand, gently rubbing his thumb against her own, causing tingles of pleasure to rush straight to her heart. Despite their hectic practice sessions, their mood remained light and happy, their practices all they had promised Whittaker they would be. They didn't give him the opportunity or any reason to separate them from one another. They maintained their focus and intensity and still made Dee weep with emotion every time she watched the program.

Costumes were designed, selected and created, glorious creations of flowing candlelight chiffon for Jordan's dress with crystal and bronze colored bead detailing and nearly indecent deep bronze colored form fitting pants for Aleksei, topped off by a shimmering copper colored tunic over an off-white shirt with flowing sleeves. The costumes were due to be delivered by noon and plans for a formal dress rehearsal were underway.

"Aren't the costumes suppose to be here already?" Whittaker barked at Dee.

"They said noon. Take a look at your watch, Whittaker. Does it say twelve o'clock yet?" Dee fired back, her patience more than a little worn.

Scowling, Whittaker did just that, scowling again and lifting it to his ear to make sure it was working.

"Whittaker, you're losing it." Aleksei offered, shaking his legs to get the kinks out. "We've still got five days until our 'debut'."

"You've never skated with chiffon slapping you in the face while you're holding someone over your head. I don't want any accidents!" Whittaker growled, casting another frustrated look toward the office at the end of the rink.

Dee couldn't take it anymore. "Thirty minutes for lunch. Make it a light one," she suggested, putting up her hand to silence Whittaker's impending argument.

Jordan and Aleksei felt the pressure building as their first competition approached, trying to dissipate the mounting tension between their coaches. All four of them were bombs ready to explode and simply looking for a place to do it. When Dee gave them the opportunity, they didn't need another excuse to escape. Quickly they skated to the doorway at rink side and slipped their blade guards carefully over their perfectly sharpened blades. Thirty minutes didn't give them much time alone so they headed for the closest place available, the work-out area off the locker rooms. Rushing like lunatics, they crashed through the double doors, laughing out loud when the doors slammed loudly against the walls then swooshed quietly closed behind them. Thankfully they were alone in the large room. Aleksei looked down into Jordan's upturned, flushed face and read the wanting expression in her deep green eyes, his own gaze questioning. Jordan carefully cupped his face in her hands and quickly offered a heated whisper, "I want you so much, Aleksei, it almost hurts."

Aleksei needed no further encouragement, quickly he pulled Jordan into a small niche separating the lockers and pushed her against the wall, his body immediately following and melting into hers. Their mouths met hungrily, their breaths blending, their hands pulling each other closer and running erotically up and down each other's bodies. Aleksei's hands clutched Jordan's rounded bottom, pulling her firmly against his crotch, leaving no doubt in her mind as to how she affected him. Moaning softly, Jordan pushed against him, her own heated response clear to him.

"Dear, God, I can't stand this much longer," Aleksei growled deeply, his teeth hungrily devouring her neck, his hands running riot over her hips and bottom.

Jordan closed her eyes in ecstasy, flashes of brightly colored lights exploding behind her closed eyelids as Aleksei tortured her with kisses and soft bites to her neck and shoulders. Her hands touched him everywhere, searing him with her heat through his snug T-shirt and then sliding beneath the worn, soft material to finally touch his bare skin beneath. "Aleksei..." came out as a sigh, then was swallowed when his lips claimed hers hotly.

"They're here!" Whittaker bellowed, pushing through the double doors excitedly, two garment bags held in his arms.

"Terrific," Aleksei mumbled in frustration, pushing away from Jordan with a last painful glance. Jordan smiled and blew him a kiss.

"Where's mine?" she asked excitedly, playfully swatting Aleksei on his butt as she skipped past him.

Whittaker scowled at Aleksei, then Jordan as she took the bag he held toward her. "Stay out of the corners!" he growled, knowing all too well the signs of rising passion. "Put these on and let's see how they play on the ice. You've got fifteen minutes."

"What about our thirty minute break?" Aleksei inquired innocently, casting an innocent look at Whittaker, then smiling mischievously at Jordan.

"It's over. Fifteen minutes!" Whittaker barked, then turned to leave only to stop, walk to where Jordan was standing and firmly grasp her hand, pulling her with him.

Jordan cast a final look over her shoulder at Aleksei, smiled and stated smartly, "Fifteen minutes!"

Aleksei's rich laughter filled the air, back dropping Whittaker's complaints as to the impertinence of today's youth.

* * * * *

Dee critically eyed Jordan's costume. Yards of flowing candlelight chiffon made up the full sleeves and flowing empire-waisted skirt, which fell to below her knees. Crystal and bronze beads intertwined in an intricate design across the demi-vest that covered her breasts; a little too snugly as far as Dee was concerned as she looked at the swelling curves of Jordan's breasts spilling over the top. The full sleeves were slit to show form-fitting under-sleeves of deep bronze.

"This is gorgeous," Jordan whispered reverently. Lifting her arms and watching the way the chiffon flowed.

"The neckline won't work," Dee stated, then tried in vain to pull it a bit higher.

Jordan eyed her uplifted breasts in the mirror and smiled at Dee. "I bet Aleksei won't mind it."

"I'm sure he'll appreciate it even more when he lifts you and you fall out of your bodice completely," she stated flatly. "Unfortunately, the judges don't give extra points for that."

"Only during exhibition," Jordan joked then apologized for the sorry attempt at the pun. "Can we give it a try and see how much needs to be added to keep me covered?"

"We'll have to, we're running out of time," Dee agreed and again checked the length of the skirt. "I'm also worried about this length. It may need to come up, we don't need you tripping over it."

"Let's try it and see where we stand," Jordan urged, turning from side to side and seeing it flow around her softly.

"You're right. Let's see if Aleksei's costume fared any better," Dee urged and led the way to the ice.

*   *   *   *   *

"Doesn't the U.S.F.S.A. prohibit pants like this?" Aleksei inquired irritably, referring to the United States Figure Skating Association who mandated the rules of competition clothing as he checked the form-fitting pants from all angles in the mirror and noted that they left absolutely nothing to the imagination.

Whittaker smiled smugly, unconcerned and slowly circled Aleksei. He was right, the pants were nearly indecent and showed off Aleksei's muscular legs and butt to perfection. Whittaker wasn't too concerned about his butt because the shirt and tunic would cover a good portion of it. "Put the tunic on and let's see how you feel before you start bitching too loudly," He growled and handed him the garment.

Aleksei pulled the tunic over his head and slipped muscular arms through the flowing full sleeves, buttoning the cuffs as Whittaker zipped up the back.

"Covers your ass," Whittaker stated, pulling the tunic into place and running his hands across his shoulders to check the fit there. "Fits up top—turn around."

Aleksei did as told and found himself facing the mirror full on. His eyes widened as he noticed the deep 'v' of his tunic and the amount of his chest showing beneath the neatly laced shirt, the curling black hair clearly visible.

"The girls will love it," Whittaker stated, his gaze running up and down Aleksei's tall form.

"These pants are going to kill me!" Aleksei complained, pulling at the clinging cloth.

"Get used to it," Whittaker stated firmly, then slapped Aleksei on the back. "Let's hit the ice."

"You get used to something creeping up your ass," Aleksei grumbled as he followed his coach to the ice, still pulling the offending fabric away as it crept into places it shouldn't.

"You've been creeping up my ass for years. Quit your bitching!" Whittaker tossed over his shoulder and continued on his way.

Aleksei's deeply voiced mimic of Whittaker's last statement caused Whittaker's shoulders to shake with laughter. "Yeah, and if you're real lucky, I'll be creeping up it another ten years!"

"Deal," Whittaker said taking a seat rink side.

* * * * *

Aleksei had never seen a more beautiful vision on the ice than when he first viewed Jordan in her costume, skating gracefully away from him, the chiffon flowing softly around her long, shapely legs. She executed a perfect spiral, one leg raised in a high straight line, her arms crossed beautifully over her chest, then as she rounded the far corner of the rink and moved toward Aleksei, she spread her arms wide, the sleeves flowing in the gentle breeze she made as she glided over the gleaming ice. Aleksei nearly fell over when he saw her breasts close to spilling out of her top.

"You were right, Dee, the skirt's too long. If I drop to my usual spiral position, it's on the ice," Jordan called, testing the length as she dipped and swayed.

"Drop any lower and that's not all that'll be on the ice!" Aleksei growled, skating toward her then sliding in next to her, his scowl clearly visible as he looked at her daring neckline.

"Don't you like it?" Jordan inquired innocently, secretly enjoying his show of possessiveness.

"You know I do, I just don't need everyone else liking it too!" he growled deeply, trying to tug the neckline up.

"Won't work, Dee tried that," Jordan stated, slapping his hands away and sliding back to take a good, full look at him.

Jordan's breath caught as she looked at him. She'd never seen anyone more handsome and virile in such a costume and her eyes widened in astonishment and pleasure as she took in his snug pants and impressive shoulders. "Isn't there a law against looking as good as you do?" she whispered, running a hand lovingly down his chest.

Aleksei's smile was at once smug and surprised. "No one will see me once they get a look at you," Aleksei countered, "Even after we fix that neckline," he finished, caressing her soft curves with a heated glance.

"If you're through, let's try this in costume," Whittaker yelled and made his way to the CD player.

"Positions," Dee stated, waiting until Jordan and Aleksei were center ice, then nodded to Whittaker.

"Ready," Aleksei advised, his deep voice carrying easily over the ice.

The music began and Aleksei and Jordan became Romeo and Juliet.

*　　　*　　　*　　　*　　　*

In all actuality, they looked more like two of the three stooges. Barely a minute into the program, Aleksei nearly dropped Jordan during their split-triple twist lift when her full skirt caused his hold on her waist to slip and she fell heavily against him. Fortunately, his size and strength over-powered the blow and he was able to keep them from falling to the ice. The next dilemma occurred on their side-by-side sit-spin combination when her skirt caught his blade, nearly ripping it completely off, throwing them both off balance and causing them to both wind up spinning on the ice on their butts. It was at that point that Aleksei's pants split up the back. Eventually sliding to a stop side by side, they looked at the wreck their costumes were and found all they could do was laugh hysterically.

Aleksei's loudly called, "I told you they were too damn tight!" sent Jordan into further fits of laughter and she could barely stay on her feet and hold the ruined chiffon of her skirt off the ice as she made her way to the side of the rink.

Dee and Whittaker looked from the pair on the ice to each other, shaking their heads and trying to maintain some dignity, eventually giving in to the sight of the tattered pair. Weeks of work on the lovely costumes had disappeared in under two and a half minutes.

"I believe we need to rethink the costumes," Whittaker suggested, wiping a tear of laughter from his eye.

"Do you now?" Dee inquired, then burst into gales of laughter as she watched Aleksei rip off the remaining bit of skirt from Jordan's costume and wrap it around his waist to conceal his split pants.

"Well, that's a look I wouldn't have thought of for Juliet," Whittaker nodded at Jordan. "I kind of like the minimal look," he suggested, referring to the now even lower neckline, full sleeves and high-cut leotard barely covering her bottom. "Aleksei doesn't seem to mind it either."

Dee smiled softly as she watched Aleksei make half-hearted attempts to pinch Jordan's bottom, while trying to avoid Jordan's hands as she tried to pull away the fabric covering his torn pants. "I think the U.S. Figure Skating Association might have a different opinion though," Dee said and called the bedraggled pair off the ice. In a tatter of torn fabrics, the two left the ice to stand before their coaches, trying their best to show some dignity.

Whittaker, as usual, came straight to the point. "Well—you two look like shit!" he boomed and the four fell apart with laughter.

Eventually Dee restored order and made the grim observation they only had a week to correct the costume problem. Ideas and suggestions were offered and rejected until, finally, changes they could all agree with were hit upon and the appropriate details were finalized. Calls to the seamstress were made and once again, they were in a holding pattern for their final dress rehearsals.

Aleksei and Jordan headed for their respective locker rooms to change back into their practice clothes, Whittaker making sure Aleksei found his way to the men's locker room. All the while Aleksei grumbled he knew Jordan's body as well as his own after all the time they'd spent together on the ice. One couldn't remain oblivious to his partner's body after hours of lifting, throwing and holding it, it was a minor detail it had always been clothed, if you could call the form-fitting leotards clothes. Whittaker hadn't bought Aleksei's argument and ushered him into his side of the locker room.

* * * * *

The time it took to change clothes was brief and within ten minutes the shredded costumes were in a pile on the desk in the office and Jordan and Aleksei were back on the ice practicing. Whittaker had them do a final easy walk-through of their Romeo and Juliet program before leaving them to work on their exhibition piece, a heart-pounding rock and roll number by a well-known group. Whittaker shook his head in wonder as he watched the two skaters shift from a highly classical number only moments before to the now high-energy, dangerously athletic number they worked on. Aleksei's lifting and throwing power amazed Whittaker, and he had to give Jordan credit for her courage. He sure wouldn't have been willing to leave his life in someone else's hands while they threw him twenty feet across the ice at thirty miles an hour. God bless the young, he prayed.

Dee joined Whittaker at the boards, tapping her toe to the heavy beat of the music, holding her breath as Aleksei launched her into a throw triple Salchow, then breathed easier after Jordan's perfect landing. "They're something to watch, aren't they?" Dee asked Whittaker, her eyes never leaving the pair.

"That they are!" Whittaker stated proudly, cringing slightly at the dangerous dismount they used from their star-lift. "I'm going to have to talk to them about that dismount—I don't feel comfortable with it."

"How do Jordan and Aleksei feel with it?" Dee asked.

"You know Aleksei, he's got the strength to carry it off and Jordan trusts him completely."

"So what's the problem?"

Whittaker shrugged. "Just a little nagging voice in my head telling me to change that dismount."

"Has it ever steered you wrong?"

"Never!" Whittaker answered quietly. "And that's what bothers me."

* * * * *

"Whittaker is uncomfortable with the dismount from your star-lift," Dee stated coming straight to the point as she watched Jordan remove her skates in the locker room.

"What's your take on the dismount?" Jordan asked quietly, her hands quickly loosening the laces.

Dee shrugged, a small frown furrowing her brow. "That whole program scares me, honestly. Too many risky moves for my tastes."

"Whittaker said we had to push the bounds of safety if we were going to get the judge's attention. We're not one of the "tried and true couples" who get points for having skated together for ten years. We've got to get our names to the front of the judge's minds and make it stick if we even want to entertain thoughts of the Olympics." Jordan stated firmly.

"At the risk of injury?"

"Aleksei's leg is fine."

"I'm not talking about Aleksei. I'm worried about you."

"What's to worry about? I'm fine, never better."

"And what about when Aleksei drops you out of one of your lifts or a dismount goes wrong?"

Aleksei's never dropped me. He promised me it would never happen."

"That's not a realistic promise. There are some things he has no control over and if he's got you over his head and hits a bad patch of ice, there's no way he can keep you from falling the ten feet to the ice."

"Nothing's happened yet," Jordan stubbornly stated.

"You're tempting fate, Jordan. Change the dismount. Please," Dee urged.

"I'll talk to Aleksei about your concerns, but I honestly think the program is amazing the way it stands," Jordan answered, frustration clear in her voice. With a final wipe of soft cloth across her blades, she slipped the soft cotton guards over the gleaming, perfectly sharpened metal, and slipped them into her bag.

"I just want to see you safe," Dee offered.

Jordan smiled softly, and quietly responded. "That's the same thing Aleksei keeps saying. Funny how everyone seems to think I need protecting. I'm not some china doll that is going to shatter if I fall. If that were the case, I would have hung up my skates the first time Hanks threw me into the boards. I bruise but I don't break."

"I'd rather see you didn't do either."

"Nice thought but not very practical. We're doing things on a sheet of ice that most people wouldn't do on a surface that isn't slippery. But an element of danger is what keeps people watching us and I want them to see what Aleksei and I can do. There was a time when I used to watch Gordeeva and Grinkov skate and wished I could slip into her skates just once, and feel his arms around me, feel what she felt when he lifted her and carried her, and yes, even threw her. And then Aleksei came into my life and he pushed his way through this wall I'd erected that kept everything calm and even and boring. He made me feel things I never thought I'd feel, pissed me off in ways unimaginable, pushed me physically in my skating that I never knew I could manage and made me laugh like I never believed I would again. I owe him my life, literally, and I'm not going to risk losing all he's given me because Whittaker is uncomfortable with our dismount out of the star-lift. I trust Aleksei, body and soul! You've watched us do the program a hundred times, there's never been a mishap. Trust and believe what you see before you. Like Whittaker keeps saying—we're magic!"

"Magic can't keep you safe," Dee argued.

"Probably not, but I like the way it makes me feel and for now, that's enough!" Jordan stated emphatically. Slipping the bag's strap over her shoulder, she slid her stocking covered feet into clogs and walked out of the locker room.

"My only concern is what happens when the magic disappears?" Dee quietly asked the silent room.

The sound of the heater kicking on was her only reply.

* * * * *

Whittaker's conversation with Aleksei didn't go any better. Heated words about trust and ability were exchanged, charges of the coach knowing what was best and safest tossed back and forth only to be trashed beneath the heels of both men, each certain their position was right.

Finally Whittaker backed down, stating that if this was their decision jointly, he would abide by their wishes but if it was Aleksei grand-standing and anything happened to Jordan, he would personally see that Aleksei never skated again. Aleksei, seething in anger, pointed out for the fourteenth time that he would never put Jordan's safety at risk and their one desire was to win a berth to the up-coming Olympics and make both their coaches proud. It was to this end that they planned to skate their risky programs.

"If it works, you're the hero, Aleksei. If it doesn't, you've put a child at bodily risk!" Whittaker argued.

"Jordan's almost seventeen, hardly a child, and the last thing I would ever do is purposely endanger her. We're here to win and we're committed to doing what ever it takes to get us there!" Aleksei growled, his eyes flashing dark and dangerous.

"Is it worth the risk?"

"If it was you, what would you do?" Aleksei asked quietly.

Whittaker ran frustrated hands through his thinning hair and shook his head as he pondered the question. Sheepishly he glanced at Aleksei, scowling at the tall, muscular man before him, strength and energy shimmering around him in waves and shook his head slightly. "Probably the same damn thing you're doing," he admitted quietly, reaching out a hand and waiting for Aleksei's response.

"We'll do our best, Whittaker. We'll make you proud," Aleksei stated resolutely, his voice deep and calm, accepting his coach's hand and holding it firmly.

"That's all I can ask of you."

With a slight nod, Aleksei released his coach's hand, retrieved his skating bag and left the locker room to meet Jordan rink-side.

Whittaker watched him go, his eyes shining brightly with tears and cast a pleading glance heavenward. "Watch over them, please."

With a final silent prayer, he slowly left the locker room.

Chapter 7

The spacious arena in New England scheduled to hold the National Figure Skating Championships was filled to capacity. The crowd noisy and excited as they awaited the debut of Jamison and Rocmanov. Dee and Whittaker had kept their pair under close scrutiny, limiting reporters and photographers to a minimum and thus ensuring a secrecy that was driving the public wild with speculation and their competitors crazy with worry. Rumors flew about the volatile new couple, ranging from constant fighting to wildly in love, from landing a throw quad-axel to missing double axels regularly. Time would tell and the time was here to prove all the nay-sayers wrong.

Scott Hamilton was commentating, along with Verne Lunquist and Rosalynn Sumners, for the competition, and all were impressed with the previous evenings short programs and looking forward to the long programs to come.

"Good evening, everyone. This promises to be one of the season's most exciting competitions. Tonight's long programs will determine the winner for the National Championship and move the winners toward the World Championship and that much closer to a berth for the Olympics." Verne Lunquist announced.

"That's right." Scott Hamilton agreed. "And the question on everyone's mind is, Can Jamison and Rocmanov hold on to their second place standing after their short program with the reigning U.S. champions,

Wyatt and Hamilton, breathing down their necks? Considering the short time this pair has been together, their chemistry on the ice is very reminiscent of Gordeeva and Grinkov and it should prove very interesting to see their long program, kept tightly under wraps until now. We all wish them well and look forward to the skating to come."

The announcement came for the pair skaters to take to the ice for their five-minute warm-up and the crowd watched with interest as Jordan and Aleksei joined the others on the ice.

The newly Zambonied ice was perfect. It shone like a glassy lake undisturbed by any breeze, free of ripples or flaws as the five pairs of skaters stepped onto its slick surface. Slowly they circled the ice, getting a feel for the ice, the size, and the smell of it. Jordan and Aleksei were the last pair to step into the arena, Jordan casting a quick look at Aleksei and smiling broadly as he quickly stuck his tongue out at her, making her laugh and breaking the tension he could feel as he held her hand.

Dee and Whittaker watched as they slowly circled the ice, noting the other people around them and watching with interest as the others practiced various moves. Aleksei bent his head to Jordan's and whispered something to her, nodding in agreement at her response and the two immediately picked up speed as they rounded the far corner of the ice. It was amazing to see the speed with which they skated, their blades barely whispering a sound as they flew over the ice, scarcely scoring the slick surface beneath them. The audience watched in anticipation as they picked up speed, holding their breaths when he threw her effortlessly into a triple axel and she landed on one foot, arms gracefully spread forward, reaching for him and gliding backwards, joining Aleksei where he met her further up the ice.

"If that's any indication of how they're performing tonight, the defending champions definitely have their work cut out for them. Jordan and Aleksei obviously are going all out this evening. It would appear this pair does not believe in an easy warm up and fully intend to make the team of Wyatt and Hamilton work for their win. Tonight will prove to be a true test of strength and courage." Rosalyn Sumners stated, her voice full of excitement.

"You're right, Roz. Jamison and Rocmanov are looking very much like the pair everyone else is going to have to keep up with." Scott Hamilton added.

The announcers returned their attention to the ice, and watched the remaining minutes of warm-up for the five pairs on the ice. Jordan and Aleksei returned to the boards where their coaches awaited them, listening intently to suggestions and comments, nodding in understanding and pushing away from the boards as they returned to their warm-up and prepared to execute a final lift. Aleksei and Jordan picked up speed, keeping a watchful eye on the other skaters, shifting their position when one of the other couples cut across their ice, then resumed their position and once again picked up speed. Jordan took her position slightly in front of Aleksei, grasping his wrists as he placed his hands beneath her bottom and lifted her over his head, holding her ten feet in the air. Her legs bent gracefully, carefully avoiding his face with her sharp blades, she raised her arms slowly and sensuously over her head, smiling serenely as the chiffon sleeves of her costume billowed in the breeze they created as they sped across the ice. Aleksei held her slight form over his head without strain, sensing every muscle movement Jordan made as she stretched her legs straight and arched her back, completing the movements of their lift.

Aleksei felt, more than saw, the sudden flash of black as it careened toward him from his left side, leaving him no room to maneuver or escape the sliding body beneath him. An audible gasp left the crowd as the entire audience watched Renee Wyatt, the female half of the defending U.S. champions, fall out of a simple throw and slide beneath Aleksei's legs, tripping him as he held Jordan over his head.

Aleksei's immediate reflex was to keep Jordan safe. Without even a split second to warn Jordan of the impending fall, Aleksei abruptly dropped his elbows, the movement bringing Jordan's lower body immediately lower and her arms instinctively forward. Despite Jordan's slight weight, the forward force had her falling face first toward the ice until Aleksei physically threw her away from him, the heel of her blade slicing into the top of his thigh. The power of his throw gave her momentum enough to get her hips over her heels so she fell to the ice on her bottom, her hands sliding painfully against the now roughened surface and causing ice burns on her palms.

Aleksei fared far worse. Having used his arms to get Jordan out of harm's way left him without anything to break his fall, and he landed heavily on his chest and stomach, knocking the wind from his lungs. As much speed as they had attained, he slid the final distance into the boards, his cheek splitting open as he hit against the solid wood and finally came to a stop.

The arena was completely silent, everyone holding their breaths as officials and medical help scrambled onto the ice to assist the skaters. Jordan crawled on her knees, ignoring the pain as the ice cut into her stockings and finally her knees, ignoring the bloody trail her palms left on the pristine whiteness of the ice. Her only thought was to get to Aleksei.

Aleksei lay completely still on the ice, mentally taking note of where he hurt, grimacing as he looked down at the leg that throbbed and saw the blood dripping onto the ice. Slowly he rolled to his left side, his eyes coming to focus on Jordan as she called his name and scrambled to his side.

"Oh, God, Aleksei," she whispered, finally reaching him and pushing his shoulders back to the ice when he tried to sit up. "Don't move," She whispered, tears filling her eyes.

"Are you okay?" Aleksei questioned, looking her over and frowning at her bloody knees and hands.

Jordan swatted away his hands as he reached for her, wanting him to lie still until the doctors reached him. "Hold still, you idiot!" She pleaded, gently pressing his shoulders back to the ice, grimacing at the bloody stains she left on his once-glamorous costume.

The doctors were there quickly, poking, and prodding, and asking questions that soon had Aleksei thoroughly frustrated, and wanting to punch something. Yes he could see the two fingers they were holding up. No he didn't have a headache or feel dizzy. Yes, he could feel his toes, bend his knees and touch his finger to his nose, if they really wanted him to. The doctors wanted to carry him off the ice on a stretcher but Aleksei wouldn't hear of it. He did agree they could apply pressure bandages to his leg and temporarily bandage his cheek, but he was determined to get off the ice under his own steam. Jordan pleaded for him to follow their recommendations but Aleksei would have none of it, and ten minutes after the accident, he was back on his feet, bandaged and bloody, with his partner at his side, skating off the ice. Thunderous applause followed them as they exited the ice, and headed for the dressing room, the doctors right behind them.

Whittaker and Dee met them as they exited the ice, concern and frustration etching their features. "What the hell happened?" Whittaker demanded, frowning as Aleksei stumbled slightly, then slipping one of Aleksei's arms over his shoulders as he helped support him.

"The champs need work on their landing. You'd think after seven years together they could land a simple throw," Aleksei grumbled.

"You'd think so," Jordan agreed seriously, a small laugh escaping her despite the adrenaline rush that was causing her whole body to vibrate.

"I could have done that well when my damn leg was in the cast!" Aleksei answered with a shake of his head and a frown.

"Don't think about that, now," Jordan offered. "Let's just see how bad your injuries are. Okay?" Jordan ended, doing her best to ignore the sudden weakness in her knees and the urge to be sick as the adrenaline in her system began to dissipate. There was a lot to be said for an adrenaline high but the downside of it sucked!

Quickly they made their way to the medical center, helping Aleksei onto the examining table, and hoping he would lie back as instructed, but not surprised when he refused to do so.

"Okay, Doc, patch me up. I've got a competition to win!" Aleksei stated emphatically.

"Are you out of your mind?" Dee and Whittaker both questioned in astonishment. "After that fall?" Dee added.

"I've fallen before. It's no big deal," Aleksei responded.

"You need stitches," Whittaker countered.

"Butterfly's will work for now," Aleksei fired back.

"You could have a head injury."

"I've had them before, and this doesn't feel like one. I'm going to skate!" Aleksei stated emphatically.

"Not if the doctors scratch you."

Dee, Whittaker, Jordan and Aleksei all looked expectantly at the doctor. Aleksei reached for Jordan's now-bandaged hand and rubbed it gently.

The doctor looked at the four people before him and shrugged his shoulders slightly. "There's no sign of head injury and the cheek is primarily superficial. The leg injury should be stitched but butterflies will probably hold. I can't guarantee there won't be scarring without real stitches but that's up to Aleksei. If he thinks he's up to it, I won't stand in his way. In fact, I'd be very interested in seeing the outcome," the doctor answered.

"I don't like it," Whittaker argued.

"So what's new. Lately, you haven't liked much of anything!" Aleksei complained, taking the two offered pain killers from the doctor and sitting back as he began to clean the wound on his cheek and bandage it closed. Jordan sat beside him, her head resting against his shoulder, one hand absently rubbing his uninjured thigh as the doctor gave Aleksei an approved pain killer, closed the thigh wound and placed a sterile dressing over the butterfly stitches.

"That should do it," the doctor said, finishing his work and gathering up the bloodied bandages and medical instruments. "Good luck to you two," he offered, leaving the four-some alone.

"Are you sure about this?" Jordan quietly asked, her hand still softly stroking Aleksei's good thigh.

"As sure as you can get. Besides, the last time you sliced me open with your blade, I won," Aleksei stated, cautiously sliding from the table and testing his legs.

"Don't remind me," Jordan pleaded. "And if it's okay with you, let's not make a habit of this. There's got to be some other way of insuring a good performance other than me cutting you into pieces."

"We'll look into it after we win," Aleksei stated positively. "Shall we skate?" Aleksei questioned, offering her his hand.

"You bet!" Jordan agreed, taking his hand, then allowing herself to be pulled into his chest while his arms wrapped securely around her.

"I was scared to death for you," Aleksei whispered huskily against the top of her head, his breath leaving a warm spot where it touched. "I didn't know what to do."

Jordan pulled away slightly; looking into Aleksei's pale face and gently touched the bandage covering his bruised cheek. "I was afraid for you. When I saw you lying on the ice bleeding, I wanted to take your place. I don't ever want to see you hurt again," Jordan whispered brokenly, a single tear tracing a path down her cheek. With a shaky smile, she raised onto the toe picks of her skates and softly kissed Aleksei's mouth. A gentle kiss to take the pain away.

Aleksei brushed the tear from Jordan's cheek and with his eyes glowing brightly, declared heartily, "Let's kick some ass!"

"Yeah, let's!" Jordan agreed smiling, and wrapped her arms around Aleksei; tightly holding him against her and wishing the competition were over.

* * * * *

"Unbelievably enough, Jamison and Rocmanov will be competing tonight. Despite their horrendous spill during warm-up, when defending champs Wyatt and Hamilton collided with them, they will be competing," Scott Hamilton announced, clearly amazed at their courageousness.

"That's right, Scott. The judges have allowed them to skate two slots later than originally planned, allowing them time to change into different costumes. Their original costumes, obviously ruined, during their collision with the defending champs," Verne added.

"Well, I for one, can't wait to see their performance. If nothing else, their courage to even attempt such a difficult program after such a spill should be an inspiration to us all!" Scott concluded.

The competition continued, but everyone's mind was on the performance yet to come, Jamison and Rocmanov's first official performance as a pair.

*   *   *   *   *

"Ready?" Aleksei softly asked Jordan, their eyes meeting and holding as he sent encouragement and confidence her way. Once again, the couple were standing beside the ice they had only moments before met disaster head on. Casting a last quick glance at the ice, she lifted her chin defiantly, daring the ice to challenge her, smiling as she nodded in agreement and squeezed his hand gently.

Aleksei looked at their hands, fingers laced together and his eyes darkened a fraction in anger when he again noticed her abraded palms. The gauze had been removed and her palms looked red and painful, he hoped she could stand the pressure on her palms during their numerous lifts. "How bad are they?" he questioned, holding her held palm up for inspection.

"I'll survive," She stated easily, running a finger between his eyes to erase the frown line forming. "Smile, it's our turn," she demanded, giving his hand a final squeeze and preparing to step on the ice.

"And now, ladies and gentlemen. Jordan Jamison and Aleksei Rocmanov," a voice out of the darkness announced.

Together, as one, Aleksei and Jordan stepped onto the ice. Holding hands, they skated confidently to the center of the ice, smiling confidently at each other and the crowd and assumed their starting positions. The crowd refused to stop applauding, showing the pair their appreciation of the courage and tenacity they had shown. After their collision on the ice with the defending champions, no one would have been surprised if they had been unable to compete and had withdrawn, and yet, here they were, center ice, awaiting their music. Jordan and Aleksei held their opening position for over a minute, absorbing the strength they felt flowing from the appreciative crowd, breathing deeply and calmly as they felt their own adrenaline begin to surge through their systems. Finally, a request to be seated was announced and the audience complied, but not before words of encouragement were called out from various corners of the arena and applause again broke out.

Aleksei and Jordan remained motionless, waiting for the silence to descend and their music to begin. Aleksei smiled into Jordan's upturned face and mouthed *nobody leaves,* causing her to smile secretly in return and nod in agreement. After what seemed hours, the soft beginning strains of Tchaikovsky's *Romeo and Juliet* were heard and Jordan and Aleksei took their first tentative strokes on the ice as an official pair.

Just as Whittaker and Dee had hoped, the audience was entranced. The only sounds to be heard were the rising and falling notes of the music. Jordan and Aleksei sped across the ice, their blades mere whispers as they performed all the required elements. The audience made not a sound, holding their breaths as the pair before them landed each jump, throw and lift without fault or hesitation, despite their earlier incident. Even the announcers were silent; each lost in the beauty of the performance being played before them.

When Aleksei lifted a seemingly dead Jordan into his arms and raised her up, the audience felt his pain, knew he was pleading with

God to join her in death and everyone understood his plight, felt his loss for the love of his life. In the deafening silence, you could feel the audience's sympathy pouring onto the ice. When he raised her over his head and then collapsed with her in his arms on the last notes of the powerful music, the arena erupted into cheers that threatened to bring the ceiling down.

Aleksei and Jordan lay still on the ice, their chests laboring to take a full breath, absorbing the applause surrounding them and smiled to each other. With a gentle kiss, Aleksei lifted her to her knees, stood beside her and assisted her to her feet. Holding her hand, he bowed to her, then the audience, forgetting about the judges and embraced the magic they had been a part of. They accepted the applause, laughing as the power swept over them and carried them forward to accept the flowers that were being tossed onto the ice. Aleksei scooped up a single white rose and presented it to Jordan, kissing one hand softly and then leading her off the ice to the kiss and cry area where they would await their scores.

Flash bulbs went off furiously, despite the request there be none for safety purposes, as audience members tried to get pictures of the new pair as they waited patiently with their coaches in the chairs. When the scores for technical merit came up, the audience voiced their disapproval at the 5.8's and 5.9's that crossed the board. When the scores for presentation came across and read 6.0 straight across, the audience went wild and it wasn't until Jordan and Aleksei took to the ice for a final bow that the pandemonium subsided somewhat.

Jordan and Aleksei won the National's easily that night, despite their near-disastrous collision with the defending champions, and it would be a night neither of them would ever forget. It was a night that would remain in their memories forever.

And as Aleksei stood center ice, holding Jordan against his side, sharing their success, he understood what his coach had wanted for him all along. The fulfillment of being a part of something that made you truly happy, truly complete. As Aleksei looked down into Jordan's upturned smiling, radiant face, he knew this small slip of a girl was the woman he was meant to share his life with, to grow old with. The thought made him throw back his head and laugh with joy toward the sky. The surprised look on Jordan's face only made him laugh that much louder. Easily, he picked her up into his arms, spinning her in circles until she was laughing as hard as he was. The audience joined in their joy, clapping even louder and stamping their feet, the sound shaking the very foundation of the arena. Aleksei returned Jordan to her feet and with a final bow of gratitude, they left the ice, their fans still throwing roses and small trinkets onto the ice.

The announcers remained stunned. "I can't believe what we've just witnessed!" Verne said. "Never in all my years as an announcer, have I ever experienced such enthusasm from an audience."

"You're right about that." Scott agreed, "The only other time I can remember the audience responding so passionately was when Katia Gordeeva took to the ice alone for the first time. You could feel the strength the audience was offering her then and you could sure feel them supporting Jamison and Rocmanov tonight."

"Ladies and Gentleman, tonight you witnessed magic at it's very best and, as far as I'm concerned, I can't wait to see their next competition!" Verne added enthusiastically.

"I can't imagine them beating this performance, because, as Verne said, this was definitely magic. Who knows, maybe we are witnessing the next Gordeeva and Grinkov," Scott finished, shaking his head in wonder as he listened to the still cheering crowd.

"From all of us up here in the booth, this is Verne Lunquist, Scott Hamilton and Rosalyn Sumners, bidding you good night."

Chapter 8

"Physicals check out, blood work shows no performance enhancement drugs present. According to Olympic rules, you're on your way to the Winter Olympics!" Dee screamed in excitement. All the medical tests and paperwork were completed and all that was left to do was to finalize reservations.

Jordan smiled broadly at her coach, her enthusiasm reaching out as they enclosed each other in a congratulatory hug. "Does Aleksei know yet?" Jordan asked, her eyes glowing brightly.

"I would assume Whittaker's breaking the news to him also," Dee said, smiling as Jordan became more animated, her enthusiasm making her giddy.

The front door suddenly slammed open, Aleksei's muscular figure filling the doorway, the sun shining brightly behind him. "We're there!" he spoke softly, deeply, yet the strength behind his words spoke louder than if he had yelled them. Rushing toward Jordan, he scooped her up in his arms, spinning wildly in circles and they laughed and cried in joy and anticipation.

Whittaker gently hugged Dee, kissing her cheek softly and the two coaches smiled as they watched their athletes celebrate their good fortune.

Jordan was dizzy when Aleksei finally set her feet on the ground and held her firmly against him, hugging her to his broad chest as he kissed the top of her head. "We made it brat!" he celebrated, kissing her mouth quickly while she frowned at him for using the nickname he seemed to favor.

"We've still got the Russians to beat," Jordan reminded.

"No—they have to beat us!" Aleksei corrected.

Jordan smiled up into his dark eyes, laying a gentle hand against his cheek, enjoying the sensual roughness of his day-old beard against her palm. "I like the way you think," She answered, stretching upward as he lowered his head toward her awaiting mouth. Their brief kiss was gentle, full of love and understanding and hope and the belief that they would reach their goal. Aleksei's arms engulfed Jordan as he hugged her closer to him, feeling her heart beat against his chest, answering his heart as it called to hers and he knew without doubt that if hearts could beat as one, theirs most certainly did.

There was nothing that could stop them. He knew, as sure as he knew there was a God in heaven, that the United States would bring home Gold this Olympics. And he couldn't believe his good fortune, that this slip of a girl—no woman—was going to be there to share it with him.

Life couldn't get any better than this.

*　　*　　*　　*　　*

"We want to spend a weekend at the cottage. Call it a final break before the Olympics," Aleksei stated, his glance going from Whittaker to Dee, then to Jordan who nodded in agreement.

"We could use the down-time," Jordan urged, her soft smile conflicting with the tired shadows beneath her eyes.

Aleksei and Jordan had been spending fourteen to sixteen hours a day on the ice, rehearsing again and again until their programs played through their minds in their sleep. Without a doubt, they could use the break but Whittaker was concerned the time-off could work against them.

"You've found your rhythm, I hate to have you lose it. You don't have the time to start all over."

"We see our programs in our sleep, there's nothing to lose," Aleksei growled at his coach.

"It's only one weekend," Jordan suggested, looking to Dee for assistance.

"It probably wouldn't hurt to give them a small break," Dee offered, holding her hand up when Whittaker opened his mouth to disagree. "You can't say they aren't ready, Whittaker. They've busted their asses and I think they could use the down-time."

Whittaker frowned again, looking from Jordan to Aleksei, holding a conversation with himself as to the pros and cons of letting them off the ice for even a few days. Finally, he relented. "One weekend, but no skiing, no hiking, nothing that could physically put you at risk. You two have worked too hard to lose because you did something stupid!" He growled, pointedly looking at Aleksei.

"Agreed," Jordan and Aleksei answered in unison.

"Couldn't it be somewhere a bit closer, the cottage is a good two hour drive away," Whittaker complained anew.

"That's the idea. We want quiet time alone," Aleksei stated softly, sending Jordan a heated caress with his dark eyes.

Whittaker caught the meaningful look and frowned again, directing his glance toward Dee. "You need to save your strength, the Olympics are only nine weeks away. I want you both healthy and strong. Weak legs aren't going to get you Gold."

"Gordeeva and Grinkov didn't have problems with weak legs and I'm sure they managed to spend some quiet time alone," Aleksei argued.

"They were married!" Whittaker shot back, his heated glance reaching Jordan.

"So because we're not married, and if we spend time alone, all we're going to do is fool around? Nothing's going to happen that I don't want to happen," Jordan answered firmly, succinctly.

"What if someone came forward and made the accusation that the two of you are, ah…involved now?" Whittaker suggested.

"Why would anyone make such an accusation and even if they did, why would it matter? We're not allowed to have feelings for each other? It's not as if I'm under age. I'm old enough to be having an adult relationship if I choose to!" Jordan stated heatedly.

"Why did Nancy Kerrigan get her leg bashed? If someone wants to win, they'll find a way to see it happens. Stranger things have happened," Whittaker argued.

" You're being paranoid," Aleksei stated.

"I'm being cautious. I don't want you two risking anything."

"We're taking one weekend, alone, doing nothing but relaxing and relieving some of the stress that's built up. I really don't think there's much at risk," Aleksei reiterated.

Whittaker still didn't like the idea, couldn't shake the feeling of trouble ahead; unseen but a pulsing threat in his gut. "I don't like it, but I obviously have been out-voted. I want you back here January ninth, no delays, no arguments, no excuses."

"Great!" Jordan yelled excitedly, throwing herself against Aleksei's chest and smiling as his strong arms enfolded her.

"You have three more weeks to abuse us, Whittaker. Be happy!" Aleksei teased, kissing the top of Jordan's head and smiling broadly.

"You're right. And by the way, did I mention I volunteered the two of you for an AIDS benefit December twenty-first?" Whittaker questioned, raising one eyebrow in defiance when Aleksei scowled over Jordan's head.

"No, you failed to impart that little bit of information," Aleksei growled, "Couldn't you find another way to put us to work any closer to Christmas?"

"Don't worry, I'm still looking for something to keep you up to speed. We wouldn't want you getting lazy."

"We can try our exhibition piece at the benefit, see if the program needs any final tweaks," Jordan interrupted, sensing Aleksei's rising temper as his arms folded tighter around her.

"That's a good idea," Aleksei answered quietly, his voice dangerously deep, his glance growing fiercer as he looked at his coach.

"I still don't like the dismount," Whittaker began, only to be cut off by Aleksei's heated response.

"I don't give a flying leap what you like or don't like at this minute, Whittaker. Back off and leave us alone."

Aleksei released Jordan from his arms and gently urged her forward with one hand at the small of her back, guiding her around the desk and toward the door. Stopping briefly, he kissed Dee's cheek, speaking something into her ear that Whittaker was unable to hear, and leaving the two coaches behind in the office.

"What did he say?" Whittaker demanded as soon as the office door shut.

"You're on a 'need-to-know-basis, and right now, you don't need to know!" Dee answered smartly, and brushed past the stubborn man, soundly slamming the office door behind her.

"The whole world's gone fucking nuts!" Whittaker yelled to the ceiling, frustration making his voice a thunderous roar that rattled the steel framework which held the dropped ceiling.

* * * * *

"Oh, Aleksei, this place is perfect," Jordan softly voiced, slipping the huge down coat from her shoulders and laying it across the back of the over-stuffed sofa, her gaze taking in the welcoming room.

The cottage was small but cozy. There was a single main room that held a huge fireplace, over-stuffed sofa, two wing chairs and assorted small tables, along with a kitchen and small eating area. Slowly she walked about the room, taking a peek inside the small bedroom snuggled off to one side, teasing Aleksei about breaking in the antique wrought iron bed that lay covered by a beautiful floral print comforter in muted shades of mauve, cream and jade. The small adjoining bathroom held a cast iron stand-alone tub complete with claw feet. When she saw the small tub, she couldn't resist teasing Aleksei about the impossibility of him fitting into it. Aleksei simply shrugged his broad shoulders and said it would be interesting trying, a lecherous glint sparkling in his dark eyes.

"I'll bring the bags in and then I'll build you a fire," Aleksei suggested, giving Jordan a gentle kiss before he went outside.

"I'll start the cocoa," Jordan offered.

"Don't forget the marshmallows," He ordered before he closed the door behind him.

Jordan looked through the cabinets in the small kitchen, quickly finding a small saucepan, filling it with water and putting it on the stove to heat. Aleksei kicked the front door, announcing his arrival and Jordan dashed the short distance to open it for him, taking a bag of groceries that balanced precariously between two suitcases. Aleksei placed the suitcases in the small bedroom, sitting on the bed and bouncing slightly to check its firmness and retraced his path past the kitchen, where he grabbed a handful of marshmallows from the bag on the counter, despite Jordan's attempts to keep them for the cocoa.

"You eat them all before the cocoa's done, you'll be making a trip to the grocery store alone," She vowed.

"You'd send me out into that wilderness alone for a bag of marshmallows?" Aleksei asked, his tone light and teasing.

"In a New York minute!" Jordan responded, tossing a handful of the soft, white puffs at him.

"At least I eat them—you're just tossing them around like popcorn."

"Oh, popcorn. That goes great with cocoa and marshmallows."

"Food of the Gods," Aleksei agreed, chuckling, and exited the door as another handful of marshmallows flew his way.

Jordan puttered around in the kitchen, putting away groceries, making cocoa and popcorn and generally discovering where everything was. If nothing else, the cottage was well equipped despite its small size and so far she hadn't come across anything she needed and couldn't find. From the kitchen she was able to watch as Aleksei built the fire in the large stone hearth, bantering with him over the proper procedure for building a fire and finally settling herself comfortably on the sofa before the hearth to watch him. In short order he had the fire blazing, it's heat and woodsy aroma filling the small room.

"Will this do, m'lady?" Aleksei questioned from his knees, his hand indicating the huge fire behind him.

"If that's the best you can do. I'd hoped it would be a bit warmer with the fire," Jordan teased, laughing lightly as Aleksei slowly stalked her on his knees, his look one of a sleek, predatory cat. On he crept until he reached her, his muscular arms caging her between them, her knees trapped between his spread legs where he held her pinned loosely against the coach.

"I can do much better than that," he stated deeply, his voice dangerously sexy, his dark eyes burning brightly "How much warmer do you want it?"

Jordan ran her hands along Aleksei's bracketing arms, loving the feel of the quivering strength he held in check, drowning in the dark, sensual look in his eyes, a look reserved for her alone. Slowly she stroked his face, running her thumb over his full lower lip and twitching when he nipped it gently, only to smile when he turned his head slightly, his heated lips scorching her palm with a kiss. The heat from Aleksei was making her dizzy, his playful kisses and knowing caresses driving her crazy, making her want him more each second, more than she'd ever desired him before. Somewhere deep inside of her a flame was growing brighter, calling her toward an unknown universe, demanding more power to reach the far away stars. Aleksei softly calling her name slowed her spinning feelings, but only marginally. She had to struggle to focus her forest green eyes on his handsome face.

"Aleksei, I'm melting," she whispered breathlessly.

Aleksei smiled softly, gently cupped her cheeks and with a knowing look sweetly kissed her, pulling away when she sought to deepen the kiss. "You're not yet, little one. But believe me, you will be before we're done."

"Promise."

"I promise you nothing but pleasure, my love," he vowed, then scooped her into his arms and carried her into the small bedroom, gently laying her across the floral bedspread and joining her on the soft mattress.

* * * * *

Aleksei softly stroked Jordan's face. His fingertips barely grazing her soft skin sent tingles of pleasure through her body, making her inch closer to the warmth and strength of his body as they lay side by side. Her breath came in small puffs, her eyes drifting closed as he pressed teasing kisses along her neck, pulling the material of her sweater aside to continue his sweet assault on the skin of her shoulder. Aleksei's softly spoken words of what was to come make Jordan flush with anticipation yet apprehensive of the unknown at the same time.

They had waited so long to consummate their love. Aleksei had shown more patience and restraint than Jordan had actually. Several times it had been Aleksei who had gently left Jordan's welcoming arms when the need to be together had become overwhelming. Aleksei had given Jordan the time she needed to decide what she wanted in her life, not just the heated passion of stolen moments but the enduring love of a lifetime. Now as he watched her eyes glaze and her skin flush with passion, he knew he had done the right thing in waiting for her to come to him.

"Sweet heaven, Aleksei, this is torture," Jordan moaned, shifting ever closer to his muscular form, her hands running heatedly up his arms and over his shoulders to delve into his thick dark hair and pull his face up to hers where her mouth could devour his. Deeply she kissed him, her tongue melting against his as he swallowed her groan of pleasure. Slowly their mouths mated, teasing, tormenting, answering each need as it arose, separating only briefly when Jordan's sweater was swiftly pulled over her head and tossed to the floor, forgotten, as their kiss resumed.

Aleksei slowed their kiss, taking small bites from the corners of her mouth as if sipping fine cognac, getting dizzier by the moment as his own passion increased in tempo with Jordan's. Wanting to make their time together last a lifetime, he took a deep, calming breath. "You taste of cocoa," he teased, his voice deep and lush with passion. Licking at her lips and evading her mouth as she sought to draw him back against her lips, he easily caught her hands above her head and laced his fingers through hers as he held her firmly, yet gently, against the pillows.

The friction of his palms against hers brought on new sensations. How often their hands had blended this way while they skated and yet this sensation had never been as full of fire and excitement; had never made her want to melt into oblivion and beyond.

"I want to touch you," Jordan gasped, her fingers flexing anxiously, her palm pushing against his even as her hips imitated the motion against his own, the movement causing the heat in his loins to burn hotter.

Aleksei closed his eyes against the sweet torture Jordan was innocently inflicting, breathing deeply and looking for strength as he sought to keep control of his raging hunger for her. She was driving him toward oblivion, knowingly, or unknowingly, it didn't really matter. Their hunger for one another was making his hopes for a slow seduction unrealistic and at this point in time he really didn't give a damn. He only wanted to insure she wasn't hurt in any way.

Seconds slowly ticked by as he struggled to slow his racing heart, trying to ignore the bolts of desire that threatened to engulf him each time

Jordan moved against him, softly imploring he make love to her; her soft perfume surrounding him with its magical power.

"Do you have any idea what you're doing to me?" he questioned, his voice husky and deep.

"What I've wanted to do to you since the first time I saw you," Jordan answered softly, her eyes widening with shock as she suddenly realized what she'd said.

Aleksei pulled back only slightly, his eyes watching hers closely, noticing the soft flush that crept up her cheeks. "Exactly which meeting would that be?" he asked softly, his breath catching as he watched her tongue moisten her full, pink lips.

Flustered, Jordan tried to think of a tart response, but her mind was empty of everything but the things Aleksei was making her feel. "What do you mean, 'which meeting'?"

Aleksei's smile widened, his eyes shining as a sudden thought struck him. "Don't tell me you've had the hots for me since Canada?" he asked quietly.

"You're crazy. I was only a kid then. Kid's don't think about those things at that age," Jordan stuttered, her eyes trying to look anywhere but into Aleksei's dark knowing gaze.

Aleksei released her hands, cupping his own around her face, his thumbs gently caressing her cheekbones. His whispered calling of her name brought her shining eyes back to his, dark green and obsidian meeting and holding, all questions asked and answered as they silently communicated. With infinite care, he softly kissed her lips, her cheeks, her eyes, branding her as his alone. "Jordan, I love you," he whispered thickly, his heart welcoming the feeling that filled him as he finally voiced his desire.

Jordan blinked in surprise, a smile, one of knowing and ecstasy at once, spread across her face. "It took you long enough to figure it out, Rocmanov!" she stated tartly, the happiness she was no longer able to contain bursting forth as bright laughter.

Aleksei returned her brilliant smile, taking in the vision she presented before him. Never had he seen anyone as beautiful as the woman before him. "What do you mean, 'it took me long enough?'"

"You've loved me forever and didn't even know it," Jordan answered cockily, her eyes flashing brightly.

"I haven't even liked you forever. What makes you think I've loved you forever?"

"I knew in Canada."

Aleksei shook his head trying to clear a path through the haze of passion so he might be able to understand her train of thought. "Explain this to me, please. Did I, or did I not, knock you on your butt in Canada?"

"Yes, you did."

"And this meant I loved you?" Aleksei questioned calmly, his gaze sweeping across her flushed, glowing face.

"Not the part where you knocked me down, specifically. It was the way you treated me afterward." Jordan explained, brushing her hand down his cheek.

Aleksei wracked his brain trying to remember everything about their encounter so many years before. "I remember something about the 'Ice Queen' and calling you a brat…"

"It was the way you called me a brat; the tone you used. You use the same tone with me now," Jordan ended softly, her hands holding his face. "It's the same tone you used, just now, when you told me you love me. It's the same tone that makes me weightless and able to touch the universe. It's the same tone that told me when I was twelve I would find the way to heaven; a place where I'd be happy and unafraid. I would find my way to you."

Aleksei could only look at her, afraid to speak for fear his voice would fail him. Slowly he leaned forward, his lips gently meeting hers, blending softly and sweetly. Barely leaving her lips, he whispered "Jordan Jamison, you take my breath away." Returning to her lips, he lost himself in their sweetness, drowning gratefully as wave after wave of passion reclaimed the pair and pushed them toward sweet oblivion.

There would be no more softly spoken words for now as their need to be one became all consuming, pushing away outside interference and distractions until they existed within the small cocoon of the bedroom. Their clothes magically dissolved beneath questing hands and lips, each piece revealing secrets to the other. Despite their having touched each other in nearly every imaginable way while they skated, the revealing practice clothes had still left them to imagine what lay beneath. Now, there would be no further secrets and both Jordan and Aleksei reveled in their exploration of each other's bodies. Erogenous zones in the most unexpected places were found, ticklish spots emerged, all under the joy and laughter of discovering each other.

After what seemed an eternity, the playfulness turned into passion and the pair sought their fulfillment, finding the brightly shining stars in the universe they traveled, clinging to one another as they shattered together in a shower of fiery sparks. Trembling, they clung together, as much out of desire to remain locked together in each other's arms as too exhausted to move. Their chests heaving together as they slowly returned to earth and regained their breath.

"Are you all right?" Aleksei asked softly, pushing aside Jordan's damp hair and kissing her flushed, damp cheek.

"Is it always like this?" Jordan asked serenely, snuggling closer to Aleksei and smiling softly when he tightened his arms around her.

"Is what always like this?" he asked obtusively, grunting when she punched him lightly in the stomach for his comment. "Ow—what was that for?"

"For the stupid response. Now, I'll give you another chance. Answer my question," she demanded, running her hand through the damp curls covering his chest.

Aleksei couldn't think straight with her touching him as she was. Despite being exhausted only seconds before, he now felt strong enough to run a marathon. Catching her wandering hand and bringing it to his lips, he kissed her palm, enjoying the way her eyes darkened at the intimate gesture and smiled into her upturned face. "No, my love, it's not always like that. But it will always be that way for us." he promised, "Nobody leaves, remember?" his lips whispered across hers just before he plundered her mouth, rolling her onto her back and into the deep pillows.

Jordan's body immediately responded, fires raging anew and she marveled at the sudden overwhelming need to again search the stars with Aleksei. This time, their union was urgent, their ascent swift and savage as they peaked within moments of joining. Their gazes remained locked together, Aleksei's obsidian eyes filling with fire, Jordan's deepening from emerald to hunter green; each watching the other as they sought their fulfillment and fell over the edge into oblivion together.

The descent to earth was slow and feather soft, their eventual return leading them into a deep, restful slumber. Aleksei's arms held her spooned comfortably against the front of his body; her warm, shapely bottom pressed against his lap, his knees resting against the back of her thighs. Jordan held his hands in hers, her head resting on the pillow beside Aleksei's, copper and deep brown hair blending across the fluffy whiteness of the pillow. Their bodies moved together as naturally as they did on the ice, as if they'd been together forever.

And they slept, the deep, dreamless slumber of lovers well satisfied, knowing when they awoke they would be together—forever.

Chapter 9

The forest was silent, as if holding its breath in anticipation. Jordan found herself alone, in the middle of a clearing, the pine needles silencing her footsteps as she slowly turned in a circle in search of a way out. Suddenly, several yards away, Aleksei stood at the wood line of the forest, his arms outstretched, reaching toward her. Jordan cautiously began walking toward Aleksei. His voice was silent yet inside her heart she could hear him calling her to him. Each step she took toward him, he seemed to melt deeper into the forest, his tall, muscular body becoming more transparent with each passing second. It was as if he was slowly fading before her eyes. But she knew that was impossible so she kept moving forward, her hands reaching out to touch him.

"Jordan, I love you," Aleksei stated softly, his voice clear in the chill winter air.

"Aleksei, wait," she implored, trying to run toward him, but stumbling on the uneven earth of the forest. "Don't leave me. Nobody leaves. Remember?" she cried, picking herself up when the dense forest floor tripped her.

"I'll never leave you, Jordan. We'll always be together," he promised, his body fading further, shimmering in the cold breeze.

"Aleksei, no…! God…, please, no…" she sobbed, stumbling forward and finally reaching the spot where the last vague image of Aleksei's body shimmered before her. "Aleksei, you promised," she cried, reaching for him *and feeling not the welcome warmth of his body but empty, cold air.* "You swore to me... Nobody leaves..." *she whimpered brokenly, collapsing to the ground.*

"You'll always be able to find me, Jordan. I'll always be with you. Perhaps not the way we want it to be, but I will always be with you. Listen to the whispers on the ice, Jordan. You'll find me in the whispers on the ice."

"That's not enough. I want you next to me. I want to be able to touch you, to hear your laughter and see your smile, to feel your heart beating against mine. Don't leave me, Aleksei," *she cried brokenly, reaching for him only to see her hands penetrate his barely discernible shape.*

"I love you, Jordan... never forget. I'll love you forever..." *he whispered and gently ran his hand down her cheek, fading away completely to leave her totally alone in the forest.*

Jordan awoke with a violent jerk, sitting upright as the last vestiges of her nightmare swirled through her mind, finally fading to leave her empty and exhausted. Touching a hand to her cheek where Aleksei had last touched her, she cringed at the coldness she felt there. Fearfully she looked to where Aleksei had been sleeping, panic surging forth when she found the bed, and the room, empty.

"Aleksei...?"

Silence was her answer. Trying to control her panic, she climbed from beneath the covers, slipped Aleksei's abandoned T-shirt over her head and inhaled deeply of his scent that still clung to the shirt. Slowly she walked through the doorway into the large room, calling his name, and still she found nothing but silence. Quietly she stood in the middle of the room, unsure of what to do next, fighting the urge to simply collapse to the floor and cry.

The door suddenly opened, it's frame filled by Aleksei's enormous form holding an armful of firewood, the snow swirling behind him as he tried to close the door with one foot and still hold the wood.

Jordan launched herself at him, ignoring his warning of being cold and wet with snow, and literally pushed the wood in his arms to the floor, easily sidestepping the falling debris. Without a word she threw herself into his arms, holding him tightly as she tried to melt into him, squeezing the breath from him.

Aleksei's surprised grunt at her behavior subsided the moment he saw her pale face. Her eyes were wide and panicky, their darkness glazed, tears that still trailed down her cheeks. Her lips trembled as she tried to answer his question. "Jordan, what is it?" he repeated when he wasn't sure if she'd understood him the first time.

Jordan could only shake her head; afraid to put her dream to words for fear it would give it the power to become fact. "Hold me, Aleksei…just hold me," she mumbled, burrowing against him.

"Come here, sweetheart," Aleksei coaxed, walking her to the couch and gently placing her on the soft cushions, wrapping the fleece throw around her shoulders. "Let me get the fire going. I'll be right here," he stated, waiting until she nodded in agreement before he left her side.

In short order he had the fire roaring healthily, the heat penetrating even the farthest corners of the room. He had watched Jordan silently watch him build the fire, the panicked look in her eyes slowly fading as she had watched his every move, never speaking aloud but communicating her fear to him clearly.

"That ought to keep this place warm for a while," he offered conversationally, leaving the hearth and crawling on his hands and knees across the floor to kneel before Jordan on the couch. The throw stayed firmly wrapped around her shoulders, her knuckles white where she held the fabric close beneath her chin.

"Are you okay?" he asked her quietly, brushing wayward curls from her temples and placing a gentle kiss on her forehead.

"I think," she whispered, leaning her forehead against his and closing her eyes, the deep breath she took still a bit shaky.

"Want to talk about it?"

Jordan's head popped up, her eyes dark and full of fear at his question, her heading shaking back and forth adamantly. "No, it might come true!" she gasped, pulling Aleksei into her arms, her body trembling. "Aleksei, please...just hold me," she pleaded.

Aleksei held her tightly, gently stroking her back as he whispered soothing words of comfort. At a loss as to what could have frightened her so much. He couldn't have been away from her for more than five minutes. The woodpile was just outside the door, not fifty feet away from where she had slept, so he had not idea what any of this was about. "As you wish, Jordan. I'll hold you all night if that's what you want," he whispered into her hair, lifting her easily into his arms and settling comfortably into the corner of the sofa. Gently he set her between his spread legs, her arms releasing the fleece throw to wrap about his waist as she snuggled her cheek beneath his chin, closing her eyes and heaving a deep sigh. Aleksei held her tightly, resting his chin on the top of her head and breathing deeply of her soft perfume.

Slowly, over time, Aleksei felt Jordan relax in his arms, heard her breathing calm, felt her trembling stop. Patiently he waited for her to come to terms with whatever had frightened her, wishing he could chase away whatever had shaken her so, knowing there were some demons she would have to fight alone. Her sudden, quietly voiced, question surprised him after her lengthy stillness.

"Aleksei—nobody leaves, right?"

"That's our promise to each other," he answered simply, releasing her when he felt her push against his chest as she moved to sit up, her eyes capturing his and refusing to break contact.

"Swear it! Swear that with the two of us, nobody leaves!" she demanded urgently.

Aleksei's hands cupped Jordan's face, pulling her forward until their lips nearly touched. "As God is my witness, Jordan. Nobody leaves!" he stated emphatically, his eyes delving deeply into hers, reaching her soul, and sharing his courage and belief in what he said.

"I'm going to hold you to it," Jordan promised, covering his hands, where they rested on her face, with her own, her cold fingers absorbing the warmth of his own. Slowly she moved the few inches forward until her mouth met his, their kiss sealing their vow to each other and chasing away her final fears left by her nightmare. Softly they explored the unhurried, gentle side of love, kisses shared simply for the joy of sharing, touching for the simple sake of feeling the wonder of love. When they finally parted, there was no remainder of the fear Aleksei had witnessed earlier, simply his shining, beautiful Jordan.

"Want to come skate with me?" Aleksei asked suddenly, his hands sifting through her copper-toned curls, a mischievous smile curving his lips.

"You brought our skates? Whittaker's going to kill you if he finds out," Jordan warned. "Remember, 'no skating, no skiing, no hiking. Nothing that could land you in the hospital!'" she reminded.

"You could land me in the hospital after the workout you put me through earlier," he teased, his smile widening as he watched the flush spread across her cheeks as he teased her about their earlier passionate encounter.

"Fine—don't expect another such threat to your health then. I wouldn't want to be the one responsible for your withdrawal from the Olympics," she threatened nonchalantly. Moving to leave the circle of his arms and making it as far as the edge of the couch before he circled her slim waist with one arm, he pulled her backwards, holding her slim back tight against his broad chest.

"Don't make threats you can't keep, brat," he whispered heatedly against her neck, his lips pressing hot kisses between his words to emphasize his point, smiling when he felt her melt against him.

"You just think you're irresistible, don't you?" her voice sexily low despite her cheeky response.

"No, you do!" he answered cockily, rubbing his beard-rough cheek gently against hers before turning her in his arms enough to face him.

"Why would I think you're irresistible?"

"I don't know. Why?"

"You want me to give you a list?" Jordan teased.

"A whole list, huh? I didn't know there were so many things about me that were irresistible," he stated flippantly, pleased arrogance clear in his tone.

"Don't get so excited. The list is *very* short!"

"You must have forgotten to poll everyone I know," Aleksei stated, his eyes sparkling mischievously.

"I only polled those females who have actual knowledge of your irresistibility. I was surprised at how willing they were to talk to me. In fact, most of them offered their opinions without being asked."

Aleksei's exaggerated cringe startled a laugh out of Jordan, "Touché, brat. Now give me this list."

"I really don't think it would interest you," she shrugged, pushing against his chest as if to leave.

"No you don't..." he started, tightening his arms and bringing her warmth and softness back against his chest, then leaning forward to give her a quick kiss. "You started this subject, you finish it. The list!" he demanded laughingly.

Jordan heaved a huge sigh, her expression one of 'if I must' and began. "Well—everyone agrees you're easy enough to look at... Ouch!" she complained, slapping at the hand that pinched her bottom. "Fine—you're gorgeous—too damn gorgeous if you ask me; but then, nobody did—ask me that is. Anyway, you're fun; whatever that means and I probably don't want to know, so we'll go on to the next thing on your *list*. You skate well. That I can generally agree with. Ouch!" another light pinch afflicted her bottom. "Your ass, unarguably, is the best in the business!"

"According to whom?" he choked out, an unexpected blush coloring cheeks.

"The only one who counts—me, of course!" Jordan stated firmly. "Therefore, you look wonderful in tight pants, and out of them, according to some who will remain nameless but can be easily spotted because they're limping. I won't say why or how they came to be that way, only that they are and that a certain ex-skater's ex-husband was happy to get the work," Jordan teased airily, snidely referring to the Nancy Kerrigan/Tanya Harding debacle.

"Moving on..." Aleksei encouraged, chuckling at her show of jealousy.

"Where was I?" Jordan pondered her face a study of innocence, "Oh, yes, tight pants. Next, there are those who are quite partial to your chest hair," she stated, pulling smartly on a few and enjoying immensely his flinch of pain. "I, personally, find them okay. All right, more than okay," she stammered, responding to Aleksei's smug look and raised eyebrows as he remembered how she hadn't been able to stop running her hands over his lushly covered chest when they'd made love.

"Ah." he nodded in understanding. "It would seem, the *list* is primarily about my physical attributes."

"You're surprised?"

Aleksei searched her face, looking for censure and found none. "I probably shouldn't be considering I spent the better part of my early years proving my manhood to everyone. It's just kind of disheartening to know that my legacy is going to be how many beers I could knock back, how many fights I fought, how many bones I broke and how many women I knew," he stated, frowning at the memories of his youthful, reckless past.

"So who says that has to be your legacy?" Jordan questioned, smiling lovingly up at him from where she lay against his chest until he returned the smile. "Why can't your past be chapter one and what we do together be chapter two and what people remember?"

"Because people tend to remember the bad and ignore the good, the bad is typically much more interesting."

"Only in a wicked, voyeuristic, sort of way. It's easy for people to say 'can you believe the wild stuff so-and-so did? I can't believe he got away with it.', and still experience the same thrill vicariously without having to take the risk. People are warped enough to scream 'that's pushing the envelope too far' and wish they'd had the balls to think of it themselves, not that most of them would have had the guts to try some of the stuff you have. Still, they may shake their fingers at you and say 'bad boy' but secretly hope you keep doing the outrageous things that keep their lives a little more exciting," Jordan suggested.

Aleksei looked at her in amazement, astonished at her insight. "Obviously, your bio is wrong. How old are you?"

"Old enough to know better than to even think about doing some of the things you've done, let alone attempt them, but old enough to appreciate the thrills you've given those who needed a little *umph* in their lives. You've given a lot of different things to a lot of different people, good and bad alike, and I can't say I agree with all you've done. But you've changed, in ways the world is only starting to find out and I think you have every right to be very proud of this new chapter in your life," she ended softly, her cheeks blushing at Aleksei's warm, astonished, dawning gaze.

If someone had told him two years ago he'd be madly in love with this slip of a girl who had verbally, and physically, knocked him to his knees, he would have said they'd smoked a bad batch of weed. Instead, here she was, sprawled comfortably between his legs, her soft, full breasts resting warmly against his chest while her fingers absently played with the dark curls, her eyes melting into his, her lips only a small breath away. The sudden belief that he could be everything she said left him stunned. The fact she wanted to be a part of it left him feeling complete, as if he'd found the part he'd been missing and searching for all his life, filling him with a joy he'd never known.

"Marry me, Jordan," he asked softly, his voice low and filled with emotion.

Jordan's eyes widened, the dark green orbs fringed by lush, black lashes filling with tears. "What did you say?" she managed to gasp.

"You heard me."

"Say it again, please," she whispered.

Aleksei released his arms where they looped comfortably around her back and brought his hands up to cup her face, his thumbs gently rubbing away the tears slipping from her beautiful eyes. His dark eyes delved deeply into hers, his reflection clear despite the tears. He could feel her shallow breathing where their chests met, almost see her breath through her slightly parted lips. "Jordan, I love you with all that I am and all that you believe I can be. Marry me, please," he whispered deeply, dipping his head to lightly kiss her lips.

Jordan could only stare, unblinking, as tears slipped from her eyes, her voice lost, her orderly thoughts scattered to the winds at Aleksei's softly voiced request. His soft, searching kiss didn't help her sort through the swirling visions that danced through her brain and restore her to some semblance of balance. Never, in all her wildest daydreams, had Aleksei even hinted at something so permanent as his sweetly voiced request. Yet, deep in her heart, she knew this was the moment her life had been building toward. All her medals, and awards and trophies were simply stepping stones toward her final pinnacle: Aleksei.

"Yes!" she whispered softly, the soft stroke of her heated word touching Aleksei's lips at the same time he heard her quiet answer.

"Thank you," he gasped, his deep voice breaking with emotion as he held her tightly against him, spreading soft kisses over her face and finally, kissing her parted mouth voraciously, losing himself in the passion that flared between them.

*   *   *   *   *

The fire crackled noisily. It's flames cast shadows throughout the room, failing to reach the far corners and leaving areas of darkness.

Shadows that gently caressed the couple lost to passion before the roaring blaze, celebrating their love and commitment to one another. Celebrating their happiness for the moment and their hopes, and dreams, and wishes for the future. A time when the world was theirs for the asking. A time when the world looked forward to a future filled with the beauty and perfection of Jamison and Rocmanov. When 'Fire and Ice' did lead to all things beautiful, and anything was possible.

Chapter 10

The soft crackling sounds of the remaining bits of wood being consumed by the coals in the huge fireplace awoke Aleksei. The subtle glow from the embers failed to reach into the blackness of the room; allowing it's glow to reach only as far as the couple laying on scattered pillows on the floor before the hearth, a fleecy throw covering them. Aleksei awoke to find himself wrapped around the warm, soft, body of Jordan as she lay sleeping cushioned against his chest, lying on his side, her hips pressed provocatively against his groin. One arm encircled her ribcage, the warm weight of her breasts resting against his forearm; his other arm lay straight, cushioning his head, his palm facing the ceiling. Jordan's head lay tucked securely beneath his chin, silken strands of her coppery hair teasing his neck and cheeks where they tangled in his beard. Her soft scent surrounded her, making him breath deeply in appreciation, then groan as needles of pain stabbed their way up the sleep-numbed nerves in his arm.

"What's wrong?" Jordan whispered sleepily, caressing the arm that encircled her ribs and wiggling closer to Aleksei's warm, muscular torso, a soft smile crossing her lips when she felt his immediate physical response at her gentle push against his hips.

"I'm too old for this," he groaned, flexing his fingers and swearing at the intense spasm of pain as the nerves began to awake.

"To old for what?" she asked quietly, her voice deep and sultry, still half-asleep, her eyes closed, rubbing one smooth leg against his own hair-roughened calf.

"Oh, God, Jordan...don't move," he implored, his voice deep and husky, trying to ignore the desires her innocently seductive movements caused.

"I'm not," she whispered, her warm breath stirring the hair on his arm that rested beneath her breasts.

"You are, you just don't realize it," he growled, swearing forcefully when he bent his numb arm, the sharp needles becoming flaming knives. "Shit!" he complained, releasing his hold on Jordan and rolling onto his back, his good arm forcefully rubbing his nerves back to life, his blood surging forward through his veins, it's path literally traceable.

Jordan rolled onto her stomach. Pushing her tangled curls out of her face, she rested one cheek on her crossed arms, her eyes watching his barely visible image. In the meager light, the soft, roundness of her bottom was silhouetted; the swelling curve of her breasts as they melted against the pillows merely hints of shadow, yet Aleksei's gaze devoured the sight of her.

"Is this how your mornings usually start?" Jordan inquired curiously, enjoying the way the shadows played across the muscles on his broad, curl-matted chest and bulging arms as he continued to massage his slowly awakening limb.

"Are you referring to waking up wrapped around a beautiful woman or my arm being asleep?" he teased, flexing his fingers, then his elbow and finally rolling his shoulder.

"Either," she quipped nonchalantly.

Aleksei had the disadvantage, with her back to the low burning embers; her face was in the shadows, her eyes unreadable. "I honestly couldn't tell you the last time I woke up with my arm asleep, but I would rather not enjoy the experience again anytime soon."

Several seconds passed before her second question was whispered, "And the other?"

Aleksei ran a hand through his thick, dark hair. "Shortly before I fell off the mountain and broke my leg," he answered honestly.

"That was three years ago." Jordan stated disbelief clear in her tone.

"Amazing, isn't it?" he replied cynically, shaking his head in astonishment at his suddenly realized self-imposed period of celibacy. "Who would believe I could have gone that long without getting laid?"

"Well, apparently, your record continues because you didn't get *laid* last night, as far as I'm concerned!" she stated arrogantly.

Aleksei rolled from his back to side, his movement bringing him beside Jordan, where he could run one hand from the curve of her shoulder, down the slim line of her back and over her round bottom; smiling in pleasure at the warmth and softness of her skin. "Oh? How, then, did we spend the better part of last night?" he asked softly, his warm breath grazing her face as he watched the coppery tresses of her hair slip through his fingers like molten metal when he sank his hand into her hair, his mouth moving toward hers.

Jordan's mind swirled madly as Aleksei's touch in her hair sent jolts of electricity throughout her body, making her body swell and lean toward his ever-growing, powerful magnetism. Like a moth drawn to the flame, without thought or will, she melted into him, her breasts flattening against his muscular chest, one hand coming up to cup his cheek. "Making love," she whispered into his mouth, just before their lips met, softly at first, then ravenous, delving into the heated cores of their passion. Desire flared anew, driving all but the need to be one from their minds, pushing them ever closer to paradise.

Aleksei nudged Jordan onto her back, grasping her hands and stretching them over her head; lacing his fingers through hers. In the failing light, he smiled into her dark, glazed eyes, certain her expression was a mirror of his own. "You're right, brat. For a kid, you're awfully smart," he stated, his voice deep and husky, his eyes running appreciatively down; then up, her curvaceous form lying beside him. "But right now, you don't look much like a child," Her beautiful body looked like finely carved marble in the pale light, shadows hinting of shapely hills and valleys, secrets waiting to be sought.

"I'm not terribly interested in how smart I am at the moment. I'm much more interested in the lessons I can learn from you. Show me, Aleksei. I want to learn everything that pleases you," Jordan pleaded softly, the sultriness in her tone belying her innocence. "Make love to me again."

"You won't be able to walk later, if I do," Aleksei scolded lightly, trying to control his body that even now pushed temptingly against Jordan.

"We can skate anytime," Jordan pouted, "I want to make love now."

"We make love again now, you won't be skating anytime soon," he reiterated, his chivalrous intentions melting away despite his good intentions.

"I don't care," Jordan insisted, trying to slip her fingers from Aleksei's seductive hold and failing. Trying another plan of attack, she sensuously ran her slim, smooth leg over the back of Aleksei's large, muscular limb, her breasts pressing temptingly against Aleksei's chest when currents of electricity jolted from their entwined legs, up her body and into the sensitive centers of her swollen breasts.

"Jordan…" The warning was seductive, his tone deep, erotic and full of unspoken wickedness. His dark eyes gleamed brightly, lit from within with fire and swelling desire, matching the swell of desire that pulsed persuasively against her thigh. "You're insatiable, brat."

"It's your own fault."

"How so?"

"You made the mistake of showing me Chateaubriand and now suggest I go back to the salad bar. I've got news for you, mister. It ain't gonna happen. Now stop stalling and make love to me the way I know you're dying to!" she demanded, pushing her hips against his turgid length, a womanly smile lighting her eyes upon hearing his harshly inhaled breath.

"You're a witch, Jordan Jamison and you know what happens to witches?" he growled, shifting his weight as he moved his body over hers, his hands releasing hers as he braced the heavy weight of his upper body on his elbows. Their chests met, rock solid muscle and flushed, softness melting to become one. Settling himself between her thighs, the heat of their passions surged ever upward, sweeping them away on rapturous waves that left them breathless.

"They were burned at the stake and sent to hell," she finally mumbled, gasping as his heat scorched her, restlessly moving against him and whimpering for appeasement.

Aleksei's passion was volatile, walking a fine line between the sublime and utter pain. Jordan's grasping, clinging hands only added to his headlong rush into oblivion, threatening to tear the flesh from his body even as they promised the paradise to be found in hers. Somewhere, deep inside, he found the power to cease his body's urgent call for completion and halt his motion against Jordan's warmth. His breathing harsh and labored, he softly called her name three times before his low voice penetrated her mist-swirled mind, her glazed, dark green eyes finally opening and meeting Aleksei's intense gaze.

"There'll be no hell for you, Jordan, only heaven. But, mark my words, before we're through, you may not know the difference between the two!" he stated determinedly, his voice dark and dangerously seductive.

Jordan lay mesmerized, both by his words and hypnotizing gaze. As if from afar, she watched his face come rushing toward her, crushing her soft lips as he plundered her mouth, his tongue hot and demanding passage into her warmth. At the same time he ravaged her mouth, he entered the heat and tightness of her body, his strength and fervor pushing her faster and higher than ever before. The wildness of his possession pushed her into oblivion almost immediately, her body shaking uncontrollably as wave after wave of ecstasy crashed over her, leaving her utterly limp, her cry of pleasure captured by her lover's mouth.

Aleksei's body followed her lead, pulsing hotly, powerfully, his strength flowing into her welcoming body. A deep growl escaped his chest as his climax crashed over him, drowning him with pleasure and stealing away the last of his strength. Breathlessly, he rolled to his side, concern his heavy weight would crush her making him leave her warmth. Still, he reached for her hand, weaving their fingers together and keeping them bound as one. The two lay silent, chests heaving as they struggled to breathe, their skin glistening damply in the semi-darkness of the room.

"Aleksei?" Jordan whispered, somehow finding the strength to turn her head toward him, smiling sleepily into his eyes.

"Yes, my love," he answered returning her smile.

"If that's what heaven and hell are both like, I'm not afraid to die," she murmured, squeezing his hand gently, her eyes drifting closed, her breathing settling into the slow, steady rhythm of slumber.

"Me either," he murmured in agreement, his eyes lovingly tracing the soft lines of her flushed, beautiful face before he slid headlong into his own exhausted sleep.

The sun rose only moments later, casting the entwined lovers in the pale pink light of dawn, the last embers flickering, then fading to blackness in the great fireplace.

Chapter 11

"Aleksei, this is ridiculous!" Jordan complained laughingly, holding his hand tightly with both of hers as he lead her through knee-deep snow toward a secret place, her angora beret pulled over her eyes. "I look like a total dope!"

Aleksei glanced over his shoulder at her, his eyes full of love and amusement at the petite woman behind him, looking very snow-man like in her off-white down parka, trudging along through the deep snow, blindly following his lead. "Hardly a dope, more like a blindfolded snowman," he teased, flinching when she scooped a handful of snow up and tossed it toward where she hoped his head was. "Almost," he offered on a laugh, brushing the small bit of snow off his shoulder where her snowball had grazed him.

"Wait until I get this hat off, then we'll see how you fare."

"Don't make threats you can't back up," he teased.

"I don't," she replied sweetly, pulling gently against his hand. "Want to slow down just a bit? My legs are long, but they're not as long as yours."

Aleksei didn't answer her question, he simply scooped her into his arms, settling her snugly against his chest and giving her a quick kiss to her cold, pink cheek. "How's that?"

"I'm perfectly capable of walking by myself: you don't have to carry me." Jordan explained, snuggling closer to Aleksei's chest and tightening her arms around his neck. "Can I take this silly hat off my eyes now?"

"No, we're almost there. And as to carrying you, I happen to enjoy having you in my arms," Aleksei stated softly, his deep voice sending shafts of warmth straight to her heart.

"As long as you don't mind."

"If I minded, you would still be knee-deep in snow," he offered, lightly kissing her nose.

With seemingly no effort, he continued to walk on through the deep snow, unhampered by her weight or the weight of the backpack containing their skates and a small CD player strapped to his back.

Jordan's other senses became more alert as Aleksei trudged on through the deep snow. The sound of the snow whispering and then crunching as it compacted beneath Aleksei's boots, the wind gently teasing tendrils of her hair against her cheeks, the steady sound of Aleksei's deep breathing as he moved ever forward, his seductively spicy after-shave.

"I smell ice and someone has a fire going," Jordan suddenly stated, lifting one hand to remove the covering from her eyes.

"No you don't!" Aleksei chuckled, quickly turning around and putting her on her feet. "The hat stays on until I say otherwise."

"Aleksei, this is ridiculous. How much further do we have to go?" she complained, her hands held securely in his. Despite still having the offending beret covering her eyes, she could feel Aleksei's overpowering presence before her, effectively blocking any view she might have had.

"We're almost there," he promised, once again taking her hands and gently urging her forward through the snow.

Two minutes later he slowed his steps, guiding her before him and slipping behind her to slide his arms around her waist. "Now you can look," he whispered the warmth of his lips a scorching heat against her cold, pink cheek.

Jordan pushed the beret from her eyes, the softness of it coming to rest against her forehead and squinted as the bright sun reflected off the pristine snow into her eyes. Blinking as her eyes adjusted to the brightness, the view before her took her breath away.

There, before her, was the largest frozen pond she had ever seen, covered in untouched snow but for a large rink-size section that had been shoveled clear and smoothed. Tall pines surrounded the area, giving them privacy and offering semi-shade from the glare of the bright sun; their branches kissed with a dusting of white powder. A portable outside fireplace was already happily burning; small bursts of sparkles showered into the morning sky as a piece of wood exploded into flames.

"My, God, Aleksei. How did you ever find this place?" Jordan asked reverently, pulling his head down for a sweet kiss.

Aleksei gratefully accepted the kiss, pulling her closer as the kiss deepened, his hands running over the full bulkiness of her parka, and moaning deeply when she ran her hands over his bottom then began a slow, torturous journey around his hips and toward the source of his manhood.

"Jordan…" Aleksei growled deeply, grasping her hands and holding them lightly behind her back only to find the position pushed her hips against his and passion flared between them yet again. "Jordan…" he warned, his voice deep and raspy.

"Aleksei, I've never made love in the snow," she suggested brazenly, her eyes shining brightly. Her cheeks flushed, whether from the cold or passion didn't matter, her lips parted as her breathing hitched, little puffs of steam evaporating in the cold air. Standing on her toes, she continued to push against his hips, his physical reaction readily visible beneath the snugness of his jeans, his warmth shimmering in waves around him.

Aleksei tried to get a grip on the situation. Rational—think rational he repeated to himself. "Do you have any idea what the temperature is out here?"

"Cold?" Jordan asked impishly, her eyes turning a dark green as she watched his go black. Suddenly her hands were free and they were gently stroking against the fabric covering the pulsing strength of Aleksei's erection.

"Jordan…" Her name escaped on a whisper, his hands pushing into her hair, her beret knocked to the snow, forgotten. His mouth covered hers, their tongues meeting hungrily, lost in passion as their bodies strained together, seeking what they knew they would find together; a place where they became one and galaxies exploded in showers of shimmering light.

"Make love to me, Aleksei," Jordan entreated, her hands tightly gripping the front of his jacket as she tried to stand on legs which refused to hold her.

Fire burned deeply in Aleksei's obsidian eyes, his breathing harsh as he struggled to control the passion that raged through his tall, muscular body, his hands reaching for the zipper on Jordan's bulky jacket. "Just remember, brat, I won't be the one who has to explain how you got frostbite on your ass."

"I'll gladly risk frostbite if it means feeling you inside me," Jordan whispered brokenly as the coat fell open beneath Aleksei's nimble fingers. His hands slipped beneath her sweater to cover her breasts, the lace of her bra lightly abrading her sensitive skin.

Magically, the front clasp on the lacy garment opened and the heat of his palms scorched her erect nipples, her gasp of surprise at the heat of his touch extraordinarily loud in the stillness of the forest, the sound echoing to all corners of the pond.

"All the animals in the forest are going to be talking about us tonight," Aleksei teased, his mouth replacing where his hands had been only moments before.

Jordan watched Aleksei suckle at her breasts, her vision growing hazy as her world spun crazily. Aleksei's touch caused her blood to race wildly through her body. Gently she cradled his face between her hands, a wistful sigh escaping her lips when she drew him from her breast, the coldness of the air brushing against the dampness on her breast where Aleksei's mouth had scalded nearly unbearable. With an unbelievably wicked look, her dark green eyes glazed as passion overtook her and she naughtily suggested, "Then why don't we really give them something to talk about?"

Aleksei's deep, wicked laugh acknowledged her request.

Not long after, the silence of the forest was broken.

*   *   *   *   *

"Can we skate now?" Jordan asked breathlessly, energized after their bout of wild lovemaking in the snow, smiling wickedly at Aleksei's sudden disbelieving frown.

"Do you really expect me to be able to use my legs after what you just put me through?" he growled, shifting slightly to escape the snow that crept beneath his down-filled coat and against his bare bottom.

"You at least got to keep your pants on. I was the one with my bare ass hanging out for all the world to see."

"But it's such a nice ass," Aleksei offered, smiling in appreciation as he watched her wriggle her legs back into her snow pants.

"Be that as it may, I still would have been the one thoroughly embarrassed if someone had happened upon us."

"Then be glad that the only voyeurs were of the four legged variety and they don't tell tales."

Jordan glanced around their secluded glade and smiled at the beauty surrounding her. "In this magical place, I wouldn't be surprised to hear the animals can speak."

Aleksei nodded in agreement, "You're probably right. Let's hope they don't have cell phones and call Whittaker and tell him what a naughty girl you're being."

"It's only because you have such a bad influence on me—just ask Whittaker!" She shot back.

"Whittaker's prejudice. He thinks you're an angel."

"He's right," Jordan agreed, smiling broadly.

"He hasn't seen you like I have. He doesn't know about your *dark side!*" Aleksei stated, his voice deeply menacing and dramatic, his look one of lechery.

Jordan laughed wickedly, offering him a look of coyness and stated brazenly, "You mean the side that has me out here, bare assed and making wild love with you in the snow."

"That's the one," Aleksei agreed, pulling her back across his chest and kissing her lightly. "And if it's all the same to you, I'd rather no one else knew about this *proclivity* of yours."

Jordan sighed dramatically, her breasts pushing temptingly against the firmness of his chest. "If I must, then I suppose I can manage to keep this small secret about myself. But it won't be easy. You might have to help me keep it by occasionally indulging me in a snowy romp," She begged prettily, her thumb seductively stroking his lower lip, only to be replaced by her lips when she gently nibbled his sensuous lips then covered his mouth.

"If I have to shave snow from ice cubes I'll take care of it," He mumbled before he deepened the kiss. Carefully he rolled over with her until she lay pressed in the soft snow, his body shielding her from the cold breeze.

"Now who's ass is hanging out?" she asked breathlessly when their lips parted, small puffs of fog dissolving into the cold air as they breathed erratically.

Aleksei glanced about him; amazed he had once again lost himself in the moment and the magic that was Jordan. "I honestly don't know how everyone can believe I'm a bad influence on you. If I remember correctly, we came out here to skate—at your insistence I might add—and here I am, literally freezing my ass off in the breeze. If you ask me, your poor influence over me should be uppermost in Whittaker's mind."

Jordan smiled softly, gently pushing her hips against Aleksei's as she listened to his half-hearted complaining, her eyes shining wickedly when she heard Aleksei's breath hitch and felt his answering nudge against her hips. "Whittaker believes I'm an angel in disguise—complete with halo and shimmering wings—just ask him."

"Yeah, well, he's been wrong before. Not often, mind you, but on occasion," Aleksei managed to growl, his voice husky, his body responding heatedly, as he valiantly attempted to fight the sensuous spell Jordan wove so effortlessly around him. With a low groan, he rolled to his side, pulling Jordan with him, where they lay facing each other, his arm a pillow for her head.

"You don't believe I'm an angel, Aleksei?" Jordan questioned innocently, yet seductively, her eyes darkening as she placed playful kisses to the corners of Aleksei's mouth, teasing him with soft kisses and gentle bites, then running her tongue torturously around his lips, only to pull away when he sought to deepen the kiss.

"I believe you're a tease that plays at being an angel," Aleksei murmured deeply, appreciatively, his obsidian eyes full of passion and promises of wicked retribution if she continued to play this game of torment, his body hardening and swelling to a point near pain.

"How can you even suggest such a thing?" Jordan asked in disbelief, her lips twitching as she sought to control the smile which threatened to spoil her indignant question. Her deep green eyes glowed brightly as further ideas of sensual torment swirled through her mind, making her light-headed as visions of them together in the snow ran wildly through her mind's eye.

Aleksei watched Jordan's eyes, truly windows to her soul, and her mischievous mind, and wondered what new tortures she had in store for him. Despite his body screaming anew for release, he worried about hurting her, knew that moments lost in passion could result in discomfort lasting for hours. They only had a few days to themselves and he didn't want her to spend them in pain, even if making love had been her idea. They had their whole lives ahead of them; there was no reason to rush. Still, she was barely irresistible laying next to him, her face flushed, her eyes bright with passion, her lips swollen and pouty, begging to be kissed. "If you could see what I see right now, the look in your eyes, you would know that angels would never be allowed to look as you do and be considered saintly," Aleksei answered quietly. His voice was husky, and sent currents of electricity through her as he nudged her gently onto her back and covered her with his muscular form. Holding his weight on his elbows, his hands slid into her coppery curls, holding her head easily as his dark eyes melted into her ever-deepening green gaze. "Still, there is a heaven to be found in angels like you, Jordan. And I will forever thank whatever God there is for sending you to me," Aleksei stated huskily, his breath whispering across her lips just before his mouth devoured hers, his tongue mating with her own, as his hips pressed in wanton invitation, despite his best intentions.

Jordan squirmed beneath him, her body taking control from her mind and pushing her ever toward the promises of abandonment and fulfillment that Aleksei offered with his loving heart and powerful body. Somehow her snow pants disappeared and Aleksei replaced them with his surging strength, filling her and sending her screaming over the edge of fulfillment immediately, waves of rapture lifting her ever higher only to momentarily slow her climb and then surge her speedily toward new heights. Aleksei clenched his teeth and sought control as she shattered around him, her muscles clenching him hotly, devouring him, threatening to pull him from the paradise he had found. The paradise he could see, and smell and fell pulsing around him; a place he never wanted to leave. Slowly he traced her beloved face; his jaws clenched tightly as he struggled to remain embedded within the paradise that was Jordan. Tremors still vibrated through her, aftershocks, and she struggled to open her eyes. Aleksei's shining black eyes gazed intently into her own of dark forest green, glazed in passion and astonishment, searching for answers to unknown questions. Somewhere, Jordan found the strength to lift her hands and sift them through the dark, curling hair only inches above her face, holding tightly. Their eyes met and held as she pulled his mouth forward to meet hers. Their kiss was sweet, tender, promising the world and giving more. Aleksei's body surged deeper, Jordan's answered and accepted, as he gave up his struggle to control the emotions racing through him and exploded into her body, his eyes still holding hers as he gave himself into her loving care. Jordan watched him careen over the edge into oblivion, followed him as he touched her deeper than ever before and held on blindly, ferociously, as their souls melted together to become one.

* * * * *

Soft strains of romantic music drifted on the gentle breeze which rustled pine boughs and sent loose snowflakes dancing through the air, the sun turning the particles of ice into sparkling diamonds, showering down on the two people who skated soundlessly across the frozen surface of the lake.

The sound of laughter and screams of delight drifted on the breeze, catching the attention of two others as a man gathered wood from a woodpile and his wife, armed with her ever-present video camera, took home movies of grandpa to send to their grandkids. The man smiled at the woman a few feet away from him, his blue eyes shining knowingly as he listened to the sounds on the wind that circled them teasingly. "Betcha I know what they're up to!" he stated with a wink, grabbing one final log and trudging toward his house.

"William, you've got a one-track mind," the woman scolded lightly, shooing him away playfully when he started to come too close. After forty-seven years of marriage, they still teased and laughed and loved as they had in the beginning.

"Let's go see if I'm right," he whispered conspiratorially, putting his hand up to block her viewfinder and growling, "Turn that damn thing off," and grabbing her hand and pulling her toward the towering trees that separated their home from the lake.

"What if you're right and we stumble on to something embarrassing?" the woman worried, following her husband's lead through the ankle-deep snow.

William looked at his wife, love clearly shone from his sky-blue eyes. He still believed she was the loveliest woman on the planet. "Well, then, I guess we'll be embarrassed together. Besides, only wild kids would be stupid enough to fool around in the snow. Can you just imagine trying to explain to a doctor why your private parts were frost-nipped? It's probably just some kids whooping around on the ice," he suggested, pulling his wife the few remaining steps through the pines to stand on a ledge overlooking the frozen lake, his arm slipping easily around her waist to hold her close.

"Oh, William," she whispered, looking at the beauty of winter's influence on the rugged terrain as it spread before her. The lake was a seamless sheet of glass, twinkling with glitter in the sun, the towering pines bowing beneath the weight of their snow-laden limbs. No matter how many times she saw it, it would always surprise and humble her to see how Mother Nature transformed her already beautiful mountain range to something even more glorious wearing winter white.

"Look," William offered, directing her gaze toward the end of the lake right below them. The music began again, easily recognizable now that they were so close, *Romeo and Juliet*, one of his wife's favorites. The two skaters began to move soundlessly across their open-aired rink, oblivious to everything but the music and each other. "You might want to make use of that stupid thing you're carrying," he suggested and smiled when she raised it to her shoulder, fidgeting with the adjustment controls and pushing the start button.

Silently William and Nora watched the pair below them, William moving to stand behind his wife and wrap his arms around her waist, her head resting beneath his chin, using his wide stance to lean against to steady her picture. Their breaths slowed, holding when they watched the man throw his small partner across the ice, releasing when she landed safely and glided back toward him. The music built, leading toward the final heart-breaking strains and they watched the skaters collapse to the ice, wrapped in each other's arms. The music ended and the male skater helped his partner to her feet, kissing her hungrily and then picking her up and spinning her in circles until she laughingly begged for mercy. Only then did he put her down lightly, kissing her again before he released her, then holding her hand as they skated toward the side of the lake.

"Have you ever seen anything so beautiful?" Nora asked, turning off the camera and brushing tears from her cheeks.

"Only you, my love," William answered, kissing away a tear she had missed.

"You're crazy, William Morris," Nora stated, smiling in spite of herself.

"Crazy about you," He agreed, releasing her waist and taking her hand to start their walk back to their home.

"Who do you think they are?" Nora asked, casting a final glance toward the couple now sitting on a blanket-draped fallen log.

"Certainly no one from around here. Those two have to be professionals or I'm a pickled herring," William answered, visions of the beauty and perfection he and Nora witnessed running through his mind. He doubted he'd ever see anything as amazing and beautiful again in his life.

"That's what I've been smelling—I was wondering about that," Nora teased, laughing at William's playful swat on her bottom. "My guess is they're going to the Olympics and came here to practice in peace," Nora imagined.

"You read too many of those mushy romances, Nora Morris. I swear, they're turning your mind into mashed potatoes."

"My mind's just fine, thank you very much. I just happen to believe that those two are the best skaters I've seen in a long time and only the best go to the Olympics. Is that such a difficult concept to accept."

No ma'am—and I have to agree with you—they're the best I've seen in a while. But that doesn't mean they're going to the Olympics. Maybe they're just a couple of kids that have been practicing up a storm and look better than they actually are. It isn't like we keep up with skating on a daily basis."

"William Morris, that has got to be the stupidest thing I've ever heard come out of your mouth. I'm going on the Internet and see if I can't find out who they might be and which one of us is right. Though, as far as I'm concerned, it's nothing more than a waste of time, since you don't have the sense God gave a brick."

"How can you say that? I watch skating with you every time you call me in. Do I ever complain about watching that stuff with you?"

"You're only interested in their little outfits and how much of their bottoms show. You don't know a lift from a throw," Nora stated laughingly.

William scowled, his eyes bright with humor despite his expression. "Why do I need to know about the technical aspect of the sport? I watch it for the entertainment value. I know what I like and what I don't like. That's all that matters, as far as I'm concerned!"

"And what we just saw? Did you like them?"

"I couldn't see much of her bottom…" he began, only to grunt when her elbow made contact with his stomach.

"William!" Nora warned softly.

"Nora, my sweet, you're too easy a target," William teased, squeezing her hand lovingly. "Those two back there damn near made me cry, and you know I don't like to cry. I don't think I've ever seen anything so—I don't know—magical, enchanting, entrancing. It's hard to explain. Something about them seems to reach out and enfold you, capture you, share with you, a feeling of a place that we all search for but few of us find. I think we saw something very special back there and I'll thank God everyday of my life for having had you to share it with me," he ended quietly, his voice husky with emotion.

Nora gently caressed her husband's cheek, placing a soft kiss to his lips and smiling into his eyes. "William, you are such a soft touch despite this grizzly bear front you put on. What ever will I do with you?"

With a lecherous smile and a wiggle of his bushy eyebrows he answered, "I have an idea or two."

Nora shook her head in exasperation, chuckling softly and cast a challenging glance to her husband. "I'll race you to the house," and took off like a shot despite her advanced years.

"You cheat!" William called, following his wife at a purposely-slower pace. After forty-seven years of marriage he'd learned it paid to let your wife win the race every now and then.

Besides, in the end, everyone was a winner.

Chapter 12

Three days later, Aleksei and Jordan awoke to bright blue, sunny skies, and snow flurries that defied the weatherman's logic.

"Aleksei, how can it be sunny and snowing at the same time?" Jordan pondered as she watched the sparkling snowflakes float through air that looked like it belonged to a summer vacation from a window. "I tell you, it pays to be a weatherman. That's got to be the only job that you can be wrong all the time, make big bucks and never worry about getting canned. What a racket," she complained, casting a final glance out the window, a sudden feeling of foreboding rushing through her causing her to shiver and cross her arms across her chest.

"Cold?" Aleksei asked, crossing the room and wrapping her in his arms, his cheek resting on the top of her head.

"No, just a shiver," Jordan answered softly, snuggling closer to Aleksei's heat.

"You're never cold. "

"I didn't say I was cold. I said it was a shiver."

"Maybe someone walked across your grave," Aleksei teased, frowning when she pulled from his arms, her eyes darkening in fear.

"Aleksei, don't say such things, even teasingly. You're tempting fate and it's more powerful than both of us!" Jordan demanded, her voice, and body, shaking with fear, her nails digging into his forearms. "Take it back. Take back your comment now!" She demanded.

"Jordan, take it easy..."

"Take it back, Aleksei. NOW!"

"Okay, okay. I didn't mean it," Aleksei relented shaking his head in puzzlement as he viewed for the first time how superstitious his partner was. Funny how you could know someone for so long and still discover new, and sometimes unusual, things about a person. "Do you think that will satisfy the fates?" he asked, semi-seriously.

"We can only hope it will. Time should tell us pretty soon," Jordan whispered, wishing and praying the feeling of foreboding that still chilled her would vanish.

"You don't really believe in all that mumbo-jumbo do you?" Aleksei asked, her expression giving him her answer immediately. "Obviously you do," he concluded.

"How can you not?" Jordan questioned sharply.

"Easy," Aleksei stated firmly. "You make your own fate. Show me where everything is written in stone and I'll believe we have no actual control over our destinies. Can you? Is there such a place? Of course not, because we aren't totally powerless to some greater force. The only thing we're powerless against are our own weaknesses and believe me, when I say, nothing—NOTHING—will come between you and I. We're partners—on and off the ice—and nothing can, or will, change that. Got it?" Aleksei demanded, pulling her into his crushing embrace.

Jordan could feel his strength seeping into her chilled body, warming her, tempting her to believe that perhaps his beliefs weren't so far fetched. Maybe together they could determine their own fate. Perhaps he was more powerful than the demons that haunted her. Maybe her nightmare had been just that, nothing more than a bad dream and not a brief glimpse into the future. Snuggling deeper into his embrace, she nodded, agreeing. "Got it."

"Good!" Aleksei breathed in relief, kissing her forehead and tucking her head back under his chin. "Then suppose we go find our way into town, grab breakfast, and see if we can't buy something special to remind us of our brief escape from Whittaker," He suggested.

"Sounds good to me. I'll be ready in less than ten minutes," Jordan stated.

"Is that ten minutes Earth time?" Aleksei called to Jordan's retreating form, appreciating the view of her southern exposure.

"Funny, Rocmanov," she called back.

The day it takes her ten minutes to get ready is the day the world comes to an end, Aleksei jokingly mumbled to himself, filling his pockets with his car keys and wallet, then shivering as a chill ran through his body. Casting a quick glance about him, he quickly took his comment back, maybe it wasn't good to tempt fate too often. When Jordan returned five minutes later, another chill surged through Aleksei.

"See, I told you, less than ten minutes!" Jordan quipped, placing a quick kiss to his cheek and then slipping into the jacket he held. His odd expression stopped her. "What's wrong?"

"Nothing."

"You're sure?"

"Yeah. I'm just surprised you were ready so fast. Typically, you're at least ten minutes longer than you say you'll be."

"Well, I guess today isn't a typical day," Jordan quipped.

"If it isn't going to be a typical day, then what kind of day is it going to be?" Aleksei pondered.

Jordan smiled over her shoulder at him, her eyes so full of love it made his heart overflow with emotion and race at the same time. "A day more special than yesterday was but not as special as our day together will be. A day, I know, I will remember for the rest of my life."

Aleksei's smile was boyishly charming and wickedly sensual at once, a bright flame burning brightly in the center of his deep ebony eyes. "Talk about performance anxiety. How can I be expected to make this day one you'll remember your entire life?" he asked mysteriously.

"That's your problem, not mine, Rocmanov," Jordan replied flippantly.

"Gee, thanks. Nothing like making things easy for me. I suppose I'll just have to be my usual wonderful self," Aleksei replied arrogantly. "No sweat."

Jordan laughed at his egotistical antics. "Tell me, Rocmanov. How does that very large ego of yours fit into that semi-large body of yours?"

"Semi-large?" Aleksei gasped in feigned horror, pulling her into his arms and ravaging her neck with nipping bites and heated kisses, his hips pressing wantonly against her own, his rising passion obvious.

Jordan's laughter turned to whimpers of pleasure, her mouth seeking his, finding, sipping, and devouring, until they pulled apart to catch their breaths. "What was the question?" Jordan asked dreamily.

"Semi-large," Aleksei offered.

"Oh yes. I suppose, depending on ones interpretation of size, your body could be considered on the large size," she offered, gasping when he pushed against her hips, his passion for her blatantly obvious. "Definitely large!" she decided, her sharp nails digging into his jeans when she grasped his hips and pulled him back to her, moving against the source of his passionate heat.

"Jordan…" he moaned, his mouth capturing hers in one final devouring kiss before he pushed away from her. "We were on our way out, remember?"

"What? …Oh, right," Jordan mumbled breathlessly, struggling back to sanity and grabbing her purse off the small table by the door, her mind still dizzy from Aleksei's siege upon her senses.

"Got everything?" Aleksei asked a final time, zipping up his jacket and checking his pockets for his gloves, there as expected.

"As far as I can tell. Anything I'm missing and can't live without, I'll just have to buy," Jordan answered lightly, smiling at Aleksei's show of gallantry as he held the door for her.

"Then we're out of here!" he stated, ushering her out and closing the door behind them.

The cellular phone lay on the counter; forgotten, a faint shadow in the shifting light that streamed through the windows of the cottage, it's shape becoming ominous as the sky darkened to a deeper gray.

*　　*　　*　　*　　*

"Do you think the storm's going to be as bad as they're predicting?" Jordan asked worriedly, watching yet another weather update flash across the TV screen in the small diner they had chosen to have a late lunch in, frowning when their county's name was shown as one directly in the path of the heaviest snow.

"What are they forecasting now?" Aleksei asked, between bites of an obscenely large bacon-cheeseburger oozing catsup and relish.

Jordan's frown deepened, "According to their latest Doppler radar reports, and all their wonderful computerized information, a.k.a. 'best guess', twenty to thirty inches by morning, with drifts of four feet or more. You'd think with all their million-dollar equipment, they could give a more educated guess than *between twenty and thirty inches*. You know," Jordan plucked a few French-fries from Aleksei's plate and emphasized her point with one before sliding it into her mouth. "I think the weather guys just have a dart board with weather pictures and temperatures on it and right this minute they're throwing sharp objects at it to give us *up-to-the-minute* weather reports. Like they know what they're talking about," she ended in disgust.

"Whether they know what they're talking about or not, we need to make a decision, Jordan," Aleksei stated, hating the idea of cutting their time together short but knowing they couldn't risk being snowed in for a week no matter how much they would enjoy it.

"Don't say it, Aleksei. I can't stand the idea of leaving early," Jordan moaned, already knowing they had no choice. With the weather forecast so ominous, they had to get out while they could. Regardless of the fact they had Dee's Jeep, even a four-wheel drive vehicle couldn't assure they could make it through drifts that high.

"Some things we have control over, Jordan, other things we don't," Aleksei stated, signaling to the waitress for their check. "Do you really want to risk being stuck up here and being disqualified from Nationals?"

"Maybe they'd give us a bye—it happens under special circumstances," Jordan suggested hopefully.

"I hardly think they'd give us one because we refused to cut our vacation short and leave when we should have."

"You have to pick now to be sensible?" Jordan asked in frustration, pushing the remnants of her salad around her plate.

"Don't blame me—it's your fault. Being around you, the sensible one, all the time, it was bound to happen sooner or later," Aleksei stated, taking the check and leaving more than enough to cover it on the table. Rising to his feet he rounded the table, pulling her chair out as she stood. "We'll come back," he promised, helping her into her jacket.

"Soon!" Jordan stated urgently, shrugging into her jacket and pulling the mittens from her pockets. "Real soon!"

"Sounds good to me," Aleksei agreed, kissing her lightly and urging her toward the exit.

The door opened just before they reached it, the freezing wind ushering in swirling snow and two hurrying forms. "Damn, it's cold out there" a gruff voice stated, pulling a snow-covered cap from his head and shoving it into his jacket pocket.

"William, watch your language. Everyone with half a brain knows it's cold outside, the snow gives it away," a petite woman beside him scolded lightly, shaking the snow from her scarf-covered curls before letting it drape over her shoulders. "Excuse my husband. He likes to state the obvious," Nora explained in a teasing whisper to Jordan and Aleksei. "That way, he's never wrong."

"Don't start, Nora. I was wrong—once." William allowed, helping his wife slip out of her coat and hanging it on the rack beside the door.

"I love a man who's willing to admit he was wrong—even if it was only 'once'," Nora laughed, her laughter bright and child-like, her eyes glowing brightly.

Jordan smiled at the pair, looking up at Aleksei, her smile widening at Aleksei's wink and knowing smile back. "How long did you have to wait for his admission?" Jordan asked.

"Forty-seven years!" Nora stated matter-of-factly, accepting William's kiss on the cheek as he returned to her side. "Don't let anyone tell you you can't teach an old dog new tricks. It just takes a little patience and a great big stick!" Nora explained, her hand reaching for her husband's, their fingers lacing together.

"See, there's still hope for you yet, Rocmanov," Jordan offered over her shoulder where Aleksei stood behind her.

William looked Aleksei up and down, shaking his head in consternation. "I think you're going to need a bigger stick than Nora did to keep this buck in line!" he suggested, his eyes suddenly squinting as if trying to remember something he should know. "Nora, why does this young buck look so familiar?"

Nora looked Aleksei up and down, her gaze shifting to Jordan and then back to Aleksei. "You're right, William. They do look familiar, sort of, like we should know them. Damn, maybe I do need some of that Ginkoba vitamin to help me remember things."

"Now who needs to watch their language?" William teased, readily side-stepping his wife's half-hearted attempt to jab his ribs with her elbow. "See, after forty-seven years with the same woman, I can finally tell when she's out to crack my ribs!" he commented with a knowing look.

"Is it worth it?" Aleksei asked, grunting at Jordan's well-aimed shot to his ribs with her elbow and pulling her tight against the front of his body.

"The bruised ribs or the forty-seven years?" William asked, watching the way Aleksei and Jordan interacted.

"Both," Aleksei answered simply.

"There's not a day I would trade or make different. Nora, here, has made every single one of those days more special than the one before it. I can't image not having her in my life and would sell my soul, to the very devil, if I had to, to keep her with me. She's my life, and without her, I wouldn't want to live," William quietly offered, his hand gently squeezing his wife's.

"William, you talk too much," Nora sniffed, embarrassed as she wiped away threatening tears.

"See? You can't win," William pointed out. "Either I talk too much or not enough. Makes a man wonder if it's worth the effort."

"Believe me, it's worth it," Jordan stated. "You're lucky to have found such a wonderful man, Nora. And to have had him for forty-seven years and still feel this way about one another is even more wonderful. I can only hope I'll be so lucky."

William watched Aleksei's eyes deepen with love for Jordan as he listened to her speak, quietly absorbing every nuance of her voice, her profile below him, her encompassing scent. If this wasn't a man up to his neck in love, William thought, he'd eat the sweat-salty brim off his favorite baseball cap. "Somehow, I think luck is running your way, little lady."

Jordan smiled softly, casting a shy glance at Aleksei; her blush deepening at Aleksei's blatantly admiring look. "Thank you," she finally managed to whisper.

The door flew open again, icy cold wind and swirling snow encompassing the lone man that struggled to close the door behind him, then removed his Michigan State Patrol Officer's hat, the clinging snow on the brim sliding to the floor silently. His reddened cheeks and blue tinged lips gave evidence the storm was worsening, information they would have all preferred not to hear. "Anyone needing to get off this mountain had better start down now. If the storm holds it's present force, they're planning on closing the roads within the hour."

"Is it really as bad as all that?" Nora asked.

"Bad and getting worse," Officer Michaels stated. "The storm's actually dumping more snow two thousand feet below us. The tough part is going to be getting through the seven-to-five thousand foot elevations. If—and that's a big if—you can make it through there, you should be okay, but I wouldn't recommend you even trying to leave in anything other than a four-by-four vehicle—the bigger the better."

"Can the jeep manage in this weather?" Jordan asked Aleksei, concern lowering her voice.

"It's a four-by-four. That's why Dee keeps it here. She said it's gotten her out when storms were rolling in before. I don't see why it won't this time," Aleksei answered, squeezing her shoulders reassuringly.

"This storms shaping up to be one of the worst ones we've had in a hundred years. You both be real careful out there and I'd recommend you take some food and coffee with you, just in case you do get stuck. You all got a cellular phone in case you do run into trouble?" the officer asked.

"In the car," Jordan answered.

"Good. Then you'd best be on your way as soon as possible if you even want to think of making it through. You both be real careful and take it slow and easy, the roads are already icy and even four-by-fours can't get through everything," the officer urged, taking the large thermos of coffee one of the waitresses handed him. "Thanks, Manda."

"You be careful out there, Jim. I want my thermos back, preferably in one piece this time," The waitress teased, trying to lighten the mood that had suddenly cooled at the officer's warning.

"Boy, break one little thermos and you never hear the end of it!" the officer countered, giving her a quick kiss on the cheek. "I'll see you later, babe."

"You'd better! Be real careful, you hear?" the waitress demanded.

The surprised look on the faces of both Jordan and Aleksei caused William, Nora and Officer Michaels to smile knowingly at their expressions. "It's okay, they're engaged," William offered, his statement seeming to explain the quick exchange between waitress and patrolman.

Completely bemused, Aleksei and Jordan nodded their heads up and down, casting a quick, confused glance toward each other. "I think we'd better take the patrolman's advice and get moving. We can't afford to get stuck here," Aleksei stated.

Jordan agreed and the pair made their good-byes, accepting wishes for a safe trip down the mountain. Together they leaned into the gusting wind as Aleksei held the door for Jordan and they carefully made their way across the icy parking lot to the jeep that was their only way out of town.

Once inside the jeep, they settled into their seats, securely latching their seat belts and started the engine, smiling when it turned over without a problem. "That's a good sign," Aleksei quipped, smiling as he adjusted the heater to both warm their feet and defrost the windshield.

"What is?"

"Engine turned over on the first try."

"Were you worried it wouldn't?"

"Not really. But it wouldn't have been a very positive sign of things to come if I'd had to get jump started," Aleksei rationalized.

"I suppose you're right," Jordan agreed. "But since it did, we're home free. Right?"

"Ask me when we pass the four-thousand foot elevation sign," Aleksei stated, sliding the gearshift into drive and pulling slowly out of the parking lot.

With a final glance through the swirling snow, Jordan watched the lights of the diner fade away and returned her eyes to the barely discernible road they traveled. "I don't think I like this. You can't see anything." She muttered, straining to see through the thick flakes that twirled and danced through the air, blanketing the narrow road they cautiously traveled.

"That's why I'm driving. I see better than you do," Aleksei teased, trying to lighten the mood and at the same time keep himself alert to any possible dangers ahead. Icy roads and steep mountain grades didn't make for a comfortable, stress-free road-trip.

"Did we wait too long to leave? We should have left first thing this morning, shouldn't have we?" Jordan questioned; her eyes widening as a sudden gust of wind broadsided the jeep, making it rock slightly. "Aleksei…" she gasped, her hand sliding through the handhold above the window.

Aleksei held the jeep steady, applying light pressure to the gas pedal, maintaining their speed and direction, seemingly without effort or anxiety. Inside, he'd held his breath, a thin stream of sweat sliding down his backbone when the wind had rocked them, when he'd seen the sharp light of fear enter Jordan's eyes. "It's okay. We knew it was going to be windy. Officer Michaels had said to expect it."

"He said windy, not hurricane force," Jordan complained.

"Can't be hurricane force winds—no oceans around here," Aleksei joked, focusing on the miserable visibility and slick road surface, wishing he were anywhere but in this storm and actually praying, which he didn't believe was worthwhile, they make it down the mountain in one piece as quickly as possible.

"Don't quibble with me, Rocmanov. I don't care if hurricane's come in off the ocean. I just want off this damn mountain."

"I know you do. It just so happens, it's high on my priority list, too. We'll make it, but it's not going to happen in ten minutes."

"How long do you think it will take?" Jordan asked, frowning. Was the snow getting heavier?

"I honestly don't know. Not anytime soon, I'd say. It looks like the snow's coming down harder. Have you seen any elevation markers?"

"I can't see ten feet in front of us and you expect me to find you an elevation marker? What are you, nuts?"

Aleksei flexed his tense fingers, one hand at a time, refusing to fully release the steering wheel. They might only be going twenty-two miles an hour, but with road conditions and visibility this bad, he wasn't going to risk losing control. Sailing off the side of a mountain wasn't his idea of a good time. He'd learned that lesson the hard way when he'd broken his leg mountain climbing. He wasn't about to endanger Jordan with such carelessness. Then again, thinking about his accident, his stupidity had brought them together and here they were, creeping down a mountain during the worst snowstorm to hit in over a hundred years and he couldn't remember ever being happier. Talk about the weirdness of life. "Tell you what, Jamison. Your job will be to find us music for our next program. There's a case of CD's Dee left for us."

"We leave for the Olympics in less than a month and Dee's already thinking about our next program?" Jordan asked in disbelief.

"They're under your seat. It will give you something to do besides worry about the weather," Aleksei encouraged, smiling when she finally reached for the case beneath her.

"I tell you, I'm going to find myself a new coach. That woman's gone over the line this time. We're on vacation and she sends a whole caseload of CD's for us to listen to so we can pick our next music? What is wrong with her?" Jordan lifted the list from the case and turned the map-light over her head on. "You know, Aleksei. This is just a gesture in futility? She's already decided on the next piece. She's only doing this to make us think we're part of the process."

"If it makes you feel any better, I put my two cents in as far as voting for my choice," Aleksei offered.

"What did she say?"

"What else? That I had good taste and she could live with my selection," Aleksei bragged.

Jordan choked out a laugh. "Right. And how many promises to skate to her music of choice did you commit us to?"

"Unless you have no objections to skating with me for the next seventy-eight years, don't ask."

"That long, huh?" Jordan asked, heaving a huge, dramatic sigh. "I hate to say this, Rocmanov, but, you got screwed on that trade."

"Maybe, but I don't see it that way. The idea of spending the next lifetime with you doesn't seem half bad," Aleksei answered quietly, his knuckles running a soft caress down her cheeks, his eyes saying more than words could in the lifetime he looked forward to with her.

Jordan grabbed his hand, placing a soft kiss into his palm and smiled in complete content. "So, Rocmanov. Which piece of music have you sold our souls to Dee for?" She asked, scanning down the list in the case of CD's.

"There were two I couldn't decide between. I figured you, in all your infinite wisdom and experience, should make the final decision. They're marked with an asterisk," he nodded toward the list she held.

"*East of Eden* and *The Prayer*? How am I supposed to decide between the two? You know how much I love both these pieces of music. Why can't we do them both?"

"Who says we can't? I'm sure if we promise Dee another hundred years of servitude, she'll be happy to choreograph them for us," Aleksei suggested, smiling into Jordan's green eyes, brightly-lit emeralds full of fire, and passion, and mischief.

"I'm up for it, if you are," Jordan promised, slipping the CD containing the title song from *East of Eden* into the car's CD player.

The music started softly, slowly filling the interior of the jeep with sedate, wistful strains of music that brought visions of floating and drifting through warm, beautiful clouds in a summer sky to mind. Jordan sighed, her eyes softening as the beautiful music stole into her soul, wrapping her in peace and warmth; a serene smile graced her full lips, "Oh, Aleksei, you're right. This music is definitely worth years of servitude and groveling."

"I thought you'd agree. I'm glad I didn't indenture the both of us for a piece of music you hated," he replied gently, his smile widening as he watched her slide further into the music's magical spell. The thought he'd never tire of looking at her flashed across his mind, reaffirming what he already knew—he loved her. Somewhere along the line he'd fallen so far in love with her that he had a better chance of drowning in the desert than he had of escaping what he'd always believed was the end of one's freedom. She had taught him, you could still be half of a whole and yet stand alone, when, and if, you needed to. Loving someone didn't mean you *couldn't* live without them, it simply meant, you *didn't want* to. Suddenly it wasn't so terrifying to admit that he loved this wisp of a woman two feet away, bundled in a winter coat that hid all the glory that was hers alone. A beautiful, petite, spitfire that spelled things out clearly, didn't waste words and didn't beat around the bush to spare feelings. Life was too short to spend it constantly worrying about hurting inflated egos, and sugar-coating the world—she'd long ago lost her rose colored glasses and saw things perfectly clearly.

"I love you, Jordan," Aleksei said softly.

Jordan turned her head to look at him, her eyes softly shining, "I know, Rocmanov. And the scariest part, is loving you back. It seems everyone I've ever loved has left me, one way or another."

"That won't happen with me—with us."

"How can you be so sure?" Jordan asked wistfully. "The best I can hope for is just that—I can hope you won't leave. But even hoping doesn't make it a given."

"I can swear to you there is no power on this earth that can, or will, make me leave you," Aleksei promised, reaching to grasp her hand and squeezing it to reaffirm his commitment. "I swear, Jordan. You are stuck with me until I'm too old to lace up your skates."

"You never lace up my skates," Jordan sniffed, wiping away tears of happiness that threatened to slip from her forest colored eyes.

"Then I guess you'll have to teach me how to," Aleksei teased, "When you're pregnant and you can't see your toes over your tummy, you'll need someone to lace your boots," he ended, the image he suggested clear in his mind and surprisingly enough, it made him even happier.

Jordan raised her eyebrows, "Pregnant and skating. That's certainly not a picture I would have envisioned you conjuring up. What's up, Rocmanov? Suddenly feeling your age?"

"No. Suddenly clear on the direction I want my life to take and what I want out of it. And unfortunately for you, Jamison, you're smack dab in the middle of it. Have you got the energy to keep up with me?"

"Keep up with you? Old man, if it wasn't for me you'd be looking for another bottle of hair color to get rid of your gray!" Jordan countered, running her hand through his thick curls, not a sign of gray to be seen.

"Wrong, Jamison. You're the cause of any gray hairs you may find and I'm damn proud to show them off. I've earned every last one of them having to deal with your temper tantrums, your fits of prima donnaness…"

"Is that a real word?" Jordan quipped.

"Close enough. Your smart-ass attitude…"

"My nice ass," Jordan corrected, smiling at the light that fired in Aleksei's ebony eyes when he tossed her a heated glance.

"Yeah, your very nice ass, too," he agreed. Where was I?" he asked with a wide smile.

"Does it matter? I get your point," Jordan conceded.

Aleksei's smile widened. "Good, as long as we've determined who's in charge here."

Jordan's eyebrows rose yet again. "I never relinquished control of myself over into your very capable arms—hands." Unable to resist, she stroked a hand over Aleksei's shoulder and down his muscular arm. Even through the thick coat his muscles were plainly apparent. "We're partners, friends, antagonists, confidants…"

"Lovers," Aleksei added, his voice deep and warm.

"Lovers," she agreed. "sounding-boards, help-mates… What am I forgetting?"

"I think I get the gist. We're everything to each other."

"Right. Can you live with that, Rocmanov?" Jordan asked.

Aleksei frowned, a crease forming between his eyes before he finally answered her. "I can't believe I didn't see it before, but now that I think about it, I'm sure that's how my life has been for the last three years. You mean to tell me, we've been a *pair* for over three years and I'm only just now reaping the benefits of said partnership. Damn, Whittaker's slipping. All this time and all I heard from him was, *don't touch her, hands off, you're skating partners—period*. I need to straighten him out or get myself a new coach."

"Don't pick on him. He was defending my honor."

"You did just fine defending your own honor. Believe me, you made the boundaries quite clear regarding when and how you were to be touched."

"It wasn't meant to torture and torment you."

"Maybe not, but it did just the same."

"Look at it as foreplay," Jordan suggested, blushing at Aleksei's burning gaze as it wandered up and down her body, his gaze returning to meet hers, his message clear, he wanted nothing more than to devour her, on the spot if possible.

"I know all about foreplay, sweetheart, and let me tell you, you sent me up in flames more times than I care to think about, let alone name. You could count the number of hot showers I've taken in the last three years on one hand!" His voice was dangerously soft—passionately heavy.

"I'm sorry," Jordan apologized on a whisper, secretly pleased by his admission.

"Don't be. It was worth the wait!" Aleksei responded huskily, his hand reaching for hers and drawing it to his mouth, his lips placing a soft kiss in her palm. "I'll love you forever, Jordan," he promised quietly, his gaze switching from the snow and ice covered road to her face and back again.

"I love you, too," Jordan whispered, running her knuckles against his strong jaw, the beginning roughness of his beard sending tingles up her arm, the lingering scent of his after-shave drawing her nearer, leading her to lean over and kiss the spot her fingers had just grazed. "I love the way you feel."

"The feeling's mutual and when we get off the mountain, you're going to have to remind me of how you feel. It's been too long since I held you in my arms."

Jordan glanced at her watch—two fifty-three in the afternoon. "It's only been a few hours, Rocmanov. How quickly they forget," she sighed dramatically.

"Believe me, Jordan, I never forget how you feel—how you taste—I just happen to like frequent reminders," he explained, suddenly leaning forward toward the windshield, straining to see through the ever-thickening snowfall that the windshield wipers never seemed to quite keep up with.

Jordan was busy changing CD's, slipping Aleksei's other choice into the player and reaching to push the play button. Her finger slipped to press the *repeat* button when she heard Aleksei's damning curse and looked up to see the snowplow sliding sideways toward them, blocking both lanes on the narrow mountain road.

Chapter 13

Aleksei slammed his food down on the brake pedal, felt the pounding pulse beneath his foot as the anti-lock braking system kicked in, barely slowing them as they slid headlong toward the looming snowplow. His gloved hands held the steering wheel steady, his mind racing through scenarios of escape, dismissing them one by one. With the snowplow taking up the entire road, there was no escape, towering mountain on their right, and a guardrail and very long fall to their left. Neither choice did much for him. He could hear Jordan's harsh breathing, wishing he could hold her hand and reassure her everything would be fine, but he couldn't. Until it was all over, he couldn't risk diverting his attention from the ever-gaining snowplow. There would be time to comfort her when all this madness was over.

Jordan could only stare in morbid fascination as she watched the snowplow slowly slide ever closer, cutting off every avenue of escape their jeep might consider, knowing the snowplow could flatten them like a bug, probably wouldn't even feel the bump as they slid beneath it's gigantic body. Suddenly she felt as if she was watching the impending accident from somewhere else, somewhere far away. She could hear shallow, labored breathing, the pounding of a heart, faint music, somehow comforting but seemingly out of place in this nightmare. She saw her right hand grip the hand-hold over her head, and felt her nails dig into her palm as she closed her hand around the bar. Dazed, she watched her left hand brace itself against the center console, saw her feet press against the floor-board, preparing for the impact that seemed to only inch toward them. Like one frame of a picture after another; the snowplow's progress was barely discernible visually but its threat loomed dangerously all the same.

Aleksei jerked the steering wheel to the right, he knew they'd never survive a head-on collision against the monster of steel only feet away. The thought that anything was better than being hit head-on flashed through his mind. He heard Jordan's soft gasp of fear as if from far away, could hear the brakes screaming metal against metal as he pushed the brake to the floor-board, gripped the steering wheel and swore to himself he wouldn't let go of it under any circumstances and hung on. With nothing else left to do, he softly called her name, his eyes drifting right, his gaze finding and holding hers, thoughts of everything he wanted to say to her flashing through his mind his mouth refusing to work. A sudden spark lit her emerald eyes, everything he felt in his heart he saw reflected in the depths of her eyes. *It's okay, she knows* he realized and with the realization, a sweeping calmness stole over him. Her gentle smile was the last thing he saw before their world exploded.

The snowplow closed the final distance and slammed into the jeep. The impact shattered the windshield, the power of the blow throwing Aleksei against the driver's door, despite his seat belt, his head hitting the side window and shattering it, glass exploding into the freezing air and blending like glitter with the dancing snowflakes. Jordan was thrown against the console, flashes of bright light dancing in the blackness assailed her as her ribs slammed against the solid surface; a far away groan. The air bags deployed—yet another explosion in the melee.

The snowplow's motion continued, catapulting the jeep forward, sounds like the staccato of gunfire echoing through the mountains as the tires on the passenger's side flattened, the sudden weight shift tilting the jeep crazily, the passengers inside were tossed to the right. Jordan moaned as her right shoulder made contact with her door, her hand still clenching the bar above her desperately; the one solid thing in her spinning world. The snowplow slid into the jeep a second time, propelling them forward and against the guardrail, a dented, rusted guardian against the long drop down. The jeep came to an abrupt stop, tilted at an angle, balanced on the flattened passenger's side tires against the steel and wood barrier that kept them from sliding down the steep slope into oblivion.

Time moved in slow motion, one millisecond at a time, as the snowplow finally slid to a stop, its back end hitting the tilted jeep at the rear and pushing it through the steel railing. In horror, the dazed snowplow driver watched the jeep leisurely slip over the side of the road, like sliding into a warm pool, and disappear into the swirling whiteness, tumbling helplessly over rocks and trees, it's path through the snow painfully visible. Finally, the battered jeep stopped its descent, upright against a stand of towering pines, their snow laden limbs trembling at the force of the jeep's blow when it came to a rolling halt. Snow gently sifted over the broken vehicle, silent but for the howling wind that raced through the mountains, it's wail mournful.

The snowplow driver sat dazed, unable to believe the tragedy he had just escaped, realizing he could just have easily followed the jeep over the side of the mountain. Clumsily he reached for the microphone on his two-way radio, barely able to hold it in his trembling hands.

"Base, this is Charlie-12, come back. May-day, may-day!" he managed to utter, his voice cracking with emotion.

"This is base, Charlie-12. What's up?" a voice responded.

"Send all emergency units. We've got someone over the side. Mile marker twenty-nine!" he cried, tears starting to run down his cheeks.

"Are you okay, Charlie?" the voice asked in concern.

"They were kids, Margo. They were just kids!"

"Charlie, take a breath and talk to me. What happened?" the dispatcher asked, pushing one intercom button to signal an emergency, and then another to put the transmission out over the loudspeakers.

"I hit black ice…sideways slide…couldn't control the rig. I saw the jeep and couldn't do a damn thing. I pushed it over the side…I watched it slide down the mountain…" he answered faintly, his tone lifeless.

The dispatcher watched the rescue crew scramble, trying to control her own emotions that threatened run wild. "Sit tight, Charlie. Help's on the way. Are you hurt?"

Charlie moved his limbs, legs worked, arms worked, ribs didn't hurt, head was still attached, no scratches. He looked into the rearview mirror, no cuts or bruises that he could see, only his haunted blue eyes looking back.

"Charlie?" the dispatcher called.

"I'm fine—not a God damn scratch! I killed those two kids and I didn't get a GOD DAMN SCRATCH!" he railed, hitting his fists against the massive steering wheel before him.

"Take it easy, Charlie. Help will be there real soon. We'll get 'em out. You'll see, everything's going to be just fine," the dispatcher offered, sending up a prayer to heaven that she would be right.

"How, Margo? How will everything be fine? You didn't see 'em. You didn't see their faces when they slide over that edge. They're just kids, Margo, with their whole lives ahead of 'em!"

"I know, Charlie. You're right—I didn't see them. But we're on the way and we're going to get them out!" Margo insisted.

"I'm going down to see what I can do for 'em," Charlie stated, releasing his seat belt. "I'll get back to you."

"You be careful, Charlie. We don't want to have to be rescuing you, too."

"I'll get back to you," Charlie ended, tossing the microphone to the seat, zipping his jacket and pulling his hat lower over his ears.

As he stepped out of his rig, the wind howled around him, pushing against him as if in punishment, demanding atonement for his error. Cautiously he peered over the side, squinting against the snow that struck his face like tiny needles, each sharp prick reminding him of how much more fortunate he was than the crumpled vehicle so many feet below him. Tears stung his eyes, freezing before they fell. Closing his eyes to block the wind, he found new pain as the vision of two faces, frozen in bewilderment, and then fear, flashed before his mind's eye with a force that dropped him to his knees. Blindly he opened his eyes, again squinting to see through the swirling blizzard in the hopes of finding the wreckage below him. "Help's on the way. You two stay put and we'll get you out real soon!" he yelled, his hands around his mouth as he sought to be heard above the wind.

For a brief moment, the wind stopped blowing. The snowflakes twirled gracefully to the ground. A sound caught his attention, making him turn his head from side to side as he sought its source. From far below him, Celine Dion's and Andrea Boccelli's voices blended in sheer beauty and power as they sang *The Prayer*. Charlie shook his head in wonder and disbelief. Of all the songs in the entire world, the fact it was this one, which drifted through the sudden peacefulness, had to be an omen. Charlie only hoped it was one of good.

*   *   *   *   *

We ask that life be kind, and watch us from above. We hope each soul will find another soul to love. Let this be our prayer, when we lose our way. Lead us to a place—guide us with your grace, to a place where we'll be safe...

Celine Dion's words beckoned to Jordan from far away, a somehow familiar voice in a world where it felt as if she was moving in slow motion, her mind refusing to put the fractured pictures, that flashed strobe-like before her eyes, and made her head pound painfully, back together. Cold wind and snow blowing across her cheek brought her eyes open, her vision blurring as the wind glazed her eyes. Her eyes drifted shut, the effort to hold them open overwhelming. The song continued, beginning anew, and slowly drew Jordan back to reality. *Aleksei's choice of music for their next program*, her mind screamed, the last flashing moments of their world returning clearly to her memory, a gasp of panic escaping her mouth as a puff of fog in the freezing air.

"Aleksei…" Jordan moaned, turning her head toward the left. "Oh, God…" she cried, struggling to release the seat-belt, grabbing her ribs as pain fired through her side, taking the breath from her lungs and causing bright lights to flash before her eyes. *Breathe—just breathe,* she told herself, concentrating on controlling the pain. She couldn't help Aleksei if she fainted. Gradually, the pain subsided and her vision cleared, her mind holding the panic at bay for the moment. She tried the seat-belt latch again, moaning when pain from her left wrist speared up her forearm and into her shoulder. A wave of nausea rushed through her body and for a moment she thought she was going to be sick. Through sheer effort, she refused to acknowledge, let alone, give into her weakness. There would be time to get sick later, Aleksei needed her now. Struggling to twist enough in her seat, she managed to push the latch with her right hand, pushing the slim piece of fabric that had saved her life away from her body.

Carefully she got to her knees on the seat; her left wrist barely supported her weight and throbbed painfully as she leaned against the console separating her from Aleksei. Cautiously she ran her hands over the parts of him she could reach, tentatively poking and grazing the right side of his body. When she pressed against his stomach, he moaned softly, his head turning toward her, his eyes blinking open then closing again.

"Come on, Rocmanov. Look at me," Jordan pleaded, gently running her hand over his left cheek and into his hair to hold his head steady, grimacing when warm blood flowed over her fingers.

"That must have been some party," Aleksei mumbled, his voice strained.

"What are you talking about, Aleksei?" She asked, her gaze switching back and forth between Aleksei and looking around for the box of Kleenex that had been in the back seat, but was now God only knew where.

"This hangover...we won Gold, didn't we?" he mumbled weakly, his eyes blinking open, squinting as he tried to focus, then his expression became confused. "What happened?"

Jordan finally located a sweatshirt stuck beneath the seat, ripping it free from a bent metal bracket. She folded it and placed it carefully against Aleksei's head, lifting his hand to hold it in place.

"Sorry." Jordan whispered at Aleksei's hiss of pain when she pushed the fabric against the wound.

"Well?" Aleksei asked quietly.

Jordan looked through the windows, void of glass, and shrugged her shoulders. "I'd say we took the express elevator down the mountain, and nothing against your driving, but next time, I'll drive."

"Not a problem," he agreed, wincing as he tried to shift position in his seat.

"What's wrong?" Jordan questioned sharply, watching his face go pale; his eyes close as he struggled to control the pain.

"My ribs," he finally answered, breathing slowly—shallowly.

"Does it hurt anywhere else?"

"I think the easier question would be where doesn't it hurt."

Jordan smiled softly. Joking was a good sign, wasn't it? "Okay, then. Where doesn't it hurt?"

Aleksei pointed to his lips, turning his head to accept Jordan's soft kiss when she moved toward him. "Thanks."

"For what?"

"The kiss and for not freaking out and falling apart."

Jordan shrugged. "Not that I didn't take it under serious consideration, but what would be the point? It's not as if freaking out is going to change anything," she stated matter-of-factly.

"Be that as it may. It's a typical reaction."

"Since when have I ever behaved in a *typical* fashion?" Jordan asked, frowning when she checked his head wound and found it still bleeding.

"Point taken," Aleksei mumbled, closing his eyes wearily. "So where are we?"

"I'd say about two-hundred feet lower than we were five minutes ago," Jordan guessed, pushing the cloth firmly against his head and looking for something she could wrap around his head to hold the cloth in place.

Both of them jerked in surprise when the glove-box door suddenly dropped open, an ace bandage clearly visible in the small compartment.

"That'll work," Jordan stated, reaching for the bandage and carefully, but firmly, wrapping the bandage around his head, and holding the sweatshirt snugly against the wound. "See, even from miles away, Dee and Whittaker are taking care of us," Jordan stated.

"I hope you enjoyed your time off. I have the feeling Dee and Whittaker won't let us out of their sights after this fiasco."

"It wasn't your fault, Aleksei. It wasn't anyone's fault. That's why they call it an accident."

"Be that as it may, neither one of them will let me forget this screw-up for a long, long time."

"It's not your *screw-up*, Aleksei. It's just one of those stupid, senseless things that we'll spend years trying to figure out. Personally, I don't think it's worth worrying about right this second," Jordan suggested, awkwardly wrapping the ace bandage around Aleksei's head to hold the sweatshirt in place.

"Could you get a signal on the cell phone?" Aleksei asked tiredly.

Jordan looked quickly about the scattered mess that covered the back seat. "I don't see it. Any idea where it might be?" she asked worriedly.

Aleksei shook his head, gritting his teeth against the pain the movement caused. "It could be anywhere on the mountain. We should have left earlier," Aleksei noted, his breathing growing shallow and hoarse.

"There was no way to know the storm would be this bad."

"We should have paid closer attention to the weather reports."

"What, and be the only people on the planet to believe those morons? Statistically, how often are those guys right? They're lucky if they're right even fifty percent of the time. I bet if their salaries were based on their forecasts being correct, they'd try a whole lot harder to get it right."

"You're jabbering, Jordan," Aleksei muttered, his voice slightly slurred, groaning in pain when he tried to push himself farther up into the seat in an attempt to ease the pain in his lower back and stop the tingle he was beginning to feel creep up his legs.

"Sorry, just trying to keep your mind off our minor dilemma."

"If this is a *minor* dilemma, I'd hate to see your version of a major one," Aleksei slurred. His breath caught, as a fit of coughing brought him upright in his seat, a growl of pain escaping into the cold air as his back arched rigidly, his right hand pressing hard into his right side.

Jordan's cry of fear blended with Aleksei's sound of pain. Gently she cradled his face in her hands, ignoring the pain in her left wrist as she cooed words of comfort and love, and promises the pain would ease. "Look at me, Aleksei. Look at me. Focus on my eyes, sweetheart. Listen to my voice, love. Relax—relax and breathe. In through the nose—out through the mouth. Remember? Breath through the pain. Focus on breathing. Push the pain away—it's someone else's." Jordan repeated over and over—a litany for them both.

Slowly Aleksei's pain eased, his body relaxing as he settled into the car seat, sweat covering his face and running a line down the center of his chest to disappear beneath his shirt. "I'm sorry," he whispered, his ebony eyes glassy.

"There's nothing to be sorry about."

"You won't get your Gold medal," Aleksei wheezed, struggling to breathe.

"We'll get it next time!" she stated softly, her eyes shiny with unshed tears, her throat thickening with emotion as she watched him struggle to control his increasing pain, and felt an unearthly calm begin to pull him from her and toward death's approaching hands.

Aleksei watched her silently, unsure how to say the words out loud. He knew there wouldn't be a next time—at least for him—but how could he explain to her that it was okay his time was over. That he felt he'd lived more in the last three years he'd been with her than he had before they'd been thrown together. That the years before her he'd been adrift, alone and floundering, looking for a safe harbor, that he'd found that, and more, in her, and he would never be able to thank her enough for her gift of unconditional, unrestrained love, humor, strength, loyalty and devotion. "How do I begin to thank you for all you've given me?" he whispered.

Jordan's shoulders lifted in a small shrug, her teeth worrying her lower lip as she sought to control it's trembling, swiping away the tears that escaped her gleaming emerald eyes and slowly traced down her cheeks. "How about I give you the next seventy-five years to try?" she choked out hopefully.

"Seventy-five years doesn't sound like such a long time. Can I get an extension after that?" Aleksei asked quietly, his voice growing weaker.

"As many as you like," she whispered.

"Good. But you're liable to be stuck with me forever."

"I'll manage. I'm very accommodating."

Aleksei's smile was soft, content, despite his snort of disbelief. "You never said which music you preferred," he stated, the music finally penetrating his tired mind.

Jordan watched Aleksei closely, could feel his strength draining, his life force fading slowly and felt helpless to do anything. All that was left for her to do was be with him and share her love, her warmth, and her strength. "If you don't mind, I think this one's my favorite," she answered, listening as Celine Dion's and Andrea Bocelli's voices blended perfectly in *The Prayer*.

Aleksei nodded haltingly in agreement. "I knew some of my good taste would rub off on you eventually," he commented amiably, gritting his teeth as a sharp shaft of pain shot up his spine. Calling her name, his voice filled with pain, he reached for her hand, his fingers interlocking with hers as she cooed words of comfort and love into his ear, her cheek resting against his; warm against cold.

"It's okay, sweetheart. It's almost over. Help's coming," Jordan vowed, praying she was right, ignoring the pain the swept up her arm as Aleksei's grip tightened on her hand as another wave of pain swept over him.

The Prayer began again, its wistful opening notes filled with hope and promise. "Listen to the song, Aleksei. Concentrate on the song. Visualize the program we'll set to this music you've picked. People will say it's our signature piece. It will be so beautiful, they'll weep when they see us perform it," Jordan whispered, tears coursing freely down her cheeks, her heart breaking as she watched the man she loved drift ever closer toward death's waiting arms.

Aleksei's ebony eyes opened, glazed with pain yet lucid and accepting. "I'll always be with you."

"I know," Jordan whispered.

"I love you, Jordan, I always will," Aleksei's voice broke, tears falling from his dark eyes as he looked into the bruised but beautiful face of the young woman he'd come to love more than life itself.

"Me too. I'll love you forever, Aleksei!" Jordan answered, pressing soft kisses to his lips, frowning at their coldness.

"Talk me through our program, Jordan. Let me see how beautiful it will be," Aleksei whispered, his remaining strength draining faster with each passing second.

Jordan pushed the CD button to start the music from the beginning and softly spoke to Aleksei, her cheek resting against his chest, listening to his slowing heartbeat. Her words clearly described the way their final program would appear; the beautiful lines they make together in their spirals as they sped across the ice, their powerful lifts and throws, seeming effortless, and the love for each other that would show for all the world to see.

Aleksei mumbled something softly causing Jordan to lift her head and look into his beautiful eyes. "What, Aleksei?"

Aleksei smiled tremulously down into her shining green eyes and gently stroked her bruised cheek, marveling one final time at the silken softness beneath his fingers. "I love you, Jordan. Listen to the whispers on the ice," he whispered fervently, accepting the soft kiss she brushed across his lips and weakly pushed her head back to his chest.

A world where pain and sorrow will be ended, and every heart that's broken will be mended. And we'll remember we are all God's children, reaching out to touch you—reaching to the sky.   We ask that life be kind, and watch us from above. We hope each soul will find another soul to love. Let this be our prayer, when we lose our way. Lead us to a place—guide us with your grace, to a place where we'll be safe…

Jordan concentrated on the final strains of the music, feeling Aleksei drift into death's welcoming arms, as the last notes of the song disappeared into the swirling wind, heard his heart slow, and then cease, beneath her tear streaked cheek, felt his grip relax where their fingers were interlaced. She remained still, unable to leave Aleksei, unwilling to break their final tie. Time stood still, marked only by the howling wind, accumulating snow, and the song, which repeated over and over. Jordan passed the time talking to Aleksei, thanking him for all he'd given her, promising she would keep his memory alive, and that she would see him again—someday.

"Hello… Can anybody hear me?" a voice suddenly called out of the wind and swirling snow.

Jordan ran a caressing hand down Aleksei's cheek, along his jaw, her thumb gently grazing his full lower lip. Leaning forward she placed soft kisses to his temple, his cheek, a last kiss against his lips, whispering a final vow to love him forever. She took a deep, trembling breath, and with a final tear-filled look, called into the air, "We're here."

* * * * *

Silently she waited for her rescuers, her hand holding Aleksei's, their fingers laced together.

Chapter 14

"The figure-skating world was stunned and saddened today by the unexpected death of Olympic, and World champion, Aleksei Rocmanov. While vacationing with his partner, Jordan Jamison, at the vacation home of Ms. Jamison's coach, Mr. Rocmanov, and his partner, were struck by a snowplow that lost control after hitting a patch of black ice. The snowplow apparently struck them twice, the second hit pushing them through a guardrail and sending the vehicle the skating partners were traveling in plummeting more than one hundred and fifty feet over the side of a mountain. The vehicle rolled several times before hitting a stand of pines and coming to a stop. Ms. Jamison was admitted to the hospital where she was treated for a broken left wrist, a mild concussion, bruised ribs and lacerations. She was at her partner's side when he died. Funeral plans have not been announced, as yet." The reporter, Mark Foster, somberly intoned, his voice emotionally strained. The same reporter who three years before had announced Jordan and Aleksei's plan to become pairs skating partners.

"Truly devastating news for the figure skating world, Mark. As everyone knows, the pair were planning to participate in next month's Olympic games and were the favored pair to bring home Gold for the United States. Those dreams and hopes are now gone and we can only wish Jordan a speedy recovery and send our heart-felt condolences. When such a tragedy occurs, it's hard to understand the reason behind it. When it happens to people so young and full of promise—it's impossible to understand." The co-anchor added, her eyes filling with tears and threatening to ruin her perfectly made-up face. "Please know, Jordan, you're in our thoughts and prayers, and we will never forget the magic you, and Aleksei shared with all of us. We will never be able to thank you enough for that special gift."

"From all of us, at Channel 5 News. Good night," The anchorman closed, the screen filling with clips of Aleksei and Jordan's all too short skating career together.

* * * * *

Jordan stared, unblinking, at the TV screen from her hospital bed. Silent tears traced a path down her cheeks; her teeth worried her full lower lip, much the same way Aleksei used to. How they'd loved to kiss and nibble each other's mouths. Each kiss seemed sweeter than the one before and they just couldn't get enough of each other. Dee cast a quick glance at her, dividing her attention between the doctor, Whittaker and Jordan, trying to remain calm for the sake of them all.

"The concussion is minor, nothing to be overly-concerned with, we're simply keeping her here as a precaution. The lacerations look worse than they actually are—most only superficial. The break in her wrist isn't causing her the pain I'd normally expect considering the severity. Shock is probably keeping the pain at bay but when the shock wears off she's going to be uncomfortable. I've already scheduled medication to handle that if it gets to be too much for her. The biggest problem is going to be her emotional state. She's been through a major trauma, no one handles it well when someone they love dies in their arms," the doctor explained, checking Jordan's chart and making further notes, glancing from time to time at the silent, petite figure covered with an over-sized hospital gown.

"Is there any memory loss?" Whittaker asked, his voice deep and grave.

"None that is discernible. It might actually have been a blessing if Jordan didn't remember the accident, at least temporarily. Unfortunately, it seems, she remembers every vivid detail. On the one hand it was good she was with Aleksei when he died—she had time alone to be with him—time to say good-bye. On the other hand, she'll always wonder how things might have been different if the rescue team had reached them fifteen minutes sooner. The paramedics said she refused to leave him and go up the mountain without him. She climbed up that steep slope holding on to his hand. The rescue workers were awed, they'd never seen anything like the devotion she showed Aleksei."

"Has she said anything?" Dee asked quietly, wiping tears away.

The doctor looked worn out, it had been a long night. "She wanted to know why she made it and he didn't. It's a typical question survivors have. It's an expected part of the whole 'survivor guilt' scenario."

"Do the survivors ever get over the guilt?" Whittaker questioned.

"Some do—some don't—every case is different," the doctor answered truthfully.

"How do we help her?" Dee asked, looking over the doctor's shoulder at Jordan, still silently crying.

"Be there for her, listen to her, let her rage. You know her best, she'll let you in when she's ready," the doctor finished, finalized his notes, shook Dee and Whittaker's hands wishing them well and quietly left the room.

Dee looked at Whittaker, noting his pale complexion and pain filled eyes. Aleksei had been the closest thing to a son he had had, and now he needed to plan his funeral. Dee squeezed his hand, trying to show what she couldn't put into words and struggled to hold back the tears that threatened again. There would be time for tears later, now she had to get through the night.

Whittaker coughed gruffly, running a hand through his gray hair and stood. "I'll be back soon, as soon as things are in order. You stay with Jordan," he stated, nodding toward the petite figure on the bed.

"Can I do anything for you—for Aleksei," Dee asked, her voice catching in sorrow.

"Take care of Jordan for him. It's what he wanted more than anything on earth—knowing she was safe," he growled, brushing away a tear that escaped his tightly held control.

Dee could only nod her agreement, afraid to speak for fear of completely breaking down.

Whittaker placed a soft kiss on her cheek, squeezed her hand reassuringly and left the room, the soft squeak of his sneakers against the shining tile the only sound heard in the otherwise silent corridor.

* * * * *

"William…William…" Nora called from the living room where she sat watching the evening news, disbelief clear in her wide-eyed gaze.

"What is it, Nora?" her husband asked as he hurried to join her on the couch.

"That's them. Isn't it? I'm sure that's them," Nora stuttered, pointing at the TV, her outstretched arm shaking.

William looked at the TV, then slipped his glasses from his shirt pocket and slid them onto his nose. The images cleared, his heart skipped a beat as the newscast on Jordan and Aleksei filled the screen. "Damn," he mumbled, sorrow filling him. He and Nora had only met them that afternoon and spoken for only a few minutes, yet the news that less than three hours later one of them was dead made him go numb.

Silently they listened to the broadcast, Nora clutching his hand tightly, tears slowly trailing down her cheeks. When the news showed footage of their *Romeo and Juliet* performance, Nora jumped to her feet. "William, that was them. They're the skaters we saw out on the pond the other day. That was the music we heard, remember?"

"Sweet God," he mumbled, shaking his head in sorrow. "How could this happen?"

"It shouldn't have happened. They were young; their whole lives ahead of them. Heavens, William, they were going to the Olympics!" Nora cried, suddenly gasping as her hands swept up to cover her mouth.

"Nora, what's wrong?" William questioned, grasping her arm and turning her to face him.

"The tape. We were the last people to see them skate together," she cried softly.

William wrapped his arms around her, resting his chin on her head. "I'd forgotten all about that. I do my best to forget when you're using that silly video camera. I always look fat in the movies and you always seem to wait until I'm bent over to film me."

"And here I thought you just liked to show me your good side," Nora teased, wiping her cheeks against his shirtfront. "We need to get that tape to that young lady. I think she might like to have it—as a reminder of better times," she suggested.

William looked down into his wife's upturned face and wiggled her nose fondly. "You're always thinking of ways to make things better for others. You're one very special lady, Nora. No wonder I love you so much!" he stated lovingly, gently kissing her forehead and giving her a quick hug. "Before we call the news station though, we better see what, if anything, came out on that tape of yours."

"You're right," Nora agreed and with a quick kiss to her husband's mouth, left to find the video camera.

William cast a final glance at the TV screen, his heart growing heavy as he watched the news report and short tribute about Jordan and Aleksei end. "God be with you both!" he whispered to the picture of the pair on the screen as he watched the credits end and the screen go dark.

* * * * *

"When can I leave?" Jordan asked quietly, allowing the nurse to write down her blood pressure reading on the chart she held.

"As soon as Dr. Barnes clears you. Your blood pressure and temperature are normal, eyes look good," the nurse answered, checking her pupils with a small flashlight. "No residual effects from the concussion are indicated. My guess is you could probably be out of here by tomorrow."

"I'm not waiting that long!" Jordan stated, her tone soft but determined, causing the nurse to look at her in surprise.

"That will be up to the doctor to decide," the nurse responded diplomatically. The young woman in the bed might physically look the size of a twelve year old, but her eyes held more pain than anyone should have to deal with. The nurse had seen death first hand, even held the hands of strangers who had been in her care, yet she'd never experienced the death of someone close to her. Thankfully, her parents, her brother and sister, even her grandmother were still alive and well, irritatingly so at times, and she sent a quick thank-you skyward. Now, looking at the petite young woman with haunted green eyes before her, she couldn't imagine the sorrow and emptiness she had to be feeling. Not only had she lost someone she'd loved personally, her professional life would be changed drastically.

All the hospital staff had been told of the accident that claimed Aleksei Rocmanov's life and they'd been advised that, until further notice, they were operating under a 'no comment' restriction. Access to Jordan would be limited to her doctor, the two nurses assigned to her, Dee and Whittaker. All other hospital personnel and visitors would need to be cleared by the security guard posted at her door. Too many attempts by the media to enter her room for an exclusive story had led to the decision to post the guard.

"Good morning, Ms. Carlen," the security guard said quietly, holding the door open for Dee to enter Jordan's room and then closing it silently behind her. The nurse acknowledged her presence with a quick nod and continued to make notes in Jordan's chart.

"Good morning, Jordan," Dee whispered, placing a kiss against her cheek and giving her a gentle hug.

"Hi, Dee," Jordan answered softly.

"How's everything look?" Dee questioned the nurse.

"I'm fine. I want out of here today!" Jordan answered for the nurse.

Dee looked from Jordan's pale face and sorrow filled eyes to the nurse's sympathetic gaze. "Is she ready to be released?"

"As I told Jordan, that's up to Dr. Barnes," the nurse answered.

"Fuck Dr. Barnes, with or without his release, I am leaving this hospital today!" Jordan stated firmly, her eyes darkening to deep green, a dangerous light flaming in their center.

"Jordan, please," Dee pleaded, her heart breaking as she looked into Jordan's flashing eyes and deathly pale face. "Everyone just wants what's best for you."

"What about Aleksei? What was best for him? It certainly wasn't me or he'd still be alive."

"How can you say that?" Dee asked aghast. "You were the best thing that ever happened to him. He knew it! Hell, he even said it. Not necessarily in words but in his actions, every second you were with him, and even when you weren't, for that matter."

"And look at where it got him. Dead. Just like everyone else I've ever loved!" Jordan yelled.

"That's not true. I'm here and I'm not going anywhere," Dee stated.

Jordan's eyes widened, her breath catching as Dee's words, the same exact words Aleksei had used crashed over her, taking her strength and forcing her back against the pillows. "Don't make promises you can't keep," Jordan whispered, curling herself into a small ball on her side facing away from Dee.

Dee looked at Jordan's small body huddled in a ball beneath the covers and her heart ached, tears slipped silently from her eyes and her fingers laced together anxiously. "Jordan…"

"I don't want to talk right now, Dee. Please find Dr. Barnes and see what it will take to get me out of here today," Jordan requested softly.

"I don't know if you're ready…"

"TODAY!" Jordan interrupted, her determined tone and one-word demand leaving no room for discussion.

Dee ran one hand through her hair in frustration, gritting her teeth to still the scream of rage about the unfairness of life that was raging to escape. "I'll see what I can do." Jordan only nodded an acknowledgment. "Do you have any idea where Dr. Barnes might be?" Dee asked the nurse who stood silently watching the exchange.

"I'll have him paged immediately," she answered and inquired if either of the ladies needed anything, received no thank-yous and left the room.

"Jordan…" Dee began only to be interrupted by Whittaker's arrival into the room. Dee heaved a sigh of relief and walked into his welcoming arms.

"How is she?" he whispered in Dee's ear, kissing her softly on her cheek.

"She wants out," The simple reply said it all.

Whittaker managed a sad smile, his lips trembling as he voiced. "The sentiment sounds familiar. If I had a dime for every time Aleksei muttered those words I'd be a millionaire."

"Whittaker, I'm so sorry…" Dee started.

"Don't be sorry. He was the best part of my life and I have to be thankful I had him as long as I did. I'll never forget him or what he added to my life but right now we've got to see Jordan through this and things are about to get a whole lot tougher," Whittaker responded, his voice cracking emotionally.

"I don't understand," Dee answered bewildered.

Whittaker held out his hand; a small velvet box lay in his palm. "This was in Aleksei's coat pocket."

Dee shook her head, denying what she already knew in her heart lay resting in the small box. Her hand shaking, she touched the velvet covering, her skin tingling at the contact. The box felt alive, full of hope, happiness and promises yet to be made. "Please tell me this isn't what I think it is," Dee whispered pleadingly.

"I wish I could. In all honesty, I don't know what it is. Maybe just a friendship ring," Whittaker answered hopefully.

Dee silently open the box, her breath escaping on a sigh as she beheld the wide gold band set with diamonds and pearls. "They were best friends," Dee muttered, turning the small box so the diamonds caught the light and sparkled brightly, tiny pin-points of light fluttering over the subdued, gentle hues of the pearls mounted between each sparkling stone.

"I know. I'm glad they found each other."

"Do you think she knows about this?" Dee asked, casting a quick glance toward Jordan.

Whittaker shook his head. "I doubt it. Trouble is, I don't know if this ring will help her or add to her pain. I don't want Aleksei's last gift to be a daily reminder of what she lost."

"That's one decision we can't make for her; it's got to be her decision," Dee stated firmly, closing the lid and wrapping his fingers around the box. "She needs to know about this, Whittaker, and it has to come from you."

Whittaker looked into Dee's eyes, recognized the pain and sorrow of his own reflected in hers and nodded in agreement. Silently he walked the short distance to Jordan's bed and ran a comforting hand over her shoulder. Pressing a gentle kiss against her temple, he placed the small box on her pillow, whispered something into her ear and left her side. Silently he walked to Dee, took her hand and the two coaches left Jordan's room.

"Should we leave her alone?" Dee questioned Whittaker as he closed the door behind them, dreading Jordan's response to Aleksei's last gift.

"Aleksei.... NOOOOO..." Jordan's painful wail of sorrow penetrated the thick door and echoed off the sterile walls, raising goose bumps on all who heard the heart-wrenching plea.

The nurse assigned to Jordan hurried from the Nurse's Desk toward her patient's door, stopping when Whittaker blocked the door. "What does she need?"

"Time alone," Whittaker answered huskily. "I just gave her the last gift Aleksei bought for her. If I'm not mistaken, it was a lifelong promise to be with her," his voice grew shaky and broke on the last word.

At the nurse's confused expression, Whittaker's frustration exploded. "It was a damn wedding ring!"

"Dear, God," The nurse whispered, swallowing back her emotions. She couldn't help Jordan if she was falling apart herself. Steeling herself against the sobs of sorrow that filled the air, she set aside her emotions and felt the blessed security of numbness surround her. "The doctor's on his way. If necessary, she'll be sedated."

Dee and Whittaker nodded, casting worried glances toward the closed door that did little to block the devastating sounds of loss and pain. "Do what's necessary," Whittaker finally agreed, leading Dee to a waiting area near the nurse's station.

Whittaker forced Dee to sit, then poured her a cup of muddy-brown coffee that had obviously been there too long from the coffee maker on a small table. Returning to the couch, he sat beside her, handing the offending brew to her and almost smiling at Dee's grimace of distaste as she took a sip.

"It's a good thing medical help's nearby. This stuff is awful!" Dee complained, swallowing another mouthful of the foul, thick liquid being passed off for coffee. If nothing else, the liquid was hot.

"Sorry. It's probably been there awhile," Whittaker sighed, resting his elbows on his knees and running his hands tiredly through his hair.

Dee watched him silently, the cup warming her chilled hands, her heart breaking yet again as she thought what the days ahead would hold. "Can I help with any of the plans?" she asked quietly.

Whittaker shook his head, one hand again making a path through his hair and stopping to rub the tension in his neck. "Everything's being done that has to be done. We'd never really discussed this particular subject before—didn't see a reason to—so I'm kind of making it up as I go along," he answered quietly, a frown appearing between his eyes as he squinted to see through eyes suddenly tear-filled.

Dee nodded in understanding, biting her lip sharply to stop the overwhelming wave of grief that threatened to drown her. "Okay. If you need anything, though, you know where to find me," she offered.

Whittaker reached for her hand, squeezing it gently and then laced his fingers through hers. "Knowing you're here makes it much easier."

"Thanks," Dee answered, a sad smile touching her lips before she rested her head against his shoulder, closing her eyes to try to temporarily block out the nightmare they were all locked in.

"You're welcome," Whittaker answered back, placing a light kiss to her head before he rested his own against hers.

In companionable silence, the two coaches awaited the arrival of Jordan's doctor. Less than five minutes later, they watched his white-coated lanky form slip into the now silent room that held Jordan Jamison.

* * * * *

"I want out of here!" Jordan stated, her tone flat; her eyes red-rimmed yet lifeless.

"Do you really think you're ready to leave just yet?" her doctor asked quietly, reading the most recent notes off her chart.

"I'm not ready to stay any longer so that means my only other option is to leave. My only real question is, are you going to sign me out, or do I walk out of here on my own?"

The doctor slipped her chart back onto the hook at the foot of her bed and walked to her side, his warm fingers sliding over her right wrist as he checked her pulse, then moved on to check her pupils with his small flashlight. "Any pain?"

"Be more specific," Jordan suggested.

"Any severe pain in your wrist, any headache, any pain today that wasn't present yesterday?"

"Nothing that isn't manageable," Jordan responded numbly, the fingers of her right hand lovingly playing with the pearl and diamond band that now rested on the ring finger of her casted left arm.

"That's a lovely ring. I don't remember seeing it last night," the doctor stated, nodding toward her left hand.

Jordan's hands flew to her heart, her right hand covering her left hand protectively, shielding the precious ring from his view. For a long moment she was silent, her breathing shallow and labored as she struggled to control the sorrow that once again threatened to overwhelm her. Finally, in a soft, pain filled, voice she answered the doctor who waited patiently at her side. "It was a gift from a friend. I just got it this morning."

The doctor caught the 'was' in her statement and understood. "Aleksei must have been a very good friend."

Jordan looked up into her doctor's eyes, saw the understanding and compassion in them and tried to smile. "He was the best—and the worst—friend I ever had. Aleksei made everyday one to remember, not that everyday was wonderful, although, I suppose, there was something special about everyday we spent together. Even the days we spent thinking about ways to torture each other, we were still thinking about each other. Isn't that strange? And now I wonder why we wasted so much time trying to drive each other crazy, when, if we'd just stopped and acknowledged the attraction, we would have had that much more time together and could have made that many more memories," Jordan wished wistfully.

"Maybe neither of you were ready to take that step," the doctor suggested.

Jordan shrugged, "I was always ready," she answered and cast a shy look toward her doctor who had pulled up a chair next to her bed. "I fell in love with him when I was twelve years old—he bowled me over—literally." At the doctor's confused expression, she continued. "There was a competition in Canada we both competed in. It was during Aleksei's *wild period* when he took great pleasure in making his coach as crazy as possible, and would disappear for hours before a competition. Well, this time he cut it a little close, and was charging through the lower tunnels of the stadium to get to the ice. Unfortunately, I happened to be coming around the same bend that he was cutting the corner close on, and he literally knocked me on my butt." Jordan smiled at the memory.

"Were you hurt?"

"Hardly, I'm made of stronger stuff than that! Granted, being body-checked by someone that outweighs you by over a hundred pounds isn't my idea of a good time, and I was plenty mad that this moron had jeopardized my skates. I'd spent weeks getting accustomed to new boots and blades and here they were being bounced off a concrete floor. I wasn't happy! And then I looked up, and saw the great Aleksei Rocmanov. Man, I nearly melted into a puddle just looking into those dark, mischievous eyes of his. You could always tell his mood just by looking into his eyes; they really were windows to his soul. Anyway, he made some snotty comment about size limitations and kids competing and I shifted into my *ice bitch* mode and let him know what I thought of his boorish behavior and non-existent manners."

"Why do I get the feeling he didn't respond favorably to your criticism?" the doctor chuckled.

Jordan smiled wistfully. "Aleksei didn't see it as criticism but more as a personal affront to his ego. Here he was, God's greatest gift to the weaker sex, knocking over twelve-year-olds. In those days he made it a point to be seen with as many beautiful women as possible. Whether they meant anything to him or not, he felt he needed the media exposure. And you have to admit, male figure skaters seem to automatically be assumed gay, and if Aleksei was out there every night with a different woman, that assumption couldn't be made."

"I can't imagine being a public sports figure and having to constantly prove yourself. How can you be happy under those circumstances?" the doctor asked.

Jordan shrugged again. "You consciously make the decision that this is the life you've picked out for yourself and learn to ignore the hurtful, vicious things that people say. For a long time, Aleksei believed that having your name in print, whether the reasons were good or bad, was better than being forgotten. Over the last two and a half years, he changed his mind. He'd say I made him change his mind, because suddenly he was concerned about my name being dragged through the same mud with his, and as they say, 'shit rubs off'. I was more concerned with making him believe in himself as a skater. It's hard to go from being solely responsible for the program you're skating to suddenly having someone else who can muck things up. There are days when you wonder why you even laced up your skates let alone decided to try to lift someone over your head while you're sliding across the ice at thirty miles an hour. That abrupt stop on cold, hard ice often makes you wonder about your career choice. Then there are the days when you step on that ice and a warm hand slides into yours, the music starts and magic fills your soul. Suddenly, you're gliding at thirty miles an hour with the man you love holding you in his arms, and there is heaven on earth," Jordan whispered. With a soft, sad sigh, Jordan looked at the band where diamonds shimmered beside the warm pink-tinged pearls on her left hand.

"It sounds like you were lucky to have found each other."

"We were lucky. I know we were. But, was it wrong to take it for granted that we would have more time together? Weren't we grateful enough? Did we ask too much?"

"If asking to love someone forever is wrong, then I guess it's a mistake every human being on earth makes. I, personally, can't believe that you did anything wrong in loving each other that caused this tragedy to happen. I can't say there's a greater purpose waiting for you and that this is the only way you would find your true path. I'll be the first to admit I'm not certain there's a God. At least in the sense that there's one being responsible for everything and everyone, that's one big job where you know you'll never make everyone happy. I do believe we learn from everything that happens to us—good and bad—and how we handle it determines our future. There are those who lose loved ones and never recover, and there are those who lift their chins and move forward, never forgetting their loss but learning to live again and eventually—maybe—love again."

"I can't believe I'll never see him again," Jordan whispered as tears traced a shining path down her cheeks.

"Would you like to see him once more?" the doctor asked.

Jordan's breath caught, her eyes flying to meet her doctor's steady gaze. "Could I? Would it be all right?" she asked softly, her chin quivering as she struggled for control.

"I'll see it's taken care of," the doctor stated, rising to his feet and pushing the chair back into place against the wall. "I'll be back shortly and take you to see him myself." Jordan could only nod in agreement, her eyes brimming with tears.

After her doctor left, a whispered *thank you* stirred the air.

Chapter 15

Dee and Whittaker watched the doctor quietly give the head nurse instructions, noted her quick look of surprise, and cast apprehensive looks toward each other. Only moments later, the doctor turned toward the couch they were sitting on and walked the short distance to speak with them.

Jordan's doctor didn't waste words. "I'm taking Jordan to see Aleksei."

Dee's knees gave way at the unexpected words and she slowly sank back into the couch's worn cushions. Whittaker dropped to the couch; his mouth falling open then snapping closed abruptly.

"Is that such a good idea?" Whittaker finally managed.

"She needs to see him and she wants to thank him for all he gave her. She needs to say good-bye one last time."

"How soon can she see him?" Dee asked quietly, her eyes shining with unshed tears.

"The nurse is taking care of him now. It shouldn't be long," Jordan's doctor answered softly.

"Good. She needs to be with him. Thank you, doctor," Dee stated, squeezing his hand and feeling his return squeeze of comfort.

With a silent nod to Dee and Whittaker, the doctor returned to the nurse's station and gave final instructions for Jordan. Five minutes later, a wheelchair was taken into Jordan's room, and soon left it bearing her petite form.

Dee and Whittaker watched as Jordan was wheeled from their view down a corridor to the bank of elevators that would take her to Aleksei one last time.

* * * * *

The doctor stopped Jordan's wheelchair before a wide, beige metal door with the word PRIVATE printed in bold black letters across a plain piece of white paper, which was taped to it. Jordan looked up at the doctor as he came to stand before her and help her to her feet. "Are you ready?" he asked quietly, his eyes searching hers and finding strength through the sorrow. At her affirmative nod, he pushed the door open and stood to the side, allowing her access into the softly lit room.

Jordan stepped through the doorway; a quietly whispered *thank you* followed by a gentle smile touched the doctor holding the door for her.

The doctor nodded once in acknowledgment and silently closed the door behind her.

Jordan turned and leaned against the closed door, the chill of the metal seeping through her robe. Her heart pounded erratically, her lungs struggled to take a full breath, her legs threatened to dissolve beneath her, yet she found herself moving steadily toward the hospital bed that Aleksei lay in across the room. Jordan's legs bumped against the steel frame of the bed, startling her as she realized she had reached his side.

Aleksei lay covered by a soft blanket pulled up to his waist, a black long sleeved T-shirt covered his upper body, his once powerful arms lay peacefully at his side. His dark, wavy hair was tussled, as usual, the same lock that he had constantly pushed away from his forehead fell forward, and lovingly Jordan pushed the silky strands back into place. Her fingertips skimmed over his face, memorizing the feel of his skin, smiling as her skin tingled against roughness of the stubble of his beard, remembering how his unshaven face had felt against her face, her neck, her body. Her knuckles grazed a caress over his cheekbones, her eyes clouding when her fingers slid over his temple into his hair and felt the stitches that closed the cut on his head. Without hesitation, she bent over and kissed his wound, nuzzling her cheek against his as she closed her eyes and breathed deeply, unsure if she actually caught a whiff of his after-shave or only imagined the scent she'd come to love. Sighing softly, she straightened, flinching as a stab of pain shot through her broken left wrist, a taunting reminder of the accident. Carefully she lifted his left arm and scooted onto the bed beside him, resting his arm across her lap, their left hips touching as they had millions of times before, both on and off the ice. The weight of his arm across her legs was comforting and she ran her hand up and down his arm, frowning at the missing warmth. "You're so cold," she whispered, steadily massaging his arm as he had countless times before done to hers when she had been cold. Her eyes returned to his face, he could be sleeping for the way he looked, relaxed, peaceful, his long, dark lashes laying against his cheeks, the tiniest of smiles turning just the corners of his mouth upward.

Jordan's gaze absorbed every nuance of Aleksei it touched, the small scar on his chin, his full lips, the dark slashes of his eyebrows that could lower in irritation or rise in arrogance. The powerful shoulders and chest that had lifted and held her; tightly, securely, teasingly, lovingly, the hands that had shown her heaven could be found on earth, and that magic truly existed. And as she held his cold hand, the realization that he was truly gone from her rolled over her like a crashing wave. Her body began to shake uncontrollably, and the tears she had somehow held back until now refused to remain unshed. The tears came in a torrent, dropping hotly onto Aleksei's cold hand as she raised his palm and laid her cheek against it, deep inside hoping she would feel his fingers move softly against her skin yet knowing she would never feel his touch again. Her throat felt raw as the emotional pain raged through her body and the words she struggled to speak sounded deep and throaty in the small, softly lit room. "You promised, Aleksei. You swore—nobody leaves. You swore you'd never break a promise to me. You can't break this one—not this one. Dear, God…Aleksei, don't leave me…" she sobbed, her body shaking uncontrollably as she collapsed across his chest, trying to get as close to him as she could. "Take me with you, Aleksei. I don't want to stay here without you—I can't stay without you… Aleksei, please. I love you. Take me with you…" she entreated to any power that was listening, fully prepared to die at that moment, if it meant being with Aleksei forever.

"Take me with you, Aleksei… I love you. Take me with you…" Jordan whispered over and over, tears spilling from her tightly closed eyes down her cheek which rested against his chest, her tears wetting the dark shirt he wore, her hands clenching and unclenching his muscular shoulders as she pleaded to join her love. "Aleksei, I'm so tired…Take me with you." Jordan whispered, closing her eyes against the overwhelming emptiness that the softly lit room offered. "Aleksei…" crossed her lips as a breathless sigh.

"Jordan?" Aleksei called softly, his right hand gently stroked her tangled curls and down her back.

"Hmm?" Jordan answered sleepily, snuggling closer against his chest.

"Jordan?" Aleksei called again, a low chuckle making his chest vibrate. Effortlessly, he rolled her on to her right side, and tucked her head against his shoulder, fitting his body against hers. He brushed her hair from her face, and lifted her chin with his finger, his mouth settling sweetly over hers.

Jordan returned the kiss, sighing as he deepened it, her left arm slipping around his back as she pulled him closer, her breasts melting against the hard muscles of his chest. "You're too sweet," Aleksei stated softly when he finally found the will to end the kiss.

"Complaining?" Jordan questioned groggily; her eyes dark green and glazed with passion.

"Never," Aleksei answered, placing a gentle kiss on the top of her head as he pushed her head back against his shoulder and heaved a sigh of contentment.

Jordan snuggled closer against Aleksei, one slim leg slipping between his muscular thighs. "That's good. It's important to keep your partner happy," she sighed tiredly, haziness slowly creeping over her.

"Tired?"

"Sort of—but not really. It's weird—kind of like watching someone else lose their energy," Jordan leaned her head back to look into Aleksei's dark gaze, "Does that make any sense?"

Aleksei's dark eyes delved deeply into Jordan's answering green gaze, a knowing smile sparking a light in the depth of his eyes as his lips lifted upward. "Yeah, it makes sense," he answered, placing a gentle kiss against her lips. "Jordan, listen to me, we need to talk."

"Let's just snuggle quietly for a minute and then you can talk all you want," Jordan suggested, closing her eyes as she rubbed her forehead against his chin, and snuggled closer against his body, her hips pressing temptingly against his own.

"Jordan, I can't think when you do that."

"Do what?" she asked sleepily.

"Wiggle against me that way. It ruins my concentration for all but one thing and we don't have time for that right now."

"We'll always have time for that, Aleksei."

"If only it were true," Aleksei sighed wistfully. "Jordan, listen to me. Are you paying attention?" Aleksei shook her gently, his tone becoming more urgent.

Jordan struggled to open impossibly heavy eyes, her vision hazy when she finally coaxed them open. "What is it, Aleksei?" she asked at his serious look.

Aleksei's gaze roamed freely over her face, her beauty enhanced by the soft light that surrounded them. "Jordan, we don't have much time."

"What are you talking about, Aleksei? We've got forever, just like you said." Jordan stated, a small frown forming between her eyes as she tried to bring Aleksei's face into focus.

"I was mistaken," Aleksei answered simply.

"You can't be—you're never wrong. You told me so yourself," Jordan argued, a small pinpoint of panic flaring somewhere deep inside her.

"Well in this instance, I was wrong."

"You can't be—I won't accept it. In fact, I refuse to accept it!" Jordan stated firmly, panic taking a firm hold and wrapping a tight fist around her.

"Jordan, I want our last moments together to be a time you'll remember for the rest of your life."

"OUR life, Aleksei. Don't you mean, OUR LIFE?" Jordan whispered, her eyes wide, fear clear in their green depths.

"My life is over, Jordan. You know that, even if you don't want to admit it. Our time together is over and now it's time for you to move on. I don't want you to waste your life mourning for what might have been. You're young, I want to see you fulfill your dreams."

"You're my dreams, Aleksei."

"Only one of them. You have other dreams to fulfill, other lives to touch. You can't move on, if you don't let me go. You have to let me go, Jordan."

"Not yet, Aleksei. Don't make me do this. I can't let you go—not yet!" she entreated, pulling him closer even as she felt him slipping from her grasp.

"Jordan, this isn't something I want. The very last thing I want to do is to leave you, but there are some things we have no control over. This is one of those things. It's time for you to stand-alone—to see how strong you are all by yourself. You don't need me, or Dee or Whittaker, you're stronger than you realize and it's time for you to show the world how great you really are."

"I can't do it—Aleksei. I can't do it without you," Jordan gasped.

"I won't be far, Jordan. Listen for the whispers on the ice, it'll be me right there beside you. I won't be far away. Every whisper you hear will be me telling you I love you."

"Aleksei, don't leave…" Jordan begged, her breath catching harshly as her throat closed, and tears coursed down her face.

Aleksei's hands held her face; his thumbs gently wiped the hot tears from her cheeks. As his tear filled ebony eyes held her deep green gaze, his mouth lowered and he gave her a sweet kiss, his own tears blending with hers. "I never wanted to leave you. Remember that, I didn't leave you willingly!" he stated fiercely, then kissed her a final time, all the passion he felt for her, and his anger at the unfairness of everything blending together until they were both gasping for breath.

"I love you, Jordan Jamison. I'll love you forever!" he whispered urgently, his eyes holding hers captive. "Never forget how much I love you. And listen for the whispers, each one will be telling you I'm right there beside you. When you hear them, close your eyes and I'll be there, holding you, loving you, for as long as you need me," He declared, a soft smile curving his lips. "Don't cry for me, my sweet. We'll be together again… I promise," he stated knowingly. "I love you, Jordan!" Aleksei's deep voice intoned emotionally as he slowly faded from her tear-filled view.

*   *   *   *   *

"Jordan…Jordan…" a male voice called, the sound faint at first, as if from far away then grew stronger. A hand shook her shoulder gently as she struggled to lift her head from where it lay against Aleksei's chest, her mind sluggish, refusing to clear as seemingly real images swirled madly through her mind. "Jordan, the people are here to take Aleksei's body to the mortuary. It's time to go," her doctor stated softly.

Jordan's eyes filled with tears as she nodded in understanding and allowed the doctor to help her to stand. "He's really gone, isn't he?" she asked in a small, pain-filled voice, her gaze wandering over Aleksei's handsome face.

"Yes," he answered simply, wondering yet again why bad things happened to good people, and if people couldn't learn how strong they were in another, less tragic manner.

"Aleksei came and told me good-bye. He said we'd be together again. He promised," Jordan offered, running her hand along his arm, up to his shoulder and with a final caress along his jaw line, bent over and kissed him good-bye. "Be seeing you, Rocmanov. I love you!" she whispered against his cheek, stood, and allowed the doctor to help her across the room.

Her doctor held the door open for her, and with a final glance over her shoulder, blew a kiss to Aleksei, and entered the hospital corridor. Two personnel from the mortuary stood beside a gurney, ready to enter the room that held Aleksei's body. Both men stood silent as they watched Jordan sway slightly, then catch herself, her chin lifting courageously as she shook her head at the doctor's offer to sit in the awaiting wheelchair.

Jordan turned her gaze on the two men, respectfully silent, and slowly walked the short distance to the gurney. "Take good care of Aleksei for me, please," she asked softly, tears filling her eyes and spilling onto her pale cheeks. "He was the best part of me."

"Yes, ma'am," the men replied in unison, nodding in understanding.

"Thank you," Jordan whispered in return, gracing them with the smallest of smiles before returning to her doctor, and sliding gracefully into the wheelchair.

The two men watched the doctor wheel Jordan down the long corridor, away from Aleksei and toward a new, uncharted life. Their eyes darkened in sadness as they watched her petite form disappear around the corner from their view, but they would always remember the haunted sadness in her deep green eyes, and soft smile of thanks.

"God bless you, Miss," one of the men offered into the silent corridor, hoping the blessing found it's way to her.

"Amen," his partner agreed, and the two made their way into the now darkened room that held the body of Aleksei Rocmanov.

Chapter 16

The winter sky had the look of impending snow, steel gray blending into ash white, the frigid wind whispered its nasty intentions, yet the lone figure, enveloped in a warm fur coat, sat unblinking on a stone bench gazing over the frozen lake in heart-broken silence. Had it really only been five days ago that she and Aleksei had gazed out across another frozen lake, had made love in the snow and skated together for the last time? Jordan felt numb; as frozen as the ice that stretched before her vision, beautiful to gaze at but ready to shatter like crystal at the least amount of pressure. Aleksei had always called her the strong one but she felt anything but strong today. Today there would be reporters and cameras and people to face, all wishing her well but all a constant reminder of what she had lost, what she wanted to forget, if only for an hour or two. She wondered if she should have taken up the offer her doctor had made her for a light sedative, something to knock back the pain when it felt overwhelming, a little pill to make her a little numb. Being numb had to be better than feeling as if she were going to explode at any moment. She couldn't deal with this feeling of being out of control and seriously wondered if being drugged was better than feeling this kind of pain. As she looked across the great expanse of ice before her, her eyes wide and unblinking, and listened intently, for the whispers that would tell her Aleksei was near. Deafening silence was all she heard.

"Jordan, the limo's here," Dee stated softly, her voice choked with sorrow, her eyes red from tears, still full of concern. Dee's words echoed ominously in the winter quiet as she looked out the back door to where the lone figure sat unmoving.

"How long has she been out there?" Whittaker asked quietly, peering over Dee's shoulder at Jordan.

The barely perceptible shrug said it all. Easily he turned her into his arms, hugging her tightly against his chest. "We'll make it through today…somehow," he stated, his voice fading into a whisper as he finished his statement.

"Will we? Will Jordan?" Dee asked brokenly, dabbing at her eyes with a damp, crushed Kleenex.

"She's stronger than both of us. Somewhere she'll find the strength."

"I hope you're right," Dee whispered, resting her forehead against his chin and trying to stop the tears that filled her eyes from falling.

"So am I," he answered simply, his voice husky. His own eyes filled with tears as he looked at Jordan's huddled, still form. "We'll give her another five minutes, then I'll go get her," he offered.

Nodding in agreement, she accepted Whittaker's soft kiss on her damp cheek and left to tell the limo driver they would be ready shortly. She could only hope it was so. But more than that, she hoped they would all survive this day, a day that should never have needed to be faced. A day they would all say good-bye to someone they had each loved in their own way. A day the world would watch Jordan say farewell to the skating partner she had found, the friend she had made, the man she had loved. The day Jordan Jamison would say good-bye to the life she had believed would last forever and take her first step alone toward the long journey that would be her future.

* * * * *

The church the limousine pulled up to was a small, quaint structure built of brick and covered with struggling vines that refused to go dormant despite the winter. The tall spire reached into the gray sky, it's lonely bell ringing sadly in the chill air, a somber reminder of death. Velvet ropes hanging from brass pedestals rested on either side of the stairs leaving a clear entrance up the stairs into the church and kept the growing crowd from invading the privacy of the famous expected to mourn the passing of Aleksei Rocmanov.

The crowd was large, yet subdued, and watched in both wonder and disbelief as limousine after limousine let out their famous occupants, now dressed in dark, somber colors that matched the mood of the occasion.

As the hour neared three o'clock, a long black limousine slowly pulled to the curb, parked and the driver opened the back passenger door. Whittaker slid from the limo and turned to assist Dee as she exited the warm interior, giving her hand a quick reassuring squeeze before turning his attention to Jordan. Dee waited quietly beside the limo.

"Ready?" he asked softly, offering his hand to her, their eyes meeting and holding, understanding the desire they each had to refuse to believe why they were here this day and yet each knowing they had to close this chapter of their lives.

"No," Jordan whispered brokenly, her eyes filling with tears even as her lungs refused to allow her to breath fully.

"Everyone will understand if you decide not to come in. You just got out of the hospital two days ago…"

Jordan shook her head from side to side and struggled to still the tears that threatened to overflow her forest green eyes. "Don't lie to me Whittaker. You and I both know no one would understand if I didn't go to Aleksei's funeral. Christ, Aleksei would never let me live it down if I didn't even give him the satisfaction of seeing me in this damn black dress."

"Aleksei always liked you in black. He once told me that when you wore black you were the sexiest woman he'd ever seen," he remembered fondly, a soft smile flickered across his lips.

"Sounds like some sexist remark he'd make," Jordan whispered past the painful lump in her throat, brushing away the tears that traced a path down her cheek. "I could have changed that chauvinistic attitude he had. In fact, he was coming along quite nicely. If I'd only had a little more time…" Jordan's voice trailed off brokenly.

"We all wish we'd had a little more time with him. But for whatever reason, our time together is over and we need to take the next step forward. It's time to say good-bye," Whittaker choked out deeply.

"I can't say good-bye, not again," Jordan moaned softly, feeling her heart break a little more as she looked toward the church.

Whittaker nodded in understanding. "No problem, Jordan. We won't say good-bye. How about, until later?"

Jordan nodded in agreement. "Until later. I like that. And we will see him later, won't we? God couldn't be so cruel as to keep us apart forever. Right?"

"No God that I pray to, Jordan. I swear to you, one day you'll look into someone's eyes and you'll see Aleksei smiling back at you. His soul is too special to keep locked away in heaven somewhere!" Whittaker stated firmly, believing in his heart the words he spoke to the petite woman before him.

Jordan cast the barest hint of a smile at the man whom Aleksei had loved like a father and placed her small hand into his larger one that waited patiently outstretched. With a gentle squeeze of reassurance, he pulled her gently out the door of the limo and to her feet, cautious of her injured shoulder and arm. Dee joined the pair and slowly made their way up the stairs and into the church.

Camera shutters clicked around them, the whirring sound of film winding forward and backward unusually loud in the cold, gray afternoon. Surprisingly enough, there were no calls from photographers to *look this way*. Somehow in death, it seemed, Aleksei demanded more respect than he ever had in life. Jordan remembered the time one obnoxious cameraman had demanded they stop while he photographed them and Aleksei had responded with an international gesture that everyone understood. After that, Jordan made sure that Aleksei always had his hands full carrying their luggage and skates and thereby made it impossible for him to be making any gestures at all. A soft, sweet smile touched her lips at the memory and she cast a loving look toward the darkening sky. The photographers caught this loving glance heavenward, and heartbreaking smile, and unknowingly Jordan took her first step toward independence. It was this picture that would grace the covers of numerous newspapers the next day, along with the accurately quoted headline, JORDAN'S FAREWELL TO ALEKSEI— 'UNTIL LATER, MY LOVE'.

Jordan, Whittaker and Dee entered the small church, their steps slowing as they joined the remaining mourners as they slipped silently into their seats. Acknowledgments were made in silence, a nod of the head, a squeeze of a hand, a soft smile. Jordan accepted the condolences silently, her composure holding precariously, her fingers playing with the pearl and diamond ring on her finger as she struggled to keep from falling apart. A priest appeared at Jordan's side and with a softly spoken question, guided Jordan toward the front of the church, where Aleksei's coffin lay draped in a blanket of gardenias, her favorite picture of him sitting atop the pewter casket. The priest held her steady when she stumbled slightly as she drew closer to his casket, offering encouragement and words she would never remember and then finally assisted her into the front pew. Whittaker and Dee followed behind and slipped in beside Jordan, their gazes traveling from Jordan to Aleksei's casket and back again.

The priest began the service and prayers were offered, songs were sung, those that had known and loved Aleksei Rocmanov spoke words of remembrance. Jordan struggled to keep from drowning in the tears that threatened to overwhelm her, her gaze on the circle of diamonds and pearls that circled her finger, Aleksei's final gift to her. As the priest asked if anyone else wished to speak, Jordan found herself standing and walking the short distance to stand beside Aleksei's casket, placing her hand on the cold surface. Beside it, she looked like a heartbroken child, but her words rang clear and strong in the silent room filled with those who had loved Aleksei.

"I want to thank all of you for coming here today. Aleksei is probably thinking all of us must have a better place to be than here, but I thank you all the same. All of you know how much Aleksei meant to me. Besides being my partner on the ice, he was my best friend, my biggest supporter and the one I loved most in this life. I can't imagine ever loving anyone again the way I love Aleksei. And so I can't—I won't—say good-bye to him. I'll simply say, until later, my love," Jordan finished softly, kissing Aleksei's coffin a last time and removing one gardenia from the blanket of gardenias adorning its surface.

The words of Celine Dion's *The Prayer* suddenly filled the room and she caught Whittaker's questioning glance, smiled in understanding and walked the few steps to meet him, sliding into his encompassing arms. The mourners filed forward, each taking a gardenia from atop Aleksei's casket and bidding their friend a final farewell. As the last notes of the beautiful music faded, Jordan ran her hand along his casket a last time and joined Whittaker and Dee as they walked through the outer doors of the church, and toward their respective futures.

* * * * *

Two weeks after the accident that shattered the future of Jordan and Aleksei, a package was delivered by Federal Express to Dee's residence addressed to Jordan. Dee signed the ever-present electronic clipboard and thanked the driver as she accepted the package and closed the door. "Jordan, a package just arrived for you," Dee called walking through the small living room and up the stairs toward the bedroom that Jordan occupied.

The door lay partially open, allowing only a thin stream of light from the hallway into the room, it's glowing touch missing the small figure that lay curled on the bed, covered with a down comforter. Dee glanced through the opening, shaking her head in concern and knocked softly against the gleaming white wood. "Jordan, something came for you. Federal Express just delivered it."

"Thanks, Dee. Just set it on the table please," Jordan responded quietly, without emotion.

Dee pushed the door open and moved to sit beside Jordan on the bed, pushing the tangled coppery curls from her cheeks and looking into her pale face. "Aren't you even a little curious what it might be?" Dee asked, waving the small package before her.

"Not now, maybe later," Jordan answered, pulling the comforter higher over her shoulder but not before Dee caught a glimpse of the sweater she was wearing that had belonged to Aleksei.

"I think you should see what it is now," Dee suggested, concern etching her eyes.

"What's the big deal? It will still be there tomorrow if I don't get to it this minute," Jordan mumbled, snuggling deeper into the comforter.

Dee groaned in frustration. Jordan hadn't left the house in the two weeks since the funeral, and worse, hadn't left her room for the past three days. Dee was worried about her health, both physically and mentally and wasn't ready to call in the professionals just yet. But her ideas were dwindling as to how to start a fire under Jordan and get her back to the business of living. Dee was the first one to admit that their lives were certainly different. There wasn't a day that went by that she didn't think about Aleksei. She'd find herself listening to music and begin planning their next program, only to suddenly realize there would be no more programs for the two of them. Their time and magic had ended sooner than anyone could have imagined, and despite the unfairness of it, it was time to start slowly moving forward. So far, Jordan was refusing to even attempt that first step, and Dee was growing concerned. Even Whittaker had commented on Jordan's loss of weight, and general loss of interest in everything. And now, as Dee looked at the small figure huddled beneath the huge comforter wearing her dead partner's sweater, she decided the time had come to force Jordan back into the living world, whether she wanted to be there or not.

"Fine, I'll open it," Dee stated, tearing the tape and opening the square box to reveal an unmarked videotape and small folded note. Dee unfolded the note and began to silently read the neatly written words before her, gasping in shock as the words before her sank in, her eyes filling with tears and blurring the contents of the note. "Dear, God…" she whispered, her fingers covering her lips to still their quivering.

Jordan heard Dee's shocked plea and slowly raised to her elbows, the comforter sliding down to her waist, the huge sweater swallowing up her petite frame. "What's wrong?" Jordan asked fearfully, her eyes wide and deep green.

Dee didn't answer. She handed Jordan the note, picked up the tape and walked the short distance to push it into the VCR, turned on the TV and walked back to sit on the bed beside Jordan, placing the remote in Jordan's lap.

Jordan watched Dee's trek to the TV and back and glanced in confusion at Dee's stunned expression, the note still unread in her hand. "Dee?"

"Read the note," Dee stated softly.

Jordan cast a final questioning glance at Dee and encouraged by Dee's nod of approval, turned her eyes toward the flowery sheet of paper and neatly written words that flowed across it's surface. It read:

Dear Ms. Jamison,

Words can never express our sadness at the loss of your partner, Aleksei Rocmanov. You probably don't even remember us—our meeting was so brief -and when I remind you of it, we hope it will not bring additional sadness to you for we met only moments before your accident. On a day that became so harrowing, we wouldn't blame you if you had forgotten meeting an old married couple in a diner. Surely, we ourselves, have met people briefly, and forgotten them soon after. But we wanted you to know how very special that brief encounter was to us, and wish you gentle, quiet days in which to heal your broken heart and soul.

We hope you will not think badly of us, but enclosed is a videotape which we hope will bring you a small amount of comfort. It was taken only days before of a pair of skaters we happened to see skating on the pond near our home. We did not know who they were, but we were entranced by the beauty of their skating, and the obvious love they shared for one another. Little did we know, those skaters would turn out to be you and Aleksei. We thought it was only right that you have this tape of the final performance of Jamison and Rocmanov. The memory of the beauty you shared with us will remain with us forever.

Thank you for your gift and may God bless you and keep you safe.

Most sincerely,
Nora and William Harrison

Jordan brushed the tears from her cheeks, her vision blurred and looked at Dee in disbelief. "How can this be?"

Dee shrugged and offered the remote to Jordan. "I don't know. Maybe one last gift from Aleksei," Dee suggested softly.

Jordan looked at the remote, apprehension clear in her dark green eyes. "I don't know if I can do this."

"Do you want me to leave?" Dee asked.

"No," Jordan answered firmly, shaking her head from side to side; her hands shaking as she started to reach for the remote then pulled back. "I'm afraid of what I'll see," her voice whispered.

Dee stroked her cheek, her thumb brushing away newly fallen tears. "What you're afraid of is admitting what you've lost. This is a gift,

Jordan, a gift most people would kill for. A last look at everything that was good, and happy between two people in love. Don't fear it, sweetheart, cherish it and know that you'll always have this final glimpse into the beauty and wonder that was Jamison and Rocmanov."

Jordan remained silent, her eyes closed as she struggled to still her fears and find the courage to face what lay before her. Moments later, she opened her eyes and Dee recognized the faint glimmer of determination in their green depths. "Are you ready?" Jordan asked quietly.

"Whenever you are," Dee agreed and held out her hand to Jordan. Their fingers slid together and held tightly as Jordan pushed the PLAY button on the remote and the TV/VCR combo came to life, the screen filling with the clear images of the final performance of Jordan Jamison and Aleksei Rocmanov.

Chapter 17

The blizzard began in earnest. Snow fell steadily, huge flakes that fluttered silently through the dark blue-black night and settled in shapeless mounds on the frozen earth. Towering pines surrounded the small cottage, struggling to hold their branches up as snow blanketed their outstretched limbs. The soft glow of candles in the windows of the cottage attested to yet another night without electricity due to the above-average snowfall. Still, to look at the cottage, one could feel the welcoming comfort of the cheerily burning fire in the large stone hearth as its flickering lights cast their glow through the night's darkness. A beacon of sanctuary and welcome in the swirling snow storm.

The cottage was small but cozy, consisting of one main room that held a huge fireplace, over-stuffed sofa, two wing chairs and assorted small tables, along with a kitchen and small eating area. The single bedroom, off to one side, boasted an antique wrought iron bed covered with a floral print comforter in muted shades of mauve, cream and jade, and the small adjoining bathroom held a cast iron stand-alone tub complete with claw feet. Though small, it was more than enough room for the lone woman who lounged silently on the cream colored over-stuffed sofa before the roaring fireplace, an open photo album resting on her lap, the soft strains of Tchaikovsky's Romeo and Juliet playing quietly in the background.

The woman inside was petite, her bone structure fine, falsely hinting at fragility, her complexion as smooth as rich cream. Her shoulder length hair waved in soft coppery curls, golden streaks threading highlights, showcasing large dark green eyes fringed with long black lashes, eyes that held too much sorrow for one so young. Her nose was small and straight, leading the eye toward full, rose colored lips that had rarely smiled in the past two years, and when they did showed a haunted smile despite her straight, white teeth. Dressed in simple chocolate brown leggings, a warm toffee colored cowl necked tunic sweater and wool socks, she looked much younger than her age of twenty-one.

Slowly she turned the pages. Her fingertips smoothing lovingly over the photographs before her, smiling wistfully at moments remembered the pictures brought to life, brushing away tears as she mourned, yet again, what could have been. The sudden shrill ring of the telephone seemed extraordinarily loud in the semi-silence, yet she didn't flinch at the noise and reached for the phone.

"Hello, Whittaker," she answered softly, knowing who was on the other end of the call. The same person had called her each January ninth for the past two years. Despite the interruption, her hands continued to trace the figures in the pictures before her.

"I heard the weather reports for your area and was worried about you. I knew the storm would knock your electricity out but I wasn't sure about the phones. How is everything, Jordan?" Whittaker asked, his voice deep and grave with concern.

"Electricity's out, as usual, but as you can tell, the phones are working fine," Jordan answered quietly, her pensive gaze still studying the photographs, her fingertips softly tracing the face of the man in the pictures, the man she had fought, laughed and cried with. The man she had loved more than life itself.

Whittaker frowned at the sadness in Jordan's voice, trying to keep his own tone light. "I imagine your place looks like some fairy land with all that snow and candlelight."

"Yeah, the way Aleksei always said a home should look. The way we'd talked about our home together looking before he…" she could barely tolerate finishing the thought let alone speak the words aloud.

"Before the accident," Whittaker supplied, shaking his head in sadness. Even two years later, it was impossible to believe something so magical had ended so abruptly. No warning—no foresight, simply a sudden, unexpected accident. An accident she would never understand. A tragedy she would never believe was for some greater purpose—there could be no plausible explanation for such waste. A tragedy that made the magical pairing of figure skaters Jordan Jamison and Aleksei Rocmanov into another tragic tale of sports legends. But more than that, a tale of beauty and love that had made the world a little more magical for a brief moment in time. A time when people envied the love and success they had found with one another and wished to experience the overwhelming emotions they saw pass between Aleksei and Jordan when they skated together, seeing only each other.

A time when the world had cheered with joy at the magic they cast when on the ice and awaited their upcoming chance for Olympic gold. When everyone waited to see where their blossoming love would lead them. Then suddenly, tragically, wept and mourned as a whole, for the loss of shared dreams, and wishes for a happy ending.

One moment magical—the next, gone forever.

"So how's Dee?" Whittaker inquired casually.

"Why ask me? You saw her just yesterday," Jordan stated impishly, a small smile curving her full lips.

"Oh, yeah. I forgot," Whittaker mumbled awkwardly.

"You forgot? Nice try, Whittaker. What's up?" Jordan chuckled, her smile widening as she came to a favorite picture of Aleksei in the album resting in her lap.

"What makes you think anything's up? I just called to see how you're doing, that's all."

"Right. I'm fine. Now, are you going to get around to mentioning the fact that you and Dee are coaching a new pair team, or do I have to actually catch you in the act doing it on the ice?" Jordan asked calmly, struggling to control the surge of threatening laughter straining to erupt.

"I'm not sure I heard you right. Jordan? Jordan? Are you there?" Whittaker banged the handset of the phone on the table.

"Whittaker, stop screwing around with me, and stop banging the damn phone on the table. You heard me just fine. I know all about your new team, and I think it's great. It's about time the two of you got back to work, and quit baby-sitting me," Jordan explained.

"We haven't been baby-sitting you. We just wanted to make sure you, ah, ah…" Whittaker's voice trailed off as he searched for a plausible explanation. In a way, it was true; he and Dee had been watching her closely over the last two years.

"It's okay. I love you both for all you've done for me. But it's time we all got back to the business of living. No matter how much I wish it otherwise, I can't bring Aleksei back. I can only thank him everyday of my life for what he gave me and keep his memory alive in any way I can," Jordan answered quietly.

"That's great, Jordan! Dee's going to be so damn happy to hear you're coming back to the ice. When can we expect you?"

"Hold on, Whittaker. I didn't say I was coming back to skate. You and Dee both know I haven't set foot on the ice in two years."

"That's okay. Give it a little time. You'll get your feet under you in no time!" Whittaker encouraged, trying to ignore the little red flag that he could hear in her voice.

"Whittaker, listen to me. I don't know if I'll ever skate competitively again. At this particular moment, I have no intention of ever skating pairs again. Once you've had the best, the idea of starting over is unbearable. And face it, I'm not exactly young anymore."

"Twenty-one isn't over the hill, Jordan."

"Not to a pair team that's been together for years, but it is to someone just starting out. Besides, Whittaker, my heart isn't into it the way it once was, and even if my body was willing, my soul isn't. It wouldn't be fair to a new partner to have to live up to a ghost that reminds me of his presence every time I stepped foot on the ice. I can't imagine someone else's hands touching me, and I'd be disappointed every time I turned to my partner expecting to see Aleksei's face and saw someone else. I'm sorry Whittaker," Jordan explained matter-of-factly.

"I understand. I think you're giving up too soon, but I understand. Maybe you'll be ready to give it a try again someday," Whittaker offered.

"Maybe," Jordan allowed.

"So what's your plan? You sound like you've got something going on in that pretty head of yours." Whittaker stated.

"I can't give up the ice completely, it's all I've ever really known. So I've decided to teach beginning skating to kids at the local ice house here in town."

Whittaker nearly choked. "Please tell me you're kidding, Jordan. That's a very noble thought, but your talent will be totally wasted on that ice."

"Whittaker, you're being a snob. I had my chance now it's my turn to help someone else. Just say 'welcome back to the living' and leave it at that."

"Have you mentioned your hare-brained plans to Dee yet? What's she think about this craziness?"

"She was the first one I ran the idea by. She thinks it's a wonderful idea and has even offered her spare time to help if I need her."

Terrific, she didn't say a damn thing about it to me. Why wasn't anything run by me for Christ's sake?"

"Whittaker, quit over-reacting. It's for this very reason we didn't say anything. We knew you'd go ballistic, the same way Aleksei and I knew you'd blow if we'd told you we were involved with each other. Some things are better left unsaid."

"Aleksei's got to be going nuts wondering what in the hell you think you're doing," Whittaker grumbled.

"That's not fair. Whether Aleksei would agree with me or not has absolutely no relevance to this decision. You, better than anyone, ought to know we didn't always agree. Besides, if he were here, I wouldn't have to make a decision like this. Hell, we wouldn't even be having this conversation! I'm doing the best I can. Everyone keeps saying it's time for me to move on, but now that I am, you're not happy with how I'm going about it. Well guess what, Whittaker? I don't give a flying fig if you're happy about it or not! I'm not ready to take a big step yet so you're just going to have to live with my baby-step, and if you can't then we don't have to associate anymore!" Jordan ended, emotion making her voice deeper.

"Jordan, calm down," Whittaker requested huskily, kicking himself for hurting her. "I was wrong to make such stupid comments. You know what's best for you and how much you can deal with. You go teach your young students. They'll never know what they're getting in you, but you do the best you can and you'll make me proud. And if you need me, you just call. Both Dee and I will be there for you whenever you need us."

"Thanks, Whittaker," Jordan whispered. "I'll call you in a week and let you know how things are going."

"Good, I'll look forward to the call. And, Jordan?"

"Yes."

"Thanks for loving Aleksei."

Jordan couldn't hold the tears back any longer, and struggled to control her voice as she quietly answered. "Loving Aleksei was the easiest thing I've ever done in my life. It's letting him go that's killing me."

"I know, Jordan. But when the time is right, you'll know. Until then, you keep on loving him."

"Forever, and always."

"Forever, and always," Whittaker agreed. "Good night, Jordan. I love you."

"I love you too. Sweet dreams," Jordan offered.
"You too," Whittaker suggested.
"I'll try," Jordan answered. "Good-bye." And quietly hung up the phone.

* * * * *

"Could you believe that snow on Friday? It took me the better part of the morning to dig my car out Saturday," a young man of seventeen commented to Jordan as he chipped away at the ice on the sidewalk in front of the entrance to the ice house. In a gallant gesture, he then held the door open for Jordan to enter the old building.

"It certainly reminded us that winter isn't through with us yet, didn't it?" Jordan answered, smiling shyly at the gangly youth in baggy jeans and huge winter jacket with a jester's cap in wild colors sitting jauntily on his head.

"I don't mind the snow, but I could certainly do without the ice. It's a bitch to break through. Oh, sorry about the language," he offered, his chagrined smile saying otherwise.

"No problem. I agree with you. Ice is meant for the rink and not sidewalks and streets," Jordan stated, glancing about uncertainly.

The young man watched her quietly, continuing to chip away at the stubborn ice covering the sidewalk in front of the doors. She certainly wasn't hard to look at, probably a new student, and from the looks of her, no more than sixteen years old tops. The thought of asking her out crossed his mind, and his smile widened at the possibility, his braces shining brightly in the sun. "You look a little lost. My name's George. Can I help you?" he asked, extending his hand in greeting.

Jordan looked at his outstretched hand, covered in a large red mitten and smiled. Anyone who wore red mittens couldn't be all-bad. "Hi, I'm Jordan. I'm looking for Cynthia Washington," Jordan offered, shaking his hand in greeting.

"Nice to meet you, Jordan. Chances are, Mom's on the ice making sure dad didn't drown the rink with too much water again. We've got a new Zamboni machine that he hasn't gotten the hang of yet."

Jordan's look of confusion gave George the impression she didn't have any idea what he was talking about so he went on to explain what the Zamboni machine was and what it's function was. Clearly, she was a new comer to figure skating, as far as he was concerned. Still, he figured the way she looked, it didn't matter if she could skate or not, no one would be looking at her feet anyway.

"You said your Mom's probably on the ice? Which way would that be? I was supposed to meet her at seven-thirty, but the roads were a lot worse than I thought they'd be. I'm sorry I'm late."

"I wouldn't worry about being late. I could count the times my Mom's been on time for things on one hand, and that would be being generous!" George quipped, setting the ice-chipper blade aside and moving to hold the inner door open for Jordan. "Let's go find Mom and she can get you started on your lesson. Is this your first time on skates?"

"My first time on skates?" Jordan asked in confusion.

"Yeah, you have the scared, glazed look of a new student. I just figured it was your first time, that's all."

Jordan laughed at the apt description, considering the apprehension she felt at the prospect of being back on the ice, she wasn't surprised her expression sent the same message. Aleksei had always said her emotions were out there for all to see, apparently, they still were. "I suppose it's sort of my first time. I've been off the ice for a long time," Jordan offered carefully.

"Bad injury, huh? Sorry to hear that, but, heh, you're back and that's what counts," George stated encouragingly.

"Yeah, that's what counts," Jordan agreed softly, hoping it was true and wondering for the millionth time if getting back on the ice was the right thing to do.

George continued to talk, non-stop, leading Jordan through the interior of the old building, pointing out the various rinks, three in all, the locker rooms, bathrooms and his favorite spot, the snack bar, stopping to reach over the counter and grab a donut out of a Tupperware container.

Jordan smiled at his youthful exuberance and wondered if she'd ever been that carefree and happy. The last two years had passed in excruciatingly slow motion. Every night's sleep brought dreams of each moment she spent with Aleksei, replaying in her mind over and over, calming and comforting yet leaving her empty, cold and exhausted each morning when she awoke and had to return to reality. Aleksei was gone, and with him her happiness. She'd spent two years trying to find a way to be happy off the ice and hadn't. Maybe she would find it back on the ice. Aleksei had told her to listen for the whispers on the ice and yet it had taken her two years to gather up the courage to step back onto the very place the two of them had loved with all their hearts and seek him out. He was here; she could feel him drawing her ever closer to the ice, to him.

"Here were are. See? I told you. There's Mom, checking out the ice," George stated knowingly, pointing toward the far end of the rink where a skater carefully checked the ice. "Mom, Jordan's here," George called loudly, his voice echoing off the high ceiling. "God, I love the smell of ice!" he quipped, taking a deep breath of the cold air.

"Georgie, go help your father with that machine, please. He's still flooding the ice!" Cynthia Washington said, her voice carrying across the rink and reaching his ears before she slid to a graceful stop at the doorway and stepped onto the rubber mat, pulling her son into her arms and hugging him tightly. "Thanks, sweetie."

"Mom…" George complained, returning the hug.

"Don't 'Mom' me. Go save our Zamboni," Cynthia encouraged, pushing him in the direction of a large set of double doors, her smile widening when she heard her son groan 'Dad!' upon seeing their new machine with it's hood open and his father holding a wrench.

"He's a great kid," Jordan offered, her eyes widening at the sound of tools hitting the cement floor and a wail of pain.

"Yeah, he is. And, thank God, a great mechanic. Unlike his father who isn't sure which end of a nail to hit. But then, I didn't marry him for his mechanical abilities!" Cynthia stated, wiggling her eyebrows humorously.

"You haven't changed one bit," Jordan stated, walking into Cynthia's outstretched arms and accepting her hug of welcome.

Jordan and Cynthia had become friends several years before when Cynthia had coached at the same rink Jordan had trained at. Jordan still was amazed that the young man who had just left to rescue his mother's Zamboni machine had once chased her around the ice when she was only twelve.

"Oh, yes I have. You're just too nice to notice. But you've changed," Cynthia held her at arms length, studying her from head to toe and back up again. "You've lost weight."

"Not enough to count."

"When there wasn't much there to start, every little bit counts. And your eyes, they're older. Does that make sense? I don't know if that's possible. Can eyes age?" Cynthia babbled, watching Jordan's eyes darken to a deep green as her emotions rolled over her like a huge wave. "Talk to me Jordan," Cynthia urged.

Jordan was silent for a moment, gathering her thoughts and her courage as she tried to put her thoughts into words. "I've spent the last two years afraid to step foot on the ice because I was terrified of being alone on it. So I spent all that time away from the very place that made Aleksei and I the happiest. The ice is where we fell in love, you would think I would want to be on the ice more than anywhere else in the world. But now it's as if something is drawing me here."

"What makes you say that?" Cynthia asked.

"I've never dreamed of skating alone in my life. There was always a partner at my side. But lately..." Jordan trailed off, running her hands through her hair, then shrugging her shoulders, "I've dreamed of being on the ice alone. Not competing or anything, but standing back and watching. I don't know. Teaching maybe? I don't know, Cynthia. None of this makes any sense at all. I'm so confused it's ridiculous. Maybe Whittaker's right, he thinks I'm nuts."

"Screw, Whittaker. You do what you want to do and don't let anyone tell you otherwise!" Cynthia stated firmly, smiling at Jordan's shocked expression. "Don't go soft on me, Jamison. Tell me, when was the last time you put those on?" Cynthia nodded toward the bag looped over Jordan's shoulder that held her skates.

"The day before the accident," Jordan answered dully.

"Tell you what. You get yourself a cup of coca and sit down while I go sharpen those blades and then we can see how much you remember," Cynthia suggested easily. Taking the bag from Jordan's shoulder, she pulled her behind her in the direction of the snack bar where she left her with her cocoa and headed back toward the double doors to the sharpening wheel where she carefully sharpened the expensive blades into perfectly balanced edges.

"How's your new student?" George asked over her shoulder, whistling in surprise as he viewed the expensive skates. "Hey Mom, those aren't beginner skates. Someone sold her up the river."

"Sssh. You make me screw up these blades, you're paying to replace them."

"You'd have to give me a raise then. Those blades are top of the line. Why would someone sell a beginner such expensive skates?" George persisted.

"Georgie, you talk too much. Is our Zamboni machine still alive?"

"Yeah, Dad was just checking the oil."

"You just changed it two days ago. Why did he think it needed to be checked? No, don't tell me, I don't want to know. How could I marry someone so un-mechanically inclined? No, don't tell me, I don't want to know."

"Mom, you're losing it. You want me to finish sharpening those blades?" George asked, anxious to get his hands on the gleaming metal.

"No, they're done. But thanks anyway." his mother offered, kissing him quickly on the cheek. "Now you stay out of trouble for a while. Jordan's been off the ice for a long time and she's more than a little nervous about getting out there again. I don't want to add any pressure by having any extra bodies watching her."

"Boy, it must have been a really bad injury to make her this anxious," George suggested.

Cynthia looked into her son's blue eyes and saw his compassion and understanding. "Yeah, Georgie, the worst kind. Be good now!" And with a final quick kiss to his cheek, returned to the snack bar and held the newly sharpened skates out to Jordan. "Ready?"

Jordan looked at her skates, her expression clearly stating she wasn't at all sure this was the wisest decision she had ever made. "I don't know."

"Good. Let's go!" Cynthia stated, grabbing her hand and pulling her to her feet. "The ice is perfect and calling our names."

"I thought your husband flooded the rink."

"That was last week. This week, the ice is perfect!"

"I really don't know if I can do this."

Cynthia stopped and turned to look into Jordan's tear-filled eyes. "Aleksei's waiting for you out there. How much longer do you intend to make him wait? Think about it and let me know. I'll be on the ice," she stated softly.

Jordan closed her eyes and breathed deeply. A sweet calm swept over her and what felt like a gentle kiss against her temple. A deep voice whispered her name softly against her ear, the curls at her temple rustling gently. "Aleksei," she whispered in return. Opening her eyes, she found herself alone. Cynthia was at the far end of the ice, too far to have been the one calling her name, and the voice she'd heard was lovingly familiar. With a quick glance at the skates she held in her hand, she walked determinedly to the bleachers, sat down and slipped into them.

The routine, familiar and comforting, returned to her as if she'd only been off the ice for two days instead of two years. Slowly she stood, wiggling her ankles and toes; her feet adjusting to the contours of the worn leather like old friends greeting each other. Slowly she walked to the doorway leading to the ice, her balance sure, her stride confident.

Cynthia watched her from across the rink, smiling to herself as she watched Jordan return to where she belonged. "Are you coming or not?"

"Yes," Jordan answered in a single word as she stepped onto the ice and glided across the shining surface, her feet secure beneath her, her center of gravity solid and un-shifting. Jordan breathed deeply, the chill smell of ice an aphrodisiac to her senses and suddenly she felt the urge to spread her arms and laugh out loud. She glided across the ice, the breeze she created stirring the copper-colored curls and sending them dancing. She picked up speed, flying across the ice, her soul free for the first time in two years and lifted her leg into a high spiral, her arms spread wide. And suddenly she could feel Aleksei's hands at her waist then sliding up her arms, his fingers lacing with hers. She felt the strength of his chest against her back, her leg stretched against his in the air. She could smell the masculine scent of his after-shave and knew in her heart her decision to return to the ice was the right one and this was Aleksei's way of giving her his blessing. She clearly heard Aleksei's voice whisper '*I love you, Jordan. Now off you go*' before feeling him push her forward away from him, sending her flying across the ice when she had been drifting slowly to a stop.

George had snuck into the arena, keeping out of sight of both women and watched Jordan gliding across the ice, amazed at her obvious ability. This was no beginner. When his mother caught sight of him, she walked to his side, wrapping her arm about his waist and together they watched Jordan fly over the glassy surface. Both watched Jordan's perfect spiral position in awe and both gasped in astonishment when she was suddenly propelled forward without changing her spiral position or taking another stroke, as if someone had pushed her physically forward.

"Mom, what was that?" George asked quietly, his voice a bit shaky.

"My guess would be Aleksei," Cynthia stated simply, casting a quick glance toward heaven and whispering *thank you*.

"Aleksei? You mean Aleksei Rocmanov?" He'd heard stories of the famous pair team from his mother until he could recite everything there was to know about them in his sleep.

"The one and the same."

"Come on, Mom. He's been dead for a couple of years now."

"I know," she replied easily.

"You mean to tell me you believe we've got the ghost of Aleksei Rocmanov on our ice? You've got to be kidding!" George scoffed, shaking his head in disbelief.

"Why not? We've got Jordan Jamison on our ice. Why is it so impossible to believe that Aleksei might still be around?"

"Jordan Jamison? Now you are nuts. When has Jordan Jamison ever been on our ice?"

"Take a good look, Georgie. You and I are seeing Jordan Jamison's return to the ice and if I'm not mistaken, what we just witnessed was Aleksei's final appearance with the love of his life."

"You don't really believe in ghosts now, do you Mom?"

"Is it really so impossible to believe there might be something for us after we die. I find it comforting to know that those we love and lose are still out there somewhere watching out for us; guiding us; keeping us on track."

"I guess it's possible. I never really thought much about it," George admitted.

"Well think about it, Georgie and hope I live a long time. Because, my sweet son, I'm going to tail you through all eternity!" she swore to her son, laughing softly at his horrified expression.

"Great—just great," George mumbled as he slipped away from his mother and left her watching Jordan continue to fly across the ice, her soul free and happy.

"Welcome back, Jordan," Cynthia whispered, smiling as she watched Jordan's face light up with joy and blew a kiss toward heaven. "See you later, Aleksei."

With a flip of a switch, she turned on the sound system, cranking up the volume so the rock and roll music shook the walls and returned to the ice, her voice rising over the blasting music. "Okay, Jordan. Time to kick a little ass!" and the two friends began a friendly competition between themselves, laughing and teasing and trying to out-do one another and, when necessary, hoisting the other one back to her feet after a spill.

It was a day Jordan would never forget.

Chapter 18

"Megan, get your chin up, sweetie, you're looking at your feet again. Trust me, they're still there—you don't have to keep checking on them!" Jordan called across the rink to her young student practicing her back crossovers. "Bend your knees a little more and sit into it, Megan," she encouraged, cringing a bit when her student lost her balance and waved her arms wildly before regaining control on the icy surface.

"That was close," Jordan offered, skating to meet Megan at the far end of the rink. "That's why I said to sit into it. When your knees are bent and you're seated you always have room to stand up and regain your center, your balance. But when you're already standing straight up there is no where to go but down, and we both know, you don't like going down."

"I know, I know. But I feel like my butt's sticking out when I'm seated," Megan complained.

"Sweetheart, you're twelve years old. You don't have a butt to worry about yet!" Jordan teased, flicking her nose playfully.

"I do too! It's just a small one," Megan shot back, turning around and wiggling her tiny rear end at her teacher and coach.

"I stand corrected," Jordan amended, pulling Megan into her arms for a quick hug. "Tell you what, because you're doing so great today, why don't you do a final quick run through of your program and we'll call it a day."

"Do I have to? Jeez, Jordan, you run me into the ground. I am, after all, only twelve," Megan grumbled.

"You're right," Jordan shrugged. "There's still another three weeks before the show. You can probably skate this program in your sleep so I suppose you're right, you don't need the practice. So I tell you what I'll do. I'll skate your program for you, sort of give you some ideas what I'd like it to look like, and then you can skate it for me and we'll compare the two performances and see what needs to be worked on. How's that sound?" Jordan asked.

"Like a set up," Megan complained.

"You're too smart for me. So how about it, do we each take a turn or should we do it together?"

"Next to you, I'll look terrible…"

"You never look terrible," Jordan interrupted. "You're a beautiful skater, Megan, and don't you dare let anyone make you believe otherwise. Every skater is special in his or her own way, you happen to be a beautiful spinner and have a spiral worth killing for. Don't you ever let me hear you down-talking yourself! Got it?" Jordan demanded in exasperation. Damn, pre-teens were a lot of work. Maybe she should rethink taking on the coaching job of two sixteen year olds that had been writing to her for months in the hopes of having her coach them.

"Okay, okay. I'm wonderful," Megan rolled her eyes in exaggeration, laughing at Jordan's mild attempt to look stern. "Still, I want to see what my program should look like."

"Not what it *should* look like but what it looks like when I skate it. You have all the moves down, Megan. You just have to let the music into your heart and let your soul lead you. Now, you go take care of the music," Jordan pushed her student toward the CD player at the edge of the rink.

Jordan skated to center ice, bending and stretching as she went and assumed the program's starting position. With a quick glance over her shoulder, she nodded her head in readiness.

Megan pushed the play button and soon the rock and roll lyrics of *The Backstreet Boys* music filled the rink. Megan sang along as the *Boys* pleaded 'Hey, Mr. D.J. keep playing that song for me' echoed off the rafters, it's sensual tempo matching Jordan's steps as she stroked and turned and jumped to it's beat. Her long legs and powerful strokes ate up the ice as she sped across its glossy surface.

Megan watched, totally fascinated and amazed at the speed and ease with which her coach flew through the routine, mentally making notes of hand and body movements she would borrow from her coach. The door behind her whooshed closed but Megan kept her eyes on the ice, enraptured.

"Hey, Meg," George called softly, his eyes catching sight of Jordan as she flew across the ice in a perfect spread eagle position, her arms lifting seductively over her head. George shook his head, amazed yet again at the glory that was Jordan. "Takes your breath away, doesn't she?" George stated.

The door behind them opened again, a clamoring of hockey bags loaded with equipment and sticks banged as the large man shoved everything through the partially opened door and dropped everything on the floor.

"Shit!" the man bearing the load growled, his voice deep yet tinged in humor.

"Nice move, Nick. You that good on the ice?" George teased, moving forward to hoist a couple of bags off the floor.

"Screw you," the deep voice answered on a chuckle.

"Hey, watch it. There're kids in here," George nodded toward Megan.

"Sorry, kid," Nick apologized, casting a brief glance at the young girl leaning against the rink's wall. Skinny as a rail he thought, and totally absorbed watching the skater on the ice. How anyone could get that caught up watching someone dance around the ice was a mystery to him. He'd take hockey any day—now that was a sport!

Nick finished gathering up his fallen hockey equipment, swinging the last large bag over his shoulder as he stood up. Effortlessly he shouldered the large, heavy bag, his muscles rippling as he settled it into place, the hockey sticks banged together noisily.

"Sshh," Megan hissed over her shoulder, her eyes widening in surprise when she caught sight of the man loaded down with hockey gear who looked at her in return. The man was huge—and gorgeous!

Nick cast a quick, dazzling smile at her, showing lots of white teeth and deep dimples. Her response to seeing him was typical; most people had the same amazed expression in their eyes when they first saw him. He'd long ago given up trying to *blend* with the crowd. At six foot four inches tall, the only people he *blended* with were the ones he played basketball with when he wasn't playing hockey. His broad shoulders and muscular build could have taken him on to professional football if he hadn't torn his left knee apart his senior year in college. And if his muscular physique wasn't enough to catch the attention of people, his blue eyes finished the job, whether shining a bright sky blue in humor or flashing a deep sapphire in anger or passion, they were eyes not easily forgotten. His wavy light brown hair gleamed with golden highlights, a testament to time spent outdoors.

"Sorry," Nick whispered in apology.

Megan cast a last glance over her shoulder and returned her gaze to the ice.

Nick followed Megan's gaze and caught sight of the small figure on the far side of the ice executing a beautiful layback spin. Nick watched silently, drawn in by the beauty of the skater before him, amazed at the strength and stamina she displayed as she continued the program, seemingly without effort or strain. In the past he'd always thought figure skating was for wimps, but watching this slip of a girl fly across the ice at full speed made him wonder if he'd been wrong.

"Amazing, isn't she?" George asked.

Nick nodded in agreement, unaware he held his breath as he watched her fly across the ice, leap into the air and turn three revolutions then land on one foot having successfully landed a triple axel. "Damn," Nick mumbled to himself, astounded at her ability, but mostly, her courage to try such a move. He couldn't imagine falling on the ice at that speed let alone throwing a jump in for good measure. "She's so small. Is she old enough to be doing that stuff?" Nick questioned.

Megan gave him a look that clearly stated she thought he was crazy. "I wouldn't recommend you let her hear you saying that. She's very opinionated about her stature!" Megan explained.

"She's only a kid. Is it safe for her to be doing that?" Nick questioned again, cringing after she landed another high jump.

"She knows what she's doing. She's been doing it for years," Megan explained casually.

"She's not old enough to have been doing it for *years!*" Nick stated, a strange urge to keep the small figure on the ice safe washing over him. The seductive lyrics of the song suddenly sunk in and he turned in disbelief toward George. "Jesus, George. Do you hear those words? What parent in their right mind would let their kid skate to music like that?"

"All the kids are listening to that music, Nick. It's the *Backstreet Boys*. It's a song, buddy, not the story of her life," George answered, bewildered at his friend's unusual behavior

Nick continued to watch Jordan, mesmerized by the way her body moved, confused by the way she effected him. "Who is she?" he finally asked.

"J.J.," Megan answered, her tone reverent, her awe obvious.

"J.J.?" Nick questioned quietly, his tone a bit confused.

"Jordan Jamison," George offered.

Nick heard George's statement as if from far away, then his left leg suddenly started to ache and he shifted his weight to the right side, rubbing the muscles above his left knee. A strange feeling washed over him leaving him dizzy and flushed, a shower of glittering lights flickered before his eyes for a moment and then vanished as quickly as they appeared. Nick shook his head to clear his vision, wobbling slightly under the weight of the heavy bag on his shoulder.

"Hold on there, pal," George urged, struggling to steady his friend as he watched him sway from side to side, grunting and straining when Nick leaned heavily against his much smaller form. "Damn, Nick, you need to go on a diet." He groaned.

In short order the dizziness passed and Nick looked dazed, confusion clear in his blue eyes. It felt as if his dizzy spell had lasted for hours but only seconds had passed.

"What was that?" George asked, concern and bafflement blending.

"That hasn't happened in a while," Nick mumbled cryptically.

"What 'that'? What the hell are you talking about?" George asked firmly.

"Sshh. There're kids here," Nick reminded him, nodding toward Megan who cast them occasional interested glances.

"Tough shit! What the hell was that little episode all about?" George persisted.

Nick heaved a sigh, his head clear again, only the line of sweat dripping down his spine remained from his dizzy spell. So what was the best way to explain this sort of thing to George without making him think he was stark raving nuts? "It's kind of a long story."

"Yeah, well, lucky for you, I've got nothing but time!" George stated.

"It's really not all that interesting," Nick offered nonchalantly.

"Try me—I'm into weird happenings."

"I don't remember mentioning the word 'weird'."

"No, you didn't. But your whole 'thing' looked pretty weird to me so I'll call it 'weird'!"

"You're being melodramatic, George."

"You nearly crushed me under your forty tons of muscle and now you're telling me it was nothing? It didn't look like *nothing* to me, now quit mucking around and spill it!" George demanded firmly.

Nick saw, and understood, the determined look in his friend's eyes, saw the concern, also, and decided to *spill it* as George had so succinctly suggested. "You're not going to believe this," Nick stated.

"Let me decide what I believe and what I don't. I just want to know if I'm going to have to be hauling your sorry ass off the ice on a regular basis," George returned.

"Okay, fine," Nick sighed deeply, ran his hands through his hair, cast a final glance toward the ice where Jordan was finishing her program and proceeded to tell George his story.

* * * * *

Jordan's t-stop caused a rooster tail of ice crystals to trail her as she slid to a stop next to the wall where Megan stood. "Okay, your turn," Jordan stated, her rapid breathing making little puffs of clouds in the cold air.

"I don't know…" Megan began to stall.

"No you don't—we made a bargain. It's your turn. Now go show me how it's done!" Jordan urged, pushing her toward the center of the ice and walking to the CD player. On Megan's cue, she pushed the PLAY button and watched her student skate the same program, smiling as she noticed the *borrowed* moves she had performed only moments before. As she watched Megan move across the ice, a tingling sensation ran up her spine, like fingers grazing sensually against her skin, like Aleksei had done so long ago. She glanced over her shoulder, noticed George talking to a tall man with very broad shoulders and light brown hair with his back to her. Shaking off the odd sensation, Jordan returned her attention to Megan and watched her work her way toward her final jump, a double toe loop. As Megan reached back to dig her toe-pick into the ice, she lost the edge on her supporting leg and hit the ice hard, sliding into the boards knee first and collapsed to the ice. Jordan was on the ice before Megan came to a stop, skating as fast as she could to her student's side and sliding to a stop beside her, then kneeling onto the ice.

"Talk to me Megan. Where does it hurt?" Jordan asked calmly, taking Megan's face in her hands and looking into her eyes. "Focus, sweetie. Look at me and breathe—real slow. In through the nose—out through the mouth. Come on do it with me," Jordan urged, catching a glimpse of George and the man he'd been speaking with coming across the ice toward them. "How you doing, Megan?"

"Crappy! You know I hate to fall," Megan complained, wiping away tears on her cheeks.

"Do we need the stretcher?" George asked, reaching their side, Nick right behind him.

"How's the knee feel, Megan? Do you think you can move it?" Jordan asked, remembering the number of times she'd found the ice with her knees and knowing how black and blue Megan's would be shortly.

"Lay her down on her side and have her try to straighten it first, she shouldn't wrench the joint from side to side if she can avoid it," Nick's deep voice suggested from behind, out of her line of vision.

Jordan looked at George, kneeling beside her and raised her eyebrows in question. "He's had enough surgery on his knees to make me listen to him," George offered on a shrug.

"Okay, Megan. Let's lay you down then. George, we need a blanket or something," Jordan stated, flinching when a still-warm flannel shirt fell in her lap, it's spicy scent teasing her senses.

Jordan spread the shirt on the ice beneath Megan and helped her lay down; lifting her hips slightly while George slipped the tails of the shirt beneath her. "Okay, sweetie, whenever you're ready, see if you can straighten your knee."

Megan looked at the three adults surrounding her, their faces filled with concern and smiled tentatively. Slowly she straightened her leg, expecting to feel shooting pains but instead only felt a minor throbbing. "No sweat," she stated, a nervous giggle escaping as she sighed in relief.

"All right, that's great!" Jordan stated, releasing her own held breath. "George, help me get her up, please," Jordan requested, slipping under Megan's left arm and crossing it over her shoulder and watching as George did the same on Megan's right side. "Okay, on the count of two, lift straight up. Megan, I don't want any weight on that left leg at all," Jordan instructed.

"No problem there," Megan agreed, looking from Jordan to George. "

"Hang on, Megan. George, slow and easy please," Jordan stated calmly. "One, two, lift…" Jordan counted and the two slowly lifted Megan to her feet.

"How you doing, Meg?" George asked, moving slowly forward on Jordan's command, careful not to jostle Megan too much.

"Great," Megan sighed, casting a longing glance at George.

Jordan smiled at Megan's wistful gaze, still wondering how George could be so oblivious to Megan's obvious feelings for him. For the past three months she'd always brought cookies or his favorite cake into him every time she came to the rink, which was almost daily. Jordan was beginning to think the only way George would realize Megan's crush on him was to hit him over the head with his hockey stick and tell him. Still, it was awfully cute to see Megan's eyes light up whenever she saw him, her shy smiles and accidental bumps against him making her sigh in pleasure. Jordan remembered feeling the same way about Aleksei all those years ago, when she'd been twelve, only Aleksei had literally knocked her on her butt—no gentle nudge for her. Briefly she wondered if she'd ever feel that way again.

Tingles ran up her spine again, making her shiver and drew Megan's attention. "You okay?" Megan asked, her arms still draped across Jordan and George's shoulders.

Jordan nodded yes. "Just a chill, sweetie," She answered with a smile. "How about you? How are you doing?"

"Fine, honest. My knee hardly hurts at all," Megan answered softly as they reached the exit off the ice, and stepped carefully onto the rubber flooring. Megan cast another shy glance toward George, who, as usual, was oblivious.

"I'm glad to hear that. Still, I want George to help you to the office. When I get there, I want to see your butt down, your leg up and a pile of ice on that knee. Got it?" Jordan stated, tapping Megan's nose.

"Yes, ma'am," Megan replied, rolling her eyes in exasperation.

"Don't ma'am me. I'm not old enough to be a ma'am," Jordan complained teasingly.

"It's a sign of respect," Megan offered.

"Well, I don't want that much respect—yet," Jordan fired back, slipping out from under Megan's arm and holding her steady while George pushed the forgotten hockey gear away from the door.

"Nick, give me ten—make that fifteen—minutes. Why don't you go get something to drink? I'll meet you at the snack bar," George called to Nick as he crossed the ice, returned to Megan and lifted her into his arms, cautious of her left leg and backed through the door. Jordan smiled at Megan's beaming face as George carried her toward the office, shaking her head in amusement.

"No problem. I'll be here," Nick's deep voice answered behind Jordan, startling her and making her twist as she sought its source. Her toe-pick caught the rubber mat, stopping her feet even as her body continued it's forward motion toward the pile of bags that George had just kicked away from the door. Her arms flailed wildly as she tried to break her fall, unsuccessfully and she landed in the pile of hockey gear with a thud.

Nick moved as quickly as he could, the remaining feet off the ice, to view her landing face first into the pile of bags and hockey sticks. His first thought, when he saw her lying across the bags was she had a nice ass, a *really* nice ass. His second thought was how to go about the business of getting her untangled from the mess of sticks and bags on the floor.

"You okay?" Nick called to the small figure lying on the pile before him.

"Just dandy!" came a mumbled reply tinged with heat. "When I get hold of George, he's going to wish he'd never heard of hockey."

"I hate to ruin your plans to kill, maim and destroy, but this gear's mine. George was just helping me with it when—is it Megan?—fell and we came to help," Nick explained haltingly, wondering why he felt so nervous around this slip of a girl.

"Ah. Then I guess my actual target to *kill, maim and destroy* is you, isn't it?" Jordan questioned, her frustration mounting when the blade on her right skate got caught on a strap and she couldn't roll over. "Would you please get that damn strap off my skate? So help me God, if these blades are nicked you're dead meat for sure!"

Nick removed the tangled strap and watched as Jordan rolled to her back, her bottom sinking between two large bags and effectively trapping her.

Briefly she struggled to lift her bottom up over the bags, but her movements did nothing more than cause her hair to fall into her face and wedge her deeper into the offending hockey gear. Heaving a sigh of exasperation, she expectantly held out her hand, anticipating an immediate hand to pull her out of the mess that seemed to be swallowing her. In frustration she brushed her hair from her eyes and looked up hoping to see the *never seen before Nick* with his hand ready to pull her up. The sight that greeted her was overwhelmingly male, broad shoulders, gorgeous face and the same sexy smell that had assailed her from the shirt he once again wore, despite the wet spots from the ice.

Nick froze as Jordan swept the shades of copper waves from her eyes and looked up at him expectantly, her deep green eyes blazing in anger. "You're not a kid!" He accused huskily.

"Who said I was?" Jordan fired back heatedly, her eyes held captive as she watched his go from sky blue to deep sapphire.

"You looked like one on the ice."

"Well I'd suggest you get your eyes checked, because obviously, I'm not! Are you going to help me up or not?" Jordan fumed, holding her hand out and wiggling her fingers.

"Shit!" Nick growled, taking her hand and hauling her to her feet, groaning when he pulled too hard and she fell heavily against his chest, the top of her head only reaching the top of his shoulder.

"Gee, thanks," Jordan hissed, trying to step away from his towering form and the heat that seemed to pulse from him, nearly falling back into the pile until Nick grabbed her arms and pulled her back against him, groaning as he felt the fronts of their bodies meet.

"I thought you wanted out of the pile?" he growled, taking a step back to give her some room, his hands still holding her arms, searing her with their heat.

"I did, but I didn't expect to be mauled on the way out!" Jordan complained, pulling from his grasp and attempting to step around him, her breath catching when her breast brushed against his muscular arm, her skin tingling in response. "I've got to go see to Megan," Jordan offered weakly, her blood suddenly rushing through her veins, feelings long buried struggling to surface.

"It's always nice to be appreciated," Nick stated sarcastically, stepping aside and bowing gallantly despite his desire to throttle her. "Later, brat," he stated softly, his deep voice a velvet caress.

A wave of long remembered feelings washed over her at his words, making her dizzy and flushed, made her heart pound so quickly she could barely breath. "What?" she asked softly, holding the door for support when her legs threatened to give way beneath her.

"I said I'll see you later," Nick answered, his sapphire blue eyes memorizing her face; a face he felt he knew, but didn't know.

"What makes you think that?" Jordan asked, her mind refusing to clear away the dizziness that made her slightly light headed and off balance, like one too many glasses of wine made you heady.

"I'm the new hockey coach," Nick stated simply, walking forward to stand before Jordan where she still leaned against the door. "Nicholas Devon, nice to meet you," he stated, offering his hand to her in greeting.

Jordan looked at his hand, large and long-fingered, calluses on his palm, a working man's hand. Slowly she slid her hand into his, gasping as his fingers closed around it, stunned at the jolt of electricity that ran up her arm at his touch. Leaning her head back, she looked into his face, noted his own stunned look and gazed deeply into his eyes, sapphire blue and forest green meeting. "Jordan Jamison. Welcome," she voiced softly, swaying toward him as if drawn to him magically before fighting the urge to lay her cheek against his chest and close her eyes. Memories of Aleksei swamped her, filling her eyes with tears. With a last look, she slid her hand from his, sighing wistfully when their fingers brushed apart and walked quickly, and a bit unsteadily, toward the office.

Nick watched her departure, completely baffled and confused by their encounter yet still appreciative of the view she presented as she walked away from him. *Save me!* He muttered to himself and the silence around him. This made no sense at all. Three years ago his life had changed when he'd undergone simple knee surgery—or what should have been simple knee surgery. Only after the fact, was he told that he'd had a nearly fatal reaction to the anesthetic they'd used. He had, in fact, been officially dead on the table for two and a half minutes before the doctors had managed to bring him back. And it was during that two and a half minutes that things had gotten really *weird*. He remembered flashes of pictures, like a slide show gone amuck, and snatches of words—maybe names—but he couldn't be sure. Vague images of a young man with dark hair and flashing eyes, a ready smile. Feelings of something left unfinished, unfulfilled. The whole thing made absolutely no sense. But after the surgery, when his knee had fully recovered, all he wanted to do was get on the ice, something he hadn't done in ten years, not since he was sixteen years old. But there was an overwhelming drive deep inside him that pushed him toward that cold, slick surface. Hockey had called to him and that's where he'd spent the last three years of his life, living, breathing, feeling hockey in every sense of the word.

He wondered why this overwhelming desire to play hockey had surfaced after his surgery. He still wondered, and now today, the same weird sense of being in the right place washed through him. He didn't like being out of control and this certainly felt as out of control as one could be. There had to be some sort of sense to all of this. But what the hell was it?

Never in all his life would he have believed his life could change in one day, but it had, three years before, on January ninth.

Chapter 19

"Is he cute or what?" Megan whispered in enthusiasm as Jordan walked through the doors into the office, a dazed expression on her face.

"What?" Jordan asked, trying to slow her still swirling mind and concentrate on checking Megan's knee which, as instructed, was elevated and covered with an ice pack. Gingerly, she poked and prodded, asking if it hurt when she did this or that, gently and slowly straightening Megan's knee as Megan jabbered on about how *cute* he was.

Flustered, Jordan sat on her heels, running her hands through her thoroughly mussed curls. "Megan, I am perfectly aware of how cute you think George is. Do you think you can put a lid on this crush you have on George long enough to answer my questions about your knee?"

"My crush on George? J.J. you're nuts—I don't have a crush on that goon! I'd have to be crazy to have a crush on some ape like George. Jeez, he likes *hockey* for heaven's sake. Everyone knows figure skaters and hockey skaters are at opposite ends of the spectrum. They never get along. Why, that kind of relationship is doomed from the very beginning," Megan stated firmly, her tone dictating she truly believed her statement.

"It worked in *The Cutting Edge*," Jordan offered, referring to the movie about such a match up.

Megan rolled her eyes in exasperation. "J.J., that was a movie, this is real life. That kind of relationship would never work."

"You must be speaking from years of experience. Where else would you get such an idea?" Jordan teased, continuing to poke at Megan's knee.

"Not experience, obviously. As you keep reminding me, I *am* only twelve years old. But it doesn't take a genius to see that the mentality difference between figure skaters and hockey skaters is monumentally different. We're thinkers—they're..." Megan waved her hands in circles as if looking for the perfect description, flinching when the office door slammed open and George barged in, grabbed a stack of hockey pucks and banged back out. Jutting a thumb toward the door George had just exited, Megan stated without pause, "They're apes with sticks and an excuse to demolish each other."

Jordan smiled, despite Megan's serious expression. "Yeah, I guess you're right. But admit it, some of them are pretty *cute* apes."

Megan's eyes sparkled in animation. "Yeah, especially that cute guy with George. Damn, he's big. Oops," Megan covered her mouth with both hands, aghast at the comment that had slipped from her usually proper lips.

Jordan laughed at Megan's disbelieving look. "Why, Miss Megan, what would your mother say if she heard such profanity coming from that well-mannered mouth of yours?" Jordan asked in a perfect imitation of Megan's mother's deep southern drawl, her smile growing as Megan stuck her tongue out at her.

"Before or after she fainted dead away?" Megan asked straight-faced, her mouth making a small moue.

"Why, after, of course."

"Well, her first response would be to ground me for a month but then she'd realize I was around too much and that might hamper her style with her latest *friend*. So, I'd probably just have to be here that much more often and be subjected to more profanity and get into more trouble and have to skate more and, jeez, this could go on forever."

Jordan watched Megan's eyes, felt sad when she saw the acceptance in them. Megan was too old for her twelve years and more often than not,

Jordan wanted to shake Megan's mother in the hopes it would make her realize just how special her daughter was. Typical—there were always those who had no business being a mother and those that wanted nothing more than to be a mother and couldn't be. Sometimes life sucked!

"Well then, Miss Megan, I suppose I'll have to let this little indiscretion slide, but don't let me hear such words coming from that pure little mouth of yours again. Got it?" Jordan stated, struggling to look like she meant business.

Megan laughed and hugged her coach hard. "J.J., you couldn't be mean if you wanted to. But thanks for the thought anyway."

"Yeah, yeah. So how's the knee?"

"It's fine. Doesn't even hurt anymore."

"Are you sure? I don't want you saying that if it's killing you. The last thing you need is to ruin your knee at your age."

"J.J., you could make a saint nuts. My knee is fine," Megan answered, straightening and bending her knee to prove her point.

Jordan watched Megan's eyes as she moved her leg, sighed in relief when there were no visible signs of pain and pushed her leg back down and reapplied the ice bag. "Okay, fine. I believe you. Still, please stay off it for a couple of days," Jordan held up her hand, forestalling the objection she knew was coming. "Don't quibble with me, Megan. I don't want you on the ice for two days."

"Jordan, I can't live without the ice that long. Don't torture me so," Megan complained dramatically.

"I'm saving your knee, not torturing you. I don't want you looking back in ten years and wondering if you'd stayed off the ice for those two days if your knees would still be there. Don't fight me on this one, Megan—you won't win."

Megan pouted, her lower lip jutting forward noticeably, her arms crossed tightly across her chest. "Can I still come here and be with you?" she asked quietly.

Jordan looked at the sad expression in Megan's eyes, felt the loneliness emanating from her small form, and knew exactly what she was feeling. The ice was home to her and without it she felt lost. Jordan's heart cried for Megan's lost expression and felt a kinship with the small skater beside her. Once, long ago, Jordan had found her happiness on the ice with Aleksei, had never wanted to leave it until January ninth when her life had changed completely. Now, Jordan struggled everyday to find her happiness where she could. Her days on the ice were both happy and heartbreaking, she still listened for the whispers that Aleksei had alluded she would find him in. Still, she refused to give up hope that he was beside her and would find a way back to her. Jordan firmly believed a soul as strong as Aleksei's could never be silenced completely and so she waited for the whispers that had not yet found a voice. For the time being, she would occupy her time with Megan, teaching her everything she knew, sharing everything she could. Perhaps, the two of them together, could be a family to one another.

"Megan, I said I wanted you off the ice—I didn't say you couldn't be here. I fully expect you to be here and believe me, I'll work your butt so hard you'll wish you were skating instead of what I plan on having you do."

"And what, exactly, do you plan to have me doing?" Megan asked, her eyes lighting up in anticipation.

This child eats, sleeps and breathes skating Jordan recognized. "You'll see. Just be prepared to go home tired," Jordan answered cryptically, flicking Megan's nose tauntingly.

"No fair, J.J., you're a tease," Megan complained, her eyes joining Jordan's as the door banged open again and they watched both George and Nick enter the small office, their large forms filling the majority of space.

Both females' eyes widened at the view of muscular male forms before them. George had always looked big to Jordan, but standing beside his friend, he stood several inches shorter and his shoulders weren't nearly as wide. George had yet to attain the mature male stature of his friend and, instead, looked a bit lanky beside him. The look in Megan's eyes when she looked at George told Jordan she thought he looked just fine, in fact, better than fine.

"Jordan never teases," George offered in an off-handed manner as he began to rummage through desk drawers. "She's the most serious person I've ever met in my life and that ain't necessarily a good thing," he finished, casting a disapproving look directly at Jordan, to which Jordan quickly stuck her tongue out in response.

Nick's deep chuckle of amusement turned Jordan's cheeks a becoming pink. "That didn't look too serious to me."

"That's about as excited and belligerent as she gets," George returned, digging through yet another drawer and slamming it closed when he failed to find what he sought.

"Don't be a shit, George. J.J.'s plenty of fun," Megan offered defensively.

"Megan," Jordan gasped, amazed at the words that seemed to be pouring from her mouth, courtesy of obviously too much time around George.

"Well he is being a shit and probably doing it just to show off for his friend. It probably makes him feel all macho and stuff," Megan suggested.

"Stuff it, Meg. I don't remember hearing that kids could enter this adult conversation," George growled, casting her a fiery glance.

"Don't call me Meg—my name's Megan. How many times do you have to be told that before it sinks into your fat head you ape?"

"Fine, Megan, this is an *adult* conversation. No *kids* allowed!" George gloated.

"I'm not a *kid*! I'm more mature than you'll ever *think* of being! Megan fired back, getting to her feet, her small hands settling firmly on her nearly non-existent hips as she glared fire at George.

"Yeah, right. Go play with your dolls, baby. You're bothering me," George taunted, returning his attention to search yet another drawer.

Megan's eyes narrowed, a dangerous sign Jordan recognized all to well, and without further thought, Megan heaved the ice pack at

George, and hit him squarely on the side of the head. The bag ripped open, spilling cold water and ice down his neck and chest, his roar of surprise turned to outrage and echoed loudly throughout the small room. Undaunted, Megan lifted her chin and proudly announced "I don't play with dolls—I haven't in years. Unlike you, I don't need imaginary friends for company."

George looked ready to explode, despite the water dripping off him and slamming the drawer, he walked around the desk to stand before Megan, his tall, lanky body so close she had to tilt her head back to look into his dark eyes. Despite the fury emanating in waves from him, Megan held her ground, her chin lifting defiantly. "I have a tough time believing anyone would want to be friends with a little shit like you, but hey, if that's what you want to believe—you go for it. I, on the other hand, have more friends than you'll ever dream of having and unlike you, I feel no need to be inflicting myself on people who only tolerate your presence because they feel sorry for your *domestic* situation!" he stated nastily.

"George, that's enough!" Jordan demanded firmly, her voice low and edged with anger as she watched Megan's eyes fill with tears at his hateful, hurtful words.

"It's time the ice princess grew up, Jordan. It's time she faced reality. She's not damn royalty who can walk over anyone, anytime she feels like it, and not worry about the shit she leaves behind," George yelled, furious with the emotions Megan brought out in him and furious with himself for hurting her so deeply.

"George, I said that's enough!" Jordan's voice growled loudly, her tone demanding immediate obedience. "I suggest you leave this room or I'll move you out of here myself," she vowed, pulling him the short distance to the doorway and pushing him through the portal then slamming the door firmly behind his retreating form. "Shit!" she hissed, running her hands through her thoroughly mussed curls then leaned her head against the door frame, shaking her head in confusion.

Megan's soft whimpers drew her attention and she spun around to find herself staring at Megan as Nick enfolded her in a comforting embrace. Jordan stared in disbelief as she heard his deep voice whisper words that soothed Megan's sorrow, heard Megan's whimpers turn to little sighs and hiccups and then finally cease altogether. Nick bent down to quietly ask Megan a question, then at her positive nod, helped her back to the sofa where she had been resting her knee before. Carefully he propped her knee back up with pillows and after slipping the flannel shirt from his broad shoulders, gently covered her upper body with it, tucking the long sleeves under her slight form.

Rising, he crossed the floor of the small office in three strides and stood before Jordan where she leaned against the door's handle, her mouth slightly open in amazement. Gently he reached up with one forefinger and pushed her mouth closed, then without thought, brushed his thumb across her full lower lip, his touch, warm and rough, against her skin made her breath catch. "Wouldn't want bugs wandering into that lovely mouth of yours, would we?" he questioned, a small, knowing smile lifted the corners of his sensuously full mouth, as her dazed expression seemed to intensify. Jordan's eyes widened in confusion, her pupils dilated as the urge to lean toward the muscular, broad chest only inches away intensified. She felt drawn to him in an inexplicable way, could almost hear him silently beckoning her into his arms. With everything in her she fought the urge to lean into him, refused to accept that she could possibly be drawn to him physically, mentally or any other way. It wasn't possible. She'd promised Aleksei she would love him forever. She would be true to her promise and wait for the day she would join him and they'd be together forever.

With an abrupt shake of her head she cleared her dazed mind and stepped aside to let the tall man before her leave the small office.

"I'll be right back with the ice, Megan," Nick called over his shoulder as he stepped through the doorway.

"Thanks, Nick," Megan answered softly, her voice shaky with emotion; her cheeks still pink and tear streaked.

Jordan closed the door behind Nick's retreating form, appreciating the view of his broad shoulders, narrow waist and shapely bottom. What was it about skater's bottoms? Figure skaters or hockey players—Jordan had yet to see a bottom that didn't make her think about running her hands over the firm curves. Heaving a huge sigh, she turned to face Megan who watched her from where she reclined on the couch, her knee once again elevated.

"Didn't I tell you he was cute?" Megan asked with a watery smile, her eyes dancing with deviltry.

Jordan could only shake her head in bafflement at her student's outrageous comment and wonder at the workings of her very imaginative brain. With a last final glance toward the door, she returned her attention to Megan and walked to join her on the couch. "Are you sure you didn't hit your head when you fell?"

Megan's joyful laughter floated through the cool air, reaching Nick's ears as he waited at the snack bar for ice for her knee.

George heard the familiar high-pitched sound and smiled at its source. His smile then faded as her sorrow filled eyes returned to his mind's eye and he once again heard his hurtful words running through his mind. What was wrong with him? Never in his life had he ever purposely set out to hurt someone, but that was exactly what he'd done with Megan. People didn't purposely set out to hurt those they loved. If you loved someone, you kept them safe and happy and protected. And as he pondered his motives behind his behavior, he froze, shaking his head in disbelief. No way—no way in hell! She was twelve years old—okay, almost thirteen—yet in so many ways she seemed much older. But still—love her? It wasn't possible. In fact, it was impossible! What he felt for her was no more than what he would have felt for a little sister, if he'd had one. But the more he thought about it, the less impossible it seemed. They'd known each other forever. He'd always been there for her whenever her mother had needed to be somewhere else or with someone else. His shoulder had been the one Megan had cried on, his arms had held her when she was scared, or sad or hurt. He'd been there to cheer her on when she'd learned a new jump or perfected her spins. He'd been her cheering section, as no one else had, forever. And today he'd done his best to destroy her. Why? To prove he could? To prove he was a man? Shaking his head in confusion, he ran his hands through his hair. He owed her an apology—a big one! But how to explain what happened, let alone why it happened? This was way too confusing to do alone. There had to be someone who could help him sort out the confusing thoughts that zinged back and forth through his brain, make some sense out of the incomprehensible meanderings of his mind. Nick. Nick could help him out with this one. Nick would know what to do. Nick had to know what to do. If Nick couldn't help him, he was surely up a creek without a paddle.

With a quick prayer and crossed fingers, he went to find his friend.

* * * * *

Jordan refused to allow Megan on the ice for a full week and instead kept her occupied listening to music for her next program, coming up with costume ideas and started her on the basics of choreography. Jordan felt if she kept Megan's mind busy, she'd forget about being off the ice for a short time. It didn't work. In the span of three hours on her first day off, she'd decided on her music, already had a costume in mind and she and Jordan were already arguing over the choreography, it was a loud exchange of opinions interspersed with laughter.

It was music to George's ears and despite the fact Jordan had banished him from the office whenever Megan was present, their voices raised in playful bantering and vigorous bouts of making their opinions known brought a smile to his face. Megan could hold her own when it came to making her feelings known and he had the feeling that Jordan was on occasion creating excuses to get Megan to argue with her and give her the chance to express herself. Something Megan's mother had never done with her daughter. Megan's mother made all the decisions—period. Fortunately, these days Megan's mother rarely made an appearance, unconcerned with her daughter's injury despite Jordan's call and explanation about the fall. Megan's mother had full confidence Jordan would do all that was necessary to see to her daughter's safety. And if it was okay, did Jordan mind watching her until she got back from her quick get-away? It shouldn't be more than four or five weeks. Jordan couldn't believe the gall of the woman and was more than ready to blast her about her non-mothering attitude when she caught the look of relief on Megan's face and her eyes lighting up in excitement at the prospect of spending all that time with her coach. All thoughts of the forth coming argument dissolved and she agreed, shaking her head in disbelief as Megan's mother jotted down the number where Jordan, or her daughter, could leave a message if she was *really* needed. But stressing, time and again, her necessity for a complete get-away—the world was just too much for her right now—so to call only if it was a dire emergency. Thanks so much. Good-bye. With nothing more than a kiss blown in Megan's direction and a quick, brief wave, Megan's mother had departed without a backward glance. Jordan had felt like crying herself at the woman's coldness but upon seeing Megan's resigned expression, simply pulled the young girl into her arms and held her, absorbing the tears Megan silently shed as her small form shook in Jordan's arms.

And now, a week later, Megan was driving Jordan crazy with the same one question. "Why can't I skate? My knee feels fine. I've been off the ice for a week—just like you said—so when can I skate?

Jordan was beginning to believe that was the only sentence Megan remembered. "Can't you manage just one more day off the ice? Would it really kill you to give your knee one more day?" Jordan asked with more patience than she felt.

Jordan's day had started out badly and was quickly moving towards miserable. With only two weeks to go before the ice show, everyone's nerves were on edge. The last thing Jordan needed was Megan's relentless pleas to let her skate. But Megan continued her assault on Jordan's goodwill and finally exploding in frustration, Jordan had told her to get out of her face, take her skates and as far as she was concerned, skate her nagging little butt off.

Megan felt about two seconds of guilt at her behavior but happily grabbed her skates and ran from the office toward the rink, shrieking in joy.

Jordan listened to Megan's happy laughter echo from the high ceilings and gritted her teeth in frustration. It wasn't totally Megan's fault she was so on edge. Over the past week it seemed she was continually tripping over the new hockey coach and each time she saw him the urge to draw closer was harder to fight. She wondered if this is what it felt like to be a leaf in a windstorm, helpless to fight against the inevitable push and pull of something more powerful than herself. Worse still, it upset her that she had to work harder to bring Aleksei's face to her mind's eye. She was so sure she had loved him with all her soul and yet when she closed her eyes, his beloved face wasn't as clear and detailed as it once had been. Suddenly his eyes would look sky blue instead of ebony, his hair a tawny brown instead of dark and wavy. She often wondered if this was the path to madness and had been more than willing to sell her soul to the devil for the chance to spend one last day with Aleksei. Of course, she knew that was impossible and so she set her goals much lower. On days like this one, she wondered what she had worth bartering with for fifteen minutes of silence, peaceful, deafening, silence.

Instead, the phone rang, its sound obnoxiously loud and with a scowl she answered it. Immediately a woman's voice on the other end of the call starting jabbering excitedly, speaking so quickly she could scarcely understand the jibberish. George then entered the office, casting an apprehensive glance toward Jordan and smiling when she held the phone away from her ear and rolled her eyes in exasperation. George's smile widened when what sounded like the voice of Alvin the chipmunk clearly echoed from the phone. Shaking his head in amusement, he dropped his hockey bag beside the door and started for the cabinet that held the schedules for the next several hockey games. Just as he opened the door, the room vibrated with a deafening crash and the entire building shook.

"Oh, Christ. Dad," George offered in explanation, slamming the cabinet door and racing for the direction of the Zamboni's garage.

Jordan mumbled an *I'll get back to you* and dropped the phone into the cradle, dashing after George as he ran toward the double doors leading to the garage. Just as Jordan cleared the double doors, hot on the heels of George, she skidded to a stop, George's back taking the brunt of her slight weight as she crashed into him, grabbing his arms when she nearly fell.

The sight that greeted them made their mouths drop open in disbelief. Briefly put, there was a new opening in the far back wall of the garage. An opening more than large enough to easily fit the Zamboni through. As they stood staring at the gaping hole in the wall, floating dust mixed with the snow swirling through the opening, and settled on the pile of splintered timbers that had once been the back wall, but now littered the floor.

George's father coughed through the dust and debris surrounding him and stepped carefully from the battered Zamboni. As he scratched his head in bewilderment, he looked from the machine to the new opening, then back to the machine, his expression clearly stating he just couldn't figure out what had happened this time. All he'd wanted to do was move the stupid machine from one side of the garage to the other. Should it really have been that difficult a task? Were all Zamboni machines so miserable to operate? Apparently so.

"Dad?" George asked, concern for his father's well being out weighing his frustration at the newest disaster instigated by his unlucky father.

"Your mother's going to shit when she sees this!" George senior stated knowingly, nodding his head up and down.

"I'd say that's a safe bet, Dad. You okay?"

"Only until your mother sees this—after that, I can make no promises."

"What on earth happened?" Jordan made the mistake of verbalizing the question on everyone's mind.

"I just wanted that damn thing out of the way. I couldn't get to the tools I needed—don't you look at me that way, junior—your mother hasn't taken away my right to use every tool around here. She's still kind enough to let me use a power drill."

"The battery operated one," George, Jr. reminded him.

"Yes, the battery operated one," George, Sr. scoffed, scowling that he was restricted to using such low powered tools. It really wasn't his fault he'd drilled a hole in his hand with the electric drill, accidents happened all the time; they just seemed to happen to him a little more frequently than the average person. "All I wanted to do was reinforce some of the scenery with a couple extra screws."

"Dad, the scenery's fine."

Jordan held up her hand, worrying her lower lip at George's father's words. "Actually, George, I asked him to do that for me. There were a couple of pieces of scenery that were a little rocky."

"See?" George, Sr. demanded, pointing his finger at Jordan and nodding vigorously. "I was just doing what I'd been asked to do."

"Okay, fine, Dad," George Junior held up his hands as if surrendering. "Still, why'd you move the Zamboni?" he asked, running his hands through his hair in frustration, his mother's shocked expression clear in his mind.

"I told you, Junior, I needed my *battery operated drill*," his father explained patiently, enunciating slowly and clearly as if speaking to someone a bit dimwitted.

"Dad..." George Junior sighed, rubbing his temples where his headache was building mightily. "Why, didn't you ask for help?"

"I didn't want to bother anyone. Everyone's running around here as if it's their last day on earth. It shouldn't have been a big deal to move that monster from one side of the garage to the other."

"You're right Dad, it shouldn't have been a big deal. But as usual, it's turned into a big deal and now we all have to deal with the fall-out," George Junior explained in exasperation. Looking again at the gaping hole in the wall, he cringed when he thought of how his mother was going to react to his father's latest mishap.

"Junior, it's not that big a deal, really! It could have been a whole lot worse!" his father countered.

"What, the whole building could have fallen around our ears?"

George Senior hadn't even gotten that far in his thinking. "Well there is that. No, I was referring to the size of the hole—it could be much bigger."

"Dad, it's big enough. It's winter. Remember? It's snowing, it's cold, there's a hole in the damn wall you could run a tank through, the ice show is two weeks away, Megan's recovering from a knee injury, Nick's going weird over Jordan and Mom's running on black coffee, chocolate and Tums. It doesn't get much worse than that!" his son demanded, oblivious to Jordan's sudden paleness and in-drawn breath.

Nick's sudden appearance through the hole in the wall surprised them all and Jordan's tension increased as she worried about George's comment regarding Nick and her. But Nick's casual statement, "I know George complains about my shoulders being wide, but honestly, I still fit through the front door," broke the tension and the small gathering soon found themselves trying to control their laughter, for the most part, unsuccessfully.

Jordan tried her best to ignore Nick, but time and again she found her gaze wandering appreciatively over his tall, muscular form. George was right, his shoulders were enormous! Thankfully, Nick's down-filled parka covered those wide shoulders and muscular arms and fell to mid-thigh, also covering his tempting bottom and upper thighs.

Maybe there is a God in heaven, Jordan thought as she pulled her wistful gaze forcefully away from the impossibly handsome man. "George, I've got to go check on Megan," Jordan offered as a way of escape. Her heart picked up it's pace every time she was in the same room with Nick. Escape was her only chance of salvation.

"You let her on the ice?" George Junior asked in disbelief. "The toughest broad I know gave in? I don't believe it."

"She wore me down—kind of like Chinese Water Torture—I couldn't stand her whining anymore so I tossed her butt out and told her to knock herself out. Hopefully, she didn't take it literally," Jordan laughed, her eyes bright, her smile wide.

"Now I know your secret—you can't stand whiners," George countered.

Jordan stuck her tongue out, her cheeks flushing when she saw Nick had caught her childish gesture and stood gazing intently at her, his eyes holding hers captive.

"I'll be sure never to whine," Nick added, his tone deep and promising, his eyes darkening a deeper blue.

Jordan's heart started to pound wildly, her breath caught in her throat and she felt captured by the power he radiated. It took all her strength to close her eyes, breaking the magnetic pull Nick had over her and with a mumbled excuse about Megan, left the trashed room, her legs barely supporting her.

George watched her sudden retreat, baffled by her unusual behavior until he looked at Nick and saw the same dazed expression in his eyes as he continued to stare at the door Jordan had just exited through. "Nick...Nick..." George called before scooping up a small piece of Styrofoam insulation and bouncing it off Nick's shoulder with an accurate throw.

"What?" Nick growled, looking around in bewilderment, shaking his head to clear the strange sensation he felt every time he was anywhere near Jordan.

"Welcome back, buddy," George offered, bumping shoulders with him as he passed by.

"What?" Nick repeated, his hands spread as if asking what the devil George was insinuating this time.

"Just off in the ozone again, Nick. No problem," George explained, starting to pick up the larger pieces of wood that littered the floor.

"Bull." Nick argued.

George's expression said otherwise.

"Shit!" Nick growled deeply, running his large hands through his short hair.

He had to get a handle on what was going on. This was getting entirely too weird! Why was he so drawn to this slip of a girl—no woman—he'd met only a week ago? She wasn't anything like the typical women he'd dated. He'd always been drawn to women who laughed easily, flirted shamelessly, were loaded with curves and knew exactly what to do with them and kept the promises they'd made, even if the promise had come after tequila shooters. Nick was certain, Jordan had never even been in the presence of a tequila shooter. And figure wise, if she had one, she did her best to keep it covered. Although, he knew for a fact she had one fine ass and even the long sweatshirts she wore constantly refused to stay in place and rode up over her hips, leaving that lovely bottom free to view. And since every time she saw him, she reversed her direction, more often than not, he had a fine view of her retreating southern exposure. A view he had come to appreciate more and more each time he saw it.

"Nick, you're slipping again," George suggested, bumping past him again, his arms filled with remnants of what had once been the back wall. "You going to help or are you going to stand there mooning over Jordan all afternoon?'"

"Screw you, Washington." Nick growled, slipping his parka off and tossing it on to the workbench, his flannel shirt followed, landing on the mountainous jacket. "So, what's the plan?" Nick asked, standing with his feet slightly spread, his arms spread across his massive chest, the muscles of his arms bulging.

George looked at his friend, a towering mass of muscle and good looks and shook his head in amazement. "You know, Nick, there ought to be laws to protect you pretty boys. No wonder you get girls so easy. They all think you're gay and they'll be the one to convert you. What a racket!"

Nick suggested George attempt a physically impossible act upon himself, threw back his head and laughed. The sound deep and husky, echoed through the building, reaching Jordan in the ice rink where she watched Megan skate happily over the ice and suddenly her heart began to race.

"Damn you, Nicholas Devon," Jordan whispered, her arms crossing her chest as her blood began to boil. With an effort, she pushed the image of sky blue eyes and a sexy smile from her mind and returned her attention to Megan as she sped across the ice.

"So tell me, Washington. How long do we have to get this hole in the wall fixed before the boss gets here?" Nick asked, grabbing another armful of splintered and broken wooden beams.

"Not long enough."

"Time to think positive, Georgie. Are we putting a door in or just putting the wall back together?"

"I think it would be best if it looked like it used to. I'd just as soon she not find out about this little incident."

"Whatever." Nick shrugged. "I'll get the list of materials together, we'll send your father down to get the stuff and be back together by..." Nick looked at his watch—eleven-thirty. "late tonight."

"Other than the 'we'll send dad to get the stuff' I can live with the rest of it," George agreed, sending his father a look that stopped the protest his father had been about to make.

"Tell you what, Mr. W., we'll go get the stuff together," Nick offered, grabbing up a clipboard and tape measure and sticking a pencil behind his ear. "In the mean time, give me a hand with measuring this hole and then we'll figure what all we need to make it disappear."

George Senior positively glowed at Nick's offer and jumped to his feet, eager to be part of the process to put the wall back together. Maybe today wasn't such a bad day after all. And if all went as planned, his wife would never know about this little *accident*.

Chapter 20

The next ten days passed in a blur of saw dust, loud machinery, and even louder explanations when George's mother got back into town two days ahead of schedule and immediately spotted the, as yet painted, replacement wall. Despite George Junior's diplomatic explanation regarding the accident, Nick's assurance the building was structurally sound and her husband's blood promise to never, never, touch her precious Zamboni machine again, Mrs. Washington spent the better part of the day stomping through the building and slamming doors whenever she had the chance. Everyone was perfectly aware her mood was less than cordial and they all steered a wide path around her, disappearing when necessary to insure they would survive to see the forthcoming ice show. Thankfully, Mrs. Washington's mood was greatly improved by the following morning, thanks to a coat of matching paint that made the new and old wall blend together so nicely one had to look hard to see where the old met the new.

With three days left until the ice show, dress rehearsals were held. Final adjustments were made for music and lighting, scenery changes were timed, modified and timed again. Final fittings for costumes were completed, sequins torn off, zippers replaced, ribbons shortened, feathers sewn on, beads and bangles glued and pinned. Blades were sharpened, boots polished, and blister pads, and Band-Aids were worth their weight in gold. All in all, it was shaping up to be one hell of a show.

Nick watched the wild and frantic motion going on around him and thought the average person would get tired just watching the level of energy that surged through everyone in the building. Yet, for the first time in years he felt truly alive and the feeling confused him. There was no reason he should feel this attraction to the chaos that went on around him, and yet he felt physically drawn to the music that made the building vibrate with anticipation. There were times he could swear his name was being called, and he'd find himself standing rink side watching the skaters. The feeling was especially urgent when the pair skaters hit the ice. There was a tangible feeling of electricity that crackled in the air, like an approaching storm, and it made his blood flow faster through his veins. The sensation built in him, despite his best efforts to ignore the pandemonium surrounding him. He felt drawn to this group of skaters, as if a member of the team, and it made him crazy because there was no reason in hell he should feel any kinship to a bunch of guys in tights figure skating. And yet, he kept returning to watch the proceedings. Silently he made notes in his mind what needed to be changed or corrected to make one program flow more smoothly into the next, why a particular jump wasn't working or, with the pair skaters, why the boy couldn't get his partner in the air for their lift. The sudden realization he was doing this was bad, what was worse was he knew what he was doing! He knew he was right! There was no reason for him to even be thinking along these lines—figure skating was for wimps. Hockey was his game. He was no namby-pamby in tight pants and flowing shirts! Give him a stick and let him knock some ones head off any night and he was happier than a pig in the mud. So what in the world made him think he knew what the hell he was talking about now? He couldn't say, but he *knew* he was right.

Unfortunately, he made the mistake of yelling out across the ice "You've got to get under her more and lift with your legs," that drew Jordan's attention.

Jordan's look of surprise at the deeply intoned command soon turned to confusion. For the briefest of moments, she was sure it had been Aleksei's voice that had shouted the command, but only Nick stood looking at her from across the expanse of ice.

Nick watched her face go from joyfully expectant to pale and annoyed when she realized it had been Nick's booming voice she had heard. With a dismissing toss of her head, she returned her attention to the pair on the ice and stopped the music. Stepping on to the ice, she made her way to the skaters, watching as the teenage boy helped his partner back to her feet after he made an unsuccessful attempt to lift her. She was beginning to think he was never going to get this lift down consistently and began to think of alternate moves for this part of their program. It certainly wasn't fair to his partner to suffer the constant consequences of his inability to get her up and balanced. Jordan looked at his partner, certainly small enough to be easily lifted, and shook her head in frustration.

Nick watched the small movement of Jordan's head and could feel her frustration. Still, Nick wasn't stupid, he didn't have to be hit over the head with a mallet to figure out Jordan wanted nothing to do with him. He, himself, felt better when she wasn't around. In fact, he could almost convince himself things were close to normal when he couldn't see her or smell her perfume or hear her voice and laughter. Although it seemed that more and more frequently she interrupted his thoughts, even his sleep, the one place he'd found refuge and silence from the strange happenings that had begun after his surgery three years before.

Nick watched Jordan explain, yet again, how the lift was to be executed. He could see the girl nodding in understanding but her partner just didn't seem to be getting it. In exasperation, Jordan explained it yet again.

Without even thinking, Nick found himself stepping on to the ice in his work boots. The slick surface felt comfortable and welcoming even without skates. Confidently he strode across the glassy surface toward the three skaters that stared at him as if he'd lost his mind. "You've got to get under her. Your knees bend, don't they?" Nick questioned the boy, whose look was rather belligerent and said without words how he felt about hockey skaters.

"They bend just fine."

"Then bend them and get under your partner!" Nick growled.

"I think I know a little bit more about this than you do."

Nick looked down at the boy who, even in his skates, stood a good half-foot shorter than he did. "That's your problem, you're thinking instead of listening. I'm sure your partner *thinks* differently," Nick stated, looking at the girl that still rubbed at her aching left hip. "Suppose, for half a minute, you turn off your macho teenage attitude and pay attention. With any luck, you'll learn something and your partner won't have to down eight Advil to sleep tonight."

Jordan looked at Nick. A new respect for him flickered to life as he patiently, but succinctly explained exactly how the lift was to be executed. When he called her name and held out his hand to her, she realized he planned to use her to demonstrate the lift. She looked at his boot-clad feet and shook her head. "I really don't think it's necessary to demonstrate the lift. You've explained it very clearly."

"I've heard you explain it to Ram-jet here several times, too, but he obviously is the type that has to *see* how it works to really get it. So, let's show him," Nick stated patiently, his hand still outstretched.

"Nick, I don't know. I don't think…" Jordan began, her voice fading to a whisper as she shook her head back and forth, her hands clasped tightly together behind her back.

"Jordan, for once, don't think. Just trust me," Nick asked softly, his hand still outstretched to her, rock steady.

Jordan looked from his reaching hand up into his bright blue eyes and for the briefest moment was sure they turned ebony. Closing her eyes to clear her vision, she opened them and stared into Nick's blue eyes, filled with patience and confidence. "If you drop me, I will never let you forget it!" she vowed strongly.

"That will never happen," Nick stated surely, watching as Jordan's eyes widened in surprise, not knowing she had received that exact promise from Aleksei years before. Jordan swayed toward Nick, her legs suddenly weak at his words and she grabbed his hand with both of hers, allowing him to pull her before him. "Okay, kid. Watch—and learn!"

As if from a distance, Jordan listened as Nick carefully explained each step of the lift, moving her body into position as he stepped before her, his palms resting against her hip bones, his fingers curling around her hips, his touch hot against her suddenly chilled flesh. Jordan closed her eyes as the first wave of dizziness washed over her. Aleksei was there, she could feel his presence surrounding her, she could feel his hands on her hips and without any effort, she suddenly was lifted high into the air and held securely. As if the past three years had never existed, she arched into position without consciously thinking to do it. Her arms spread wide as if she was flying, her heart soaring as she felt her blood pump furiously through her veins as it had every time Aleksei had held her, either on or off the ice. She heard his voice as he instructed her on their dismount and blindly she obeyed. Her hands reached for his shoulders, her fingers wrapping around the muscles of his upper arms as he lowered her then sliding down the length of his arms and finally running her finger tips over his palms until their fingers laced together. Sighing deeply, she leaned against his body, her cheek coming to rest against his chest where she listened to the comforting, steady beat of his heart. She whispered his name on a sigh. *Aleksei.*

"Jordan?"

"Huh?" came her quiet reply. She didn't want to leave the safe haven she'd found. It had taken her three long years, but she'd wished Aleksei back and somehow he'd found a way to return to her. Jordan promised they'd never be apart again.

"Jordan?" The voice was more insistent, different than before, a bit deeper.

Jordan felt Aleksei's fingers slide from hers and frowned at the loss of his touch. "Come back, Aleksei."

"Jordan!" Nick's voice broke through the final threads of fantasy that surrounded her.

Her eyes sprang open and she realized it wasn't Aleksei she stood before but Nick. Nick watched her eyes go dark and fill with confusion and her cheeks flush rosily in embarrassment. With a small push, she backed away from him, mumbled a small "I'm sorry", announced there would be a ten-minute break and left the ice.

* * * * *

Cynthia Washington stood beside her son and they watched the unusual scene play out on the ice before them. Her breath caught and held as she watched Nick lift and hold Jordan above his head in a lift that looked all too familiar, as if he'd been doing it all his life, which she knew he hadn't. Even George's eyebrows raised as he watched Jordan and Nick perform the lift.

"This is too weird," George muttered.

Cynthia looked from her son to the ice and back again. "What's this about, Georgie?"

George shook his head. "You wouldn't believe me if I told you, Mom."

"Try me," Cynthia encouraged and listened as her son told her the story Nick had told him about how his life had changed on the operating table three years before. Cynthia could only shake her head in astonishment. She had learned anything was possible and never to discount love as being a stronger power than even death. "Has Nick ever seen anything on Aleksei? Any of their programs?"

"Nick thinks figure skating's for wussies!" George snorted. "The fact that he's drawn to Jordan and doesn't know why is making him crazy.

Makes him a madman on the ice come hockey-time but it's making him really edgy come downtime. I worry about him, Mom. I don't know how to help him," George concluded, his eyes returning to the ice.

"Georgie, I think it's time Nick met Aleksei Rocmanov," Cynthia stated, nudging her son toward the ice. "I'll see him in my office," She offered, heading through the double doors to her office and searching through her collection of videotapes of Jamison and Rocmanov. When she found the program she wanted, she popped the tape into the VCR, settled into her chair and awaited Nick's arrival.

*   *   *   *   *

Nick sauntered into Cynthia's office five minutes later; a frown still creased his forehead as he tried to figure out exactly what had occurred on the ice with Jordan.

"George said you wanted to see me. What can I do for you Mrs. W? George Senior on the move again?" he asked, trying to take his mind off Jordan and the strange sensations that still crashed through his body.

"No, George Senior is being a perfect angel and busy putting together programs—with any luck, he won't staple his finger to one of them."

Nick nodded in understanding, a small smile crinkled the corners of his mouth. "So, what can I do for you?"

"I was hoping to help you," Cynthia offered, picking up the remote to the VCR and handing it to Nick.

"I'm not very good at fixing electronic gadgets, did you check the batteries?" Nick suggested, surprised at Cynthia's sudden burst of laughter.

"The VCR's fine, Nick, and the remote doesn't need batteries," Cynthia watched Nick's expression become more confused and sat forward, resting her elbows on her desk. "I wasn't aware you were so knowledgeable regarding the intricacies of pairs lifts. If I'd known, I would have taken you off hockey skates and put you back on real skates."

"No disrespect, ma'am, but hockey skates are *real* skates."

"George told me you thought figure skating was for wussies."

"Yeah, well, George has a big mouth!" Nick growled.

"Yes, I know," Cynthia smiled. "So how long have you been an expert at pair skating?"

Nick's look slipped from surprised to aghast. "I don't know anything about pair skating."

"That's not how it looked to me just now when you were lifting Jordan as if you'd been doing it forever," Cynthia stated plainly.

Nick started to open his mouth to say something, closed it, opened it, closed it and finally shrugged and groaned. "I don't know where the hell that came from!" he muttered, running his hands through his hair in frustration. "I was watching the kids out there practice their program, saw Ram-jet drop his partner for the forty-second time and something just snapped. The next thing I knew, I was out there, telling that snot-nosed punk to pay attention and Jordan was over my head before I even realized what was happening. Let me tell you, it was *fucking weird*!" he growled deeply.

Cynthia nodded understandingly. "You're right, it is strange. But what you're about to see is probably really going to throw you for a loop," she said, turning on the TV/VCR combo. "I want you to watch this, and when it's over, we'll talk."

The screen came to life, two figure skaters alone on the center of the ice. Nick immediately recognized Jordan and a slight chill shook his body as he looked at the tall, dark-haired man holding her in his arms, familiar but not. As he watched, the two began their program, picking up speed as they covered the ice and the man lifted Jordan into the air, holding her high as they circled the corner and carefully lowered her back to the ice. Her hands traced down her partner's shoulders and arms as Jordan had his own only moments before. Nick directed a startled look of surprise at Cynthia who only nodded in acknowledgment, and told him to keep watching. Nick watched the program, saw his own skating style matched the man's on the screens and shook his head in disbelief. None of this made any sense. The longer he watched, the more he recognized himself in the skating style of Jordan's partner, the more confused he became.

Finally the program ended and Cynthia stopped the tape.

"What the hell is going on?" Nick asked, obviously bewildered. "Who is that guy?"

"That, Nicholas Devon was Aleksei Rocmanov, Jordan's partner, both on and off the ice."

"Was?"

"Yes, was. They were in a car accident, he died in her arms."

"Christ!"

"It's been a difficult three years for Jordan."

"Three years?" Nick mumbled, confusion warred with disbelief, he rubbed suddenly cold hands together in an effort to warm them as a wave of strange sensation crashed over his head.

"Yes. Aleksei died on January ninth…" Cynthia began.

"The same day I had my knee surgery and was dead on the table for twenty minutes." Nick ended.

"Georgie told me about the *visions* you had while you were officially dead."

"Georgie has a big mouth!" Nick repeated, stunned at the realization there were too damn many coincidences to be coincidental.

"What did your doctors say?"

"You mean besides oops? That it was probably an allergic reaction to the anesthesia, probably nothing more than hallucinations. What are the doctors going to say? *Don't worry, you just picked up someone else's soul who isn't ready for heaven just yet?* They might as well have had me wrapped up in rubber padding if that was their only explanation," Nick looked back at the screen, now blank, and asked if there were any other programs he could watch. Maybe—just maybe—it was only a coincidence that their lift had been identical to Jordan and Aleksei's in the program he'd just watched.

Cynthia watched Nick and felt helpless to assist him. Everyone had to find their own way in this world, despite her own beliefs that sometimes shit just happened and no matter how hard you fought it or how loud you screamed against it, it just happened, with or without your agreeing to it. "Do you remember much about your visions? Does anything ring a bell or pull at you that you remember?" Cynthia asked as she gathered together videotapes of Jordan and Aleksei for Nick to view.

"Only bits and pieces that are so vague and hazy they don't make any sense." Nick offered, accepting the stack of tapes from Cynthia and heading for the door. As he opened the door, he stopped as a surge of something flashed through his memory. "Cynthia, have you ever heard Celine Dion's song, *The Prayer*?"

Nick's question completely stunned her and she leaned against the desk as her legs threatened to give way. Slowly she nodded up and down, her mouth dry as she finally got her one word question out. "Why?"

Nick shrugged his wide shoulders. "I've never heard it played, I've never seen the sheet music to it. And yet I know the words and can hear the music as clearly as I can hear Jordan's blades whisper across the ice. Yet there's something that won't allow me to listen to that piece of music alone. Why is that? Why should one piece of music mean that much to me?"

Cynthia swallowed the lump that threatened to choke her, wiping away tears from the corners of her eyes. "That piece of music was the one they had decided on for their next program. As it turned out, it was the piece of music they were listening to when the accident occurred, it was the piece of music they were listening to when Aleksei died in Jordan's arms."

"I don't understand," Nick stated softly, his mind whirling as he tried to make sense of the insensible.

"Sometimes we're not suppose to. Sometimes all we can do is hang on and believe that things happen for a reason and that someday that reason will be revealed," Cynthia offered.

"I don't know if I can do that," Nick stated.

"What's the other option?" Cynthia asked.

Nick shrugged and shook his head back and forth.

"Be patient, Nick. Good things come to those that wait."

"Yeah, and Santa Claus is real," Nick grumbled and left the office.

Cynthia watched him walk away, his head held high and proud, his swagger so much like Aleksei's it made her want to cry. With a look toward heaven, she closed her eyes and said into the silent room. "I knew you hadn't gone far, Rocmanov. We've all missed you so much."

The clear sound of blades as they whispered across the ice filled the small room and seemed to return the sentiment. Cynthia smiled.

All would be well very soon, she felt, and on that thought, left the small office, closing the door behind her. Seconds later, the soft strains of *The Prayer* filled the room, yet the sound system remained dark—the power off.

Chapter 21

The day of the ice show dawned with crystal clear blue skies and a disguised temperature of twenty-two degrees. Jordan had to once again remind herself that just because the sun was out, it didn't mean the heat was on. As she stepped from her SUV, she wished she had worn her down-filled coat instead of her fleece skating jacket. Shivering as the wind blew through her hair, she grabbed her oversized bag, which held her skates, make-up, sewing kit and anything else she had felt might be necessary this hectic day and dashed toward the front doors of the ice house. Side-stepping George Junior as he spread salt over the sidewalk, Jordan laughed a hello and dashed through the double doors, pushing the second set of doors open with her bottom as she answered George's yelled question from the walkway and collided with Nick as she quickly spun to face forward.

Jordan's breath left her body on a whoosh as she hit the solid wall of his chest. She felt herself bounce backwards, her large bag slipping from her shoulder, the straps tangling with her feet and tripping her up. A small cry escaped her lips as she felt herself falling helplessly backwards. Suddenly, large, strong hands grabbed her forearms, their grip firm, but not hurtful, and she found herself pulled quickly forward, and against Nick's rock-hard chest. Jordan's cheek rested against his chest, his heartbeat a steady, comforting rhythm in her ear. Closing her eyes, she sought to calm her own racing heart and frowned as she felt her heart slow and then match the rhythm of Nick's until she couldn't tell if it was Nick's heartbeat she was hearing or her own.

Nick stood still, despite his desire to wrap his arms protectively around her and tried to ignore the heat that radiated from her body and seeped into his. With a silent moan of loss that seemed to roar in his ears, he released her arms and stepped away from her. At the loss of his closeness, Jordan looked up into Nick's eyes, now a deep blue, and stumbled yet again as an all-too-familiar look gazed back at her, one of hunger and yearning.

Nick steadied her yet again, keeping her at arms length and shook his head in amusement. "It's a good thing you're not skating today or we'd be scraping you off the boards within the first thirty seconds after you hit the ice," his voice was deep and sexy in spite of his insult.

Jordan lifted her chin a notch and did her best to look down at him despite the fact he towered over her. "If I wanted to skate today, I would. I had my time in the spotlight. Today belongs to all of our students. And besides…" she picked up her skating bag and slipped it over her shoulder, "I'll have enough on my hands seeing to the show without needing the additional worry about performing," she ended and turned to head toward the locker room.

"I don't remember you ever being nervous or worried about a competition or exhibition before," Nick called to Jordan's retreating back, his voice challenging. Jordan stopped and turned to look at Nick; ready to engage in the next verbal volley when his next words made her freeze. "Except after that fall at the Nationals when you sliced my leg open—again."

Waves of dizziness crashed over Jordan as visions of the fall he referred to flashed before her eyes. Bright red blood splattered across the pristine whiteness of the newly groomed ice and ruined their beautiful costumes. Her hands and knees were scraped and bloody, his leg cut open from her sharp skate blade, his cheek cut and bleeding from his collision with the boards, and yet, they had skated, and won. No, she and Aleksei had skated, and won. This was Nick before her—not Aleksei. No matter how badly she wanted it to be Aleksei, it wasn't. It was Nick! And suddenly she was furious, at Aleksei for leaving her, at herself for still wanting Aleksei so badly she saw him everywhere and in everyone. But especially, at Nick, for making her feel things she didn't want to feel.

"You don't know what you're talking about, you weren't there. You don't know anything about me!" Jordan accused from across the room.

"I know more about you than you think. Cynthia gave me tapes of all your programs and told me to watch them, closely, and then to watch them again."

"Why would she do that? There's no reason you need to know about me. I don't want you knowing anything about me—I don't want anyone knowing anything about me! This is my life!" Jordan stormed.

"You're right, it is your life. And from what I've seen, for the last year you've been hiding out in this hole of an ice house teaching kids to skate for nothing and going through the motions of life."

"So what? It's my life. It's my right to spend it however I want and if I want to spend it in this 'hole', then dammit, I will and if someone doesn't like it, they can go screw themselves!"

"You're a champion, Jordan. You shouldn't be here, you have so much more to show the world!"

"WAS! I was a champion. A long time ago, but I learned there were more important things in this world than medals and trophies and ribbons. Unfortunately, I learned it too late and it cost me the one thing that mattered most to me in all the world."

"It wasn't your fault Aleksei died," Nick stated deeply. "You wanted to stay at the cabin another day. Remember?"

Jordan's mind swirled anew, her blood roared in her ears as her heart pumped dangerously fast. How could he know such things, she'd never told anyone, not even Whittaker or Dee about that particular detail. How could Nick know? "You don't know what you're talking about,"

Jordan yelled, holding up her hand to ward Nick off when he started to approach her. "You couldn't know!"

Nick stopped, his breath caught as he took in her large dark eyes so vivid against her pale skin. Her coppery hair became a mussed maze of curls as she pushed her hands through her hair in an effort to control their shaking. Her breasts rose and fell rapidly as she fought to breathe normally. "You're right, I shouldn't know, but I do. For the first time in three years my life feels *normal*—or at least more normal than it has since *things* started happening. For three years I've felt disconnected, like a part of me was missing, and then I saw you, and suddenly everything made sense. This is where I was being lead—to you."

"You're out of your mind!" Jordan stated in disbelief. "Georgie said you were weird."

"Yeah, well Georgie talks too much!" Nick growled. "And this has nothing to do with Georgie, it has to do with you, and me, and Aleksei."

"There is no you and me, and don't you dare even mention Aleksei's name. You know nothing about him other than what you may have seen on the tapes Cynthia had no business showing you."

"Jordan, Aleksei was a man, not a god. He doesn't want you spending your life mourning his memory and simply marking time, he wants you to laugh, and be happy, and love again."

"How would you know what Aleksei wants?" Jordan questioned, her voice filled with pain.

"Because the son-of-a-bitch has been leading me toward you for the last three years!" Nick yelled.

Jordan's wide-eyed look of disbelief said it all. "And I thought I'd heard every pick-up line out there," Jordan stated in disgust.

"It's not a line—it's true—and believe me, I'm not happy about any of it!"

"Well, that makes two of us buddy. The idea that you think you could simply say *Aleksei sent you* and that I'd fall over at your feet in rapture and thanks makes me want to throw up. There was more to Aleksei than good looks and a great body."

"So you think I look good and have a great body?" Nick asked belligerently.

"I never said that."

"Your eyes say differently."

"You're reading something that isn't there," Jordan parried. "Aleksei was kind and caring and funny…"

"And opinionated and obstinate and infuriating!" Nick finished, crossing his arms over his chest, his muscles clearly defined through his turtleneck shirt.

Jordan's mouth felt suddenly dry as she watched the play of his muscles beneath his shirt. With an effort, she returned her attention to Nick's face and found herself staring at his mouth. "You could have learned any of that from the articles Cynthia keeps in her scrap books. Information she had no business sharing with you by the way," she mumbled.

"I didn't have to look at Cynthia's scrap books to know about you. All of a sudden I knew things I'd never had any interest in, let alone a reason to know about, like figure skating. I'd always hated figure skating because it was for wussies…" Nick charged.

"Nobody *hates* figure skating. It's not possible to *hate* figure skating!" Jordan interrupted.

"I've got news for you, Jordan. There are a lot of people out there that think what you do is the epitome of stupid and reckless. Think about it. How smart is it to strap a narrow razor blade to your feet and go as fast as you can on a slippery surface?"

"You make it sound dangerous," Jordan argued, her look clearly stating she thought he was crazy.

"It is dangerous. How many times did you wind up in the hospital? Did you ever count how many bruises Hanks gave you or how many times you wished you'd make it through a program while he was your partner and not be thrown into the boards?"

"That's part of pairs skating. You learn to live with it," Jordan's answer was simple—it was a fact of life as far as she was concerned.

"But that changed after you became partners with Aleksei. He promised you he'd never throw you into the boards."

"And he kept that promise!" Jordan agreed.

"But why would I know he'd even made such a statement?" Nick growled. "Why would I suddenly have all this knowledge in my head about a subject I'd never paid any attention to—never had any interest in whatsoever—until after I nearly died on an operating table? Why would my body suddenly be able to do things on skates I would never have even considered doing on a solid surface? Why would I suddenly know where my hands had to be to lift you into the air when in the past I'd have said you had to have a death wish to even let someone do that to you? Think about it Jordan. I went into surgery to have my knee fixed, died on the table, was *visited* by God knows what and after the doctors managed to bring me back, I knew all this shit. I didn't look or ask for this knowledge—hell, I didn't even want it! But for the last three years I've needed to be on the ice the same way fish need to be in water. Before that, I didn't even like ice cubes in my drinks. So you explain it to me, Jordan. Why do I know so much about you and your ex-partner? Why do I feel drawn to music that you and Aleksei used for your programs? Why do I visualize you skating in my arms when we've never done it before?"

"I don't know. Maybe you were brainwashed. Maybe they played the same music during your surgery and your subconscious locked on it for some reason. I don't know. It's your problem—not mine!"

"You're wrong! You're part of the problem and like it or not you're going to have to deal with it!" Nick growled.

"I don't have to deal with you at all Nicholas Devon. You've got your ice and your stupid stick and you can chase your little piece of plastic around it until hell freezes over. There's no reason our paths have to cross at all!" Jordan stated furiously.

"Do you still wear sheer stockings when you perform?" Nick asked quietly, his gaze skimming up her warm-up pant covered legs. Closing his eyes, he could visualize her long, shapely legs and his fingers flexed at his desire to run his hands over her soft skin, he just knew her skin would feel like silk.

Jordan's heart skipped a beat at his softly spoken question. "That's none of your business," she answered softly, her voice quivering as Aleksei's voice vowed in her memory she'd be able to wear sheer stockings again because he'd never throw her into the boards.

Nick watched her eyes fill with sorrow and pain crease her brow and wanted to draw her into his arms, he could almost feel Aleksei pushing him toward her. "Aleksei never wanted you to stop skating. He loved watching you skate as much as he loved skating with you."

"Then he shouldn't have left me," Jordan demanded, wiping the tears from her cheeks away angrily.

"It killed him to leave you," Nick stated knowingly.

"Yeah, well, it killed me to. I've been dead for three years—one of the walking dead," Jordan answered flatly.

"He wants you to be happy again."

"So he sent you to replace him?" Jordan asked in astonishment. "That sounds like some stupid macho stunt he'd try to pull. Even in death he wants to call the shots!" Jordan snorted in contempt. "Sorry, Nick. I'm not looking for a replacement—I had the best. I'd rather be alone than settle for second place!" She stated nastily.

"Don't be a bitch, Jordan. The *Ice Queen* bit never worked with me," Nick warned without thinking.

"You're wrong—it'll work just fine with you. I'll grant you, I let my guard down and let Aleksei into my heart. Don't think for a minute the same thing will happen with you. And don't try to pretend to be someone you're not just to get in my knickers, Mr. Devon. I'm not interested."

"In me or in life?"

Jordan's slight shrug was the only answer he received as she turned and walked away from him, grabbing her bag from the floor and slamming through the women's locker room doors.

Moments later, Nick heard George Junior's laughter as he helped Megan through the doors, her skating bag slung over his shoulder, her costume bag draped over his arm. With a scowl, Nick looked at the two young people, obviously attracted to each other and growled a greeting as they passed.

George and Megan's bemused expressions met and held, breaking apart on a nervous laugh as they reached the locker room doors and George handed over Megan's bags. With a quick, light kiss to her cheek, George wished Megan luck and ran off to see what the next thing on the *short list* of to-do's was before the show began.

With only two hours until show time, a lot could happen!

*   *   *   *   *

Cynthia Washington made the mistake of entering the locker room before Jordan had left it and found herself the center of Jordan's glaring attention. "How could you do that to me, Cyndi. How could you give that bastard access to my life?" Jordan growled, slipping her foot into her skate, setting her heel in place with three solid kicks to the padded floor and furiously lacing up her boots.

Cynthia didn't have to be a rocket scientist to figure out who the *bastard* Jordan referred to was. "He's been lost and drifting for three years, just like you. He had questions, I thought maybe you had the answers."

"How can I have answers to his questions when I have so many of my own I'm still trying to figure out? Cyndi, I can't believe you set me up like this?" Jordan hissed angrily, standing up and squatting slightly to settle into her boots.

"You're over reacting. The show's making you edgy," Cynthia suggested, watching as Jordan paced back and forth before her.

"My edginess has nothing to do with the show—I'm fine with the show."

"Then why aren't you skating in it?"

Jordan stopped abruptly, her fiery gaze meeting Cynthia's calm, steady look. "This show isn't about me. It's a way for our students to show their family and friends how much they've accomplished. Whether or not I choose to skate—and I choose not to—has nothing to do with the show."

"I think you're afraid to be out there under the spotlight alone," Cynthia stated bluntly.

"I skate everyday *alone*, Cyndi."

"Not by choice, but because you have to skate, just like you have to breathe." Cynthia corrected. "Why aren't you skating in the show, Jordan? Every student in this building has asked me that question a dozen times. And I've never been able to give them the real reason, even though I know what it is."

"So tell me, knower of all things. What is that reason?" Jordan asked sarcastically, her anger growing.

Cynthia took in Jordan's defiantly raised chin, her flashing eyes and hoped she was doing the right thing. "Because you're afraid if you're a success alone on the ice people will forget Aleksei and that part of your life will have been a waste. It's easier to stay hidden in the shadows crying over what could have been and screaming unfair than it is to put yourself out there on the line and make a fool of yourself. Well, Jordan—you're right—it's easier not to try but then there's not much satisfaction in hiding and wallowing in your own self-pity."

"It's my life. I'll live it as I choose and if I choose to spend it alone then it's my damn business and no one else's!" Jordan stormed.

"You're right, it is your life. But I don't have to stand by and watch you die a little more each day. Do you think Aleksei's happy knowing you're just biding your time on earth? Do you think it would make him happy if you threw yourself off a damn cliff so you could be with him?" Cyndi yelled, grabbing Jordan and turning her to face a full-length mirror. "Look at yourself, Jordan, you've changed. You're twenty-two years old but for all the life in your eyes you could be two hundred. The last thing Aleksei would have wanted you to do was mourn him for your whole life. He didn't expect you to. If he was here now he'd kick you in your skinny ass and tell you to start living again."

"If he was here we wouldn't be having this conversation," Jordan answered flatly, the tone filled with pain.

"But he's not here—he's gone—forever, and no matter how much you wish it could be different, if can't be. It's time to let Aleksei go. It's time to thank him for all he gave you and get on with the business of living," Cyndi stated softly.

Jordan lifted tear filled eyes to her friend. "I don't know how to start."

Cyndi wiped tears from Jordan's cheeks and kissed her softly on the forehead. "Listen to the whispers on the ice, Jordan, they'll show you the way," Cyndi offered and left Jordan alone in the silent locker room.

Jordan sank to the bench when her knees refused to hold her any longer. Cyndi's words recycled through her mind and Jordan knew she was right—she was afraid to succeed on her own. Aleksei had been the best part of her life and no matter how much she raged against fate and its cruel hand, she was alone, and had to learn to stand on her own. The very thought of standing alone scared her to death, let alone the thought of being on that huge piece of ice under a spotlight by herself. What if she failed? She wasn't sure if she even wanted to try to be a single skater. And if she did, what if she couldn't make it as a single? What if no one was interested in seeing Jordan Jamison skate any longer? There were so many *what ifs?* to worry about.

On the other hand, what if she did become a single skater? Or for that matter, who said she had to return to competition any way? Wasn't she happy coaching and teaching? Didn't she find joy in watching her students accomplish a new move? Didn't she feel their excitement when they won a competition? Wasn't there more to life than competitions, exhibitions and injuries?

Yes! As sure as the sun would rise the following morning, Jordan knew she could find joy in her life as long as she had the ice beneath her feet, one way or another. She'd hidden behind her grief and fright long enough. Aleksei had always told her she was stronger than she realized; maybe it was time to see if he was right.

Feeling both emotionally and physically stronger than she had in years, she rose to her feet, the comforting feel of her blades beneath her made her smile. As she pushed through the locker room doors, the haunting notes of music she hadn't heard since the accident reached her ears and sent shivers coursing through her body. The melody to *The Prayer* crashed over her like a wave pounding the sand and nearly sent her to her knees. It was common knowledge at the ice house that that particular piece of music was never to be played, under any circumstance, and yet the music concluded and began again, it's softly pulsing beat drifting from the rink used only for hockey.

Jordan realized it could only be Nick who would be belligerent enough to play that piece of music. Obviously, since he'd been unsuccessful in his attempts to seduce her, he'd decided it was his job on the planet to torture her in every way possible and somehow he'd discovered this piece of music would be the best way to twist the proverbial knife.

"Nicholas Devon, you bastard..." Jordan yelled as she forcefully pushed through the double doors leading to the rink, her strength making them slam against the walls sounded like gunshots in the large rink. Yet the sound didn't disturb Nick as he skated to the music. Jordan watched him in silent awe, her breath barely making a sound as she watched the beauty of his skating as he circled the ice, his blades soundless against the freshly groomed ice.

Nick skated to the far side of the rink and lifted the remote to the sound system and started the piece of music over again. Jordan watched him skate to the center of the rink, his brow furrowed as if he was struggling to remember something just out of reach then smoothed as if the puzzle was solved and the pieces fit. Nick began to skate again; his feet secure beneath him, even though he wore hockey skates. His strokes were strong and lengthy, eating up the ice as he gained speed and suddenly leaped into the air, spun around three times and landed backwards on his left foot. He held his backward glide position for several long seconds and then turned as if he were lifting a partner into his arms and then setting her back on the ice.

Jordan watched Nick in silence. Chills raced up her spine as memories of the program she had described to Aleksei, as he lay dying in her arms, suddenly came to life before her. How often had she visualized this program in her mind, too afraid to actually attempt it on the ice for fear of it not being all that she had promised Aleksei it would be? And yet, now before her, their program was being performed by a stranger whose style and strength was nearly identical to Aleksei's but who physically looked nothing at all like him.

Jordan looked from the ice to the exit door she had only moments before slammed through and knew in her heart she was on the brink of something life-changing. Her mind screamed for her to run as fast and far away as possible to escape the power that beckoned to her from the ice. Yet her heart reassured her there was peace and love and comfort to be found on the shining, mirrored surface that had always been home to her. With a final glance at the exit sign, Jordan removed her blade guards from her skates, and stepped on to the ice and into her future.

Chapter 22

The clear, soft whispers of sharp blades as they scored spider web-like designs into the ice lead Jordan forward, encouraging her to move toward the ever-strengthening power that drew her on toward the future that awaited her. Soft music tickled a vague memory and reached her from far away yet grew in volume as she focused her attention on the soft, beckoning notes, the musical strains causing waves of warmth to flow through her. Warm fingers traced a gentle path down her arm and interlaced with her fingers, a light, reassuring squeeze offered comfort.

The whispers grew, becoming more insistent, urging her ever forward, and her eyelids twitched at the sudden splashes of bright light that flashed before her eyes.

"Jordan… Jordan…? Can you hear me?" a familiar—yet not familiar—male voice called from far away. A bright light crossed her line of vision again, hurting her eyes and she weakly turned her head away from the source of discomfort, a small groan escaping her lips.

Pain stabbed through her brain like a hot, sharp knife and she gasped in surprise, struggling to understand the chaos that suddenly surrounded her. Had she fallen and struck her head when she stepped on to the ice to confront Nick? Portions of questions formed in her mind in slide-like flashes, incomplete and scrambled, and the more she tried to concentrate, the more her head hurt.

"It's okay, sweetheart, relax. Come on now, Jordan; breathe for me, in through the nose, out through the mouth. Remember? Just concentrate on breathing, push the pain away." his voice, deep and familiar, coaxed softly into her ear, his warm breath stirring the hair at her temple as a pair of hands slipped into her hair, and held her head still, while his thumbs gently caressed her temples.

Jordan stilled at his softly spoken words and gentle touch, her subconscious blindly following his lead. She tried to concentrate on the man's voice, deep and calm, and fought to open her eyes in the hopes of making some sense of the madness that still swirled confusingly around her. Finally, after what felt like an eternity, the pain receded and her body went limp, as she was able to relax again.

She sighed in dismay as he pulled his hands from her hair and gently laced his fingers with hers as he held her hand, missing his gentle touch. The brief thought, *'Toto, we're not in Kansas anymore'* flashed through her brain, making her laugh at the absurdity of the thought.

The sound came out as more of a croak, and everyone in the room cast concerned looks at each other. All silently voicing the same question. *Well?*

"Come on, Jordan. Open your eyes—try sweetheart," the voice requested, his tone soft yet insistent.

Jordan did try, but her eyes felt weighted down and refused to obey her command, and when she tried to verbalize her dilemma, her mouth felt as if it had been stuffed with stale, gritty cotton.

"All her stats check out, Dr. Devon," a nurse stated quietly, handing the chart toward the doctor that stood at the foot of the bed.

"Come on, Jordan, vacation time's over, quit screwing around and open your eyes, brat."

Jordan groaned, a hoarse, raspy sound, and swallowed, groaning again when she took a deep breath and felt fire spread through her chest. Her hand clutched convulsively at the fingers still laced with hers, squeezing tightly as she struggled to control the pain that stole her breath away.

"She hasn't lost her grip!" the voice stated dryly, surprised at the strength of her hand in his. "Come on, brat, open those gorgeous eyes for me," he coaxed yet again.

"Go away, Rocmanov, you're a pain in the ass!" Jordan complained, her voice barely more than a whisper as she turned her head away from the voice beside her.

The sudden silence in the room was deafening, and everyone held their breath in anticipation.

"Who?" the voice asked, his hand reaching her cheek and gently turning her face to his.

Jordan's eyes fluttered open, blinking at the bright lights above her head, fighting the desire to succumb to the peaceful darkness that hovered at the edges of her consciousness. Her eyes dropped closed, then opened again, squinting as she sought to bring the face before her into focus. "Don't screw with me now, Aleksei, I've got a hell of a headache. What did you do, drop me on my head?" she asked softly, her eyes absorbing every detail of the face before her. Dark hair fell haphazardly over his brow; his ebony eyes glowed brightly with a hint of tears, despite their arrogant expression. A bandage covered his cheek, hints of the bruise beneath it visible. His beautiful mouth smiled widely, stretching the stitches at the corner of his lip, even as it trembled with emotion he could barely contain.

"No, I didn't drop you," he answered quietly, his eyes memorizing every detail of her pale face, the fading bruises that encircled both her eyes barely noticed as his grateful gaze blended with her confused glance, his smile growing as tears filled his dark eyes. Tiredly he laid his head against her shoulder and heaved a sigh of such utter relief he could no longer hold his emotions in check, the blanket caught the silent tears that slipped from his eyes.

Jordan felt Aleksei's pain, radiating in waves, and struggled to raise her hand and lay it against Aleksei's head, her fingers sifting through the dark waves of hair the texture of silk. The light caught the glimmer of diamonds on the ring firmly settled on her left hand as she ran her fingers through his hair and she paused, momentarily stunned, at the sight. A soft smile lit her face as she watched the diamonds catch the light and cast miniature rainbows over the pearls. Lifting her gaze from the beautiful ring, she looked about the room, not surprised to see Dee and Whittaker there, looking exhausted but wearing grins that stretched from ear to ear. Whittaker's quick, happy wink spoke volumes. A doctor leaned over her. Tall with sandy colored hair, and the most startling blue eyes she'd ever seen, eyes that seemed somehow familiar. She tried to figure out why she should know him, as she followed his instructions while he flashed a small light across her eyes, listened to her heart and took her pulse, then nodded in approval, yet she was still unable to determine where she should know him from.

"What happened?" Jordan asked hoarsely, looking from Dee to Whittaker to the doctor and finally Aleksei.

The question hung in the air. How much did she need to be told now and how much could wait until she was stronger? Aleksei looked from Whittaker to Dee to the doctor, they all seemed to be waiting for him to take the lead.

"It's a long story," Aleksei finally answered, his voice deep and filled with such relief he felt exhausted and exuberant at the same time. Jordan was back, and safe, and there would be plenty of time later to tell her the whole story of the accident. Time to tell her how close he'd come to losing her forever, how he'd spent the last five days beside her in the hospital, refusing to leave her side. Talking to her; bullying her; begging her to fight to stay with him, telling her what their future would be like if only she'd quit the possum routine, and get up off her butt. But mostly, praying, as he had never prayed before for her to find her way back to him—and he'd been heard. Somehow, someone had heard him, felt him worthy, and answered his prayers. For now, just the fact that his prayers had been answered and Jordan was back was enough for him. He only hoped one day he would understand why he, of all people, had been granted this most magical of miracles.

"So fill me in," Jordan coaxed softly, her smile gentle and filled with love.

"There's no rush—we've got plenty of time. Nobody leaves, remember?" Aleksei stated, his voice a husky whisper, as his hand again slid into her hair, his soft touch causing tingles to run over her scalp.

"Of course, I remember, nobody leaves," Jordan agreed and smiled into his eyes as their lips met in a soft kiss that was filled with love and tenderness. "But at least let me know if the story has a happy ending," Jordan pleaded softly, grazing the knuckles of her left hand down Aleksei's cheek, a small smile forming at the rough texture of his unshaven face against her skin.

Aleksei grasped her hand, his lips kissing her palm and laid it against his cheek. His ebony eyes sparkled with hope and happiness and a belief that everything was really going to be okay. "How can anything concerning us have anything *but* a happy ending?" he asked huskily.

"Do you think?" Jordan asked simply, her eyes searching his for the truth.

"I *know!*" Aleksei answered firmly, his voice deep and sure.

"Still think you know everything, don't you, Rocmanov?" Jordan teased quietly, her eyes glowing tiredly but brightly behind the bruises.

Aleksei brushed his fingers through Jordan's coppery tresses, spreading the shining curls against the stark white pillowcase and smiled at Jordan's response. "Yeah, as a matter of fact, I do, and don't you forget it!" he answered arrogantly.

"That shouldn't be a problem, Rocmanov, especially since I'm sure you'll remind me *if* I should ever forget. But trust me, you truly are unforgettable!" Jordan stated softly on a sigh, a peaceful smile lighting up her bruised face.

"You're pretty unforgettable yourself, brat," Aleksei countered and watched Jordan's eyes drift shut, watched her chest rise and fall as she breathed slowly in and out. Over the last five days he'd come to know the meaning of every electronic beep, buzz and whistle in the Intensive Care Unit, and as he watched her heart beat a steady rhythm across the Heart Monitor, he knew she was merely slipping into a normal sleep.

With a final kiss to her cheek, Aleksei slid his fingers from her hand and stood, stretching his muscular arms over his head in an effort to relieve the tension of the past five days. Aleksei walked to Dr. Devon's side and cast a glance at Jordan, peacefully asleep. "Well?"

Dr. Devon looked at the three people, now all staring at him, and smiled broadly. "From all indications, I'd say she's on her way back. I won't lie and say it's going to be a cakewalk because she'd looking at some heavy-duty rehabilitation. The internal injuries were corrected surgically, and should pose no problem. But a double compound fracture of the same leg takes a long time to heal without throwing in a crushed knee on top of things. I honestly can't promise she'll ever walk without a limp, let alone skate again. I'll be happy if she gets back eighty-percent usage of that leg, I wouldn't even hope for a hundred percent."

Whittaker's snort of disbelief alerted the doctor of the absurdity of his statement and Aleksei added his own opinion. "You don't know Jordan, Dr. Devon. Mark my words, she'll skate again and if she has her way, you'll see us win the Gold Medal at the Olympics four years down the road!" Aleksei stated surely.

"A positive attitude is very important during rehabilitation. I just want you all to be aware that her recovery is going to be neither short, nor easy, and just in case the worst occurs, be prepared for the possibility that her skating career is over."

"Thanks for the observation, Doc. We've listened to you give us your worst case scenario regarding Jordan's injury, and now we're going to offer you a little bit of advice—don't count her out, and I recommend you make your reservations for the next Olympics now, you're going to want a good room!" Whittaker suggested heartily.

Dr. Devon looked from Whittaker, to Aleksei, to Dee, and finally at Jordan, still resting peacefully in her bed, and smiled at group. "I'll do that, Mr. Whittaker. And if they don't win that Gold Medal, I'm sending you a bill for my expenses," Dr. Devon stated, offering his hand to Whittaker.

Whittaker looked at the offered hand, then Aleksei, and finally Jordan, and grasped the doctor's hand, pumping it as he stated firmly. "Doc, if they don't win Gold, I'll personally promise you and your misses a month-long vacation anywhere in the world."

Dr. Devon shook his head in amazement, just a tinge guilty about accepting such a sucker bet. The possibility of Jordan ever skating again was remote let alone throwing in the possibility of winning Gold at the Olympics. Still, he felt compelled to be part of this group of close-knit people that had been beside Jordan throughout her ordeal. "I'll start collecting travel brochures right away, my wife's been after me to take her to Australia for years," the doctor answered, his broad smile reaching his bright blue eyes.

"The closest you'll come to seeing Australia is visiting the *Out-Back Steak House*, Doc. Dress warm, the ice rinks can be chilly!" Whittaker suggested.

"I'll keep that in mind," Dr. Devon responded, shaking all their hands one last time before he left the room.

Aleksei returned to sit beside Jordan, linking his hand with hers again, and smiling as he felt her steady pulse beat against his thumb.

"I'd thought we'd lost her there for awhile," Whittaker whispered over Aleksei's shoulder from where he stood behind him looking down at Jordan. "You brought her back, Aleksei."

"I couldn't let her go," he answered quietly, his voice breaking with emotion. "She's my life, and if we ever skate again, or don't, it won't matter. She's alive and I can touch her, and hold her, and laugh at her bad jokes, and make love to her in the snow again, and that's all that matters. Skating will just be icing on the cake—if it happens.

"Well, it damn well better happen. Otherwise, you're going to pay half the expenses for that doctor to take his wife to Australia!" Whittaker chuckled.

"You made that bet—not me," Aleksei countered.

"Yeah, I did, but you gave me the *look*."

"What *look*?"

"You know, the *look*! That look that says 'take him, he's ours'!" Whittaker stated.

"Whittaker, you are a lunatic!" Aleksei laughingly stated, shaking his head in disbelief.

"Yeah, well, the two of you made me one," Whittaker complained, his look encompassing both Aleksei and Jordan.

"And if you're very lucky, we'll continue doing so for many years to come," Aleksei offered, smiling up at his coach.

"Promise?" Whittaker asked quietly.

"We promise," Jordan answered softly for both herself and her partner, sleepily smiling into Aleksei's and Whittaker's surprised faces.

"I thought you were sleeping," Aleksei offered, kissing her lips gently.

"Just dozing."

"Well doze some more," Aleksei suggested.

"I've been away from you long enough, I don't want to be away from you anymore," Jordan stated.

"Tell you what, you doze, I'll stay here with you," Aleksei suggested.

"Hold me?"

"I don't know—I don't want to hurt you."

"You could never hurt me, Aleksei. Please?" Jordan pleaded prettily.

"Just for a bit—you need your sleep," Aleksei agreed, carefully climbing on to the bed, laying on his side and gathering Jordan into his arms. Aleksei rested his head against the top of Jordan's head, silky strands of coppery hair teased his lips and he blew the strands away from his mouth. "I've missed you!" Aleksei stated softly.

"Me, too," Jordan agreed, inhaling the scent that was Aleksei's alone. "You smell wonderful."

"I can just imagine. I haven't been real concerned with regular showers lately, I've had more pressing matters on my mind and had to make due with quick sponge-baths."

"Alone or with assistance?" Jordan inquired off-handedly.

"Well, you were here but didn't offer much assistance."

"You've been with me the whole time?" Jordan asked in amazement.

"Where else would I be?"

"Exactly how long have I been here?" Jordan asked seriously.

"Long enough," Aleksei answered cryptically, refusing to answer her further questions about the accident. There would be time later for all the details. "You're supposed to be sleeping, remember?"

Jordan lay quietly against Aleksei, absorbing his warmth and strength, smiling as visions of their time in the cottage entered her mind. Jordan snuggled closer against Aleksei and sighed in pleasure. "Aleksei…"

"Sshh. You're supposed to be napping."

"Just one more question."

Aleksei's exaggerated sigh was his answer.

"What did *we* promise Whittaker?"

Aleksei's chest rumbled as laughter rolled through him. "You're suppose to know what the deal is, before you promise to fulfill it."

"So how bad did I blow it?" Jordan asked sleepily.

"Nothing too far out there. You—I mean *we*—promised Whittaker Gold in four years," Aleksei explained.

"Is that all? I thought it was something really tough," Jordan mumbled as she slipped back into a peaceful sleep, wrapped in Aleksei's arms.

Aleksei kissed Jordan's head and snuggled against her. "That's what I thought, too!" he agreed and moments later, joined her in a peaceful sleep filled with dreams of their future together, their breaths matching as they inhaled and exhaled in unison.

Epilogue

Four Years Later

"Good evening ladies and gentlemen, and welcome to the Long Program portion of pairs figure skating competition of the Winter Olympics." Scott Hamilton intoned as he commented the evening's events. "With the pair of Jamison and Rocmanov leading after the Short Program, I spoke with the pair before their Long Program and this was what they had to say…"

"How are the nerves tonight, Aleksei? Are you happy to be the third team on the ice?" Scott asked Aleksei, who stood alone outside the ladies locker room.

"In all honesty, we would have been happy going first. The waiting is probably the worst. We would just as soon get it done, and over with." Aleksei answered, casting anxious glances toward the door.

Scott chuckled, "You seem to be waiting now."

"These days I do a lot of waiting. Patience is something I've developed in the last eighteen months." Aleksei answered, his smile growing as he watched Jordan exit the locker room and hand over their smiling, laughing son into his arms.

"Who's your friend?" Scott asked, laughing as the baby grabbed the microphone and tried to wrap his drooling mouth around it.

"We'd like to introduce, Sergei Francis Rocmanov—our *greatest* achievement," Jordan answered softly, her hand gently stroking the dark, wavy curls that covered her son's head, smiling into the ebony eyes that smiled back at her, so like his father's.

"He's got potential in the broadcasting booth, he's not afraid of a mic!" Scott suggested with a laugh, gently tugging the microphone from the baby's grip. "I'd say things can't get much better for you two."

"Yeah, Scott, life's pretty damn good!" Aleksei agreed, flicking Jordan's nose playfully at her censorious look.

"So, Jordan. How are you feeling tonight?" Scott asked.

"I can't tell you how much I'm looking forward to going out to eat at the *Out-Back Steak House* after we're done here tonight," Jordan stated confidently, laughing at Scott's baffled expression, smiling up at Aleksei and returning his knowing wink. "Don't worry, Scott, next time you've got an evening to spare, we'll tell you the whole story. It's one for the books!"

"I'll hold you to it," Scott agreed. "Good luck to you both and be sure to root for mom and dad, Sergei," Scott suggested, chuckling as baby drool ran down the side of the microphone and onto his hand.

* * * * *

"It's impossible to believe, that four years ago, the pair of Jamison and Rocmanov, were involved in a horrendous accident, that left Jordan Jamison seriously injured, and doctors with severe doubts as to her ability to ever walk—let alone skate—again. Tonight, however, the team of Jamison and Rocmanov, are celebrating their greatest achievement on the ice, as they did, indeed, win the Gold Medal for the United States!" Scott Hamilton later stated as he smiled broadly into the camera.

* * * * *

In the audience, Dr. Nicholas Devon, and his wife, watched the pair team of Jordan Jamison and Aleksei Rocmanov win the Gold Medal, as promised, and cheered wildly as the arena erupted in excitement, even as they knew they would be paying their own way to Australia.

* * * * *

From rink side, Whittaker, Dee and a squirming Sergei, watched the pair skate a perfect program and fulfill every promise they had made to themselves and each other.

Their near-perfect scores reflected the judges' unanimous agreement.

Gold was the color for the evening.

* * * * *

"Ladies and gentlemen, Gold Medal winners from the United States, Jordan Jamison and Aleksei Rocmanov." A voice in the dark boomed and the spotlight caught the pair as they stepped onto the ice and skated to their starting mark to perform their exhibition program.

And as the musical notes from *The Prayer* began, Aleksei voiced a silent *thank you* toward heaven, and whatever power had granted his prayer. The pair began to skate the program that had begun as a nightmare but turned into a beautiful vision of faith, trust and loyalty, but most of all, love.

And, as they had promised each other so many times—nobody left.

Printed in the United Kingdom
by Lightning Source UK Ltd.
122930UK00001B/224/A